He tilted her ... ...his, softly at first, t... ...ency, more warmth, until Lyndell's very soul melted. And yet ... and yet she was a lady. She wasn't any light-skirt to be tumbled in the hay. She wasn't any mousy old spinster, either. She was, for the first time in days, Miss Lyndell Markham, a lady. ...

AN EARLY ENGAGEMENT

"It's growing colder. I don't suppose you'd care to continue this discussion under the covers?"

"Smoky!" She snatched her hand back and jumped up, breasts heaving.

His sigh was not entirely feigned. "Well then, what about a good-night kiss?" Who knew where that could lead?

She shook her head, smiling. Damn if the chit wasn't up to snuff after all.

"No? What if I said Mr. Butler advised it? I understand you listen to him."

She grinned, stuck her little nose in the air, and solemnly parodied: "I regret, my lady, that it would not be in our best interests. ..."

By Barbara Metzger:

CUPBOARD KISSES*
BETHING'S FOLLY
THE EARL AND THE HEIRESS
RAKE'S RANSOM
MINOR INDISCRETIONS*
THE LUCK OF THE DEVIL*
AN AFFAIR OF INTEREST*
CHRISTMAS WISHES*
A LOYAL COMPANION*
LADY IN GREEN*
AUTUMN LOVES: An Anthology*
AN ANGEL FOR THE EARL*
A SUSPICIOUS AFFAIR*
LADY WHILTON'S WEDDING*
FATHER CHRISTMAS*
VALENTINES: A Trio of Regency Love Stories for
    Sweethearts' Day*
MY LADY INNKEEPER and AN EARLY
    ENGAGEMENT*
AN ENCHANTED AFFAIR**

*Published by Fawcett Books
**Forthcoming from Fawcett Books

Books published by The Ballantine Publishing Group
are available at quantity discounts on bulk purchases
for premium, educational, fund-raising, and special
sales use. For details, please call 1-800-733-3000.

MY LADY INNKEEPER
AN EARLY ENGAGEMENT

Barbara Metzger

FAWCETT CREST • NEW YORK

Sale of this book without a front cover may be unauthorized. If this book is coverless, it may have been reported to the publisher as "unsold or destroyed" and neither the author nor the publisher may have received payment for it.

A Fawcett Crest Book
Published by Ballantine Books
My Lady Innkeeper copyright © 1985 by Barbara Metzger
An Early Engagement copyright © 1990 by Barbara Metzger

All rights reserved under International and Pan-American Copyright Conventions. Published in the United States by Ballantine Books, a division of Random House, Inc., New York, and simultaneously in Canada by Random house of Canada Limited, Toronto. *My Lady Inkeeper* was originally publishcd by the Walker Publishing Company in 1985. *An Early Engagement* was originally published by Ballantine Books in 1990.

Library of Congress Catalog Card Number: 95-90825

ISBN 0-449-22447-3

No part of this book may be reproduced or transmitted in any form or by any means, electronic or mechanical, including photocopying, recording, or by any information storage and retrieval systems, without permission in writing from the publisher.

All of the characters and events portrayed in these stories are fictitious.

Manufactured in the United States of America

First Edition: April 1996

10 9 8 7 6 5 4 3 2 1

Contents

My Lady Innkeeper

When I was little, my grandfather would call my sister by her name, Carole. He also called me Carole. When we were together, he'd say, Hi Carole, who's your friend? This one's for Carole, anyway. With love.

Chapter One

"*Toads!* All men are toads," declared Miss Lyndell Markham as she paced around her aunt's sitting room, waving a scrap of parchment. "They seek a woman for her money, her family name, her looks or her virtue—not an honest motive in their hearts. A woman can't trust any of them!" Miss Markham paused in her agitation to seek confirmation from her audience of one, her cousin Isabelle, whose advanced state of pregnancy proclaimed her trafficking with the enemy. Bella murmured "No, dear," without missing a stitch of her embroidery. Miss Markham's complaints were not new ones. Nor were they without foundation.

Unfortunately for man's baser motives, Miss Markham was blessed, or cursed, with a multitude of temptations. As for wealth, she was one of the foremost heiresses of the realm; for lineage, the sole child of the late Earl of Markham, whose title was ancient and impeccable. As to beauty, with her vibrant red-gold hair now cropped into fashionable curls, startlingly clear green eyes, a peach-blush complexion and a graceful figure of ideal proportions, the whole carried with an elegance of manner and garbed in exquisite taste, Lyndell just missed perfection by a nose. The Markham Nose, to be exact; patrician to be polite; less than straight to be truthful. As her father had predicted, "As long as my money is inherited with my nose, they'll still call her a Beauty." If not an Incomparable, she was often called the Magnificent Miss Markham.

As for virtue, in certain baser circles, such as White's betting book, she was dubbed the Unmountable Markham. Lyndell had managed to attain her twenty-fourth year with virtue intact despite importunities by every expert with rak-ish ways and roving hands. These importunities provided one, but only one, of the day's grievances. In a swirl of am-ber crepe and green riband, Lyndell flicked the letter at her inattentive cousin.

"It's not enough I have to suffer every puppy's drooling and every basket-scrambler's begging to pay his addres-ses—to my estate!—but now every loose screw feels I've been on the Town so long I'm past the age of innocence."

With a faint smile, Isabelle denied the possibility. "Come, Lyndy, no gentleman would treat you like a . . . a . . ."

"A light-skirt? Bella, you are such a babe! Yes, I know you're an old married woman of twenty-six. But you're a prelate's wife." Before Isabelle could make any disclaimers, Lyndell recommenced her pacing, her steps the strides of a tall, confident woman. "Here, do you know Lord Nay-bors?"

"Yes, I mct his wife at—"

"Last night at the Bellinghams' ball he asked me to stand up with him and I accepted, thinking to have some rational conversation at last. He kept dancing toward the balconies and then almost pushed me out, for some fresh air, he said."

"But Lyndy, it was freezing! It's November!"

"Exactly! And his wife is at home with a sick child! I put a flea in his ear, you can be sure, but it's always the same. Society says a woman's reputation is all-important, and every man is out to help her lose it. Then she'll be la-belled 'fast,' Society will turn its back, and no one will marry her! Well, I am tired of those games."

"Is there no man who can inspire a *tendre* in you?"

"What, Bella, you too?"

Isabelle flushed and lowered her eyes to her needlework again, fashioning rosebuds to an impossibly tiny bonnet.

"Are you joining the throng to see me wed? Aunt and Uncle are despairing, and even Lady Jersey hinted I was too long in the tooth to be so particular."

"No, Lyndy, you know I only want to see you happy!" Bella didn't say, "As I am," and Lyndell didn't say, "Married to an old stick as you are?" but she gave an unladylike snort. "Not likely, among the lobcocks and loobies one sees at all the ton parties. I've met all the eligibles, and I'd rather stay on the shelf!"

"Perhaps Father could speak to an older gentleman, one with wealth of his own . . . ?"

"You mean a marriage of convenience? I think not! I've found them to be damnably inconvenient, especially for the woman! She gives up her freedom, hands her finances into his keeping, in exchange for what? The right to bear his children! The husband now has her properties to gamble away without touching his own holdings, and the right, no, the responsibility, to enjoy his mistresses in Town, while his wife sits in the country breeding. No, thank you!"

"But, Lyndy, don't you wish to be married at all?"

There was a moment of silence as Lyndell seemed to lose some of her bravado. She sank to the floor near her cousin's chair, fingering the tiny cap.

"Yes, Bella." She spoke in a subdued tone, and with a tinge of wistful sadness. "I would dearly like to be married, to love and be loved, to *share*. But I cannot give my hand without giving my heart, and I've not found the man I could love and trust and . . . and cherish, the way my parents did each other. Do you understand, cousin, that I could never do what Mama did, after Papa died? I may stay on the shelf forever, but I'll never marry just so I'll not be alone."

Lady Markham's second marriage, a scant year after the earl's passing, was a mistake, and a further tragedy for the grieving twelve-year-old Lyndell. She simply couldn't understand how her sweet, gentle mother could transfer her affections from the Earl of Markham, a noble in every respect, to the very common Joshua Riddley. It was not that the young Miss Markham was a snob, but Riddley was far beneath her father in education, civility, gentility, everything that makes for a cultured gentleman. In fact, Riddley was no gentleman. A member of the most minor landed gentry, his main interests were gaming, drinking and riding to the hounds. When he couldn't chase the fox, he chased serving girls. This was the man Lyndell's mother chose to succeed the earl. Despite capable managers and her own brother's assistance, Lady Markham simply could not face the responsibilities of the vast King's Mark estate and a willful daughter, combined with the bleak future of years of loneliness ahead, or having to face the London Marriage Mart as a no-longer-young widow. And there was Joshua Riddley, a widower with a young son. He was jovial, undemanding, known for years; he was ready to shoulder all her burdens.

If Lady Markham's burdens were the sweetest windfall Riddley had ever known, he managed to hide his true colours. At least for a few months after the wedding, that is, until he saw exactly what was his directly, through his wife's settlements, and what he could carefully glean as overseer of the earl's unentailed properties—Lyndell's inheritance. Suddenly he could indulge his habits to excesses he had only dreamt of, embarrassing his new wife, infuriating and mortifying his new daughter. He abused the servants, misused or neglected the tenants and the lands Lyndell had been taught to honour. He used Markham money to set his own son Jasper up as a wastrel, a fribble with no need to earn a living or learn a trade, just another gaming, drinking leech.

Neither father nor son had the mental scope to beggar the estate nor, with the capital investments untouchable in London, to greatly affect Lyndell's wealth, yet the lands, and her pride, suffered. For four years she could do nothing. Then her mother died. Faded, tired, isolated by embarrassment from all social life, Mrs. Riddley drifted from weakness to illness to death. It was, or seemed to the then sixteen-year-old Lyndell, another solution of least effort, another betrayal. Before leaving King's Mark to take up residence with her Aunt Lillian and Uncle Hardesty in London, Lyndell threw the Riddleys off her lands. The father she threatened with court action if he ever approached her again. To her step-brother Jasper, an ineffectual ne'er-do-well, she offered a one-time sum of money to purchase an army commission, or passage to America, or a university education so he might find a profession, whatever, just to be gone. Now, eight years later, after the Bath Seminary for

Young Ladies, after her presentation and warm welcome to the ton, Lyndell still carried the scars of distrust and disdain.

Today she also carried a letter from Jasper Riddley.

Shaking off the despondency of sad memories and loss, Lyndell jumped to her feet and tossed her head, as if to rearrange her thoughts along with her curls. Laughing, she proclaimed, "Men are all fools. They must inherit it from their fathers!"

Isabelle was relieved at the lightening of her cousin's mood and hastened to change the topic. "I collect you mean Jasper—you said he'd written—but I can't understand what has you in such a taking. He is not asking for more money, is he? I thought that was settled years ago."

"Oh yes, well settled! I paid his debts and thought to provide for his future in some respectable way. Instead he and Joshua went to London and proceeded to gamble the sum away. If Joshua hadn't been killed in a duel over some marked cards, they would both have landed in debtor's prison, and I'd have let them rot there."

"You know you wouldn't have been so hard, Lyndy, especially not on poor Jasper."

" 'Poor Jasper,' is it? You always had a soft spot for him, even as a child, after he rescued your kitten from the goldfish pond. I always thought he'd tossed it in himself just to tease you, but no mind. I don't know if I actually could have let Jasper die in prison, but I would certainly have let him sit there a while. It might have averted his next actions."

"You mean the inn?"

"Yes. To take what remained of his money—my money!—and return to Suffolk, not ten minutes away from King's Mark, and purchase a tavern! Not even a respectable coaching house on the Norwich road where he might have made a profit, but a dreary little wayside inn, little more than a hedgerow pub. And he had the nerve, the sheer gall, to call it King's Pass!"

Isabelle smiled. "Perhaps he was acknowledging his debt to you."

Lyndell merely gave her cousin a dark look. "It never

9

mattered overmuch, since no one in London knew of the relation, and everyone near home knew I had cut the connexion, but my . . . my . . . step-brother"—the words almost choked her—"a common innkeep! And none too successful either. His principal income came from fleecing at cards any well-heeled traveller unfortunate enough to be stranded at the place. If he could. More often Jasper would lose. The noddy couldn't even cheat right! But that's nothing, nothing, I tell you, to this! Here." She handed the letter over to her cousin. "See for yourself."

" 'Dear Sister,' " Isabelle read, ignoring the unladylike growl coming from Lyndell's throat. " 'Here is the deed to King's Pass Inn, made over to your name. No fear, they'll never connect you with the spies.' Oh dear."

"It gets better. Keep reading."

" 'I swear to you I thought the Quinns, the previous owners, you know—they stayed on to run the inn for me— were merely involved with the Gentlemen. That's smugglers, if you don't know the term. But it turns out they were also waylaying couriers bound for the army installations at Southwold Barracks, drugging the wine and copying orders, or getting the soldiers jug-bitten enough to tell secrets, and passing the information on to the Frenchies, with the help of some London swell. The messengers would never reveal they'd stopped off for a wet, or a wench, so no one was the wiser till a courier was found dead and his papers gone, and a Captain Drew Jamison started nosing around. The Quinns shabbed off, leaving me in a pretty pickle, I can tell you. Quinn said his London connexion—it could have been any of several nobs who stopped here occasionally—would be watching to make sure I didn't snabble on them or they'd dim my lights too.' "

Bella looked up enquiringly.

"That means kill him," Lyndell informed her tersely.

After a quick horrified gasp, Bella continued to read:
" 'With Nappy defeated the whole should blow over eventually unless the magistrates connect me somehow to the dead messenger, or to a few robberies at the coaching inn by Framingham. Then I'd be finished either way, so I'm hiding out for a while. Dilly, I'm depending on you to save

10

my skin. Yours too, if it comes to that. You wouldn't want your brother up on King's Bench warrants, I'm sure. I know you can pull it off with all your influence in Town. You're my only hope. Your affectionate brother, Jasper.' " Isabelle's voice faded away, as she sat in stunned silence.

"Spies, smugglers, highwaymen. What do you think of Jasper now? I'll bet he knew all along what was going on. Even a skitter-wit like Riddley can recognise French brandy and despatch cases. As long as he was being paid, he'd not question the French Army's landing force putting up at his miserable inn! And how true to character, running off, leaving me with a witches' broth abrewing!" Spots of colour highlighted Miss Markham's cheeks as her redheaded temper again took control.

"But Lyndy, what are you going to do?"

"Do?" she sputtered. "What should I do? Run to the Admiralty and say my step-brother knows a spy in London but he's too cowardly to identify him, so please forgive him? Or tell the magistrate Jasper would never exert himself so far as to murder anyone, but he's simply gone on a repairing lease, so you must not suspect him? What kind of fool would I look?"

"Good heavens," Isabelle said as it all sank in, "he'll be deported, giving aid and shelter to criminals."

"Oh, no, he won't." Lyndell countered. "They hang traitors."

Chapter Two

$\mathcal{I}$nactivity and indecision made up no part of Lyndell Markham's five-foot-six-inch frame. Having taken control of her own life at the age of sixteen, and capably too, she was not about to yield her fate to mere chance now. Especially with the London Season growing so tedious, and what looked to be high adventure beckoning. Murder, mayhem, treason, a high-born villain—the Minerva Press couldn't equal Jasper's bumblebath. Lyndell knew exactly what she had to do: leave London with as little fanfare as possible, set herself up at the inn, and trap the spy. The details could be worked out later.

The first part of the plan involved swearing Isabelle to cooperative secrecy. From years of experience with her headstrong cousin, Isabelle knew better than to try dissuading Lyndell from her hey-go-mad start, but she did inject some practicality by mentioning such items as danger and propriety. It was unthinkable for a well-born lady to be staying at an inn unchaperoned, and everyone within miles of King's Mark would recognise the earl's daughter. Furthermore, what could a single woman do in the face of such ruthlessness that Jasper couldn't? Lyndell was forced to agree that her plan had flaws, but with a little thought she could correct the major problems: first, she would pretend to be Miss Lynn Riddley, Jasper's sister and the new innkeeperess, and she would wear a disguise, which, to Isabelle's dismay, seemed to make the plot even more attractive. Lyndell would stay away from her home, and take no London servants who could gossip. Instead she'd ask the Bennetts to travel with her, for protection and to satisfy convention. Sarah Bennett had been Lyndell's nurserymaid and Joseph had been her father's groom. Pensioned off to a cottage in Islington, there was no more respectable, loyal pair. Isabelle had to be content.

Lady Hardesty was even easier for Lyndell to persuade, by the simple expedient of lying. Miss Markham appeased her conscience by reflecting that the truth would only worry Aunt Lillian, and what way was that to repay all her kindnesses? Besides, Lyndell had to start practicing subterfuge somewhere, if she was to be any good at thief-taking. So she claimed a serious problem at the manor—not far from the truth—and exhaustion from the constant London rounds, as her reasons for begging off all their engagements. If Lady Hardesty was a little quick in her acceptance of Lyndell's departure, Lyndell could understand. It could be no pleasure for Aunt Lillian either, despite the many dis-claimers, to be still chaperoning her niece after all these years, listening to the tattle-mongers link Lyndell's name with one bachelor after another, and have the girl still, dis-appointingly, on her hands. After all, Lady Hardesty had married her own daughter off before Bella was eighteen. Of course, she'd often said, it was different; Lyndell was an heiress. But no, as long as she knew the Bennetts were along, Aunt Lillian could see no objection to the Suffolk trip.

The Bennetts, however, were not so easy to convince.

Lyndell straightened the bow on her chip-straw bonnet as the carriage drew up before the neat white cottage with its kitchen garden off to the side. She had to laugh at herself, a grown woman, tidying up to face people who'd known her as an infant. That they still shared a comfortable affec-tion was obvious in the warm greetings, the cosy hominess of tea and fresh-baked strawberry tarts in the tiny kitchen. There could be no untruths here, Lyndell knew, not when she was asking them to share the danger. A little subtlety, perhaps, but no outright lies.

"Do you remember the inn Jasper Riddley purchased, just to the south of King's Mark?" she asked, after the table had been cleared and Bennett's clay pipe had been lit. "The one the Quinns used to have?"

At their nods she continued, "Well, Jasper's run into a bit of difficulty and I wish to go there to see what help I can be. And it occurred to me you might enjoy a holiday in the country as well."

"How nice for you to think of us, dear, wasn't it, Mr. Bennett?"

Joseph raised one brow and thoughtfully tapped his pipe on the fireplace.

"Then again," Lyndell continued, figuring in for a pence, in for a pound, "I'm fairly certain Jasper will be removing from the area permanently and I thought you might be in-terested in taking over the inn." She had an awful moment of self-reflection when she saw herself enmeshed in the life of crime: cajolery, then lies, now bribery, and she'd only

13

been at it for a few hours! What next? Go for the weak spot! She turned to Sarah. "You know you've been saying how the city is getting so large it'll be at your doorstep soon, with all its noise and dirt and bother. And you, Benny, I know you'd rather keep horses of your own than work for hire at that livery, and you'd still have your pensions. I thought we could all travel together, and stay a short while to see if you like it, before making any decisions. Of course we'd have to start out soon."

Bennett's dour "of course" received an answering twinkle from Lyndell, but Mrs. Bennett was enthusiastic. "Just think, Mr. Bennett, a big garden and fresh country air and good, honest folks, all in visiting distance of King's Mark." She looked around and lowered her voice. "I shouldn't be saying this to you, Miss Lyndy, but Islington is getting Fast. It is too, Mr. Bennett, don't you laugh. That little house at the corner, the one with the nice primroses, was sold last month to Lord Ainsley—and for what? To house his . . . his . . . oh dear."

Lyndell smiled, showing a dimple, and patted Sarah's hand. "All the more reason to consider a move. What do you think, Benny?"

His wife looked at him anxiously but Mr. Bennett only studied the tobacco in the pipe, poking at it and puffing, before turning to Lyndell at last. "This bit o'difficulty young Riddley found himself in, just what might that be?"

Flushing slightly and lowering her eyes, Lyndell told them about the letter, all of it, and her plan to clear Jasper's name and safeguard her own, with their help. "It's not that we'd be so all alone, either. There's this Captain Jamison, and the whole King's Mark staff if we need it."

"It's not quite what I'd like," Mrs. Bennett confessed. "You pretending to be what you're not, and people not like to treat you as a Lady of Quality, but we're good loyal Englishmen too, aren't we, Joseph?"

Bennett thought he knew enough about traitors to be fairly sure none would return to a scene of so much suspicion, so he hadn't many misgivings on that score. He also thought he knew enough about young creatures, horses or otherwise, to probe a little deeper. "Won't you be missin'

14

out on all those fine parties and such? The missus'n I could go on and see what's in the wind, without you comin' along."

Lyndell almost squeaked, "Without me? Oh no! What are a few parties—they're all so boring anyhow, after the first few—compared to this? I wouldn't miss it for anything!" When she noted Bennett's grin, she added, "And don't you start on me about wasting time when I could be finding a husband, either. I'd rather catch a spy!"

"But, dear," Sarah started, looking from one to the other, before she was interrupted by her husband's muttered, "The gypsy fair again."

"What was that, Mr. Bennett?" she asked, but Lyndell was blushing, a curse of her fair skin.

Bennett had to pause to relight his pipe. "The gypsy fair. Miss Lyndy was nobut six years or so, and I was undergroom. Th'earl and Henesley were off buyin' horses and little miss here, red hair in braids down her back, 'n no front teeth, comes up'n tells me to saddle her pony, she's goin' to the gypsy fair. So I asks if the earl said she could and she tells me he didn't say she couldn't."

"Well, he didn't," Lyndell put in.

"Then she says she'll go anyway, if I don't help her creep out where no one's lookin', because she has two pence all her own and wants to have her fortune told. I wasn't going to saddle up that pony no how, but she looks up at me with those green eyes all watery and a quiver in her voice, sayin' she'll be my friend, forever, if I go with her. I was cotched, all right and tight. That little grey pony—"

"Peasblossom."

"—barely come up to my stirrups, but Missy sat so tall in her saddle, off adventuring."

"And a fine adventure it was, too, Benny."

"Until we got home. Henesley wanted to have my hide, but the earl, he understood."

"Understood? Gammon, I couldn't sit for a week!"

"He told me there'd always be women who could wrap men around their little fingers—like his puss, he called her—and there'd always be men spineless enough to curl

15

up tight for them. Like me, I guess. Inevitable, is what he called it. And he weren't mad, just so's long as I kept her safe." He stared at his wife, then grinned. "So when are we off to the gypsy fair?"

It wasn't till Lyndell's fine carriage had pulled away, plans made, times set, that Sarah said to her husband, "Adventuring indeed. That girl needs a husband," and he answered, "Amen to that."

Chapter Three

After an early morning start, they changed carriages at the posting house in Chelmsford, the first stage out of London, so as not to inconvenience Lord Hardesty any further, Lyndell told her uncle's driver. It looked like snow, and she didn't wish the coach and horses stranded in the country. If the London servants thought it too smoky by half for Miss not to be driven direct to her destination, they were too used to the ways of the Quality to be bothered overmuch, and Bennett's largesse also helped quiet their reservations, and their tongues.

So Mrs. Bennett and Lyndell, the hood of her green cloak pulled over the unmistakable coppery curls, her head lowered, were shown into a private parlour while Joseph Bennett hired a chaise to continue their journey. At the next stages, Lyndell and Sarah stayed in the coach while the horses were changed, an unremarkable young woman and her companion, taking refreshment from the hamper at their feet. It wasn't till just past Framingham, well into Suffolk, that any change occurred. First Lyndell opened her cloak and laid it aside to reveal a grey merino gown of fairly good quality, but with no embellishments to mark it a fashionable creation. It had a loose enough fit to hide Lyndell's own notable figure and at the same time proclaim to the experienced eye that Miss Lynn Riddley bought ready-made clothing. Serviceable and unpretentious, the grey merino, along with a dreary brown bombazine and a plain navy kerseymere hidden under Lyndell's muslins and silks, was Isabelle's prepregnancy visit-the-poor clothes. From the portmanteau at her feet Lyndell next pulled a huge droopy nightcap, a relic of Isabelle's mother-in-law's last visit. Unlike the scraps of lace most ladies perched on their heads to denote their attaining "a certain age," this item more closely resembled a dairymaid's mob-cap—after the cow had worn it too. It did have the advantage of hiding every stray curl of Lyndell's hair and, flopping over her brow as it did, of shadowing the sparkle in her green eyes. Right now those eyes were alight with merriment as she pulled from her reticule a pair of spectacles, Uncle Hardesty's unknowing contribution, and placed them low on the bridge of her nose, right at the Markham deviation. A touch of powder to dull her fine complexion, a slight stoop to the shoulders, and voilà, Miss Lynn Riddley, spinster. Poor but respectable, meekly come to hold house or inn for her brother. What a great actress she would be, Lyndell decided, if she ever got tired of the ton.

Unfortunately, there was no one but the hired driver and his postillion to behold her performance, and they had seen nothing more than the green cape before. Instead of being impressed by her transformation, or even noticing it, they wished only to discharge their passengers and head back toward Chelmsford while some grey afternoon light still remained. And before the snow started.

Bennett's knee-slapping guffaws almost compensated, but there was no mistaking that her grand entrance was marred by the lack of an audience. The place was deserted. A dog barked somewhere, the only sign of life, so Lyndell took the spectacles off before she tripped, straightened up to help tote parcels in, and jauntily set off to inspect her new surroundings.

The tavern sign, a faded blue horse running, hung crookedly. Someone, Jasper most likely, had crudely painted a

17

crowned figure on the horse's back. The King, passing by, as any sane customer would do. The inn's exterior was something less than dramatic; it was dingy. A two-story brick-and-beam construction, it hadn't so much as a single rosebush to relieve the dreariness. The inside was no better. The large common room smelled of stale ale and staler bodies. The one tiny private parlour was dark, and showed none too clean in what weak light filtered through the smoke-grimed windows. To the rear were the kitchen, a nearly empty pantry, a few minute rooms for maidservants, and what must have been the Quinns' quarters. . . . They'd left the bed and the wash stand.

"How nice," Mrs. Bennett declared firmly. "We'll have lots of room for our rugs and furniture from Islington. If we decide to stay, of course."

Lyndell was doubtful. "There's a great deal of work to be done . . ."

"And best it got started. I just knew you'd ought to have a lady's maid with you. 'Tisn't proper, no one to bring you hot water to wash. Well, there's no hot water either. You, Mr. Bennett, go find the woodpile and see to lighting some fires while I air these rooms and check the stores, so's we can have some tea. Things'll look better with some warm food in us. And Joseph, the trunk and that hamper . . ."

Lyndell escaped upstairs, travelling case in hand.

At the top of the stairs the corridor branched to left and right, with doors showing on either side of the hall. The opened rooms were tiny, but at least neat, waiting for the occasional merchant or family travelling to Yarmouth, Lyndell supposed. They were certainly nowhere as fine as the least grand room she'd ever stayed in, so *any* noble putting up here was either down on his luck, lost, or a suspect. Selecting the right-hand corridor and wishing she'd brought a candle, Lyndell continued on till she found Jasper's apartments at the end of the hall. A small sitting room and the bedroom beyond had his unmistakable stamp: clothes strewn all over, racing papers and playing cards spilling from the bureau, empty bottles guarding the corners, an article of feminine apparel dangling from a wall sconce. Definitely Jasper's rooms. She carefully sidestepped piles of

18

papers and account books, deciding to leave it all untouched till she could make an organised search for any hints Jasper might have left. Another bedroom opened off the sitting room—for Jasper's lady callers?—and this Lyndell selected for her own use. It was clean and dry and convenient for her investigation, and logical for Jasper's "sister." By the light of a candle finally located, Lyndell unpacked a few of her belongings, straightened the cap over her curls and repowdered her face. Her grumbling stomach taking precedence over immediate exploration of the left-hand corridor, Lyndell returned to the kitchen, where she found Mrs. Bennett bustling over kettles and a welcome fire.

"Tea will be ready in a minute, dear. I've just been making lists for Mr. Bennett to fetch from market, if the snow holds off for him to drive tomorrow. Jasper left his carriage—there's a dray for supplies, and some horses—Joseph is seeing to them now. Why don't you fetch him?"

The cold wind was blowing leaves about as Lyndell hurried across the rear yard. With her head down and one hand holding on to her cap, she almost came too close to a huge dog chained to a post. Its low snarls warned her when she was just outside its lunge distance, as she quickly found out. Saying "Good doggie, nice doggie," to a creature showing foot-long fangs made Lyndell feel like a fool, but the animal went back to a pile of meat—probably its previous owner, Lyndell decided. Eyeing her warily, but not as warily as she eyed it, the dog ate while Lyndell edged toward the stables.

"You could have warned me about that dog, Benny," she called into the dark reaches of the barn.

"Didn't know you was comin', did I?" he answered as he backed out of a stall dragging a bundle of . . . sticks? Rags? "I got it some food from the missus, but there's no getting near it. Prob'ly have to shoot the poor beast in the mornin'." At those words whatever he was holding made a noise a lot like the dog's and dashed for the stable door, right into Lyndell's arms.

"Why, it's a boy!" she exclaimed. She could see the tatters he was wearing and feel the skinny arm trembling, but

19

she only heard those animal-like noises when she asked his name and what he was doing there.

"He don't talk much, it seems, but he must've took care of the horses when Jasper left. There's plenty of grain and hay. Not much for a boy or a dog, what I can see. Best take him to the missus. C'mon, lad, we'll get some warm food in you."

Lyndell wasn't taking chances; she held firmly to the small hand, to make sure he didn't escape, she told herself. The boy might also be a safe passage through the chained beast's territory, herself added, honest to a fault.

There was still another surprise waiting in the kitchen, one more of Jasper's bequeathals. If the authorities didn't hang him, Lyndell decided, she would, gladly.

Sarah made the introductions: "Miss Lynn Riddley, this is Molly. She says she's serving girl in the tap room."

As Molly bobbed an awkward curtsy, her ... endowments ... nearly bobbing out of the low-cut blouse, it was all too easy to see just what Molly served to the customers. The rouged cheeks and impossibly yellow hair proclaimed her no better than she ought to be, and probably a lot worse.

Surprisingly, it was Joseph Bennett who told Molly she might as well stay on, in spite of his wife's sniffing disapproval. "For if you're to cook, Sarah, and I'm to see to the horses, that only leaves Miss Lynn here to see to the customers else." That immediately quieted any protests Mrs. Bennett might have made. Her Miss Lyndy serving ale in a common tap room to a bunch of drunken farmers? She'd see the devil ice-skating first!

"Well, if that's all right and tight I'll just go freshen up," Molly announced. "My room's the end of the other hall from Jasper's, Mr. Riddley, that is, if you need me. With the fires lit and some lanterns out, maybe we'll have some business tonight."

Lyndell nearly choked with laughter on Molly's unfortunate phrasing, and the look of horror on Sarah's face, but she had to ask about the boy. "Him?" Molly tossed over her shoulder as she flounced out of the kitchen. "He's just the moron Quinn took out of the workhouse to see to the stables."

The boy's growling noises were too much for poor Sarah. She threw her apron over her face and blubbered into it. "A . . . a light-skirt in my own kitchen! Am I to sit to supper with that Jezebel and a lice-ridden, horse-fouled, savage half-wit? I can't do it, Miss Lyndy, I just can't."

Traitor that he was, Bennett went to fetch more wood. Lyndell dragged the boy to a chair near the fire and told him to sit, out of hearing, before returning to pat her old nurse's hand. "There," she said soothingly, "it's just for a while, you know it is! And we can't get rid of Molly. Like Benny said, she has to serve at the tables. She can even eat there, not with us! But she's been here since the Quinns too, so she might have some information."

"I know all about the information women like her have and I don't want her giving any of it to you, you hear me, Miss Lyndy?"

"Of course, Sarah, and I'll stay far away from her, I promise." Lyndell carefully did not promise to stay away from Molly's room, which she intended to search the moment it was unoccupied, if the moment ever came. What she did say was, "But we all have to listen in case she mentions any London gentlemen, or soldiers with important messages. That's what we're here for, remember?" When Sarah nodded, reluctantly, Lyndell went on, lowering her voice still further: "As for the boy, why, he's just cold and hungry and maybe a little dirty. You wouldn't put him out in the snowy night in those rags, with no supper, would you?"

"He took good care of the horses too, Sarah," Bennett added, coming in with a pile of wood and stacking it by the hearth. The boy bent to help him.

"You see, Sarah, he's no savage, just frightened," Lyndell said. "Here," and she took his hand, drawing him to the table near Sarah, where she knelt to his level. "You do understand me, don't you?" The sad little head nodded. "And can you talk if you want to?" A pause, then another nod. "Good! Now, do you have a name?" A vigorous nod. "Of course you do! Well, I am Lyndy, and this is Mrs. Bennett, who is the finest cook anywhere in England. But we have a problem. You see, Mrs. Bennett won't have strangers at her supper table, only friends, and friends always know each other's names so . . ."

A whisper: "Sam'l, ma'am."

"Fine! Well, Mrs. Bennett, this is my friend Sam'l. Will he do?"

"Of course he will, as soon as Mr. Bennett washes him up some. Here, young Sam'l, have some bread and butter to tide you over."

When the boy was shyly nodding his appreciation, Bennett touched his shoulder. "Come on then, Sam'l. I like a lad what doesn't jabber."

By the early suppertime the weather was even more threatening, dark an hour too early, but King's Pass Inn looked almost cosy. Fires had taken the chill off the common room and private parlour, and a quick sweep with a broom had gotten most of the cobwebs. Lyndell's trunk was unpacked and she'd had a warm bath, and a start at Jasper's rooms, though she couldn't have said what she was looking for.

Downstairs, the Bennetts had also unpacked and their rooms looked brighter, with furniture and bedding from one of the unused guest chambers. Sarah and Lyndell had even found an old jacket of Jasper's they cut down for Sam'l— "The least Jasper could contribute"—which they'd sew up later. Scrubbed and fed, warm and dry, he still would not talk much. Lyndell managed to find out that he was eleven, or maybe twelve, and that the dog's name was Ajax—the important things. Sam'l either didn't know or wouldn't say where Jasper was, what he'd been living on these past days, or if any London gentlemen visited frequently. For the most part, Sam'l kept his eyes firmly on his shoes. So much for that source, Lyndell decided, as she sent him off to bed in the stable with the last of Sarah's apple tarts, a pile of warm blankets, and a promise to see about Ajax in the morning. He looked at her, actually *at* her, just for a moment. She thought his eyes were brown; she thought he may have smiled. And he whispered, "My friend," then ran off.

22

Lyndell didn't know if he meant her or the awful dog, but it gave her a warm feeling anyway.

The snow began that evening, lightly at first. Bennett shoved an old bench out near the dog so it could have some shelter, and the beast missed his leg by a full inch, out of appreciation. Muttering about the dog keeping away all the customers if the snow didn't, Benny sat down with his pipe.

Just in case anyone *did* venture out, Lyndell was prepared. Wearing the navy kerseymere—even more sacklike on her than Isabelle's grey—and the rest of her disguise, she stationed herself in the small private parlour where she could see the front entrance and hear what went on in the tap room. Dust cloth in hand, she was ready to save her country, if not her reputation. What she wasn't ready for, certainly, was Molly.

Coming into the parlour, snooping on *her*, most likely, Lyndell thought indignantly, Molly looked even more fallen by candlelight. She'd changed into a red satin-bodiced gown with lacings that didn't, or couldn't, do the job. Depending on the job, of course.

Lyndell had seen light-skirts before; one couldn't help but be aware of certain women in the park or at the opera. Those were high fliers, though, elegant mistresses of the wealthy. She even knew some well-born widows, said to be "in keeping" as one would say "in mourning." Straw damsel, fancy piece, the muslin company, no euphemism quite fit the overripe Molly so well as whore. But Molly was here, and Mrs. Bennett wasn't, so Lyndell could just stop being so old-maidish—perhaps her own dismal appearance was making her catty—and start snooping on her own.

"Do you think anyone will come out tonight?" she began. "It seems to be snowing harder."

"This is just the first of it. The ground's not froze up yet so it won't last. Some folks from the Manor'll stop by. Jake the groundskeeper'll see the lights. That's from King's Mark. D'you know him?"

Who was doing the questioning? Lyndell wondered. Of course she knew Jake, and of course he didn't know any Lynn Riddley. She improvised rapidly: "No, I don't know

23

anyone in this area. I went to live with my mother's family when my father and Jasper came to King's Mark."

"Then you don't know Jasper too well, do you?" Molly asked, still probing.

"Well enough" was Lyndell's totally honest answer. "I haven't seen him recently, but we keep in touch with each other. That's why I'm here, of course."

"And did he happen to mention why he left so sudden like or when he'll be back?"

Lyndell couldn't tell whether she was being asked for answers, or just to test how much she knew. Molly had to know about the smuggling, and the dead courier at least, but she wasn't offering any information. Lyndell decided to give nothing away either. "He mentioned that he had a few problems and a few possibilities. Did he discuss anything with you?"

"No . . . He owes me some back wages, so I was just curious like."

It appeared to Lyndell that whatever else she knew, the other girl had no more knowledge of Jasper's whereabouts than his sister did. This was getting nowhere. Wiping industriously at a window pane, she casually enquired about the usual customers. "Besides the local working men and farmers, of course, I was wondering if any, well, titled gentlemen ever visited here."

Molly almost doubled over, laughing. "What, the country folk too rough for you? So you thought you'd throw your cap at some fine-breeched cove?" Still laughing, she made for the door and winked. "Let me tell you, dearie, no fancy gent's goin' t'offer the likes o'you nobut a tupenny tumble, and that only if'n it's real dark."

The night wore on, tediously. It was Wednesday; she could be dancing at Almack's. A few locals clumped in, stomping the snow off their heavy boots in the hall. From her parlour she could hear them call for ale, joke with Molly. One or two even recognised Bennett, and many welcomed him back. From what Lyndell could hear of the conversations, none were anxious to talk of Jasper or the Quinns, most likely because of their own connexions with

24

the smugglers. The talk centered on the snow: how long, how much, how bad for the crops and herds. Lyndell was yawning, considering going upstairs to bed. She didn't dare search Molly's room. Who knew how a lonely drover got ready for winter? And Jasper's belongings wouldn't offer much but dirt and debts. If he had any evidence of who was behind the smuggling or spying, he'd have given it to the authorities himself, to clear his name. On the other hand, he might more likely have used the proof to blackmail the traitor. Either way, he wouldn't have run. And where could he have run to?

Her thoughts were broken by a commotion outside: a carriage pulling up, the dog barking, carriage doors slamming, angry shouts, the sound of horses being whipped up and away. Lyndell stepped out of the parlour just as the front door crashed open. Cold air, a billow of snow, and a petite blond beauty holding a hatbox and wearing an ermine cape rushed in. The girl, sobbing hysterically, flew right into Lyndell's arms. Almack's was never like this!

Chapter Four

*L*yndell pushed the newcomer through the parlour door and shut it on the gawking faces of the inn's customers as soon as she'd called for some hot tea. The girl was already standing by the fireside, holding her hands out to the warmth, still weeping. Lyndell helped remove the cape . . . and gasped. Under the fur, under exquisite gold ringlets only a trifle disordered, and enormous blue eyes just a bit reddened, and a magnificent collar of pearls too heavy for such a young, small girl, was the unmistakable black uniform and tiny white apron of a lady's maid.

25

"Good heavens, you've run away with your mistress's cape and jewellery!"

A watery giggle issued from the rosebud mouth. "It's the other way around, ma'am. I stole my maid's uniform, but the pearls are mine." Tears again. "And I am running away, but that awful man wouldn't take me to London after he took my money. He said it wasn't enough unless I . . . I . . . and the snow . . . and now I don't even know where I am!"

Lyndell quickly handed over a handkerchief. "You're about an hour from Framingham, if that's a help, and I'm Miss Riddley. My brother owns this inn. Where did you . . . run away from?"

"From Yorkshire, but I shan't go back, I would die first! Couldn't I stay here, please, ma'am? Only till I could earn enough for the coach to London? I'd work. I . . . I could be your abigail?"

The dubious look that accompanied the question struck Lyndell's sense of humour. They both knew no self-respecting lady's maid would permit her employer to face the public rigged out the way Lyndell was. Her own Betty would have kittenfits at the very idea of the navy wool. Just in time to save Lyndell from having to explain her chuckle in the midst of such a dramatic plea, Sarah walked in with a tray.

"Ah, Mrs. Bennett, here is my maid from London, arrived at last." Lyndell spoke loudly, for the benefit of the tap room clientele.

Taking in the pearls, the cape, the kidskin half-boots—and the uniform—Sarah raised her eyebrows. Nobly, though, for the listeners, she replied, "And not a moment too soon."

Lyndell ignored the cryptic remark, directing Sarah to place the tea, then see to a fire in the room next to Lyndell's for her "maid." The instant the door was shut again she turned back to her teary visitor. She looked at the angelic face over the top rim of her uncle's spectacles—the only way she could see anything at all—and announced: "I'd be the first to admit that things are not always what they seem, and there are times when deceit becomes a necessity. This is not one of them, however. If you wish me

26

to help you, you'll have to tell me the entire tale, with no roundaboutation, mind. No, I'm not going to toss you out in the snowy night like some unwashed baggage, you peagoose, so stop crying."

Perhaps it was the tea, or Lyndell's firm authority, or the reassuring "peagoose" she'd heard all her life, but the sniffling stopped and the story began.

Her name was Felicia Fullerton, she was seventeen, and, as Lyndell suspected, she was well born. Though the family was undistinguished, her parents were well connected and wealthy. Unsaid but implied was that they were also unable to cope with their headstrong, romantically inclined daughter. After hearing of the few "minor scrapes" this tiny beauty had landed in while still in the schoolroom, Lyndell could sympathise with them. The French tutor, the vicar's son, half of a naval installation—the chit had more hair than wits! Exasperated, the father decided to marry her off. . . .

"I just grew out of my braids and I'd have had to put on caps!" Miss Fullerton took one look at Lyndell's voluminous head-covering and began sobbing again, which didn't exactly help her cause. "No London season, no balls or parties!"

"Don't be silly, married ladies get presented too. They go to quite as many balls and with fewer restrictions. An arranged marriage mightn't be perfectly what you had in mind, but . . ."

But there was worse to come, she learned, between blubbers. Felicia's father had been in contact with an old friend, whose nephew was of an age to take a wife. Not only was the nephew *old*—at Lyndell's exclamation Felicia wisely added that thirty was too old for seventeen—but he was a retired soldier who'd been used to giving orders and being obeyed, just what her papa felt she needed.

"It . . . it might have been all right . . . some arranged marriages do work for the best. . . . I wouldn't mind being a marchioness, I think, and I would have tried to love my husband, and make him love me. But Cheyne is . . . is a rake."

"Good Lord. The Marquis of Cheyne?"

"You see? Even you have heard of him."

For the past month or so, since the marquis had returned from the war in Belgium, Lyndell had heard of little else, though she'd never met him. He didn't attend Almack's, only the Cyprians' Ball. He wasn't seen at Sally Jersey's rout but he was spotted in Harriet Wilson's theatre box. He disdained the ton, choosing instead the demi-mondaine, the other-world of gaming and fast women. *That* was the arranged *parti* for this innocent child? "Good heavens" was all Lyndell could think to say.

"He'd never love me! He has his pick of every beautiful woman in London. They're sophisticated and . . . and smart. So you do see why I had to run away? He was coming to visit, his uncle wrote. I just had to leave."

Lyndell could see all too clearly: a loveless marriage to an unscrupulous libertine. She herself had been rejecting such offers for years. At least the marquis was known to be well-to-pass, so he wasn't after Felicia's money, unless he'd already gambled his considerable fortune away, but no, Felicia certainly would not be forced into this particular marriage. Lyndell would see to that!

Felicia giggled. "Well, I don't quite see what you can do, ma'am. I thought if I could just get to my aunt, Lady Forrester . . ."

"Lady Forrester has gone to Berkshire for her daughter's lying-in. You'll do better right here, you'll see."

Felicia nearly gaped. "Do you . . . that is, could you . . . know my aunt?" Felicia may have been a green country cloth-head, but she knew very well that her aunt did not number among her acquaintances dowdy ladies from hole-in-the-corner inns.

Lyndell did some long and hard thinking—an instant's flash of intuition, her best kind—and decided to reveal her own identity. "You'll recall that I mentioned things weren't always what they appeared. I'm not really Lynn Riddley, thank goodness; I'm tired of her already. My name is actually Lyndell Markham and, yes, I do know your aunt, and your cousin Elizabeth."

Laughing, Felicia said, "Miss Riddley, if you are the

Magnificent Miss Markham, one of the most fashionable ladies in all London, I must be Princess Charlotte!"

Ruefully, Lyndell joined in the laughter. Then she removed the spectacles and the gruesome cap and shook out her curls. She wiped her face on a napkin while the younger girl watched, entranced. Finally Lyndell swept Miss Fullerton's ermine cape over her hideous navy sack and sank into her deepest court curtsey. "Your Majesty."

Later, in Lyndell's bedroom, the two young women made plans.

"You'll have to write to your father, saying you are visiting me at King's Mark. That will keep him from worrying, or searching. By the time he sends for you, the marquis should be long gone. If not, I'll take you into Berkshire myself. First we must catch a spy."

Felicia was suitably impressed and wide-eyed at Lyndell's tale of High Treason. Shivering delightedly at the warnings of danger, she clapped her hands when Lyndell assigned her the role of Felicity, lady's maid. She went off to her room vowing this was the most thrilling thing that had ever happened in her whole life, and Miss Markham— Miss Riddley, that is—would never regret her new ally.

Lyndell, however, already did. She went to bed feeling remarkably old for twenty-four. Instead of having her own Grand Adventure, she felt more like the director of a play. A farce actually, even with the threat of violence. Her hero, Jasper, was a coward, her damsel in distress was a delightful widgeon. She had numerous disguises and false identities—and no clue as to the next scene.

Chapter Five

Mrs. Bennett brought Lyndell's chocolate early the next morning. She grumbled something about the "maid" being fast asleep, so Lyndell had to explain Felicia's predicament, and her decision to let the girl stay on.

"You'll see, it's working for the best. I've decided to visit Jasper's Captain Jamison this afternoon while Mr. Bennett goes to town. I'll make sure Benny has Miss Fullerton's letter to post, and a note for Tyler at King's Mark, in case anyone enquires for me. You have to remain here, naturally, so my maid Felicity is the perfect one to accompany me, the ever-so-respectable Miss Riddley." Her enthusiasm for Miss Riddley evaporated with the donning of the brown bombazine. Isabelle must have been four months increased when she had it fitted! "Did Joseph learn anything last night?" she asked, pinning her hair under the cap.

"He learned he's still good at draughts, naught else. The local folks're wary of strangers, even if some knew us once. It takes time, Mr. Bennett says. Come now, miss, the egg-man stopped by, so there's fresh for breakfast, and I've asked him to fetch us some chickens for dinner."

"Your chicken pie? Famous! Did the egg-man say how the roads were?"

"He said fair now, with the sun just out, but apt to turn mucky if it warms. Mr. Bennett says it feels like more snow in the air, in his finger joints likely, so you'd best get along with your errands for him."

When Lyndell reached the kitchen, Bennett was already out, "Seeing about that cur with Sam'l." Lyndell hurried through her eggs and muffin, then made for the back door.

Sarah stopped her with a smiling, "It's right cold out—you'll need this."

"This" was an ancient and lumpy squirrel-lined wool shawl that must have done battle with moths—and lost. A relic of the departed Mrs. Quinn or left by a guest in lieu of payment, it undoubtedly matched Lyndell's outfit far more suitably than her fur-lined green cloak.

"Complete to a shade, am I?" Lyndell asked, pirouetting across the kitchen. "But I shan't wear it when Felicity and I go to see Captain Jamison. He'd wonder that they had maids in the poorhouse!"

The dog's surroundings were improved by the bench for shelter, one of Sam'l's blankets for warmth and a bowl for fresh water. Its temper, if anything, was worse.

Bennett and Sam'l stood out of range, tossing small chunks of meat. Whenever they took a step closer, however, the huge brown beast charged, snapping.

"Here, let me try," offered Lyndell, but Bennett would have none of that.

"Oh, no, miss. The dog's mean. Most likely been whipped so often it won't let anyone near. See the marks on's back?"

"How terrible! No wonder the poor thing is mean. But Sam'l, I thought he was your friend. Won't he let you touch him either?"

Sam'l just looked down, so Bennett answered for him: "Likely Quinn whipped the boy too, so he feels sorry for the beast." The small figure in his cut-down jacket just shivered.

Lyndell felt her throat close up. She wouldn't cry though; that would help nothing. Instead, she firmly declared, "Well, no one shall hurt either of them again, ever. Give me the bowl. If it was Quinn who hurt the dog, maybe your voice and the smell of horses remind him. . . . Here Ajax, nice dog; good dog Ajax," she called softly, crooning as she slowly inched forward, tossing small bites of food until she was almost close enough to offer a bit in her fingers. Her method seemed to be working, for Ajax made no effort to charge at her, and he'd stopped making the gnarring sound

31

deep in his throat between swallows. Very gingerly Lyndell held her hand out and just as fearfully Ajax accepted the morsel. Another step. Maybe he'd sniff her hand or let her pet him? At the last step what she saw made her gasp and jerk her arm back. Her sudden movement caused Ajax to go stiff-legged and snarly and *his* return to hostility made Lyndell back away. Very slowly.

"It's awful!" she told Bennett when she reached his side. She barely noticed that he put down a sturdy log he'd been holding. "The dog's neck is all raw and the rope is cutting right into it! He must be vicious with the pain! Who could do a thing like that?"

"They must have tied him as a pup, then he got too mean to handle so they just left him. Happens that way. Couldna' been too long. He's not full growed, for all his size."

"Well, we'll just have to cut it off him." A knife appeared from under Bennett's leather smock. "Right. *I'll* have to cut it off him." This time she waited to make sure Bennett had a firm grip on the log before approaching Ajax.

Maybe the poor brute saw a man with a weapon; maybe he'd just had enough to eat. Either way, he wasn't letting Lyndell get near him.

"Good Ajax. I know someone hurt you, poor doggie," she chanted, approaching step by slow step. Ajax retreated, growling low. Lyndell put the bowl of food down, thinking that she would work on the rope collar while Ajax lowered his head to eat, but the dog didn't lower his head. Just as she reached her hand out again, saying, "We're only trying to help you," the dog lunged and snapped his jaws shut a hair's breadth from her fingers.

"I don't think he understood about our helping," Lyndell gasped, again next to Bennett, handing back the knife. "What do we do now? If we untie the chain, he'll just run away and die. If we leave him . . ."

"He'll die. Infection or chokin' or starvin' when he can't swallow no more. It'd be kinder to end his sufferin' right now. I'm sorry, laddie," he told Sam'l, "but you can't want him to go on hurtin' so bad, now can you?"

Lyndell couldn't see the boy's face, his chin tucked so tight against his collar, but she saw his head shake, then a tear fell on his scuffed and ragged boot-top. What about the boy's suffering?

"Not yet, Benny. We can give it a few more days, can't we? He's not sickly and he's eating fine and—you saw—he almost let me pet him. I can keep trying, bringing him treats, talking to him. Maybe he'll let me work on the rope tomorrow, or the next day. What do you say?"

"I say you never listened to me about tryin' to fix a busted sparrow neither." He pulled a handkerchief from his pocket and turned away to blow his nose.

Lyndell was finding it a little hard to swallow herself. She cleared her throat before telling Bennett and Sam'l she had to see about writing a letter for the butler at King's Mark.

Chapter Six

*L*yndell was driving Jasper's curricle, wearing her green cloak. "Felicity" was sitting beside her, wearing the decrepit squirrel shawl and a frown. She couldn't quite see why, if she couldn't wear her ermine cape because a maid *wouldn't*, she couldn't flirt with the egg-man, which a maid would. Lyndell was dizzy from trying to explain how pretending to be a serving girl had nothing to do with acting like a lady. She almost thought she was doing the Marquis of Cheyne a favour.

For now she had to push Felicity's problems to the back of her mind. There was the dog, and there was Jasper—*where* was Jasper?—Molly, and this Captain Drew Jamison at the Southwold Barracks, the one who was investigating the murdered courier. How much of Jasper's letter could she reveal? For that matter, how unentangled was Jasper in the whole affair? On reflection, she realised that she had only his word that he knew nothing of Quinn's doings, and Jasper's word was something less solid than Stonehenge. So what was she doing here, driving the sorriest nags she'd ever been behind—trust Jasper to own retired plowhorses—over slush-covered roads that she couldn't even see? She snatched the benighted spectacles off her nose and threw them into Felicia's lap.

"Take these," she said, "and remind me to put them on when we arrive."

The reminder of Lyndell's own sacrifices seemed to moderate Felicia's indignation. She brightened up, under the dreadful grey shawl, and began questioning her dear Lyndy about "the Season." If Lyndell had ever been that eager she certainly couldn't recall it. Of course, she'd never been as sheltered as Miss Fullerton; she had attended small parties well before she was officially "out," becoming accustomed to Society from her earliest days. Maybe that was why she was so . . . well, jaded was the word she thought of, so bored with Society. Maybe she should retire to Suffolk permanently, and grow roses (which made her sneeze). Maybe she should just reconsider Isabelle's advice about a comfortable hus—

"Halt, who goes there?"

Captain Jamison took thirty minutes to decide to see Miss Lynn Riddley. During this time she sat in the carriage, chilled, impatiently tapping her foot on the floorboard, while Felicity/Felicia smiled at every passing soldier, and every soldier in the whole fort found a reason to inspect the carriage and its dainty occupant. Felicity was adorable, despite the shawl, which she managed to slip off her shoulders, baring enough to the chill air to raise goose bumps on the pink flesh. The black of her uniform, crisply pressed again, hemmed and gathered by Mrs. Bennett to mould the plumply rounded figure, well became the girl's rosy colouring. The blond curls, which neither Lyndell nor Felicia had been able to manage creditably, were gathered up onto Felicia's head with a scrap of black lace ribbon from one of

Lyndell's petticoats, letting the ringlets fall down her back. Not quite right for a lady's maid, but extremely pleasing to a handsome young corporal begging to know where such a lovely flower had sprung from. Lyndell had the dreadful thought that Felicia might mention the King's Pass Inn by name, filling the tavern with panting soldiers. Lyndell's vivid imagination could see Bennett beating them off with his log while Molly got rich. Not a moment too soon, Lyndell kicked her companion soundly on the ankle, causing that young lady to blush and finally lower those blue eyes. Miss Riddley, at her own haggish worst, froze the soldier with a daunting grimace through the distorting lenses.

Then a young private, a boy really, stammered to Felicia that the captain could see her mistress now. The rush to hand Felicia down could have routed the French years earlier; Miss Riddley had to accept the reluctant hand of what looked like the company cook. At least his stained apron suggested that, though why he'd be standing near the gate was beyond her. If this was how the army was run, no wonder secrets could be stolen . . . unless caution was much relaxed now that the war was finally over and these men would soon be civilians. No matter. She firmly gripped Felicia's upper arm and pulled the girl along with her after the private.

Captain Jamison greeted them in an anteroom, buttoning his uniform jacket, with effort, over a low paunch. His eyes gave Miss Riddley the merest glance at the introduction, straying to Felicity for a thorough look. While he was thus discourteously occupied, Lyndell conducted her own investigation, over the spectacles' rims.

Jamison was fortyish, one of those gentlemen who try to act younger and succeed in seeming older, or foolish. He had thin blond hair of a wishy-washy colour, combed into a wish-he-had-more style, streaky bands pulled across his head and spread out to cover more territory. His eyes, travelling up and down Felicity's charming figure, were dampish, with disappearing white lashes. There were crumbs in his yellow moustache. Altogether Captain Jamison was not Lyndell's ideal picture of an English officer.

When she explained that her mission was of a private,

35

delicate nature, he gruffly gestured her to the inner office. Lyndell pushed Felicity into one of the outer chamber's two chairs and whispered as forcefully as she could, "Sit there and *do* be quiet." She gave a last vicious look to the young private, who reddened and then fled outside, before she followed Jamison, shutting the door behind her.

Jamison was already at his desk, lighting a cigar with brown-stained fingers. He impatiently waved the foul item in the vague direction of a chair, then sat down. If she'd come as Miss Lyndell Markham, she thought, this pompous little twit would be hopping up and down, offering her wine or tea or the best seat and hanging on her every word. There was a lesson to be learned there, Lyndell realised, one she would have to consider seriously at a later point, a moral she knew would be good for her soul. Right now, however, the lesson she was learning—had learned quite well already—was that she enjoyed being Lyndell Markham far more than she did being Miss Lynn Riddley! This afternoon, however, she had to be plain—Lyndell chuckled to herself at that double-edged word—Miss Riddley, with no authority and no right to demand courtesy. She was simply Jasper's spinster sister, come to see if she could help clear her brother's name.

"No, no, ma'am, there's nothing you can do ... unless of course you know where Riddley might be right now. My superiors were not pleased with his disappearing."

"Is ... is he suspected of anything?"

"There's no certain proof. They merely want to talk to him."

"His nerves were so overset by this whole situation, he had to take a repairing lease. His health, you know, has always been delicate."

The captain picked at his fingernails with a penknife. "No, I didn't. Frankly, ma'am, I don't see what you're doing here. If Riddley has nothing to hide, he should be out in the open. If not, he's well out of it. So why don't you just go back to where you come from and let us handle it."

Of all the patronising pap! He may as well be patting her on the head, while fitting Jasper for a hemp necktie! "Sir, I feel I'd do better at the inn waiting for the London gen-

36

tlemen Jasper mentioned as having some connexion with the messenger who was murdered."

Jamison gave her a hard look. "A London gentleman, eh? He didn't speak of it to me before he loped off. What else did he happen to mention?"

"Why . . . why nothing else. Just that a murder was committed, secret documents were involved, and you were questioning him. That must mean you suspected the inn was involved. But it was the Quinns who ran off—"

"Aye, the Quinns. Let me tell you, Miss Riddley, the Quinns may have had more to hide than your brother. Maybe not. But Mrs. Quinn was found drowned up near Yarmouth this week. Maybe in a scuttled smuggler's boat trying to escape to France, and just maybe made to look like a drowning by someone who didn't want her talking." He held up three fingers of one hand, fingernails still dirty, Lyndell noted, even in her horror. "Maybe that someone was Quinn"—he bent down the first finger. "Maybe your London gentleman." The second. "And maybe your precious brother Jasper."

She gasped, but he went on, brutally: "I'm not saying what I suspect, but I am saying it's no place for you. Traitors don't sit around drinking tea, ma'am, and reading sermons. And murderers, two-time murderers, don't care much for manners! So go do your good works, lady, somewhere else." His voice had raised to a bellow at the end, but Lyndell did not flinch.

"Jasper is not a spy. Nor is he a murderer." She stood in quiet determination. In some belated regard for the amenities, Jamison stood also. His efforts at placating her having failed, and his attempt to frighten her away as well, he gave up in exasperation. "Very well, go back to your flea-ridden inn and wait for your Town nob. Send me a message if you find any proof."

"Thank you, Captain, I'll certainly do that."

She extricated Felicia from a knot of soldiers—someone had offered *her* tea—and stalked out to the waiting carriage. The captain handed her up, then Felicia, who turned to wave gaily back at her new admirer.

"Abominable girl! Don't encourage them. Especially not that despicable Captain Drew Jamison."

"Isn't he though? He even pinched me on the way out."

Despite all the turmoil raging in her head, Lyndell still had an ounce of pity to spare for any man unfortunate enough to marry this brazen chit. She snapped the reins to get her team to a steady gait, one just possibly faster than she could walk, and removed the eyeglasses as soon as the Southwold gates were behind her.

Even before Miss Riddley had her back to him, Captain Jamison stomped to his office, shouted for a messenger, stubbed out his cheroot and scrawled a note:

"Jasper Riddley's sister here, asking about London gent. Advise."

Chapter Seven

*L*yndell was depressed. Things were going from horrid to hellish. She could have done Jasper as much good by staying in London! And then she wouldn't have involved her dear friends the Bennetts in this maelstrom. Nor would she have encouraged Felicia to stay where the girl's very life might be threatened. As for the boy and the dog and this wretched inn, how in the world did she get to be responsible for all of them?

She'd returned from the visit to Jamison at another cloud-early dusk, to a scene of perfect tranquillity. Bennett and Sam'l were counting harness, the boy nodding as Benny slowly and clearly gave each a number. Mrs. Bennett was at the kitchen table, her pots bubbling on the stove, stitching new curtains from the fabric Joseph had fetched back from Entwood, the nearest town. Tiny red

38

roses on a cream background. Another murder, and Sarah was sewing curtains! She already knew about the murder, it seemed, gossip in Entwood being full of that. No one had actually blamed Jasper, Bennett had reported, but everyone was wondering where he was, that was certain!

"Tongues running on wheels, I'd wager. But why shouldn't I be making new hangings? It's no great expense, and'll make the place ever so much more homey. If we decide to leave, why, the new people will have a friendlier welcome. And as for the boy, he'll need to count just as well in Islington, now won't he?" Sarah looked so content, so sure the world was a good place for her and hers, Lyndell hadn't the heart to argue.

She took a bowl of chicken scraps set aside for the dog, and tried that futile task once more. Ajax let her approach, and even licked her fingers. But when she attempted to bring the knife toward his neck, he lurched away. He didn't try to snap at her and wasn't growling so loudly; he would not let her touch him, however. She was hesitant about trying again, not for fear of being bitten anymore so much as of injuring the dog worse with the sharp knife if he continued the sudden moves. He ate the chicken, but he held his head to one side, stiffly.

Sam'l was watching her face intently for a sign of hope, and she had none to give him. She placed a dry blanket under the dog's bench.

Dinner was a dismal affair, despite Sarah's chicken pies. Lyndell had tried to convince Felicia to return home. It was just too dangerous here, she told the girl, without, for Sam'l's sake, mentioning the fate of Mrs. Quinn. There was a world of difference between a genteel spy, she warned, no matter how treacherous, and a hardened killer. Bennett could go into Entwood and hire a carriage and driver, trustworthy ones, so Felicia would be safe.

The girl would have none of it, especially now that things were getting exciting. No, she wouldn't go to her aunt in Berkshire, to Lyndell's aunt in London, not even to stay at King's Mark. No threats of possible scandals could shake her determination to remain. Besides, Lyndell needed her. Hadn't she been handy this day? Wasn't she to stand guard while Lyndell searched Molly's room? When the cornflower blue eyes started to fill with tears, Lyndell relented, against her better judgement. Felicia instantly decided to be a proper maid and bounced up to serve the coffee, spilling some, of course. The stain wouldn't be too visible on the brown bombazine. That was the bright side.

Bennett had nothing more to report from his visit to the village. And no one at King's Mark seemed to know about Jasper, "though old Tyler's getting past it, miss. I expect you could hide the Prince Regent and his cronies in that great barracks of a place 'n Tyler'd not notice." Bennett would have to make a less overt visit sometime, to get a better look. He'd given Tyler Miss Markham's note, saying she was on her way, but if anyone asked, she was simply not receiving. Bennett didn't hold much confidence in the old man's understanding, though, so if any London acquaintances should stop by, by chance or Aunt Hardesty's direction, they might be told she hadn't yet arrived! What a furor that would cause! Another thing to worry about; a worry she scarcely needed.

The search of Molly's room, while she was safely at her own supper, prolonged by Bennett's conversation, was another wasted effort. Lyndell learned a great deal about a tart's tastes (garish) and habits (sloppy), but nothing about spies. Unlike Jasper, Molly didn't seem to accumulate possessions, just a hoard of paste jewellery and tawdry bonnets with wax cherries. Even the false cherries had chips in them.

Jasper's rooms were being made neater, in stages. Felicia was delighted with this task, learning more about a gentleman's habits than she'd learned in her short lifetime. Or than was good for her, according to Mrs. Bennett. Lyndell had to agree, but it was either keep the chit busy with Jasper's discards, or listen to her pleas to go downstairs to serve the customers!

The only evidence that Jasper was guilty of anything but decadence was a nearly empty bottle of fine brandy—obviously French. Obviously smuggled. The inch remaining must have been an oversight, which Lyndell decided to correct once she was alone in her bedchamber. It was the least she could do.

It took Lyndell's coach six or seven hours to reach East Entwood from London, making a few stops. A neck-or-nothing rider on army business, changing horses often, could make the round trip in just over ten hours. So it was that at two-thirty that Friday morning, when Lyndell was fast asleep, having disposed of the evidence, Captain Jamison received the reply to his message:

"Jasper Riddley has no sister. Tell Quinn to get rid of the woman."

Chapter Eight

$\mathscr{I}$t may have been a cold, stormy day in November, but the fates were playing Maygames with Lyndell's future. There she was, safe and warm in her bed, for the present, while in London at that same fatal hour, Wesley Richardson, Marquis of Cheyne, was living up to his reputation.

Not his reputation as a war hero, though that was considerable, Cheyne having served as a much decorated aide under Wellesley and often been mentioned in the despatches. Nor his reputation as a lady's man, if ladies they could be called, which he'd been earning this past month since his return, as if there were no women in Spain, Portugal or Belgium. No, it was his reputation for disdaining the polite world, for pursuing his own pleasures—and conventions be damned. In other words, my lord marquis was in his shirt-sleeves, in a low dive, dicing and drunk. His companions around the baize table were as jug-bitten as he, young members of the idle upper class, using Cheyne's return from the wars as a good enough reason to celebrate.

If any chance observer was asked to pick the ex-soldier from the bunch, his unerring choice would be Cheyne. Not the tallest nor the broadest, he was still the most substantial looking, the most well-muscled of these gentlemen, although they were all Corinthians, sportsmen who worked out at Jackson's boxing parlour, Manton's shooting gallery and Antoine's fencing school. His skin, darkened by seven years of rough outdoor living, contrasted with his companions' fashionable city pallor. His face, also, while certainly handsome with its square jaw and sculptured lines, was more lined as if, at thirty, he had lived longer and harder than his associates, mostly his cousin Willy's cronies. Not all the lines were from polite laughter; there were scars of bitterness from a war that was not all political debate and military tactics. Call it an air of weariness mixed with that of strength and confidence; he was easy to spot.

What was hard for some to understand was why this member of the nobility was not attending Princess Lieven's rout, not being lionised at the Prince Regent's salon, not being fawned over by every matron and macaroni in the ton. The solution was simple: Cheyne did not trust himself in polite society. When he'd first returned, there were the unavoidable family homecoming dinners, the obligatory royal receptions. The men all wanted to congratulate him on the smashing victory at Quatre Bras—later to be known as Waterloo—and the ladies wished to gossip about the Duchess of Richmond's battle-eve ball . . . at which all the young lads had their last dance, their last stolen kisses, before marching off to war, some still in their satin breeches and silk stockings, to be found days later, their bodies rotting on muddy fields. Hundreds upon hundreds, and only the lucky had died quickly. The horses were more fortunate—details were sent out to despatch the wounded and dying, to stop the awful screaming.

. . . Heroic victory, scintillating ball . . . the worst nightmare that Wesley, Lord Cheyne had ever seen, would ever see, for all his days on earth. No, he'd go no more to listen to the chitchat, to smile while his gut wrenched, to dance with all the pretty little girls who wanted to know the man of the hour. Here, in Willy's and his friends' company,

Cheyne could forget it all, even if it took a bottle of Blue Ruin to do it. And these men would not bother him for battle facts, not these grown boys who'd stayed home. Some were embarrassed that they hadn't done their duty, while others envied him the chance to go. They all respected him . . . and everyone but his own cousin feared him.

It was Willy, William Richardson, Baronet, who teased him, who chivvied him with swaggering bravado, to bring the laughter back to those tired eyes. And it was Willy, best loved and almost-brother, who still resented not being able to join up when his hero Wes, at twenty-three five years Willy's senior, went off to war.

Willy's father had still had two years of control over his nephew before Cheyne came into his full inheritance, and Viscount Richardson was bound and determined to keep his cherished nephew out of danger as long as he could. The young marquis, even then strong-willed and steady of purpose, was just as resolute about buying colours and fighting for his country. It took him a long time to convince his Uncle George, but he succeeded, after getting up to every rig and row in Town—and letting Willy tag after him. There'd been duels and demi-reps, nights when poor Uncle George had to stand bail for both his wayward charges, and days when he had to listen to his wife's weeping.

When it came to Cheyne, the viscount bowed to the inevitable, but not for Willy. Oh, no, Willy was too young, Willy was the heir, not just to his father's considerable estates but to Cheyne's vaster holdings and titles. Willy had to finish school. Willy had to console his mother for her dear nephew's absence, after she'd raised the boy from childhood to be her other son. So every time in the seven years of his service that Cheyne returned on leave, or to be reassigned, or was sent to plead before Parliament for more funds for the struggling armies, Willy tried his best to prod his cousin to battle. He wanted the chance to whip old Wes at fisticuffs, to outshoot him, outride, or outdrink him, even outargue him. Sometimes he even managed to do it, too, which made Willy feel a lot better about things in general. It was that kind of night. For his part Cheyne seemed to sympathise with Willy's need to prove himself. He enjoyed

crossing wits or swords with his cousin, and just as cheerfully lost as won, cementing a friendship begun when Willy
was still gurgling in his cradle.

Occasionally Cheyne had even been known to goad the
quick-tempered Willy, just out of a quirky humour. It was
that kind of night, too.

"No, bantling, I still say there's no such thing as an honest woman; they're all selling something. Take a whore,
now"—ribald laughter from the company—"she at least
sets a price and gives fair value." The marquis smiled at his
companions, a lopsided grin that took years off his age.
"But your so-called virtuous woman—hah! She's only
holding out for higher stakes! A man's name, his title, his
money, his home. And what does he get? Some sweet
young thing to warm his bed at night? To see to his comfort? No, he gets a headachy shrew or a watering pot
'doing her duty'!"

Willy was no more in the petticoat line than the other
young men present, yet just to contradict his cousin, he felt
he must defend the fairer sex. After all, his mother was a
woman, and his sister. "Beg to differ with you, Wes, but
you've been out of the country too long. Maybe your
señoritas and mademoiselles can't be trusted, but English
girls—"

"Englishwomen? They're the worst! They're bred to be
warmblooded mistresses or coldhearted ladies, and they've
never understood the two could mix. Not that you'd want
to marry your mistress, but damn, these 'ladies' your
mother trots out for me every time I'm home are like ice
maidens!"

While Willy was thinking of a rebuttal, even his wine-
fogged head saw the trap: he was going to be forced to defend the institution of marriage itself. The next thing he
knew, *he'd* be getting legshackled instead of Wesley. He'd
known his cousin too long.

Then Ferddie Milbrooke, notoriously mild-mannered,
tried to change the subject. "But what of affection, Cheyne?
Haven't you ever been in love?"

44

The marquis tossed the dice in the air. "Love? Why yes, I've been in love," he drawled. "Sometimes thrice a night."

At the other men's laughter, Willy reentered the discussion. "And what of the lady you'll marry someday? Shan't you love her?" he asked curiously.

"If you are thinking of the little northern heiress your father's picked out for me, there's a greater chance I'll grow wings and fly to Yorkshire. Those country girls are the worst of all, rigid morality and no social graces to compensate. No, halfling, just because I'll put a ring on some girl's finger doesn't mean she'll put one through my nose."

Willy *had* in fact been thinking of Miss Felicia Fullerton, a girl he'd known for years. He recalled a tiny china doll—certainly not some cloddish milkmaid—and it didn't suit his new-found ideas of propriety for Wesley to be bantering about his intended like this. With inebriated belligerence, Willy demanded, "Then why in blazes are you going there?"

"Why, to look over the merchandise, of course."

Now, the real reason the Marquis of Cheyne had acquiesced to his uncle's wishes, after listening to innumerable lectures on his duties and responsibilities, how he owed it to the ancient and honourable name to settle down, etc., was because the trip to Yorkshire fit his plans. There was a bit of business the War Office wanted him to look into, some loose ends to tidy up, and here was the perfect alibi for leaving town. He had no intention of offering for the girl, of course. He'd see to his errand, then he'd politely suggest to Miss Fullerton's father that she should know more of the world before making a choice, then he would excuse himself. As he explained to his Uncle George, perhaps he was ready for a little peace and comfort, learning to manage his estates and be a country gentleman. But not with a seventeen-year-old schoolgirl bride! He had nothing against Miss Fullerton, of course—he'd never even heard of the chit before—and he actually had nothing against marriage—for the right fellows!—and women he thoroughly enjoyed. No, his words were mostly the result of the wine and his desire to rile poor Willy. They had the intended effect, of course.

"To look over the merchandise, you cad! To speak of Miss Fullerton like that is insulting and degrading. I won't have it, do you hear?"

"But my dear William, I'm sure I never mentioned Miss Fullerton by name. You did! And if she's my intended, or shall we say intended-to-be-seen, I don't see what you can do about it."

"Well . . . well," young Richardson sputtered, "she's to be the head of my household, so I have the right to defend her honour! And I will and I do! You'll meet me for this!"

As the other men laughed, Cheyne called for another bottle. "But of course, cuz, I always do! What's it to be this time? Pistols or swords?"

Willy was laughing now too. "Come, Wes, you have the choice, I challenged you, remember?"

"So you did. Well, my poor battered face don't need another scar, and I'm too foxed for swords, so let's try pistols. They're quicker anyway."

Chapter Nine

There were rigid codes for *Affaires of Honour*. Seconds for both sides would meet and discuss conditions and select a secluded location. A surgeon was hired for the injured; a carriage often stood waiting to whisk the victor out of the country in case his man stuck his spoon in the wall. Being illegal, duels were secretive, hushed affairs. All parties would gather at dawn in formal dress, the seconds would make a last *pro forma* effort at conciliation, the weapons would be inspected, the ground marked out. . . .

In the trash-heaped, snow-blotted back yard of the Goose and Garter Tavern, Sir Fenton Crestwicke was making bets with a pickpocket and a rag merchant while the attics-to-let Richardson cousins staggered outside, holding each other up and singing the fifth chorus of "The Mermaid from Dover." So much for *Affaires of Honour*. The Marquis of Queensbury be damned. All of Willy and Cheyne's friends, all more than slightly on the go, were having a delightful time, laying odds, clearing a space of rubbish, setting out torches in the snow. It was just another exhibition of skill as far as they were concerned, by two of the best shots in England. Usually the Richardsons shot each other's hats off, though once Cheyne had managed to pop Willy's new beaver while aiming upside down and backwards between his own legs. That was the stunt which finally got him his army commission. That was also why Wesley and his cousin now simply struck while the iron was hot, as it were, before Uncle George got wind of anything, before Aunt Wilhelmina could develop palpitations.

The pistols were primed. It was to be seven paces, turn and shoot, no dropped handkerchiefs or "Gentlemen, take aim." Back to back, Cheyne, the taller by some inches, told his cousin, "Loser buys breakfast," and Willy answered, "As always." As they took the first step, however, Cheyne was telling himself that maybe he really *should* think of settling down and stopping such tomfoolery. So at the third step he called "Hold." He bent down, as though to remove an obstacle or adjust a bootstrap. It was hard to tell, in the shadows, and Cheyne's greatcoat hid his actions from Willy and the observers. In a moment he straightened, said, "Sorry. Let's continue." Four steps . . . five, six and seven.

Cheyne turned, raised his right arm, and fired—a snowball, which hit Willy smack in the face!

"Wesley Richardson, you blackhearted shabster! Of all the low-minded—" Willy squawked, his friends hooting. Then Willy bent low, dropping the pistol in order to gather his own like weapon for counterattack. A primed and loaded dueling pistol, however, is not the type of inanimate object that can be so casually treated, which the young baronet would have recalled if he weren't so castaway, or so anxious for revenge.

The pistol exploded, the noise echoing off the buildings facing the lot, deafening in the sudden silence.

"By all that's holy, Wes, I think I've shot m'toes off!"

It could have been worse, Cheyne realised. Hell, a dropped pistol could have taken the fool's head off. Instantly cold sober, Cheyne found himself shaking. So many friends lost, and now this most precious of all almost killed without even the pitiful excuse of a war. Never again, he vowed. As they got Willy back to their shared lodgings where Farrow, Cheyne's ex-batman, was competently slicing Willy's boot off, Cheyne kept repeating, "No more chances." His uncle was right, they were too old, they had to settle down. Life was suddenly much too valuable. When Farrow declared that Willy's foot was one bloody mess, but not like to be serious at all, barring fever or infection, the marquis made his decision: Willy'd go with him to Yorkshire. He couldn't be left to face the viscount's lectures alone—even Cheyne wasn't that hardhearted—nor to have Lady Richardson fuss over him. No, first they'd make excuses to the family, then travel to Suffolk where Willy could recuperate and Cheyne would take care of his errand. Then it was on to Yorkshire: settling down, matrimony, securing the succession and all that—for Willy. Cheyne vowed to see his cousin safely settled and out of harm's way by the new year. Naturally, he didn't tell Willy. Handing him a glass of port while Farrow sprinkled basilicum powder over the now-cleaned foot before bandaging it, Cheyne told his cousin to drink up.

"We've got to appear thoroughly foxed if we're not to make mice feet of getting by the governor."

Willy would have fallen right off the couch, laughing so hard, if Farrow hadn't held on to his foot. "Damn, Wes, if I weren't thoroughly foxed now, do you think I'd be here like this?"

The two cousins staggered up the front steps of Richardson House, Grosvenor Square, holding each other up, singing the sixth chorus of "The Mermaid from Dover," very loudly. Since it was now four o'clock in the morning, it was very loud indeed. They let themselves in with Willy's key, and stood in the entranceway, arms around each other, beginning the seventh verse. The eighth verse did it. Doors opened up and down halls, servants came running. But it was the governor himself, Viscount Richardson, in his nightcap, who outdid his son and nephew in volume.

"This is the finish! I've had my fill of the two of you! I'll disinherit you both, see if I don't! Get out! Get out and don't let me see your faces till you've learned some respect. Do you hear me?"

There must have been no one in Grosvenor Square who didn't hear him. Willy grinned and nodded foolishly, but Cheyne, worried for his uncle's health—the viscount was turning red and quivering with indignant rage—was politely reassuring. "Yes, shir. We jusht came to say g'bye—off to Yorkshire, don't ya know, to get reshpectable. Takin' Willy for courage. . . . He's always been up in the boughs when I didn't take him before, don'tcha know."

"Yes, yes, get out! 'Tho I wouldn't let a daughter of mine marry either one of you! Now go before the whole household is awakened."

Even the dead, of course, were nearly wakened, so loud was the prior discussion, but it sufficed. The door was almost slammed in their faces and Farrow and Cheyne could half drag, half carry Willy to the coach. Farrow bundled him in with fur rugs and hot bricks, amid the hurriedly packed bags, while Cheyne checked the horses tied behind. When the marquis walked around to the front to take the ribbons, Willy leaned out of the still open door.

"Say, Wes, are we really going to Yorkshire?"

"Yes, you clunch, and maybe you'll be sober by the time we get there!"

Chapter Ten

$\mathcal{F}$riday morning was grey: grey overcast sky, Isabelle's grey good-works dress, grey face powder over her own peach complexion, a grey, grey mood. Miss Markham was so rarely out of sorts that she had no patience now for her own ill humour. Surely she wasn't missing the empty-headed frivolities of Town, nor the adulation of her prosy admirers. She couldn't be that shallow. Nor would she own that her Great Adventure was turned into a tedious, frustrating interval. No, it must be the weather that had her in the mopes, and she chided herself. The sun was sure to come out sooner or later, and something just had to relieve this idle waiting. If not, she decided, in a few days she'd move the whole ménage, except Molly, up to King's Mark, resume her own identity, perhaps even invite some guests for a country visit. Bennett could keep an eye on the inn, and Jasper could pull his own coals out of the fire. That's what she'd do—in a few days. This morning after breakfast, however, she'd tackle Jasper's accounts, what smidgens of bookkeeping she could find, to see if they told her anything. Just having a constructive course of action cheered her spirits. Something was bound to happen.

Mrs. Bennett was singing to her fresh dough, encouraging the loaves to rise. Obviously there were no clouds on *her* horizon, except Molly, of course. There would be girls from the village coming to help clean this morning, some apples she'd found put up to make into pies. Her man was content gossiping with the tradesfolk and farmers, though he mentioned having to obtain better horses, if they stayed. And the boy had mumbled the whisperiest—and sweetest— "Thank you" she'd ever heard, just for some slab bacon and eggs. If only Miss Lyndy would forget her notions about smugglers and spies, take the pretty little miss with her back to London so Mrs. Bennett didn't have to worry over them, then everything would be just perfect. Except Molly.

"That ... the trollop must go, Miss Lyndy! Why, last night she pinched Mr. Bennett's cheek!"

"Sarah, I think you're jealous!"

Although the older woman's face reddened, she denied it with vigour. "Fustian! At his age? But it isn't right, what with that sweet Miss Felicity to see such havey-cavey carryings-on."

Lyndell was spreading jam on a bun. She paused to lick her fingers before reassuring Mrs. Bennett. "I misdoubt Molly could teach Felicia anything! That girl could smile at a grandfather clock and have it skip an hour! Molly has to stay a while longer, you know, in case our London beau ever arrives. So we can tell if she knows him or not. Don't worry, pet, it can't be long now, something's bound to happen!"

Another futile session with Ajax—he was weakening, but not in his distrust—forced her to admit that time was shortening there too, without much to show. Her only hope was that by the next day he'd be too sick to struggle.

Jasper's books, what there were of them, were more enlightening than Lyndell had expected. Sitting at Jasper's desk trying to decipher his crabbed hand, she first attacked the ledger, and discovered why any gentlemen ever came to such a backwater inn. In amongst "J. Anthony, locksmith" and "T. Phutts, merchant" were interspersed entries like "Lord F. and Lady T. . . . Sir J. and Miss L.R. . . . Lord H-M. and companion." All those couples ... all those unmarried couples! Jasper was allowing the inn to be used as a trysting place! Goodness, let them try it with Mrs. Bennett in charge! Lyndell chuckled, until she realised what a great opportunity this gave the spy to be where he shouldn't. No one would think it remarkable if just another London swell was at King's Pass, waiting for his "companion" to arrive.

Turning to the accounts books, scraps of tradesmen's

51

bills stuffed in envelopes, Lyndell made another observation: while there were the usual expenses for salaries and supplies, these were mostly for foodstuffs, fuel, ale and horse feeds. Nowhere was there a bill or a receipt for wine, or brandy, or port, not even a note from a whiskey distributor. Yet Lyndell had seen the well-stocked shelves, the nearly full wine cellar. She'd even partaken of some herself. The only conclusion possible, she acknowledged sadly, was that Jasper simply wasn't paying for those bottles. If he wasn't paying in cash, he must be trading—what? Silence? A place for the free-booters to store their loads as they brought the stuff inland? Use of his horses and wagon? There was no way of knowing the degree of Jasper's involvement, but it must be considerable. So what should she do now? Go to the authorities? He was still her stepbrother. Burn the evidence? The bottles would still be there without their customs stamps. No, what she had to do was find Jasper, and get him out of the country once and for all! If it took threatening him with his own account books, she'd do it! In the meantime, Lyndell stashed the records in her valise. If the authorities chose to search Jasper's rooms, there was no need to make things easier for them, and if they happened to find them in his sister's closet, no matter. She was studying them—to learn the business.

One part of the business the accounts didn't teach had to do with salaries. The Quinns drew theirs monthly, the inn's maidservants were paid weekly, occasional village help, daily. Sam'l was paid twice, a shilling each time, with expenses for his boots and pants marked in. The curious part was Molly, not mentioned anywhere that Lyndell could find. That afternoon, passing the common room on her way to the front parlour, Lyndell thought to ask the girl about it.

"It's a trade of course, my room 'n keep in exchange for waitin' on tables. And what the gentlemen give me I get to keep for myself. A girl's got to get along, you know." She snickered, bringing an urge to do mischief to Lyndell's usually well-controlled temper. "Or maybe you don't."

Lyndell fled to the parlour before her urge to throw something got the better of her. Felicia was waiting there, still in her maid's outfit, since she had only brought a nightgown and an evening dress with her. A disguise was "more exciting by half anyway." Of course, Lyndell couldn't help remarking to herself, the girl naturally found a disguise exciting; Felicia looked adorable in hers! To Miss Fullerton's regret, Lyndell plunked herself down to read aloud from Miss Austen's latest novel, which she'd brought from London. The younger lady found Miss Austen prosy, much preferring Mrs. Radcliffe, or Maria Edgeworth's Gothic Tales . . .

"You know, where the beautiful heroine is always being kidnapped or ravished or thrown off a cliff. In Miss Austen they only talk. In Miss Edgeworth's books, something is always bound to happen!"

When she heard the carriage drive up, Lyndell's first thought was, Oh, no, Ajax isn't even barking anymore. Her second was to remedy her disguise by snatching the spectacles out of her pocket and pulling the mob-cap down farther on her forehead. She had no time for a third as a tall, dark-haired gentleman in a stylish many-caped greatcoat filled the doorway, shouting orders: best rooms, private parlours, his cattle bedded down.

In two minutes it was as though he owned the inn. Bennett was running this way and that, yes, my lord this and right away, my lord that. Sarah was up and down the stairs, opening up doors, turning down covers, starting hot broth and warming bricks. Sam'l was put to work fetching water for the horses and even Felicia—Felicia of all people!—was told by his high and mighty lordship to run up and light the fires in the rooms. Lyndell, it appeared, was beneath the gentleman's notice; he assigned her no tasks, at any rate. Just as she was gathering her dazed thoughts for a majestic setdown, another gentleman, slighter and younger than the first one's thirty years or so from what she could blurrily see, entered the doorway, supported by a servant.

"This way, Farrow," the first interloper commanded the servant, and led the way up the stairs. Before the younger man, his cheeks flushed, turned to follow, he caught a glimpse of the maid in the hall. "Fel . . ."

"Fell down, did you? Poor sir. Let me help you up the stairs." And Felicia rushed to his side, leaving Lyndell even more dumbfounded. She trailed after the cavalcade to the upper bedrooms in high dudgeon, stumbling over the bottom step.

Upstairs, the man Farrow was helping the younger gentleman out of his coat, a difficult enough task without Felicia still clutching one of his hands. Lyndell said, "The fire, Felicity" and the girl immediately ran over to the fireplace where she stood looking perplexedly at the logs, the kindling sheaf and the tinder box, without having the faintest notion of how to go on. Obviously the ninnyhammer had never started her own fire! Lyndell went to assist, just as she heard his lordship send Bennett for the doctor.

"Oh no!" Dr. Kane was sure to recognise her; he'd brought her into this world! Unfortunately, there was no hope for it, Dr. Kane being the only physician around. Even more unfortunately, she'd uttered her dismay out loud. Bennett's look was a warning, but the large gentleman's glance was only mildly curious.

"Nothing serious, ma'am, I assure you. My ... ah ... friend caught a chill."

"I thought he fell?"

"Well, yes, in the snow. That's how he became feverish. Damp clothes ... Miss ... Miss ... ?"

"Riddley, Miss Lynn Riddley. I am in charge of this inn."

"Ah, I see. Here, Miss Riddley, perhaps we might return to the parlour so Farrow can make poor Willy more comfortable till the doctor comes. And Farrow, there seems to be some difficulty with the fire. See to it please."

Lyndell held firmly to the railing on the way down—dratted spectacles! She couldn't even get a good look at him! But his darkly handsome appearance, that aura of fearless command and the condescending politeness, all convinced her that here was the villain at last! His jacket bespoke Weston, or she hadn't been on the Town for six years; the necktie tied in a Mathematical, the black curls just brushing his high collar labelled him a man of fashion; the diamond stickpin meant wealth, ill-gotten or otherwise. He'd made no demurral when Bennett addressed him as my

54

lord, so here he was, Jasper's fine London gentleman! With an ill companion he couldn't be here for an *affaire*. Why else, then, besides evil designs?

Once in the parlour, she couldn't resist testing her supposition. "I'm surprised you didn't put up at the Golden Bell in Ipswich, sir. They would have better facilities for your horses and sick friend."

Cheyne finally took a hard look at his hostess. Gad, what a quiz! The little abigail must be as inefficient a dresser as she was a maid. Miss Riddley was totally colourless, with a slouch and an awful squint despite the spectacles. She looked like the founder of some religious order, and acted like the village busybody. He'd put an end to that presumption, at least. "Because I didn't want to answer a lot of foolish questions about Willy's injury," he told her dampeningly.

Aha! So he had something to hide, did he? Falling in the snow indeed! When Sarah had brought brandy and the gentleman thankfully sipped it, Lyndell took the opportunity to study him in detail, over her rims. Yes, he was the perfect scoundrel, one to make Maria Edgeworth proud: dark curls, thick unruly brows and long, nearly black lashes for a brooding look; a full mouth, firm chin, and sculpted bones for a sensual, rakish quality. Too bad his eyes were such a warm, friendly brown; they quite ruined the overall effect. Oh well, Lyndell charitably allowed, not even traitors could be totally bad. Traitor he was, though, not even commenting on the fine French brandy, after years of the blockade. Of course he wasn't surprised; he'd helped get it here.

Lyndell had to warn Captain Jamison—and get away from the inn before Bennett returned with Dr. Kane! She excused herself, made a gracious speech about hoping for his comfort at King's Pass, and made her escape, only stumbling slightly over Miss Austen's *Emma*, left lying on the floor. That was not a muffled laugh she heard; it was an evil snigger.

Chapter Eleven

"*J*ump, you blasted bonerattler, jump!" Kind words were not going to make the recalcitrant beast take the gate, so with an unladylike oath Lyndell got down and opened it, and it was not the first gate, either. For that matter, there was nothing ladylike at all about Miss Markham, from the buckskin breeches to the Belcher-style scarf at her neck to the beaver hat pulled low over her short fiery curls.

With Bennett gone to fetch the doctor, and Felicia encamped in the sickroom, there was no one to lend propriety to her afternoon's call on Jamison. Besides, Bennett had taken the carriage and team, leaving only a sway-backed mule and Jasper's broken down hunter, with no side-saddle at hand. Lyndell didn't hesitate for a moment, just proceeded to rummage through Jasper's clothespress. With the breeches tucked into old boots and pulled up with a belt, a fustian coat to cover her ill-fitting jacket, and the casual neckpiece, she thought she made a passable boy. Her hair was short enough, and, with the hat at a cocky angle, gave her a ragtag look she found a lot more appealing than her guise as the dreadful Miss Riddley. After the humbling experience of being an antidote, she was cheered by this jaunty lad. For a finishing touch, she used a pencil to add freckles, before creeping down the stairs and out when Mrs. Bennett's back was turned. She'd managed to saddle Riddles—the only riddle being why Jasper had bought such an iron-jawed hay-burner and why he had given it a family-related name—with Sam'l's wide-eyed help, swearing him, unnecessarily perhaps, to silence. After a regretful sigh for the spy's fine cattle in their stalls, she was off. She should have taken the mule.

At first, the ride was exhilarating. Riding astride, the cold wind in her face, *ventre à terre* to report a criminal . . . this was what she'd come to Suffolk for! It didn't take long for her hardheaded realism to recover from this latest burst of fancy. Riding astride when one hadn't done it since the age of twelve was agony; the cold wind was actually a bitter dampness, chilling already protesting muscles; and riding across farming country on a steed that insisted on keeping all four feet on the ground was downright impossible. She had almost gone right over the gelding's neck at the first fence, and was forced to seek out breaks in hedgerows and crumbling sections of stone walls. What kind of hunter are you? she'd asked the dumb brute, opening yet another gate. Riddles couldn't have chased down a hedgehog, nor he it one curled in a ball! But the final, most devastating prick of her bubble of glory was at the realisation, not twenty minutes out, that she didn't know her villain's name! She could describe his broad shoulders and well-muscled thighs, the straight nose and the scar on his temple, and most of all the feeling of power about him, but could not give him a name.

Captain Jamison had been less than impressed. At first he had refused to see any Master Dell Riddley, then he was incredulous that the lad Dell should be the same person as the righteous Miss Riddley. Next he made her remove the coat and turn in front of him, to see for himself. He saw enough of rounded breast and backside to make him lick his thin, greasy lips. All of this before he'd even hear Lyndell's "evidence." While she was blushing furiously and longing to slap that leer down his hairy throat, he finally offered her a seat. She still couldn't look down her arrogant nose and turn her back on him as Miss Markham would have done; she needed this worm.

"Now miss, or is it master? Shall I offer Madeira or brandy?"

"Neither, thank you, and miss will do. The disguise was necessary to deflect any suspicion a single female riding abroad would have roused."

"That's this disguise. What about the cap and glasses? Why hide your light under a bushel, hm?"

"For personal reasons that have nothing to do with this investigation which, if you could just listen, would be over shortly."

He stopped fondling his moustache. "I told you I didn't need your interference. This has nothing to do with you!"

"But it has to do with my brother Jasper."

"Ah, your . . . brother."

"Yes, my brother, who is under a great deal of suspicion while the real culprit is at the inn right now!" Noting that she finally had his attention, Lyndell hurried on, telling all about the formidable stranger. Jamison laughed.

"You say he's strong. Was he carrying a smuggler's keg under each arm? He gives orders, so maybe he has a lot of servants. His friend's mysterious injuries? Maybe he got caught in milady's chambers, you understand, and doesn't want it known. And as for not answering questions, let me tell you, miss, no man likes airing his linen, especially to a meddling, pushy female. You have no proof, damn it, not even a name, and you take my time with these vapourish imaginings! Leave be, ma'am."

"Then you intend doing nothing?" She jumped up, scrambling into the coat, cramming the hat on any which way.

He stayed seated, again stroking the stained bristle above his wet lips. "Now, I didn't say that, did I? I'll take a ride out tomorrow to look over this spy of yours . . . and maybe you and I can have a little, you know, private conversation too."

She knew. She turned on her heel and stomped out of the office in Jasper's too-big boots.

So there she was, cold, aching and indignant, trying to keep Riddles to a pace that would see them home before spring, if not nightfall. Shadows were bunching up around trees, and every once in a while she thought she heard another horse. Vapourish imaginings, indeed! Bushes don't form conspiracies and rabbits don't wear iron shoes and the sooner she was soaking in a hot tub, the happier she'd be.

"Come, Riddles, you can almost step over this one. Up, you—"

She would have been gratified at how easily Riddles cleared the wall if she wasn't too busy hanging on for dear life, and she would have been surprised at the frantic speed the beserking horse could maintain, if she wasn't already in a state of shock. She wasn't imagining it, they'd been shot at! That was a bullet that had whisked by her ear. If Riddles hadn't been so reluctant a jumper, she might be dead! She crouched low in the saddle, making a small target, or was that for duels? Don't panic, she told herself, the horse is doing that for you. Just hang on, even if your fingers get numb on the mane and your thighs are chafed bloody, just hang on. If you don't break your neck falling off, someone'll come along and shoot you, so just hang on!

Chapter Twelve

*H*ome! Never had a dark foul-smelling stable looked so much like heaven. Lyndell skidded off Riddles's back but kept her fingers twined in the mane. Her knuckles didn't want to unclench and her legs didn't want to hold her up. Muscles unfamiliar with riding astride be damned, it was muscles unfamiliar with being shot at. She cushioned her head on Riddles's warm sweaty neck and just stood there, trembling.

The gentleman stood by the one window in his tiny room, frowning out at the muddy rear courtyard and stable. His mind was on the next room, where Willy lay in a laudanum-induced haze. Gads, what a cock-brained thing to do, dragging him out in the cold! That Dr. Kane had clucked his disapproval, but thought a week's bed rest should see Willy fully recovered, thank goodness. At least now there was an excuse for staying on at this bedevilled

59

hostelry, and no awkward questions from Willy, who seemed content with grinning idiotically at that little maid ... Felicity, was it? And that was just one more small detail about this havey-cavey place he'd store away for future reflection: the stable boy who wouldn't say where his master Jasper Riddley was; that Bennett fellow scooping the doctor away nearly before he'd rolled up his bandages, and before Cheyne could ask him anything; that little chit who had a strange idea of a lady's maid's job; and that Friday-faced landlady! Most likely she'd been reading a book of sermons when he came, the exact type of self-righteous priggery he abhorred most in English womanhood. But what was she doing in this place then, at best a secluded hideaway for wayward lovers, at worst a way station for smuggled goods and stolen information, if the War Office was correct? Well, that was his job, collecting all the niggling inconsistencies and using his trained observer's instincts. He had best start soon, with that fellow riding hell-for-leather through the back woods and directly into the stable.

Lyndell's heart was beating so hard she could hear it. Oh God, it wasn't her heart, it was footsteps! It was him—the man who stole government documents ... who may have killed a soldier ... and whom she had just reported to the authorities! Whatever she did, she mustn't reveal her suspicions, lest he run off before Jamison get there. As matter-of-factly as possible, she tied Riddles to the crossbars, took the saddle off and began rubbing him down. She wished she hadn't lost Jasper's hat on the mad ride home, but her hair was short enough, with luck. She wished she knew how to whistle, just a lad hard at his work, but she could not. While she was wishing, she decided, she may as well wish his lordship would check his own horses and go away. He didn't.

While Cheyne walked down the central aisle of the stable toward the horse and rider, his eyes were adjusting to the dim light from the widely spaced lanterns. Closer, he could see that the horse was dark with sweat, as if it had been running hard for some time. The rider was no more than a gangly youth, awkward in his movements, about sixteen. His face was narrow, almost delicate, saved from being effeminate only by the ridged nose and the smudges on his cheeks. In the shadowy light, the boy's hair looked carroty, and the curls were a trifle too long for fashion, most likely his proud mama's doing. When he filled out some and stopped listening to his mother, he'd be a handsome enough young man, if he lost that trapped-rabbit expression. Shy youth . . . or something to hide? To try to reassure him, and gain his confidence, Cheyne picked up a handful of straw and began rubbing the horse too.

Lyndell immediately walked behind Riddles to the other side, trying to keep the horse between her and this man whose very presence shouted *Danger*. At least, if she kept to the dark side, away from the lights, her expression mightn't tell him how horrified she was at being near a traitor. Somehow, in all her plans to save Jasper, she'd never considered holding conversation with a real criminal, even one as devastatingly handsome as this! She thought she'd take a lesson from Sam'l, too, and say nothing lest her voice give her away. So she touched her forehead in deferential acknowledgement of his presence and assistance, then lowered her head, working on Riddles's legs.

"Nice horse."

What a clanker that was, Lyndell thought. One look at his lordship's team would tell what a fine judge of horseflesh he was. One look at Riddles, the mean little eyes, the ears laid back, that flat head and short neck, would tell the merest whipster that this was not a "nice" horse. Nevertheless, she bobbed her head and said, "Yessir."

"Been riding far?"

Far, as in Southwold Barracks? A simple no wasn't enough; the horse was still blowing. "Nosir, I've been teaching him to jump." A pistol shot was a novel teaching method, but it *had* worked.

Lyndell was running out of horse to rub. When the gentleman asked if she was from around the area, she could finally answer truthfully "Yessir," then she added, "I have to walk the horse, sir, he's hot," which was also true. And, she felt, a brilliant excuse to be gone from this villain's disturbing presence. Riddles, however, didn't agree. He saw his stall, he knew it was dinnertime, and he was not budging. Lyndell tugged on the lead line, pulled on it, jerked on it, while the nag glued his feet to the floor and the large gentleman looked on.

Yes, there was something decidely girlish about the lad, in spite of the nose, the marquis noted. The hands were white and slim, and there was certainly no strength in the wrists. His heavy brows lowered in thought, which Lyndell happily couldn't see, busy as she was whispering promises in Riddles's ear, if he'd only move. Then his lordship brought his hand down, hard, on Riddles's rump, and move he did, almost trampling Lyndell. She barely got the gelding out the stable door, but once out she vowed to keep walking the blasted horse till the gentleman returned to the inn, no matter how her aching legs protested.

After watching for a bit, though, Cheyne decided to stay. The gait was off—the boy's, not the horse's—and there was an ill fit to the clothes, on closer inspection, that didn't complement the cultured accents. Cheyne inspected his own horses, all bedded down nicely, and spent a few minutes stroking his own mount, Alcibiades. He considered the boy's lack of openness all of a piece, and realised he'd have a long wait, if left up to the young man. Instead he met boy and horse on a turn and walked along, one hand on Riddles's back, and continued his questions. Amazing how quickly the horse was cooled down enough! All he found out was that yes, the boy was staying at the inn, and his name was Dell—Dell something or something Dell?— before the lad had his horse back inside and in its stall, this time with Riddles's cooperation.

Lyndell thought about bolting for the inn's back door, but there was no saying this infuriating man wouldn't follow her, or hear Sarah's screams when she saw her Miss Lyndy. No, she was safer in the stable. He couldn't stay here all night, could he? And Bennett was bound to return soon, to extricate her. With Bennett gone, too, she could fill more minutes with chores, bringing hay, grain and water to Riddles, while keeping away from her nemesis, she thought.

He was there, however, taking the heavy bucket from

62

her, asking about Jasper. She was becoming rattled, but honestly didn't know Jasper's whereabouts, so she could answer that one decisively. He was there, even closer, almost brushing against her when she filled a pail with oats, asking about the inn's clientele. And he was there, when she reached up to get a load of hay and her coat opened.

"Ah, that answers a lot of questions," he said.

Not understanding, Lyndell looked at him, then followed the direction of his eyes till she could see her own thoroughly unmannish chest straining against the white shirt. Blushing as only a redhead could, she dropped the hay and made to button Jasper's coat. A large, firm hand on her wrist stopped her. The other hand tilted her chin up. His indrawn breath gave her the only satisfaction of the whole afternoon, though why that should be, she wasn't sure. Here she was, found out by an archfiend, alone and at his mercy, and she was pleased at the obvious admiration she read in his soft brown eyes, the twitch of his lips to a smile.

Still holding her wrist with one hand as if he'd forgotten he had it, he followed the arc of her cheek, ever so gently, with his fingertips, smudging her "freckles" even worse, then traced the line of her nose. And his smile broadened, not wickedly to frighten her, but warmly, and she smiled back, staring into his eyes.

"Ah my sweet . . . Dell. Della? No, it must be Delilah, for surely you are an enchantress with those green, green eyes. But why the masquerade, love?" His smile faded, and the tiny yellow flickers stopped dancing in his eyes. "Of course, the King's Pass Inn. You're meeting your lover here!"

"Don't be foolish," was Lyndell's answer. Somehow what he thought of her was important, even if he was to be hanged shortly. Her sudden look of dismay didn't help alter his conclusion.

"Don't worry, I won't tell. No, don't bother denying it." His fingertips brushed her lips, then continued to her chin, her throat. "You're no country wench, no more than you're a schoolboy, and ladies don't frequent low taverns dressed in breeches without good reason. Unless . . ." His lopsided smile returned as Lyndell watched, nearly mesmerised by

63

his deep voice, his steady gaze, his ever-so-whispery stroking on her neck. "Unless you're no lady."

And he drew her close with subtle pressure on her back, and tilted her head to touch her lips with his, softly at first, then with more urgency, more warmth, until Lyndell's very soul melted. Her legs, complaining for hours, finally quit completely, and she would have been a puddle at his feet if his arms hadn't held her. And still the kiss went on, teeth meeting, tongues caressing, his hands starting tremours down her back.

And yet ... and yet she *was* a lady. She wasn't any light-skirt to be tumbled in the hay, nor an unfaithful wife taking hey-go-mad chances to meet her paramour. She wasn't any mousy old spinster either. She was, for the first time in days, Miss Lyndell Markham, a lady.

She took one step away, drew back her arm, and smashed him across the cheek with every ounce of strength her outrage lent her.

"Just who in blazes do you think you are?" she spit out.

"Cheyne," he answered, just as angrily.

"Chain, as in necklace?" she asked hopefully, but already knowing, fearing, dreading, the horrid truth.

"C-h-e-y-n-e, as in marquis."

"Good Lord!"

"I try, sweetheart, I try."

Chapter Thirteen

Her palm burned, her cheeks burned, and if her lips burned, well, she'd think about that later. "Don't say it," she told Mrs. Bennett, who stood letting a spoon drip on the floor, her mouth open in amazement at Lyndell's appearance. "I need a bath." She could hear her old nursemaid's jaw snap shut, before she heard a very dignified, "Yes, my lady."

Before her bath, though, Lyndell had to warn Felicia that the . . . the ogre she was running away from was here. Cheyne, the famous soldier, the profligate, the proposed bridegroom—Why, he ate children like Miss Fullerton up for breakfast.

Miss Felicia giggled. She'd known since that morning, in fact, as soon as she'd had a moment with Willy, whom she'd known forever, of course, their fathers being such good friends. Willy turned out to be Lord William Richardson, a cheerful young fribble with whom Lyndell was vaguely acquainted and whom she would now have to avoid. Another complication! At least he had sworn not to give Felicia away. He thought it a great joke to pull on his cousin who, he assured the girl, would rather marry the devil's daughter than a little peagoose like her. As for his landlady's not being all she was supposed to be, Willy knew naught of it, Felicia vowed; she'd never give her dear Miss Markham away, after all she'd done for her, and Willy was too ill to look through her disguise. Lyndell swore he'd not have the chance. She'd simply stay out of his room, which brought another matter to hand: it wasn't at all proper for Miss Fullerton to be in his lordship's bedchamber, especially if he knew she was no maidservant.

With another giggle and a quick look at Lyndell's breeches, Felicia reminded Miss Markham that propriety wasn't exactly her own long suit these days either! On her way out, she did reassure her friend that Willy was too ill to lift his head, much less threaten her virtue. Oh, and yes, she'd certainly steer clear of Cheyne, without any urging. The man was dangerous.

How dangerous, Felicia would never know, Lyndell hoped. She didn't have a chance to pursue that thought, either, as Bennett came in just then, toting two cans of hot water and wanting to know what she'd done to put his Sarah in such a swivet. One look at the breeches made him smile, but when Lyndell told him how she'd ridden to warn Captain Jamison of the traitor, his craggy face seamed up in a grin and he slapped his knee. Tears were streaming from

65

his eyes, it was such a good joke. His Miss Lyndy riding cross-country on a plug to turn in one of the most heroic veterans of the Peninsular campaign. Aside from Cheyne's being one of Wellington's hand-picked aides, entrusted with carrying the most secret orders of the whole war, he'd been out of the country till two months ago, as any lobcock who read the papers knew. All she'd had to do was check the ledger, the very same one she'd told Bennett to fetch out, and she would have saved herself a peck of trouble. As for the gunshot, Bennett pooh-poohed it. Just poachers undoubtedly, and nowhere near her. Shots just sounded close in the dark. Bennett couldn't wait to go tell Sarah how Miss Lyndy'd left her wits in London.

At least she'd given her friends something to laugh about, Lyndell thought ruefully as she lowered her poor sore body into the tub. Her legs were still like porridge, with the top layer of skin gone, stuck to Jasper's breeches. And her lips . . .

She sank down lower, shut her eyes and, her fingers to her lips, recalled that kiss. It wasn't her first kiss by any means, not at twenty-four, but the others had been flirtatious, suggestive, quick and, well, cool. None had left her with more than a mild curiosity, or a pleasant tingle; none had left this heat, minutes later. And the warmth wasn't just in her lips, she recalled and, remembering, felt it again. At last, after reading all those books where the heroine felt a fire in her loins, Lyndell knew where her loins were! What a world of difference there was between pleasant and passionate, for though she'd never known passion before, she recognised it instantly.

Too bad its instigator was such a rogue, she thought dreamily, even if he wasn't a spy. If he wasn't a spy, how far could coincidence stretch to bring him to the inn? There was Felicia, but she'd been blown off course; what would Cheyne's excuse be for leaving the main roads, the major posting inns, unless Willy had urged him here? Unless William Richardson, the carefree young Corinthian, was the traitor. . . .

She'd made enough wretched errors for one day. Right now she wanted to think of the marquis. He was an unprincipled rake who took advantage of young girls, but he'd let her go the moment she protested. He was a practised seducer, but she'd let herself be entranced by his voice, his touch, his eyes. He was dangerous. Persistent in pursuit, wickedly observant, and he could ruin her if he knew her name. Dell Riddley had to disappear for good, and Miss Lynn Riddley had to avoid the gentleman like the plague, much to Miss Markham's regret. There it was, as plain as the raw places on her legs: for all his knavery, the indignity and outrage of his behaviour, Lyndell's major emotion, besides the one felt in her new-found loins, was one of relief that the Marquis of Cheyne wasn't her villain after all. And if he wasn't the villain . . .

On her way to dinner, scurrying past the closed front parlour door, Miss Riddley paused, however belatedly, to inspect the ledger, open on the hall table in the innkeeper's niche under the stair. There it was, by the oil lamp's light, in sure, firm letters, *Cheyne, et al.* She touched the signature briefly in what, for a middle-aged spinster, was a remarkably romantic gesture, before hurrying on to the kitchen.

Sarah was still disgruntled, more so when Felicia begged to be allowed to bring the younger lord his supper. Lyndell sided with the girl, especially since that would free the man Farrow to wait on his own master, getting the manservant out of the kitchen too. Lyndell had to talk to Bennett. It was imperative he go up to King's Mark that very night and search out Jasper. She urged him to try the unused grooms' quarters over the stables, or the gatekeeper's cottage, for Jasper had used to be a favourite of old Diccon.

With Bennett gone, though, Lyndell couldn't just flee to her own sitting room where she and her thoughts would be safe. She had to bide downstairs, in case any travellers came. Molly could handle the tap room customers, and Sam'l could take care of the horses, but if someone wanted a room, which they might, the weather not worsening any, Lyndell had to be at hand.

That's why she was still in the kitchen when Dr. Kane returned to check on his patient and see if perhaps Mrs.

Bennett had any of those Bath buns left over. Sarah introduced Miss Riddley, of course, but the old doctor just said "Hmm," giving her a good look.

"There's those that can be fooled, and then again, there's those that can't." He held up his hand to stop any disclaimers. "Take me for instance. Now I know better'n any that Elvira Riddley had no daughter; I birthed Jasper myself, and another stillborn babe that she died bearing. Then again, I'd never heard of the Earl of Markham leaving his butter stamp about the countryside." At Mrs. Bennett's reproachful tsks, he cleared his throat. "Now I'm not putting my nose"—he chuckled at his own wit—"in anyone else's business, but I'd suggest, miss, that I'm not the only one with eyes in my head."

There was only one set of travellers that evening before Bennett returned: *Mr. and Mrs. Blackburn*, the man wrote in the hall ledger, requesting adjoining bedrooms. No maid, no valet, no baggage. They were so busy staring into each other's eyes they gave the dreary landlady no second glance. Lyndell, however, even in the light of the single lamp she'd let burn in the hall, recognised them instantly: Lord Naybors, he of the wife and sickly children, and Sophie Davenant, whose husband was in Vienna with the diplomatic corps.

Naybors she put in Room Ten, across from Cheyne. Sophie Davenant she put in Room One, across from Molly. And let that be an object lesson, my fine lady.

Chapter Fourteen

*C*heyne saw the Blackburns come in. If those two were married he was the King of Persia, but he went back to his dinner of good English country fare. A short while later he heard Mr. Blackburn expostulating over the room arrangements with Miss Riddley, and he grinned. Just like an old prune, if she wasn't going to enjoy herself, no one else was going to enjoy himself. And anything less likely than Miss Riddley enjoying herself—much less in a bedroom with a man—was hard to imagine. Quite unlike his little temptress of the afternoon, he thought, rubbing his slightly swollen cheek. She actually was not so little for a woman, and not quite in the first blush of youth, but she was certainly no milk-and-water miss. He couldn't help smiling in remembrance of her spirit, no more than he could forget the sweetness of her kiss. But who in hell was she? The one-page-old ledger had yielded no information, he and Willy being the only recorded guests, and a quick look showed the rooms near theirs untenanted. He knew she was still in the inn, since her gelding was still in the stable; he'd checked. But he couldn't very well go opening every door down the corridor. Well, he would, if he was sure Miss Riddley wouldn't catch him at it. Cheyne didn't think the girl could be a servant, not when she stood right up to him that way, but that only left a connexion with Riddley or his sister. Miss Riddley was out. What could she have to do with a hoydenish, glorious, green-eyed witch? On the other hand, the idea of his Delilah with that loose screw Riddley soured his wine. He'd just have to wait to puzzle out his mystery woman, along with the rest of this mess.

Damn the War Department anyway. Just go look around, they'd said. The usual thing, there's a good fellow. Well, this wasn't the usual thing, not by a sow's tail. He'd expected to deal firmly with Riddley, talk sociably to the locals, find what he needed, and straighten it out. Instead, he was enmeshed in some deuced petticoat intrigue! Women! And the list of the creatures was growing; even the doctor grumbling about misplaced chits. But which? There was the prudish Miss Riddley who turned down corners when she saw him coming. Her skitter-witted little maid, who had taken to blushing and squeaking in his presence, though she seemed rational enough with Willy, for which Cheyne would have to berate his cousin. The chit was a regular pocket Venus, but gads, a lady's maid! If Willy was too ill to take what she was offering, why was he making sheep-eyes at her in his every waking moment? The boy definitely needed a nice, respectable wife to take him in hand. Then there was the mysterious visitor in the stable, his Delilah. The possessive seemed to come as natural as breathing. Lastly there was Molly, the barmaid, who was the only one of the bunch to show him any friendliness. Right then a little friendliness seemed not such a bad thing. It had been a long day, starting way before the nightmare of Willy's accident in the snow. Besides, Molly was the likeliest source of information he was going to find this long, cold night. Sitting alone in the private parlour with his port—damn fine port too—thinking about Willy lying there in the snow bleeding, or a pair of green eyes sparkling with passion's fire, wasn't going to solve anything. He carried his bottle, now three-quarters empty, and the glass into the common room.

The man Bennett was back from wherever he'd ridden off to earlier. That was one of the most closed-mouthed chaps the marquis had come up against, off on an errand instead of giving an answer every time. The stableboy was worse. Who ever heard of a barn brat not taking a bribe for some information? If Cheyne hadn't heard Bennett call the lad, he'd not even know his name. But there was Molly, with her voluptuous bosom and yellow hair, winking at him as she brought tankards over to a pair of workingmen, swinging her hips in exaggerated motion on her way back to the bar.

Cheyne set his bottle down on a table near the men, in case their talk should yield any clues. All he heard though was, "What's old Molly after now, awaggin' her tail like a bitch in heat?"

"Not for you, you old gaffer. Finer feathers nor yours, she has in mind, I figure." And the speaker nudged his companion in Cheyne's direction. The marquis raised his glass in acknowledgement, hoping to encourage the men's familiarity, but they just turned back to their ale and their talk of fixing the roads, come spring.

Cheyne's bottle finished, he signalled for the barkeep,

who came over, wiping his hands on his apron. Before the marquis could even hint at a question, however, Bennett informed him that Molly would be taking over now, as Bennett had to be up with the horses in the morning. Anything his Lordship wanted, just ask Molly, he said, leaving. Aye, a knowing one was that Bennett, with the look of a horse trader in his eye.

Molly brought him another bottle. Fine French Burgundy this time. She managed to rub against his shoulder putting the bottle down, and gave him a generous view of her admirable cleavage leaning over to wipe at the table.

"Excellent wine you serve here," he mentioned casually. "I wonder if there'd be any way I could purchase a case or so to take home with me."

"Well, I don't know, love. Jasper usually handles that 'n there's no telling when he'll be back."

"Surely you could procure me a few bottles at least, couldn't you?"

"Mayhap I could, if it was, you know, worth my while."

"And what would it take"—laughing brown eyes looked at her over the rim of his glass—"to make it worth your while?"

"I'll have to think on it," she said, going over to settle the farmers' accounts. "Maybe we could talk about it later."

Cheyne had another glass. Then another, while the workers put on their heavy overcoats, their mufflers, their mittens. Finally Molly came back to him, and he merely had to hold an arm out to have her in his lap. Like the gentleman he was, he offered her some of his wine. "Don't mind if I do; not many of the customers offer the good stuff. You're a real fine gent, you are."

With a little snuggling and some friendly fondling and as much wine as it took, he hoped to find out just where this Jasper was, where the wine came from and who her other gentlemen friends were. When she started nibbling on his ear and shivering, saying what a cold night it was, with the downstairs fire put out and all, he knew the lady wasn't giving anything away free. When her hands started roving lower, and she mentioned that maybe, just maybe, she could find the name of Jasper's wine dealer, upstairs,

71

Cheyne decided to make the supreme sacrifice. For God and country.

"I have to lock up down here, love. Go left at the top of the stairs; it's the last door on the left."

Willy was sleeping peacefully when Cheyne looked in on him, Farrow dozing in a chair next to the bed. He'd have to make it up to poor Farrow, but at least the goosish maid wasn't spending the night! He went back to his own room and undressed, putting on only a paisley silk dressing gown and a lopsided smile . . . all in the line of duty, sir. He took a candle with him as he padded to the door in his bare feet, then came back and stuffed a few pound notes in his pocket.

At this moment, the marquis's thinking wasn't quite at par with the battle-heightened acumen for which he was famous. He'd been without sleep for well over two days, and had been living at a fast pace for months before. He'd had too much to drink tonight, and every night this week. He'd had the shock of Willy's accident, his own remorse, and the affecting incident in the stable. In other words, his wits were gone begging. What he was using for brains at this moment was located entirely elsewhere.

Therefore, when he reached the top of the stairs, he went left, and continued on to the last door on the left, just like Molly had said. Of course Molly's directions were from the bottom of the stairs, looking up, not from his room near the central hall.

There was no answer when he scratched softly on the door. Maybe Molly was still closing up, in which case he could do a little snooping, though he didn't really expect to find contraband goods hidden beneath her bed. The door he opened showed a room in darkness, except for snow-reflected moonlight through the rear window. It appeared to be a small sitting room with two equally dark bedchambers to either side. The nearest bedchamber, he could see by his candle's light, was obviously a man's, with jackets, boots, harness pieces and neckcloths strewn about. It didn't take much to deduce that the missing tenant was also the disappeared innkeeper, Riddley. The room was too cluttered for any transient guest, and its corner location gave the best vantage of both the roadway and the stableyard. If this was Jasper's chamber, the other must be Molly's. It followed, to Cheyne's reasoning, that Molly was therefore Riddley's mistress, and his estimation of that gentleman, not high to start, dropped another notch. Not because Riddley had a mistress, not even because she was a rustic like Molly, but that he'd share her with anyone with the price. Unless, of course, Riddley didn't know. It didn't matter a ha'penny. What did was that if Molly shared Riddley's suite, and his bed, Delilah didn't!

With that tortuous reasoning concluded, Cheyne realised his candle was burning low and his bare feet were getting chilled and he could barely keep his eyes open. He could light the fire in the sitting room, offering Molly a chance to sit and chat when she came up, or he could wait for her under the covers. Major Richardson of the Fourth Cavalry would have braved the elements and put aside personal considerations, for the cause. Wesley Richardson, Fifth Marquis of Cheyne, after his second bottle and after bruising his toes on a pile of books, chose the bed.

Molly's bedroom was smaller than Riddley's, very austere by comparison. Surprisingly, there was nothing lying about except there on the bed. "Molly?" he whispered. He got no answer, but obviously she was there before him, playing coy. It seemed there'd be no genial conversation first, after all. Trying to feel regretful that it was to be pleasure before business, and failing, the marquis placed his candle on the dressing table. Then as noisily as he could, he uncrinkled the pound notes from his pocket and placed them under the candleholder, to show he understood the game. He dropped his dressing gown on the side of the bed and got in. The light was even poorer—the moon must be cloud-covered—and his candle was on the other side of the room, so he could barely make out the light curls on the pillow, and he only vaguely noted that the figure under the blankets didn't seem quite what the satin bodice had promised.

Moving closer, he called "Molly" again, and chuckled at

73

her silence. He gently kissed one eyelid and then the other, and placed one of his hands on her breast. The eyelids snapped open.

Cheyne was just considering how this wondrously soft, warm, rounded breast had appeared so . . . so flabby earlier, when a voice hissed in his ear: "It's you!"

"Of course it is, sweetings, you invited me," he answered and covered her mouth with his. This was no tentative kiss, nor sweetly intense. It was hard and demanding, with a fiery tongue. It vibrated with the intent to arouse her to passion. And it succeeded. With one arm she gave him a shove and with the other arm Lyndell gave him another clout on the side of his head.

"I never did, you . . . you libertine!"

The marquis sat up in horror. My God, he thought. It's the landlady! But no . . . he couldn't see the red-gold of her hair, or the green eyes he was sure were smouldering, but there in the unreliable light of the moon was that same profile, that same nose and, yes, it had been that same roundhouse right. Thank heavens!

"Get out, you reprobate, you ravisher, you—"

He got out of her bed before she had the whole house out of theirs, and stood there, trying to apologise. "I . . . I thought you were Molly, you see . . ."

What she saw, in that same moonlight haze, was *his* profile, and evidence that his interest, so to speak, was at the highest. She screeched one more "Get out, you evil man" while pulling the blankets over her head.

Not even when the enemy had charged Valdoz had the marquis moved so fast. He was out of the sitting room, stubbing his toes again, and on the other side of the door before he had his sash tied, and before Lord Naybors had closed his own door, down the hall.

By Jupiter, Naybors gasped, Cheyne and the landlady! That's bravery indeed!

Chapter Fifteen

The first thing Lyndell did the next morning, after unbarricading her door, was have it out with Molly: No flirting with the customers. No painted lips or low-cut dresses. And no men in her bedroom.

"If you're worried about your 'tips,' you will now be receiving a salary." Lyndell smacked Cheyne's five pound notes down on the dresser. "Here's your first payment."

Gads, was all Molly could think of, roused so roughly from her sleep to hear her employer's diatribe. What had Miss Prunes-and-Prisms in such a pelter now? She wiped her eyes. Then, as her mind started to wake up too, she recalled last night's ruckus, and began to laugh.

"So that's what happened to his nibs! What a shock he must have had!" She took in Lyndell's shapeless navy wool gown and the limp cap and laughed even louder. "There's not many women I know as would throw such a handsome buck out of their beds."

"I don't doubt that for a minute," was Lyndell's retort as she slammed the door behind her, leaving Molly flushed with hilarity at the ways of the gentry.

Miss Markham was furious. She was burning, and this time it wasn't with passion. It *was* physical yearning, to be sure, an intense desire to box that lecher's ears. Hang the molester up by his thumbs! Pull out every one of those shiny black curls!

It wasn't just the kiss, though that was bad enough. The kiss itself was actually one of the more stirring moments of her life. She'd never been kissed lying down, and there was a big difference, she'd found. That wasn't the point, however. The rake had come unbidden into her rooms in the

75

·middle of the night, assaulted her virtue and, the supreme insult, apologised for mistaking her for Molly! Boiling in oil was too good for the dastard.

What she needed right now was Jasper: Jasper coming forward with his evidence, even confessing his part in the smuggling if he had to. Then Lyndell could go home, taking the innocent Miss Fullerton out of the old goat's way. What she needed was Jasper to lend her countenance. Much as she deplored the fact, a woman under her brother's or father's or husband's protection was less likely to be harassed, which was why proper ladies were never unescorted. Even if she couldn't see clear to her weakling step-brother's defending her honour against such a virile man as the marquis, she needed his actual presence.

What she got, however, was Bennett's report that yes, he'd located Jasper, and yes, he was hiding out with old Diccon, in the gatehouse attics where he'd go undetected. And no, he would not return to the inn. Jasper felt he did not have enough information to go to the authorities with, Bennett gloomily reported, but he knew too much of the goings-on for the criminals' safety. If he wasn't arrested, he'd be killed, so he was not budging. Unless, of course, Lyndell was willing to lay down the blunt to see him safely out of the country. She considered it, then discarded the idea. His name—and hers—would still have the tarnish on it, even more so if the mess was never resolved. She'd see the lily-livered coward out of the country, all right, but not yet.

The first thing the marquis did when he awoke, after laying a cool cloth on his aching head, was to see how Willy was doing. His cousin seemed to be making a great recovery, grinning like a cat in the cream, while the little maid spooned porridge into him. As if his arm was hurt, and not his foot, Cheyne fumed. Still a little warm to the touch, Willy was in high fettle, but the girl, Felicity, was even more clothheaded than usual. Instead of blushing, as she had previously, now she jumped up and ran to the other side of the bed, spilling hot gruel on her poor patient.

It was Cheyne's turn to blush; obviously the chit had

76

been warned of his own wanton lust. And here he'd been about to chide Willy for dallying with a maid! His own actions looked even worse by daylight. What was he about, making great gaffes like that, nearly ravishing innocent maids? Of course his maid wasn't quite the innocent, not if she was in Jasper Riddley's keeping. Yet there was something so pure about her kisses, and she'd seemed so sweetly willing, up to a point. If he hadn't had such a weathered tan, his cheek would be a discoloured yellow by now. That was the point. At least she wasn't a lady, thank God, with duennas and chaperones and ten male relatives clamouring for his blood. He could just see some stiff-rumped baronet demanding satisfaction unless he married the girl. But a light-skirt?

He'd apologise, possibly buy her a gift if there was a store in the village with some gewgaws, a fan or parasol perhaps, and that would be that. After all, not much had actually happened, certainly not as much as he wished! In order to apologise he had to find her, but without knocking on the door he knew would be locked to him. He didn't even know her name, really, or what she was doing here. For that matter, he didn't know what *he* was doing here!

He had to do better than this, he told himself. Where was all that vaunted intellect, the perspicacity that had kept him alive through all those years of war? If he couldn't untangle this little inn's messy web, he'd be ashamed to face the general again.

"This is the most ramshackle hostelry it has ever been my misfortune to visit. Poor rooms, discourteous service, midnight carryings-on. This is the last you'll have of my custom, Miss Riddley, and I'll be certain to tell all my friends. Good day."

Good riddance to bad rubbish, Mr. Blackburn, Lyndell thought, nearly biting her tongue to keep herself from sending regards to Lady Naybors. No sense in drawing attention, nor in speaking more than she had to, lest he think her voice was familiar. Yet it was remarkable, Lyndell thought, how little people really noticed, especially the upper classes. If you weren't fashionable, or good ton, you barely

77

existed. Just by wearing unfashionable gowns, a cap and spectacles, she faded right into the background. Cheyne had barely nodded to her when they met; Naybors felt he could treat her like a servant; Jamison like a half-wit. A Mrs. Cox, in ermine and emeralds, took one look at Miss Riddley, the squint, the stoop, and requested her rooms through her maid, as if she needed an interpreter. Of course, when a Mr. Bushnell arrived, in corsets and eye-threatening shirtpoints, asking for a room next to his sister, Mrs. Cox, Miss Riddley-the-nonentity took great pleasure in announcing that the inn was full.

Lyndell was wrong, at least about the marquis. At the moment he was very much interested in her. He had just finished shaving and was about to tie the neckcloth Farrow had handed him when a commotion of shouts and snarls and screams in the stable yard below drew him to the window. His first thought on seeing the crowd of people out there was that his red-haired vixen wasn't one of them. His next thought was that with the drab Miss Riddley outside, it was a good time to search the rest of the upstairs rooms. But what in the blazes were those people doing out there? Bennett was holding a pistol, in a very businesslike way. Mrs. Bennett was doing the screaming, flapping a blanket in the air. The sulky stableboy had a jar of something, and Miss Riddley, wielding a large knife, was advancing on a mangy cur that was growling and snapping. The marquis left without tieing his neckcloth.

It vaguely registered in Cheyne's mind that Miss Riddley wasn't wearing her spectacles, but his attention was focussed on the dog. Bennett explained the situation to him, in the most pessimistic of terms, and the marquis assumed charge. He took the blanket from Mrs. Bennett, admonishing her to be still, lest she upset the poor beast further.

"Bennett, do you know how to use that thing?"

"Aye, well enough."

"Let's hope so," the marquis said, advancing closer to Miss Riddley and the dog Ajax, the blanket loosely wrapped around one arm. "Miss Riddley, do stand to the side more, that's it, out of Bennett's line of fire. Right. You, sir," to Ajax, "stop that noise. Down, Ajax!"

Ajax was weak, and terrified of all the people surrounding him, but he heard that voice of authority, the same firm voice used to give orders to the greenest of raw recruits. He was not conceding to it yet, certainly not lying down to be kicked or beaten or whatever, but he did stop lurching about. The marquis approached touching distance.

"Miss Riddley, at the count of three, you will clap your hands and shout, to get his attention. One . . . two . . . three." As Ajax turned to the new threat, the marquis made his move. With one fluid motion he had an arm around the animal's neck and the other hand firmly encircling the dog's mouth, keeping those jaws tightly shut. Ajax whined and struggled to get away, but the marquis's grip was like iron. "Good fellow, steady there. Now Miss Riddley, whilst I hold the mouth, take the blanket—no, take my neckcloth. Tie it firmly about his snout."

Lyndell did as she was told, having to come closer still to remove the white linen from his neck. She was blushing furiously, but luckily Cheyne was concentrating on the dog. She had to brush his fingers with hers, wrapping the cloth. Hers trembled; his were strong, brown, unmoving. She lapped the cloth two or three times around the beast's jaws before the marquis directed her to tie a knot, tightly, behind Ajax's head, "So he can't just scratch the muzzle off."

When that was done, the marquis was able to shift his position for a better grip on the dog's body while Lyndell attempted to cut the rope on his neck. The cord was too deeply embedded, however, the raw oozing skin having swelled about it. Both Lyndell and Cheyne were kneeling in the mud of the yard, his buckskins and her navy skirt fouled now, and she felt like weeping with frustration. "I can't do it without cutting his skin! Oh Ajax, I'm so sorry." Without loosening his hold, the marquis inspected this new problem. Then he turned to Sam'l. "You, boy. Go ask my man Farrow for my shaving razor. Quick now."

Sam'l stood there, rooted in the mud, looking at Lyndell beseechingly. "Sam'l . . . he doesn't talk much, my lord," she told the marquis in a low voice. "We think he was beaten too."

"Damn," with feeling. "But I can't hold the mutt forever. Bennett, can you—" But Sam'l was gone, running into the inn.

While they waited, Lyndell tried to soothe Ajax, stroking his ears, talking softly. Her arm touched the marquis's hand and he looked up. "You're not wearing your spectacles."

"No. I don't . . . that is, sometimes . . ." Giving it up, she took them out of her pocket and put them on, but not before Cheyne had seen green eyes, as clear as sunlight on a spring leaf. With the lenses the eyes seemed blurry, cloudy. Maybe he just had emerald eyes on his mind. No, there, right where the glasses sat on the bridge of her nose, a bump, a ridge . . .

The razor was thrust at him by a grinning Sam'l. "Good lad! Now, ma'am, let's do it before my arm goes numb." If he noticed that she removed the glasses before starting, he didn't comment. "Watch, the blade is sharp. That's it."

At last the rope was off. Sam'l brought the jar of salve Bennett had found in the stable and Lyndell slathered it on Ajax. Shrugging, she wiped her hand on her skirt, already trailing in the muck. She looked up to catch a one-sided almost-smile on Cheyne's handsome face. Embarrassed, she looked down at Ajax. "Now what, my lord?"

"Now comes the tricky part. We must remove the muzzle, without getting bitten, of course, then get him to a place where he can't run away. The stable?"

"Of course. Sam'l, take a blanket and make Ajax a bed in one of the loose boxes—lots of straw so he doesn't get a chill."

"Right. Now, ma'am, undo the knot, but don't loosen the cloth until I have my hand on his jaws again . . . there. I have him. Good Ajax."

With both hands around considerable poundage of dog, the marquis was getting up slowly. Bennett started to come forward in assistance, which caused Ajax to start struggling again. Cheyne ordered Bennett to back off. With a deep breath, the marquis stood up, Ajax in his arms. When he staggered a bit, Lyndell steadied his elbow with her hand—

it seemed the thing to do—and so they made their slow way into the stable.

The marquis was covered with dirt and dog hairs and breathing heavily, but Ajax was in his stall, with Sam'l offering him a bowl of water.

"He'll do, I think," the marquis told Lyndell. He was trying to study her face, but the stable was dark, and his eyes were not adjusted from the morning's sunlight outside. Besides, she had the blasted spectacles on again, and her head down. If only she wasn't wearing that atrocious cap! There was a definite similarity. He was positive of it. It was hard to think of any relation between his vibrant Delilah and the inflexible Miss Riddley—sisters? By Jupiter, maybe his nymph was Miss Riddley's by-blow? The lady had unbent some in the stable yard, and she'd certainly shown great fortitude. What she'd been trying to do may have been foolhardy, but it had taken more courage and generosity of spirit than he'd seen in most ladies of his acquaintance.

He tried to tell her so, though the governessy Miss Riddley couldn't even take a compliment. No practise, obviously. She stiffly thanked him for his impressive actions, awkwardly twisting the neckcloth she still held in her hands, not meeting his eyes. She would give Mrs. Bennett the cloth to be laundered, and was terribly sorry for the inconvenience, sincerest appreciation—and she was gone, nearly bumping into the center beam of the barn.

The marquis stayed in the stable a long while after, thinking.

Chapter Sixteen

Why did that dratted man have to be so charming? Here she thought he'd sleep until noon like all the Bond

Street beaux. She knew for a fact he hadn't been to bed early. She hadn't even considered that she might encounter him, thus the missing spectacles, while he'd been up at first light, like a soldier off to battle. If his sole purpose was to torment her, he was doing a fine job! How dare he be so cool and efficient with Ajax, so kind and gentle with Sam'l, so damned polite to Miss Riddley! Somehow she couldn't regain her indignation of the morning. Of course, she told herself, that's what made a rake: a lack of scruples sugar-coated with appeal. If a rake couldn't make a girl's heart beat faster, he was no good at the job. The marquis was very good at it, lurking in the corridors, seeking her out in the kitchen, watching her with that lazy smile. The man was a positive hazard to womankind! She managed to avoid him, staying occupied with the inn's business. Saturday was market day in Entwood, so the livestock dealers, merchants and well-to-do farmers from farther away stopped in for their suppers, with some bespeaking rooms for the night. A few London visitors came through, as out of place as peacocks in the chicken coop.

"Lord Beaumont and Lady Anabelle Beaumont, a room for the night? Let me see." That was Lord Beaumont, all right, all twenty stone of him, and his companion nearly matched him in girth. Lady Ann, however, a good friend of Lyndell's Aunt Hardesty, was a tiny wraith of a woman.

"I'm afraid Number Four is the only room available. Market day, you know."

Room Number Four was a converted dressing room, equipped for a servant, valet or maid. It contained one extremely narrow bed.

The Bennetts had agreed: it was better to run an honest inn where decent people would stay than to make a profit on sordid assignations. Sarah was especially vehement: she wasn't having such goings-on under her roof! Let them sleep in the fields like animals if that was how they conducted themselves. Silk waistcoats and lace smallclothes— and no better nor rabbits. The only question was, would they also be turning away the man they were waiting for?

What if he were clever enough to mask his true motives with a ladybird? Lyndell thought that if his business at the inn was important enough, he'd make certain he stayed. Bennett agreed.

"Squire Asgar and family? Welcome to King's Pass. We have a lovely suite with a sitting room, and I'm sure Mrs. Bennett has some gingerbread for the children."

"Captain Drew Jamison?" Gads, she'd forgotten all about him! Here he was, come to arrest a spy, and all she had was one silver-tongued devil with a scar on his forehead. The only traitor was the flutter in her heart.

"Captain Jamison, I meant to send a message, but we've been so busy. The thing is, the man I thought was the saboteur couldn't be him. He—"

"Come, ma'am, let's just see the blighter and be done. Then you and I can have a little *tête-à-tête*, hmm?" He winked. Lyndell excused herself, flew up the stairs and demanded Felicity's presence in the front parlour. "Do not leave me alone with that man!"

"Which man?"

"Either of them! Bring tea or something, but hurry!"

She took a deep breath before returning to lead the captain to the parlour. Before the marquis said "Come in" to her knock, she thought of developing a sudden headache, but Jamison had her elbow and was propelling her inside. The marquis was at ease by the fire, reading a book. He'd changed his soiled buckskins for buff-coloured pantaloons, and his cravat was tied—

He caught her looking at it. "I call it the Ajax Knot," he told her, getting to his feet and smiling. Then he noticed the man behind her and the smile died. "Captain Jamison."

"Major." Jamison saluted.

Heavens, thought Lyndell, they were friends!

"Not major," Cheyne corrected, motioning them to seats. "I sold out some months ago. Time to settle down. And what of your plans, Drew, do you intend to stay on now that the war's over?"

"Aye, I'll stay. Some of us aren't so fortunate to have estates to fall back on."

"As you say. Well, what brings you here? Are you still

83

at Southwold? Will you have some wine, Miss Riddley? Drew?"

Reminded of her presence, Jamison turned to look at Miss Riddley, who was busily wiping her spectacles. Jamison stared at her, then back at the marquis, then burst into loud snorts of laughter. Cheyne raised one dark eyebrow.

"I thought, that is, I felt—" Lyndell began, ready to confess her suspicions. The eyebrow rose higher.

"Miss Riddley thought you might wish to see an old acquaintance, Cheyne. I heard you were in the vicinity so I decided to call. By the way, we've had a bit of a problem in the neighbourhood. Don't suppose you've heard about it?"

The marquis inspected the tassel on his Hessians. "No, nothing. I have been too busy in London to take an interest." At Jamison's knowing leer, he continued, "But what's the trouble? Perhaps I can help. I did have a lot of behind-the-lines experience, you know."

"No, no, nothing to concern yourself about. Highwaymen, most likely." Jamison looked sideways at Lyndell. "You know how females are, though. They fret and fidget. Delicate nerves."

If Cheyne had his own suspicions about the scowling Miss Riddley, they did not include die-away airs. He surprised himself by resenting Jamison's slurs. What he really resented, he realised, was the coxcomb's leering familiarity with her. With the straight-laced Miss Riddley? *No one* would flirt with Miss Riddley unless . . .

To Lyndell's relief, Felicity brought the tea tray. She bobbed a curtsey, rattling the china, before Lyndell could take it from her. "Do not leave," Lyndell whispered. Jamison transferred his ogling to the pretty little maid—Cheyne had his suspicions about that too—while Miss Riddley fussed with asking the gentlemen's preferences. Felicity passed the muffins.

When Jamison had his cup, his moustache dripping tea down the front of his uniform, to Lyndell's disgust, he asked the marquis, "So what brings you here, hm?" His damp eyes went from Miss Riddley to her maid; his tone

84

was one of heavy-handed insinuation. Presumptuous ass, thought Cheyne, before his quirky sense of humour took over. This was as good a time as any to put one of his theories to the test. A spark of deviltry lighting his smile, he answered: "I'm going north on an errand for my uncle, Viscount Richardson, you recall. Looking over some prime breeding stock."

Lyndell gasped. Miss Fullerton, however, tossed the plate of pastries in the air and fled.

Muffins rolled under the chairs, muffins trailed crumbs over the carpets. If Lyndell had her way, his lordship would have a muffin crammed down his throat! It looked as though he was already choking, but on a smothered laugh. "Dratted girl," was all she said, staring significantly at him, so he would know who else was in her black book. Who knew what else he might say? For that matter, who knew what else he suspected? She had to keep him away from Jamison at all costs now, lest he feel inclined to explain the maid's dismay or, worse, compare notes on one Dell Riddley. "I'm sure you're anxious to return to your men, Captain. You mentioned a private matter . . . ?" Her stomach almost turned at the thought.

Instead of leading him back down the hall, or to a corner of the nearly empty common room, she went out the front door, near where his horse was tied. Surprisingly, there were no other men waiting. Had he come to make the arrest single-handedly? Either way, this was going to be a brief conversation, if she had anything to say about it.

Jamison dropped his oily urbanity the moment they were outside. "What do you mean, dragging me out here? Master spies . . . London gentlemen? Wellington's right-hand man, more like it! I don't know what game you're playing, missy, and I won't have it! No one plays Drew Jamison for a fool."

"No, no. You don't understand. It was an error, I tried to tell you. But . . . but his cousin is here, with some odd tale of a wound. He could be the one." Lyndell didn't really believe it, though she tried to sound convincing. Willy Richardson, that devil-may-care park saunterer? Absurd.

"Proof, ma'am, I need proof!" He seized her hand. "See

85

that you don't make any more errors, and stay out of what don't concern you. I'll return another time, when his lordship"—with a sneer—"isn't watching." He indicated the window, where Cheyne's broad shoulders were framed. Then he lifted her hand and kissed the palm of it. "For our little talk."

Cheyne saw the gesture. Miss Riddley and that cad Jamison? From what his directives mentioned, that meant she was in it up to her eyes after all. Too bad, and he'd dared to hope that his theories were correct. Foolish notion, of course. Damn. He did not see Miss Riddley furiously rubbing her hand off on her skirt. And neither one, naturally, was aware of Jamison's mustache-stroking deliberations, once back at the barracks. Crumbs fell on the page in front of him as he hastily wrote: "Cheyne here. Did the War Office send him? What now?"

"Mr. and Mrs. . . . Jones? Yes, we ought to be able to accommodate you. I'll just go see if the rat-catcher is finished. . . . You've decided to push on after all? Perhaps another time . . ."

When Cheyne asked Miss Riddley to dine with him, she could find no gracious way to refuse. He was to spend a week there, he pleaded, and his own company was already beginning to tire him. With Farrow and the maid seeing so well to Willy's comfort, there was nothing to occupy him. The parlour door would remain open, of course.

Lyndell didn't recall being so nervous since she'd curtsied to the queen, wearing those clumsy hoops and crinolines. Now she was dressed in cast-offs, but at least she didn't wear the spectacles. He'd already seen her without them, and, aside from the danger of spilling her soup, she needed all her senses about her. She could barely remember whom she had told which lies to, and he was such a . . . a knowing one, despite those friendly eyes. She squared her shoulders. Miss Markham had been giving set-downs for years, and Miss Riddley was certainly stiff-rumped enough to deflect any personal question. It was only the lad Dell Riddley she had to worry about.

To her relief, dinner was actually pleasant. Instead of the inquisition she'd expected, there was polite conversation. No mention was made of Jamison's visit, Felicity's awkwardness, the missing Jasper or, thank goodness, Dell Riddley. Lyndell was at ease over the braised veal and the turbot in oyster sauce, enjoying the marquis's company. He'd changed for dinner into black knee pants and a perfectly fitted coat of blue superfine, and his manners were superb. Polite without being encroaching, he made Lyndell forget her own dowdiness, her fear of revealing too much.

They talked of the war, and he complimented her on the depths of her understanding, beyond that of most of his London acquaintances. They talked of books and the theatre, with Lyndell bringing the marquis up to date with what he'd missed. Politics and the antics of the Regent, architecture and the new buildings Prinny was commissioning Nash to build, art and opera, they discussed it all, intelligently and as equals, to Lyndell's delight. And she hadn't given anything away, or had she?

Chapter Seventeen

On Sundays the upright, moral, God-fearing went to church. Lyndell and Felicia took the gig. The marquis stayed at the inn.

"He knows," Lyndell said, as soon as they were on the short way to the little village of Entwood. There'd been a discussion of the wisdom of the trip, but Lyndell thought it would draw more comment if she didn't attend services. She could go, properly escorted by her maid, and relieve the townsfolk's curiosity, before many were tempted to stop at the inn. She had a black bonnet with a veil, borrowed from Mrs. Bennett, so she felt she could meet any unexpected old acquaintances with safety. It was easier to keep up the masquerade if she could direct the play, as opposed to her dealings with the marquis, who seemed unwilling to follow the script! "I don't know how he knows, but he does."

"Willy swears he didn't tell. He says his cousin is just a 'downy cove,' whatever that is."

"It means he is clever."

"Oh."

Lyndell had to smile, but this was serious. If the marquis made her presence there known, Felicia's future would be doomed. She'd never get vouchers from Almack's, invitations to all the balls. She'd never meet her Beau Ideal, that handsome man who would love her to distraction, and she him, for ever after.

"Please, Felicia, please consider returning home before anything worse happens. Most likely Cheyne will keep still out of regard for your father, so we can squeak through. Otherwise your chances will be ruined."

Felicia giggled. "My chances would be ruined a lot faster if I left now."

When Lyndell took her eyes off the horses, not so chancy a move with Jasper's plodders, the girl was blushing.

"Why, Felicia Fullerton, I believe you are setting your cap for someone!" For an unnamed reason the thought that Felicia might have reconsidered her father's arrangements, now that she'd met the marquis, caused Lyndell's throat to tighten. No, the girl was still terrified of him; Lyndell could swallow again. "Willy!"

"Isn't he the most handsome gentleman you know?"

Willy?

"And so fine and brave. He was telling me how he almost ran away and enlisted, because Lord Richardson wouldn't purchase his commission. Instead he gave up his own wishes to stay back and help manage his cousin's properties. *So* noble, don't you think?"

88

Happily Felicia was content to ramble on about the myriad splendours of the young man, with Lyndell only murmuring an occasional "Indeed," or "How true." Felicia and Willy? Yes it might do, if her father permitted it. Richardson wasn't up to Cheyne's weight as a prize on the Marriage Mart, of course, but he was well-to-pass, a cheerful, likeable young fool, and with any luck could keep Felicia out of harm's way. They'd make a remarkably handsome couple, both fair and blue-eyed. Their children would be perfect cherubs . . . and perfect widgeons. The ideal match, if Willy was agreeable.

"That's why I must not leave. Willy said he'd take me home himself, as soon as his foot is healed, and explain to Papa. And I'm almost sure, well nearly positive, that he'll stay to ask Papa's permission if . . ."

"If you have a few more days to work on him! Well, if anyone can bring him up to scratch, you can. In the meantime, don't let on that Cheyne is right. Maybe he's only guessing. And Felicia dear, please do stop smiling at the blacksmith."

The village of South Entwood was hardly big enough to merit a name of its own. Beside the church and the smithy were Patchin's Dry Goods and Mr. Beck's Emporium. Beyond was a cluster of labourer's cottages, and the more substantial houses of the vicar, the doctor, Mr. Beck, and the Misses Pelham—Miss Millicent, who gave music instruction to the neighbourhood children, and Miss Serephina, who did fine sewing. The two prim ladies ran the parish charities and held genteel at-home teas.

Miss Riddley glided past all of them in the churchyard, with just the proper degree of courtesy. A nod, a small bow. Nothing unfriendly, but nothing to encourage familiarity. She was a solemn stranger in her black veil, intent on her devotions, the little maid two steps back. It was a magnificent performance, till Lyndell nearly botched it by almost marching right up front to the Markham family pew.

The marquis was on his hands and knees, but not in prayer. He was searching the innkeeper's apartments. The

89

results seemed to please him or, if not please him, then at least satisfy him, to judge by the smile he later gave Willy, pulling up a chair near his cousin's bed.

"You know, I've had a lot of time on my hands, and I've been thinking about Miss Fullerton. Perhaps it's not such a bad idea after all . . . so I thought, while you are laid up, I might just go on north and get the job done, and fetch you on the way home. I'll leave you Farrow, of course. With that ministering angel who has adopted you, you should do quite well. What do you think?"

Willy was twisting the bedclothes into knots, getting red in the face and stuttering. "But I . . . She won't . . . You can't . . ." His cousin finally took pity on him and burst into laughter, waiting for Willy's sheepish grin in return. "How did you know?"

"You gave it away yourselves, you clunch. The moment you saw the girl you told her you fell. Fell? I couldn't for the life of me imagine why you'd tell clunkers to a perfect stranger." He brushed some dust off his fawn trousers. "I hadn't, at that moment, precisely recalled Miss Fullerton's first name. Then she was so attentive, and you appeared quite taken with her."

"Well, I've known her forever. Our fathers are good friends, I told you."

"Forgive me for being a bit slow . . . I had other things on my mind. Where was I? Oh yes. It wasn't in your usual style, cooing over a lass—and a maid at that," said the marquis, ignoring his cousin and pursuing his own train of thought, "which brought to mind the last female I'd heard you mention. Did I say mention? I mean proclaim, and jump to her defense at the slightest insult. That was what our absurd duel was about, wasn't it?"

Willy coloured up. "But I couldn't let you talk like that, not when Fel—Miss Fullerton is such a sweet, innocent—"

The marquis held up his hand. "Enough! Belatedly, I must admit, I did recall your description of Miss Fullerton as a perfect china doll, all guinea-gold curls and blue eyes."

"Wasn't I right? Isn't she the most beautiful, pre—"

"Quite. But more obviously, the chit was no maid at all. Have you noticed how she dresses Miss Riddley?"

90

"I try not to."

"See? Well, to tie it all up, I inspected her room." When Willy started to bluster about indignities and taking liberties, Cheyne told him, "Don't be a gudgeon. I had to know what she was about, didn't I? You, most loyal cousin, were keeping mum. No, I realise you were sworn, or some such. At any rate, the lady travels light: one bandbox with the initials FF on it, two fashionable muslin gowns, some lacy things I did *not* examine so you can stop scowling at me, a string of very expensive pearls, and a fur-lined cape. A pleasure to travel with, I'd say, without all the trunks and cases women usually tote around. Handy thing to have in a wife . . ."

"A wife? Wes, you're not . . . no, gammon, you're teasing again, aren't you?" At his cousin's expectant, encouraging smile, he went on: "You don't mind if I . . . That is, Wes, you were . . ."

Cheyne laughed. "No, Willy, as long as your intentions are honourable I don't mind. I'm relieved, in fact, and I wish you all the best."

"It's a bit early for congratulations, Wes. Want to see her father, do it all in form, you know."

If the marquis was amazed at Willy's new respect for the conventions he hid it well, thinking only what strange effects love had on its victims.

"There's one more thing, Wes," Willy was saying. "I know that you know about Felicia, and she *thinks* that you know, but could you pretend not to know? You see, Felicia thinks it's the most romantic thing ever, right out of a Minerva Press novel, to be secret lovers." Cheyne cleared his throat; Willy stammered. "No, not that kind of lovers. You know what I mean, Wes."

"Say no more, cuz, the lady shall be allowed her flights of fancy." Actually, it suited the marquis perfectly to have the heiress continue masquerading as a maid. She'd be safer from recognition and possible scandal that way. Compared to what else was going on at the inn, her charade was mere child's play. Which reminded him . . .

"Will, have you ever taken a good look at the landlady?" he asked nonchalantly.

"No, thank the gods. What a fright!"

"But does she remind you of anyone?"

"Only m'sister's dragon of a governess, why?"

"Just a notion I had. Would she seem familiar, do you think, if she had glorious reddish hair with golden touches, and brilliant green eyes?"

Willy was hooting. "Don't tell me you're developing a *tendre* for Miss Riddley, that stick! The only lady I know anywhere near your description is Miss Markham, a real Incomparable, and anyone less like your dowdy innkeeper I've never seen. You know, I think the Markhams used to come from this area. Maybe Riddley's from the wrong side of the blanket, and that's why you see a similarity. Didn't know you were acquainted with Miss Markham though."

"I'm not. It was just a foolish idea, as I said."

However far-fetched, Cheyne's search of those rooms had given him the notion. The clothespress had yielded two sturdy, serviceable gowns—Miss Riddley was wearing a third—and a handful of others in muslin, silk, sarcenet, and crepe. Frocks designed, if he knew anything after two months of footing the bills for opera dancers and actresses, by the finest London dressmakers. Most of the fashionable gowns were in shades of green or a peach-rose, colours to compliment coppery hair and green eyes to perfection. There were no boys' clothes here, but Jasper's closet could have held enough. A valise was crammed full of old account books, whatever that meant. In the bedroom where he had accosted the red-haired imp Dell were Miss Austen's novels, no book of sermons, and Miss Riddley's spectacles.

There were two possibilities, as Cheyne saw it. The first was that the proper Miss Riddley shared the room with Delilah. But there had been only one woman in the bed with him; no mistaking that. The other possibility was that my lady innkeeper shared a great deal more with the madcap Dell.

Chapter Eighteen

When Lyndell was a child, Reverend Smallwood always seemed to direct his sermons at her. Of course he knew all her sins, he lived there right next to God's house, didn't he? The day he raged against pride in his deep voice, he stared right at Lyndell. That very morning in the church-yard, she'd boasted to Cynthia Highte about her new bonnet, when Cynthia had none. And the week Reverend Smallwood shook his fist on high declaring Thou shalt not covet thy neighbour's property, well, that was the week she and Allen Bromley had raided the squire's peach orchard.

The Reverend Smallwood had long since passed on to his final calling, most likely berating the angels for rumpled wings, and a Mr. Teppler had taken his place. The new vicar hadn't the white hair, or the thunder in his voice, and he could not be addressing Miss Riddley when he spoke of the temptations of the flesh. She almost looked around to see if Molly was there, trembling in the back row. She doubted it. When the preacher's monotone droned on about wanton lust, Lyndell let her mind wander. After all, she'd only been sorely tempted twice in her whole life, both by the marquis, and that was finished. He'd shown Miss Riddley the correct deference that evening at dinner, without any sensual overtones. He could act the part of a gentleman, if presented with a proper lady, which Lyndell was determined to be. Dell Riddley was retired. And Lyndell would swear she had done more this week at the inn to discourage illicit fornication than all the Reverend Teppler's speeches on the Serpent in the Garden. The Devil in Disguise meant nothing to Lyndell. As for the wolf in sheep's clothing that Teppler was mumbling about, Lyndell pictured a laughing-eyed rogue in buckskin breeches. She'd already been warned, thank you.

The marquis, meanwhile, was also considering sheep. Mutton dressed up as lamb, to be specific, an age-old subterfuge. But why in this world, he wondered, would anyone take tender lamb—he smiled—and try to pass it off as stringy old mutton? He was determined to find out.

"I thought I would look in on the dog after luncheon, Miss Riddley. Would you accompany me in case he needs further attention?"

"That is not at all necessary, my lord. The boy Samuel is taking care. Ajax lets him do anything now."

"Still, he's only a lad, and you wouldn't want all our efforts to be wasted?"

What could she say in the face of such civility—No, I don't trust you in dark places? She went, taking the arm he offered to see her over the mud.

Ajax was in fine shape, chasing the sticks Sam'l threw up and down the stable length. The dog dropped the stick the moment Lyndell and Cheyne entered the building, standing stiff-legged a moment, then rushing toward them. He sniffed Lyndell's skirts, gave a vague tailwag, and then practically drooled on the marquis, frisking about him, stirring up the stable dirt in excitement.

"Ungrateful cur," Lyndell called him, laughing. The marquis only ordered, "Down, boy, you're getting dirt on my Hessians," but he too was smiling. Ajax calmed enough for them to be able to see that his neck was healing, his eyes were clear, and his coat was unmatted and shiny with brushing.

Cheyne looked at Sam'l and said, "You've done a fine job, boy. He'll do. He might even make a good gun dog. What do you think?" Sam'l nodded his head vigorously. The marquis bent over the dog again, his back to the boy. "Maybe we can take him out tomorrow and get some rabbits for Mrs. Bennett's pot. Would you like that?" When there was no answer, Lyndell was about to make the reply, until she saw the marquis frown at her. "Hm?" he asked again, still not facing Sam'l. When the low "yessir" finally came, Lyndell let her breath out, and the marquis stood up, holding his hand out to the boy. Sam'l rubbed his hand on his pants before offering it. "It's agreed then," Cheyne said, his grin matching the boy's. "Now I think you ought to take him out in the sun for some exercise. Build up those muscles again."

"But, my lord," Lyndell asked, "what if the dog runs away? We can't put a tie on him . . ."

"Oh, I think he knows who his friends are now, don't you, Sam'l?" The boy nodded happily and ran out, the dog at his heels.

Lyndell said, "That was very well done, my lord," and turned to follow, but Cheyne said, "Wait," quietly, half-plea, half-command. She waited. If she were a child playing with the sea, running or getting splashed by the waves, it was time to run. But she waited. Cheyne took the four steps separating them, looking into her eyes—the spectacles were back in her pocket—or her soul. He slowly reached up and removed the cap from her head and while she stood, almost entranced, he ever so softly used it to wipe at the powder on her face. It was much too late to run. He said nothing; his gaze was intent on her mouth.

Lyndell could no more have moved than she could fly, and Cheyne could have not kissed her as easily as he could have not breathed.

The kiss was joyous and natural, like coming home. Lyndell responded fully, putting her arms around his neck, touching his cheeks, his hair. So much for Reverend Teppler's sermons.

"You're so beautiful," he breathed in her hair, "much too good for Riddley."

"What do you mean? Jasper and I—"

"Come now, precious, Jasper's sister wouldn't have any reason to be in such a disguise, would she?"

Lyndell was coming out of her golden trance. She stepped back, out of his embrace. "You mean, you think . . . Jasper? Oh you—"

He was holding her hands. "Oh no, you'll not slap me again," he said, laughing. So she kicked him. Her soft kid half-boots absorbed more of the blow than his Hessians,

95

and that was fair too, because Lyndell was more furious at herself than at Cheyne. "Ow!" she shouted. Then, "Let go of me, you . . . you brute!"

Sam'l rushed in, launching his small body at the marquis, flailing at him and gnarling. "Hold," ordered Cheyne, letting go of Lyndell and pinning the boy's arms to his sides. So Sam'l kicked him. The marquis's brow was lowering and his mouth was forming into a thin line when Lyndell cried, "Don't hurt him!"

Still holding the boy, Cheyne looked at her quizzically. "Just what kind of ogre do you think I am?"

Spy, seducer, cradle-robber—she didn't get to begin. He shook Sam'l lightly and said, "No more of that, my boots have taken enough punishment. As it is, Farrow will have my hide. It was very brave, lad, coming to Miss Riddley's defence against such a foe, and I admire you for that, but I swear I did not harm her. Did I, ma'am? Tell the boy."

Lyndell murmured, "No Sam'l, he did not hurt me."

"And I never, ever would, I promise." Sam'l nodded, believing him, and Lyndell knew she believed him too. He might ruin her reputation, he might even break her heart, if she let him, but no, he wouldn't purposely hurt her.

Her reputation, Lyndell Markham's, she would guard twice as zealously, and as for her heart, she simply would not permit herself to fall head over heals in love with such a plausible rogue. She simply wouldn't.

"Come, Sam'l, let's go see if Mrs. Bennett needs help with supper."

Intelligent and witty, spirited and sensual, exquisite and exquisitely formed. That was how Lord Cheyne catalogued Miss Riddley, whoever she was. Everything a man wanted in a woman. He still hadn't answered the questions of why a woman, perhaps connected to a noble house somewhat illegitimately, would need to be in disguise, or how involved she was in the other business, the one he'd been sent here about, however secondary it seemed now. The answers would come soon, he was confident, since, in his experience, a man had only to bed a woman to find her secrets. Have her warm and well contented, and she would babble on, if you let her. He hadn't tested the theory recently, Molly suddenly being indisposed toward company, but he was sure of Miss Riddley. The marquis, of course, was forgetting one of his own theories: lose your heart and your head will follow. Not seeing the danger signals, he was dreaming plans for the evening, remembering that kiss, how readily she came into his arms. Gads, what a mistress she'd make.

Chapter Nineteen

"Sir Martin Blazer and Mrs. Blazer? Of course. Rooms Six and Eight. Enjoy your stay."

It was Sunday evening and Lyndell was steadfastly entrenched in her nook under the stairs, in the cap and powder and spectacles. She was not going to be enticed into more indiscretions, not wine before dinner, not another shared meal, not tea after. Nothing. The Marquis of Cheyne was nothing to her, and would stay that way, behind the partly opened parlour door. Not many people chose to travel on Sunday, although Molly and Bennett were kept busy in the common room. So Lyndell was reading Miss Austen by the light of the single oil lamp on the wall behind her.

"Sir Frauncis Hammerly . . . and nephew." The fop in yellow pantaloons and a striped waistcoat dripping fobs and chains was indeed Sir Frauncis, the middle-aged, pouch-faced dandy who'd once paid ponderous court to Lyndell's fortune. His nephew was a weak-chinned young man with pomaded curls. Before Lyndell could think of a way to get rid of Hammerly, one of the worst gossips in London, Lord Cheyne casually stepped out of the parlour, leaned against the door frame, and asked if there was a problem. Lyndell stammered something about no available rooms.

"Good evening, Sir Frauncis. Poor Miss Riddley is embarrassed that the inn is nearly filled; the snow I suppose. If I can help though, the single room next to mine is vacant, and your nephew can bunk in with my cousin Willy."

There was an ornate eyeglass fixed to the top of Sir Frauncis's walking stick, and he raised this now to one red-lined eye to peer first at the marquis, then at Lyndell.

"Servant, Cheyne. Miss Riddley, is it? No, no, wouldn't dream of disturbing Richardson. We'll just push on to Ipswich. 'Ta."

When the door was shut behind them, Lyndell gave the marquis a puzzled look of enquiry.

"The nephew, ma'am."

"Oh? Oh. Oh my. I . . . I see. Thank you, my lord."

He bowed and returned to the parlour.

At about ten o'clock Lyndell decided to retire to bed. She had been yawning over the book, and the only new customers to come in were for the tap room. She went to the kitchen to tell Mrs. Bennett to listen for the bell, and she stayed to share a cup of tea before going up.

The marquis followed about fifteen minutes later, according to his own preplanned course. He would wait another few minutes—give her enough time to get settled, not enough to fall asleep—then knock softly on her door. He intended to say he needed to ask where he could hunt the next morning, which was private land, etc. She wouldn't believe his excuse, certainly, but he was willing to wager she would open the door. On the way to his own room the marquis noted that Molly must be back in business: a heavy-set man was entering her room at the end of the corridor. He knew the right one now. Cheyne shut his own door and considered whether he should remove his boots now . . . or later.

Lyndell was sitting at her dressing table, scrubbing the wretched powder and the top layer of skin off her face. She had changed into her lawn nightgown, and had brushed out her hair, and had congratulated herself on her noble behaviour. She had vowed not to be swayed by his entreaties, and she hadn't. The only problem, she thought angrily, was that there had been no entreaties! The marquis had not offered her wine, dinner, conversation—or insult. It was one thing to be ready to repulse advances, quite another when the advances did not come. She threw the towel down in disgust. Blasted unpredictable man, didn't even give her the opportunity to say no!

Now that she was wide awake, and in a righteous mood, she decided to see what Felicia was up to. It would not do for her to be so long in Richardson's room, even if the man Farrow was there too. Now whose idea was that? she wondered. Either way, a valet was not adequate chaperone for a young girl's good name. Her virtue, perhaps, but not her reputation. Lyndell put on her wrapper and the white mobcap, just in case.

Felicia was sleeping peacefully. No moral dilemmas there. With her hair in a braid, she looked like a child in Lyndell's candle's light, so Lyndell quietly shut the door behind her and turned toward her own apartment. A movement caught her eye, a man, leaving Molly's room. How dare she, after Lyndell had expressly told her no. And how could she? As the man walked closer, nearer to the hall lamp, Lyndell could see that he was heavy and coarse-looking, with thick black hair and straggle-brows. There were even black hairs growing from his ears and nostrils—disgusting! And why was he still coming down the corridor, past the stairwell? Lyndell didn't want any such scurvy character loose in the halls, so she waited for him to turn and leave. Except that he didn't. He kept coming closer and closer, and suddenly grabbed at her! Before she could even think about screaming, he had one hand over her mouth and was dragging her back toward her own room. In his other hand he held a knife, right in front of Lyndell's face. She stopped struggling and the knife moved a few inches away. She could see the black hairs on the back of his hand. Dear God, it was the last thing she was going to see!

The marquis opened his door. "What in blazes?" Cheyne did not consider the odds—the attacker had the weight, the weapon, and his boots on, but he also had Miss Riddley.

The ex-soldier lunged at the intruder, who spun around, freeing Lyndell though catching her shoulder on the knife edge. She reeled back, holding her upper arm, while the hairy brute turned on Cheyne. The man feinted once with the knife, but doors were opening up and down the corridor. Rather than take on the entire inn, the man shoved past Cheyne, clouting him against the wall, then fled down the stairs. The marquis shook his head to clear it before taking off in pursuit, down the stairs and out the door, shouting for Bennett.

By now Farrow was out, looking for something to aim his pistol at. Willy was hobbling down the hall in his night-shirt, and Felicia was rubbing her eyes, wanting to know what was going on. Lyndell was still leaning against the wall, blood now beginning to ooze between her fingers, when Mrs. Blazer put her curl-papered head out her door and hissed, "This is not at all what I am used to!"

Lyndell gave a shaky laugh. "Do you think *I* am?"

By the time Cheyne returned, Felicia had swooned twice: once in the hall when she first saw the red stain on Lyndell's arm, and again, right into Willy's thankful arms, when Mrs. Bennett told her she looked like a fallen woman, out in the halls in a ha'penny's worth of lace.

Things were well under control when the marquis entered Lyndell's room. Felicia, more than amply covered in his own paisley silk robe, was hovering over Willy's chair. Willy, from a distance, was giving Miss Riddley—a Miss Riddley *sans* cap, glasses, baggy gown—a very puzzled inspection. Before he could express his bewildered thoughts to his cousin though, he was silenced with a pinch from Felicia, and a whispered, "Later," which the marquis overheard. He would have been amused, except that he was so intent on Mrs. Bennett and Farrow, just now spreading a bandage to Lyndell's shoulder. Mrs. Bennett covered Lyndell with the bedthrow blanket.

"Damn!" said the marquis, astonishment turning to concern as he saw blood-stained rags. "How bad is it, Farrow?"

"Not bad at all, my lord," Lyndell answered for herself.

100

Farrow nodded his agreement. "More a slice than a stab. I don't think he even meant to do it. Did you catch him?"

"No, he got away. He had his horse tied right out front, and took off through the hedges. By the time we could have saddled up, he'd have been long gone."

"Who was he, Miss, er, Riddley?" Willy put in.

Lyndell gave him a wan smile and a nod of appreciation. "Never having seen him before, I haven't the faintest idea."

"You never saw him before?" the marquis asked, giving her a strange look. "The boy Sam'l knew him."

"He did? Did he say who—no I suppose he didn't."

"As a matter of fact, he did. He must have thought it important enough because he came right up to me and said, 'Quinn.' That's all, just Quinn."

Mrs. Bennett gasped, but Lyndell murmured "Ah," as if that answered many questions. It didn't for Cheyne and he decided to clear the room. "Farrow, please take Will back to bed before he has a relapse, out in the night. And thank you for your help. Mrs. Bennett, perhaps you would see Miss Felicia to her room"—no one seemed to notice that he used Miss Fullerton's real name—"and then see about some tea, with a little brandy, I think, for Miss Riddley. Thank you." He added, "You needn't worry about Quinn. I doubt he'll return, now that so many people can identify him, and Bennett is downstairs with a shotgun in any case. Farrow, you keep the pistol handy; I'll do the same."

When they were all gone and the door was shut, he faced Lyndell, huddled under her quilt, and demanded, "Now what is this all about? What in blazes did he want?"

Lyndell gave a weak giggle. "I think . . . that is, it seemed, well, I suppose he wanted to kill me." And then she was in his arms, weeping against his chest, and he was soothing her, telling her what a brave puss she'd been.

"I'm usually not such a watering pot, you know."

"Of course you're not, it's just a reaction to everything," he said, wiping her cheeks with his handkerchief. "Now come." Without giving her a choice he scooped her, blanket and all, over to the chair by the fire and into his lap. "Tell me what's going on here. You know I'll help you."

"Yes, my lord."

He gave her his one-sided smile. "Most ladies in my lap manage to call me Wesley or Wes. 'My lord' seems a little formal, under the conditions, don't you think, Miss . . . ?"

"Lynd—Lynn."

"Lynn? It's not—no matter. About Quinn?"

She started to tell him, without making much sense, so she got up to fetch Jasper's letter from the pages of her book. Without a second's hesitation, she climbed back into the marquis's lap before handing it to him. He pulled her closer and read, " 'Dear Sister.' Damn!"

"What?"

"You really are Riddley's sister?" Lyndell chose not to add the "by marriage only"; she saw no reason to lay quite all her cards on the table just yet. She nodded. "And you really are a respectable female?" She nodded again; he swore again. Disturbed, she questioned: "Wesley?"

He kissed her nose. "I was all set to offer you a *carte blanche*; now you're too proper!" He read on while she blushed.

"It seems Jasper had his fingers in a lot of pies, smuggling, robberies, but he drew the line at treason. That should save his skin. Too bad he couldn't name the London contact. That would satisfy the War Office. Do you know where Jasper is now?"

"Yes, he's up at King's Mark. That's the manor a few miles back. There's a connexion," she said before he could ask. "Do you think Quinn will go after him?"

"It he thought Jasper would talk, most likely, or if he knew anything. It's too late to warn him now. Quinn would already have been and gone. I'll send Bennett in the morning. But tell me, precious, why would Quinn come after you? What was your part in this, and why the disguise?"

Lyndell took a moment to choose her answer: "I really don't know why Quinn wanted to kill me, unless he thought Jasper had told me something, or he thought I could find some evidence. That was my plan. I was going to wait for the London traitor and trap him."

Cheyne squeezed her harder. "Foolish beyond permission, my love. Look what it's got you. And you've been tossing every suspicious character out of the inn anyway."

102

The endearments were being stored away for future examination. Right now Lyndell confided, "That's the good part. Anyone who makes a fuss about staying, unless there is a good excuse, has to be a suspect. So I report him to the authorities and—"

Cheyne burst out laughing and Lyndell could feel it up and down her body. She wriggled closer still. "What amuses you?"

"You do, sweetheart. I'm the authorities!"

It was her turn to laugh. "And I thought you were the spy!"

A few minutes of friendly bantering passed, and a few not so comradely kisses. Then Lyndell asked, "But what now?"

"Tomorrow," he told her firmly, "you let me handle it. But right now—"

"Ahem." Mrs. Bennett cleared her throat and set the tray down with a thud. She stood there glaring, her arms crossed over her chest, the light of battle in her eyes. All good soldiers can recognise a *force majeur* when they see it. The marquis retreated to the sounds of Mrs. Bennett's final warning: "And you needn't worry, my lord, I'll be sleeping right here, keeping Miss Lyndy safe from harm . . . from *all* harm."

Chapter Twenty

*F*or someone who had been shot at and stabbed, Lyndell was in a remarkably cheerful frame of mind on Monday morning. Her shoulder was stiff, but the sun was out and it was one of those nearly perfect early winter days, clear and bright without a chilling wind. Lyndell's spirits matched the day. For the first time in a long time, she had a feeling of eager expectancy, a sense of something wonderful about to happen, almost like Felicia's excitement over her first Season. Lyndell had been intrigued by the cloak-and-dagger adventure, like an exercise in logic, before it grew so personal. She had certainly often been pleased over a special ball or spectacular fete, but now she felt that a cloud of tedium had just been lifted, even if she hadn't been aware of its presence. Suddenly she was living a little more fully. The air was crisper, the sky was bluer and she was in—No, she would not call it love, not yet. She would acknowledge infatuation, attraction certainly, but for that final, irrevocable and chancy commitment, no, not yet.

What Lyndell felt was a little kernel inside her, warm and glowing, waiting to burst into full flower. She could cherish that, for now, but not let it grow. The marquis was a rake. It was simple; he could not be trusted, not to be honest or loyal or sincere, and without those qualities, Lyndell could not give herself to any man, no matter what the inclination of the moment!

For much the same reasons, she had not revealed her real identity. If Cheyne was ever to love her, and love her enough to give up those wild bachelor ways, two very separate things, then he also had to love her for herself. Cheyne was not after her fortune, that was not even a question—but what of her social position, her family name? If he could love the plain middle-class Miss Riddley enough to offer for her, Lyndell decided, his love could be trusted. And then . . . If her heart had hands, it was warming them by that little glow.

While Lyndell sat humming, mending linen in the kitchen, the marquis was out hunting, tromping through the woods, teaching Sam'l to whistle. Their noises would scare off any game, of course, but well worth it, considering the boy's laughter. For the very first time in his memory, Cheyne found himself thinking what a pleasure it might be having a son of his own to teach things to, things like shooting and fishing and following tracks around snow-brittled pine trees on a glorious winter morning. The whistling could not interfere, since the quarry whose tracks they were following had been long gone in any case. They traced Quinn's trail through the hedgerows and across some fallow acres, nearing a sizable estate, then through the forest, doubling back to the road, where the prints, heading north, were obscured by cart tracks. Convinced that Quinn wasn't lurking about anywhere close, the marquis gave his full attention to Ajax, blundering through the woodlands, crunching through the ice crust and woofing.

A pointer he wasn't, and it was obvious after the first rabbit that he'd never been taught to retrieve without tasting. Somehow, out of the dog's sheer exuberance, the gentleman's crack shot, and the boy's quick gathering of downed prey, they managed to bag a pheasant, three rabbits and a brace of woodcock, all of which Sam'l proudly presented to Mrs. Bennett, who fussed about congratulating the hunters, fixing them hot drinks, chocolate for Sam'l, mulled ale for the marquis, and reciting aloud possible menus.

Lord Cheyne took a seat next to Lyndell's and recounted the morning's activities: "The dog is a natural hunter. What he doesn't step on, he frightens half to death, then he eats it! We'd be going hungry if not for Sam'l here. Incidentally, we followed the man Quinn's path back to the road. He never went very near that manor you spoke of."

"Yes, that's what Bennett said. He went anyway, to warn Jasper, who is considering whether the inn wouldn't be a better place right now. Safety in numbers, you know. I'm almost embarrassed for him, he's such a spineless gudgeon."

"I'd like to speak to him anyway," the marquis said with a smile that could mean anything. Lyndell thought it the height of ludicrousness for the marquis to ask a Riddley for her hand in marriage, if that was what he wanted of Jasper, but she had no opportunity to discuss it, since the bell at the manager's desk was ringing, over and over.

"I'm sorry to keep you waiting, my lord . . . ?"

"Crowley; I want a room, brandy and hot food, in that order. And who, pray tell, are you?"

"Miss . . . Miss Riddley, my lord, Jasper's sister."

"Didn't know he had one." Crowley looked Lyndell over, then said, "See why he never mentioned it."

Lyndell gasped at such rudeness, before recalling what she knew of the Earl of Crowley. He was one of London's prime eccentrics, sometimes of the Carleton House set, when he chose to socialise at all. More often he was found at racing meets, horse auctions and stud farms, where his unkempt appearance and rough tongue were better suited than in the drawing room. Past his fortieth year, he had still not married, the talk went, because no mere female could interest him as much as a sweet-going mare. It was also rumoured that his whole income went to finance his obsession, perhaps, Lyndell thought, even to the point where he would be forced to crime to support his stables.

"We do have a room, my lord, if you want it. The thing is . . . well, have you ever had the measles?"

"Measles? What's to do with measles?"

"You see, we had a family staying here, and the children came down with something, then the maids . . ."

"No matter, girl, just get me a key. I must've had the spots when I was young."

"But, my lord, I . . . I feel I had better tell you that we fear it may be smallpox. So the inn at—"

"Measles, smallpox. I don't care if it's the French pox! I've been riding since sun-up and I'm not putting my arse back in the leather today. That's final!"

He might not worry over his own health, but his horses were another matter. Lyndell was about to create a dire disease in the stables to challenge his determination to stay, when she noticed Cheyne, leaning against the door frame. He'd changed from his hunting clothes into dove-grey pantaloons, a black coat and black waistcoat embroidered with silver. What a contrast between him and the newcomer in his stained buckskins and bulky frieze jacket. Both were tall, well-built men, but the earl merely looked crudely rugged; Cheyne elegantly virile. The marquis was smiling, most likely enjoying her discomfort, and shaking his head. No, don't discourage the earl more, or no, don't let him stay? Drat them both!

"Room Five, and your groom can bed down in the

106

stables. I'll see to luncheon in a half hour in the tap room. Our private parlour is already spoken for."

"Cheyne, eh? I saw his team out back, prime goers, I'll bet. Oh, there you are, Wesley. Had them off Folger, eh? Set you back a pretty penny. . . ." And Crowley wandered off, forgetting about his hot bath, his brandy and his key.

"Room Twelve, Lord Dodgett? I'm afraid that room is occupied by a . . . a button salesman. Won't another do?"

"No, no, it must be Twelve! Well, perhaps Fourteen. I'm tracing the path of a certain star, you see, and I come here to check its progress every month. Mr. Riddley understood. Are you sure he's not here? Oh, dear. My experiment, my papers for the Royal Astronomical Society—"

"My stars." Lyndell had to smile to herself; Cheyne was unfortunately still talking to Crowley. "If it's that important, perhaps I can move the button merchant. Room Twelve, you say? Would you mind waiting in the common room while I see?"

Lyndell flew up the stairs and gave Room Twelve a quick survey, opening the empty drawers and checking behind them, feeling the mattress for suspicious lumps, even tapping for loose floorboards. Stargazing indeed! A likely story for the Duke of Burfield's second son. About as likely as pigs flying. There must be something, but Lyndell couldn't find it. The bell summoned her back downstairs as she was wondering if secret codes could be sewn in the curtain hems. She'd have to search later.

"Sir Hammerly, you're back." That sounded cloth-headed even to Lyndell. Of course the aging macaroni was back, now in a red and gold waistcoat and red-heeled shoes with sequined buckles; he was staring at her through the glass on the top of his walking stick, almost searching for flaws, she felt. "And your nephew?"

"Oh, I sent the dear boy back to school. Too, too tiring. Then my valet developed a putrid throat, so I left him at Ipswich, couldn't travel with him of course. What was one to do? I simply couldn't show my face in London without being dressed properly; luckily I remembered this quaint

107

little inn. So refreshing, you know. Perfect for a repairing lease. I trust there's a room for me?"

Chapter Twenty-one

*W*illy was to be allowed down for dinner for the first time that evening, and Cheyne invited Lord Crowley and Sir Frauncis to join them in the parlour. Felicia had offered to serve, an idea quickly vetoed by Mrs. Bennett, Willy and Lyndell, who together finally convinced the girl that she'd never be able to take her place in Society if she was found out. Besides, she would most likely spill something. The problem was, however, that Molly had decamped for good, dresses, bonnets and all, sometime during the day, before anyone could question her about Quinn's presence. With so many travellers, especially those used to special services, the inn was short-handed, even with the marquis's man Farrow assisting. Lyndell's offer to pour ale in the common room didn't even merit a tongue-click from her old nurse, who simply assumed she'd been teasing. The work was finally apportioned: Bennett would take care of the tap, Farrow would serve the titles, Mrs. Bennett would cook and dish out supper for the common room, Sam'l would watch the stables, Felicia would mash the turnips (the only kitchen task Mrs. Bennett would assign her) and Lyndell would again mind the hall desk, and help ferry dishes from Mrs. Bennett to Farrow. So it was that, amidst all the comings and goings, when the parlour door was left ajar, she could overhear parts of the conversation.

"Fine table they put on here. Much better than before." Obviously Lord Crowley.

"You've been here before?" Cheyne's deep tones.

"Too damn often. There's a good breeder an hour north.

108

Hard bargainer, old Eckles, but prime stock. I got my bay colt off him in—"

"Why don't you try some of this hock, Crowley? It's quite fine. What about you, Sir Frauncis, have you stopped here before?"

"Occasionally. On the way to my nevvie's school, of course. But tell me, does the proprietress seem familiar to you?"

Cheyne said no, he was positive he had never seen her before coming here; Willy, a few glasses of wine in him, started: "It's 'cause she's—"

"Related to some of the better families," Cheyne finished. He didn't want Willy babbling on about Miss Riddley's possibly illegitimate connections with any local noble houses.

Lyndell was thankful to the marquis for protecting her, as it appeared, until Willy persisted: "But she's not just plain Miss Riddley. She's—"

"My dear boy," Cheyne drawled, almost in imitation of the dandified Hammerly's affectations, "if you are finding Miss Riddley anything *but* plain, you'd best go back to bed. The wine has been too much for you."

All four men laughed. Lyndell wasn't quite so appreciative anymore. She positively glared at Lord Dodgett when he came wandering down the hall, heading toward the kitchen.

"If it is dinner you want, my lord, Mr. Bennett will serve you in the common room."

"What? Oh yes. I forgot I wasn't at home, of course. At home I simply see if cook has left me something, whenever I'm hungry. It's much too difficult otherwise, leaving an experiment in a crucial stage, just because others call it dinnertime."

"Of course." Enough of this, Lyndell decided. The gentlemen would be a long time over dessert, then port and cigars, maybe even cards later. And with Dodgett out of the corridors too, she could not miss the opportunity. She signalled Bennett to listen for the bell, then went up.

Dodgett's room was nearest, so she began there. It was much the same as before, except there actually was a telescope set up on a tripod at the window, with stacks of note-books on the chair. The notebooks really did seem to record dates in monthly intervals, times and distances for various planets, comets or whatevers. It could be a clever device for noting full moons for smuggling, perhaps too clever, since every farmer or fisherman knew the times and tides without such equipment. The rest of Lyndell's search revealed a single change of clothes and some books, many in Latin. They could contain hidden messages, for all she knew, but she doubted it.

Hammerly's room was closest to her own, so she saved it for last, certain she could make a dash for the corridor, seeming to be innocently on her way, if she heard anyone approach. That left Crowley's and Willy Richardson's, of course, now that he was out of it for the first time. No, not Cheyne's own cousin. She opened the door to Crowley's room. What a mess!

She had seen the man carry in his luggage, a satchel and his saddlebags. The stuff must have grown on being un-packed. There were discarded clothes and only barely fresh ones, a sack of sugar lumps and some ancient apples. There was another set of notebooks, and a leather wallet, right in sight, on the dresser with used towels. The man was a fool; the wallet was stuffed full of money—money borrowed, stolen, extorted? The first notebook listed mares and foaling dates, with sires, stud fees and breeders. Another diabolical code!

When she had the second book in her hand, she heard steps on the stairs. She dropped the book and ran. Damn, she was on the wrong side of the corridor. There was Cheyne, helping Willy into his room, and there was Crow-ley, coming straight at her.

"Good evening, my lord, I was making sure the room was adequate. Is everything to your liking?"

Cheyne was scowling at her, suspicious of what she'd been at. She didn't look at him.

Crowley looked at her though, looked at the door to his room, and said, "So the old maid's still got a race in her yet, eh? It ain't what I'd have bet on, but if you've a mind—"

110

Lyndell spat out, "Sir, this is not the stable!" and stalked off. Cheyne was smirking, while Crowley muttered something that sounded like "heated-up spinsters."

She opened her own door, turned and slammed it behind her, then locked it. There! She took a few steps across the sitting room toward her bedchamber when a shadow moved and a man came toward her. Oh God, Quinn was back! "Cheyne!" she screamed.

The man said, "Hush, Dilly. It's me, Jasper."

By now Cheyne was pounding on the door. Lyndell took a deep breath, requested her heart to beat less loudly so she could think, and shoved Jasper into the bedroom. She went to the entry and opened the door enough to give a view of the empty sitting room. "I'm sorry, I thought I saw a mouse. Good night."

She could hear Crowley mutter, "Yup, skittish, just like an old mare in season."

"Jasper, what are you doing here?"

"Zounds! Dilly, you look a quiz. What's that? Oh, I thought you wanted me to come. Bennett kept nattering on about your reputation and rakes and Quinn. Did he really try to stab you?"

"Don't you try to tell me you've finally found your conscience, Jasper Riddley, and you've come to protect me, for I won't believe it for tuppence! Bennett said you'd show, for fear of Quinn. Well, you can end it all now. Your spy's most likely here so you can identify him to Cheyne and settle the whole thing. Cheyne says if you do, the other charges will most likely be forgotten."

"Cheyne, huh? Is that how come you called for him just now?"

"He ... The War Office sent him. I'll go fetch him, Jasper, except please remember he only knows I'm your sister, Lynn Riddley."

"Wait up there, sis. How is it, if he's so trusty, he don't know your real name, huh? And besides, what am I supposed to tell him?"

"Jasper Riddley, you have your attic to let! Do you think I'd want anyone to know I'm running an inn, fraternising

111

with smugglers, all in this dowdy rig?" She didn't add the clincher, "And that I'm really related to you," but she was thinking it! "As for what you'll tell him, you'll say which man spoke most with Quinn, or the couriers, and who was here when that messenger was killed, Crowley, Dodgett or Hammerly."

"They're all here at once, and Cheyne too, you say? Damn good opportunity for a hand of faro."

"Jasper!"

"Shush, Dell, unless you want to bring 'em all in here. Listen, I don't know why you'd think I'd know who it was; they all come and go regularly, and Quinn, well, he was always around. I didn't watch who he talked to."

"Don't you have a suspicion?"

"No, and for that matter I can't figure why you'd think the real traitor would come back here. Now that the government's in on it, he'd be a fool to show his face."

"Unless he wanted to finish you off too!" When Jasper whitened, she said she was sorry. "That was mean."

"No, you're right. If it is one of them, and he sees me here, he'll think I'll name him to Cheyne—and I'll be found when the snow thaws in the spring. Better be going."

"Tell me one thing first, Jasper: if you had no evidence, and you weren't involved in this, why did you write to me? What did you think I could do?"

"Oh, I . . . ah . . . I thought you could go to someone in the War Office, say, and, you know, get them to drop the whole thing. For a favour, like."

"For a favour? You mean you thought I'd—Jasper, how could you?"

"What about Cheyne, huh? You and he—"

"Get out!"

Jasper poked his head out the door, making sure no one was stirring. Then he tiptoed down the hall, boots in hand, and down the stairs. Three doors shut softly after he'd gone: Lyndell's, Cheyne's, and one other.

Chapter Twenty-two

ℒord Dodgett paid his shot Tuesday morning and left after breakfast with only his telescope, reserving Room Twelve for next month. He returned about noon for the forgotten suitcase of clothes. Lord Crowley spent the morning in the stable with Cheyne and Bennett, and departed after luncheon. He left rubbing his cheek, finally convinced that Miss Riddley was not ripe for a tumble in the hay. Sir Frauncis was keeping Town hours, sleeping till noon, then requesting breakfast, which was not forthcoming due to rebellion in the kitchen:

"Ham and buns, indeed. If his fancy lordship is so 'dreadfully famished,' he can just lay his own eggs! Who's going to cook lunch, I ask? And serve it, and clean the turnips off my stove top? And who, Mr. Bennett, is going to put my closet back to rights? There's Miss Lyndy nigh murdered in her bed, and now some ... some swine is pawing through my dresses and tossing them all about. Dirty, that's what it is, and I won't stand for it. You go right into town, Mr. Bennett, and hire me some more help. Two chambermaids mornings, is it, so I can slave all afternoon and nights while you argle-bargle with every sot in the tap? *And* not keep an eye on what's ours. I know the way back to Islington, I do."

Bennett went into town. It was Farrow, fetching his employer's luncheon of rabbit stew with dumplings, who kindly offered to carry the eggs in to Hammerly, who again was sharing Cheyne's once private parlour. Lyndell herself carried in the coffee and stayed to pour it, a perfectly lady-like service that Mrs. Bennett, even in a pet, couldn't argue with. Lyndell was busy noticing how Cheyne's smile grew,

113

just for her, right up to little gold flickers in his eyes, when Hammerly's drawl caught her attention.

"I always take a walk after meals, so healthy for one's digestion, you know. A brisk jaunt on a sunny winter's day is the perfect thing. Perhaps you'd care to join me, Cheyne?"

"Sorry, I promised Willy a hand of piquet. Perhaps Miss Riddley would like an outing, put some colour in her cheeks." And he winked, behind Hammerly's back, knowing full well her ashen look was due to powder, not lack of fresh air.

"Thank you, but no. With Mr. Bennett off to town to hire new help, I must stay to look after the desk."

She stayed about two minutes. After Hammerly minced out the door, all fussily muffled and mittened and in boots at least, instead of his high-heeled shoes, she raced up the stairs to search his room. She was deciding whether to start on the dresser or the clothespress when the marquis quietly, cautiously, entered. He was not exactly pleased to see her there.

"You little fool," he raged, shaking her at the same time. "What in all damnation are you doing here? Haven't you had enough excitement, almost getting killed? This is not some ladies' tea party, my girl, and I will not have you in any more danger, do you understand?"

"Yes, but—"

"But nothing! I said I'd handle it, blast it."

That was too much for Lyndell. His concern was touching; his high-handed domination was intolerable. "Is this how you intend handling it, my lord, by shouting at me? I suggest we get on with the search instead, before Sir Frauncis comes back and finds us here squabbling like children."

The marquis sheepishly acknowledged her logic, going so far as to admit his ill temper was due to worry over her safety, before turning to the wardrobe, patting down each garment.

Lyndell gingerly lifted handkerchiefs and neckcloths, putting everything back in its precise place. "What of your game of cards with Willy?" she thought to ask.

"Oh, he was teaching Felicia to play piquet. Something about winning all the money now, so no one can say he's after her fortune later."

"You know, then. Do you mind?"

"Mind? I'm delighted. It's about time Willy settled down and made a life for himself. He can't go on just being my heir and nothing else. Especially now."

Now that the marquis was thinking of setting up his own nursery? It was something to think about. Right now, though, Lyndell watched him squeeze the shoulder padding on a jacket. "Wesley?"

"Yes, my love?"

Ah. "This may sound foolish, but could you please tell me what we're looking for?"

"Seals. I thought you knew."

"No, I had no idea there was any evidence here. I just thought it was worth a look. Jasper couldn't have known either; he said last night the spy would be insane to come back."

"So that was the mysterious Jasper. I was hoping so, and not some new beau of yours creeping about at night."

"What, did you think I was like Molly, with gentleman callers?"

"Of course not," he answered, wisely, if not honestly. The thought had crossed his mind, to be instantly dismissed.

Content, Lyndell kept searching: "Tell me about the seals. How many? What kind?"

"As for what kind, stolen and counterfeited, from the War Office. At least three or four, we think. I'm not positive they are here either; I don't think our man would be carrying them around. In addition, the attempt on your life makes me more sure that someone doesn't want you stumbling over anything."

"Yes, but what were the seals here for?"

"It's fairly complicated, and still conjectural, but London pieces it together this way: At first the traitor in London collected valuable information himself. You know, the kind mentioned at parties and discussed at clubs. He located

115

Quinn, who we know had business dealings with the French, to transfer what he learned. Then, our man realised he could find out when couriers would be passing through here with more substantial information—reports, orders, et cetera. He could not simply steal the documents, but he could copy them, hence the false seals . . . and hence Quinn's part, besides his role of carrying the stuff to Napoleon, in exchange for the brandy and silk. Quinn or his wife would drug the wine, or get Molly to, uh, distract the courier. It only took seconds to read the documents and reseal them, using the counterfeits. The riders never knew the packages had been tampered with, so the plan went undetected a good long time, I'm afraid."

"The dead courier?"

"Exactly. He must have noticed, or protested, and they had to get rid of him. After that, the investigation showed a great many of the riders would stop here as the last stage before Southwold Barracks. A few finally admitted dallying with Molly. Incidentally, if you are interested, that's why I was . . . visiting her that evening, to try to get information."

"Why should I be interested?" Lyndell wasn't going to fall into *that* trap. She'd heard lots of sweet names and sweeter hints. What she hadn't heard, loud and clear, was any kind of declaration. She started checking behind the drawers now. She found a shilling, nothing else. "But if it's Hammerly, and he didn't carry the seals with him, why should they be here? In this room, I mean? I could have given him any room in the place."

Cheyne stopped trying to get the high heels off the red shoes to see if they were hollow. "Damn, what fools we've been! Of course they're not here. And he's certainly too clever to travel about with evidence that can hang him. But he'd have to come back, to make sure they were safe, and not likely to be discovered . . ."

"Outdoors!"

"Exactly! I thought it strange that that Bond Street stroller would crave vigourous activity, much less chance mussing his clothes."

"Yes, the road is muddy and the fields and bypaths are

116

still snowy. It's not a very good day for a walk, not in yellow-lined top boots. Let's go!"

"Let *us*?"

They were well chaperoned: Ajax doing his rambunctious best to muddy the trail, and Sam'l studiously following the tracks as Cheyne had taught him. Just beyond the inn they passed Hammerly coming back.

"Your idea of a walk sounded so enticing after all, I decided to follow your lead," the marquis told him. "Miss Riddley kindly agreed to accompany me so I wouldn't lose the way."

Hammerly raised his glass to examine Lyndell in that obnoxious way of his. She hadn't found the ratty squirrel shawl in Felicia's clothespress, and wasn't about to ask Sarah if it was in the Bennetts' ransacked closet, so she wore her own green cape. Hammerly stared long and hard at it, as if trying to recall it or to remember whether the inn proprietress had been so slouchy the day before. He lowered the walking stick and moved on, with a brief "I trust you will enjoy it," leaving the distinctive imprint of left boot heel, right boot heel, then small circle where the cane made its mark. He should have been easy to trace, but none of the visible tracks they were following had that third impression.

"So the cane is just another affectation, only for the public, I suppose?"

"Yes," Cheyne replied, "just like his drawl. And just like your stoop and those absurd spectacles. You can take them off now, before you walk into a tree. Here," and he removed them for her, taking the opportunity for a gentle kiss. Lyndell motioned toward the boy and Cheyne laughed. "The ideal chaperone; he won't tell anything! But, Sam'l, did you notice the snow on Hammerly's boots? He must have left the road at some point not too distant, so keep an eye out. Here, try Ajax on this." He presented a glove taken from Hammerly's room. Instead of sniffing it to fix the scent in his head, the dog grabbed the glove for a game of tug-of-war, then stood shredding it when the marquis let go, laughing.

117

The boy and the dog dashed ahead. Cheyne took Lyndell's hand in his, as if it belonged there. It did.

"Wesley," she asked as they walked, off the hard-packed road now and through snow, "are you so sure it's Hammerly? What if it was Crowley or Dodgett, or someone else entirely, who hasn't even come yet?"

"I was not quite so sure until this morning. As for the others, Crowley was sent by Lord Wilkerson to see if I needed any assistance."

"That old reprobate, working for the government?"

"Oh no, my dear. Earls don't work, they volunteer. He's very handy, you know. Gets everywhere, talks to everyone. He's really a fine chap."

"Well, what of Dodgett? He could have stashed the seals in his telescope and no one would be the wiser."

"Sorry. Dodgett is one of the foremost tacticians for the Admiralty."

"That moonling? I can't believe it!"

"You'll have to, pet. The stargazer's a brilliant logistics expert. Advises the entire fleet on weather, tides, windshifts. His loyalty is unquestionable."

"What about Willy, then?"

Cheyne laughed. "My cousin Willy? He hasn't two thoughts to rub together! Whatever made you think of him?"

"I didn't, not really; it was just your suspecting the Bennetts, who practically raised me."

"The Bennetts? I never even considered them. They'd just arrived, for one thing. And Mrs. Bennett is one of the starchiest ladies I know, a lot more moral than the Almack's patronesses!"

"Then you didn't search their rooms last night?"

"Of course not. Why do you always think the worst of me? I wonder, though . . ."

Ajax was barking and hopping around excitedly while poor Sam'l tried to restrain him before the dog obscured the trail ahead. It was not easy, without a collar on the animal, the dog so big, the boy so small, until Cheyne ordered him down. The dog sat, wagging snow all over his back, but he sat. Lyndell and the marquis were able to see where the footsteps circled right around a large tree, before doubling back toward the inn on a path a few feet away. At the rear of the tree there was a hollow in the trunk, and a large stomped-down area. Cheyne looked in the depression, then felt around it with his gloved hand.

"Nothing. But I doubt the seals were here. See how he paced around in back? And there doesn't seem to be a dry spot where a package rested. No, I think this was an old hiding place and he came here out of desperation, thinking Quinn may have moved the seals from the inn before leaving. I'd bet they were supposed to be in Quinn's quarters, Mrs. Bennett's rooms. Hence last night's search."

"But they weren't there, nothing was. And Hammerly didn't find them, or he'd not have come out here. So what now?"

"Now he should have to contact Quinn, unless he already has. He should be getting anxious. Anxious enough to make a mistake. Then we've got him!"

Chapter Twenty-three

"No, Lord Cheyne, you shall not spend the night in my bedroom!"

"What happened to 'Wesley'?" Lyndell and Cheyne were having tea in the parlour alone, and he was quietly explaining his plan. "It's the only way, pet, besides my most favourite wish. And here I thought . . . ?" There was that devilish grin, the one that made her insides feel like pudding. "No? We shall have to talk about it later. For now, it is one thing to use you for bait, quite another to throw you to the wolves. If I hint to Sir Frauncis that you have the seals, and you're ready to go to the authorities, he will have to try something, something you couldn't handle but I could. Therefore, during dinner you will disappear, with everything you'll need for the night. An empty room or Felicia's or mine—no, I wouldn't trust Willy. Either way, you will not be seen in the halls after dinner. If Hammerly comes to your room, which I'll leave unlocked, he'll prove his own guilt."

"What makes you think he doesn't share your interest in sharing my bed?"

"You would most likely slap me if I told you. No, he'll be there for less pleasurable purposes, and I'll be waiting for him. Farrow will be on the alert, and I'll tell Bennett to keep watch."

"What about Jamison? Shouldn't we notify him?"

"Ah, the captain. I have a feeling he'll know. We can send for him tomorrow if this plan fails."

"But what if Hammerly sends Quinn or someone else, another smuggler? Or more than one?"

"You are borrowing trouble, Miss Riddley. Quinn would not dare show his face, firstly, and secondly, Hammerly is only expecting to deal with one female. He won't send in the troops. To make sure, I'll tell Bennett to see that no one else gets up the stairs. We'll have to make certain anyone seeking rooms is turned away. The fewer people around, the safer for everyone."

For everyone but you, Lyndell thought, but she did not say it.

"How lucky, Signora Fravielli, some of your country-women are staying here too. Sisters of the Blessed Virgin, I believe. You'll be able to converse with them at dinner. You can't stay? How unfortunate. I'll give your regrets to the sisters."

"A room, Lord Minhard, for you and your . . . *two* companions? Room Fourteen is the only one available. I think they'll have removed the bodies by now."

"I'm so sorry, Lord Reynald, we have no suite for you and . . . Lady Reynald. Most of the inn is let to the Slovak-

120

ian National Dance Band. They are practising here before touring London. We do have a small room ..."

Dinner was stuffed goose and gossip. The marquis skillfully directed the conversation down light, non-personal routes, alternating between *on dits* and sporting talk, for Willy's sake. Willy and Sir Frauncis had almost nothing in common, neither age nor interests, and it was only the younger man's courtesy that hid his boredom and disdain. He excused himself before the port, at his cousin's nod. Then, not having to face any awkward questions from Willy, the marquis was able to come to the point.

"Tell me, Hammerly, do you think old Crowley could be right about Miss Riddley, that she's just a vapourish female, given to imaginings?"

"Did Crowley say that?" Hammerly swirled the wine in his glass, looking at Cheyne through pale, red-rimmed eyes.

"Oh, you know Crowley. He thinks every woman would be better off with a quick toss. But that woman does have some dashed peculiar notions."

"Oh?" The man was good, Cheyne decided; he'd be a hard one to read at cards.

"Yes, she keeps nattering on about some evidence in a courier's death. Something about a spy ring. If it's true, she ought to go to the authorities, I told her. But I don't know, it could all be a hum. You've been in this neighbourhood before. Do you know anything about it?"

"I do recall something of that nature, rather dreadful occurrence, to be sure. Does the lady have the evidence though? You'd look foolish calling in the Home Guard or whatever one does, on a woman's whim."

"Just what I thought! She said something about seals, but she wouldn't let me see them, doesn't trust me, I suppose." It occurred to the marquis, and not for the first time, that Miss Riddley did not, in fact, trust him at all. He had given her every opportunity to unburden herself, to tell him one good reason for the blasted disguise, to tell him just what she was hiding. He felt he was almost ready to accept any excuse she might give, no matter how damning, as long as she gave it. He knew she thought him a libertine and a phi-

121

landerer; he could cross that bridge with time. This deeper mistrust, the basic lack of sharing, was an insurmountable gulf, a chasm between them.

"Perhaps she just doesn't like men. You know those dried-up shrews."

Cheyne remembered those kisses, and smiled. "Perhaps. Ah, well, I suppose we'll never understand women. What do you say to a hand of piquet to while away the evening? Fine. I'll just look in on Will first. He was looking a trifle peaked. Be back immediately."

What Cheyne was doing, actually, was offering Hammerly a chance to stew. The marquis didn't want to give him too much time, or a chance to flee altogether, just enough to come up with the most likely solution: stealing the evidence. Cheyne also wanted to warn Willy and Farrow that the trap was sprung, to be on guard. He brought a book of poems of Sir Walter Scott into Miss Riddley, safely, but not serenely, locked in the maid's room.

"Thank you. How kind. Did you tell him?"

"Hmm?" The marquis was lost. Here was the real Miss Riddley, whoever she might be. The soft reddish curls, the glowing skin, an emerald robe making her eyes appear even greener. Maybe it didn't matter, after all.

"Sir Frauncis—did you hint to him that I had the seals?" She spoke a little louder, breaking his reverie.

"Shh. Yes, and he seemed so indifferent he's either a masterful actor, or thoroughly innocent. I had better go keep him occupied, and you had better stay in this room, my love, or it will be bellows to mend with you. Do you understand?"

"Yes, my lord," she answered demurely, then added, "Please be careful."

He winked at her before turning to go back down.

Lyndell paced. Then she read a poem from Cheyne's book, trying to think of him reading it, wondering which were his favourites. Then she paced some more. This was absurd! It could take hours, most likely would, before Hammerly took any action; it wouldn't be until long after all the lights were out, and the men were still downstairs. And how was Cheyne to get into her room without Hammerly seeing or hearing him? Felicia had not even come to bed, so Lyndell had no one to talk to, to tell of her doubts and fears. What a stupid plan!

As it turned out, it was not so much the fault of the plan, as the failure to account for all the players. Cheyne had overlooked Hammerly's hole-card, the joker of the deck, and had misdealt the queen out of the game. The marquis found himself playing solitaire, while Lyndell gambled at Hazard.

When Felicia finally came to bed, she was carrying a note addressed to Miss Riddley. "I found this on the table in the hall. Who is it from?"

"It does not say," Lyndell murmured, distracted. What it did say was: "If you ever want to see your brother Jasper alive, be at the King's Mark coach house at one hour past dawn, and bring the seals. Come alone." There was no signature, but none was needed.

Lyndell's first thought was to go straight to the marquis. But no, he had told her to stay. Her second thought was that if she got a message to him in time he would insist on going with her, or instead of her, putting himself in danger again. The hours she had already spent worrying over him convinced her to keep her own counsel for now. She knew the coach house—of course, she did—and how it was situated on a rise, away from all other buildings, with the grooms' chambers upstairs giving an open view of anyone approaching. No, stealth could not save Jasper; nor could a whole troop of rescuers, not without the seals. If she rode to Jamison to fetch a company of soldiers, to surround the coach house and demand surrender, Jasper would be killed and named as the traitor, with no way to prove otherwise. Then again, what if that slimy Jamison did not believe her, would not bring his men? No, she would have to do it herself, with or without the dratted seals.

There was something of the night's tension in her resolution, and something of rebellion against her recent thoughts of giving up her hard-won independence. And there was something else, a lesson she had learned long ago, taking a horse out of the stable without permission. That mare had been too big for a twelve-year-old Lyndell, but her pony was no more challenging than a rocking horse, and she would just show Bennett and those Riddleys how well a Markham could ride, see if she didn't. It had taken a great, painful while for her to mount, the stepping block still not giving her the full height she needed. Then she had stood on the fence beams, but the horse moved and she was on the ground. Her next effort sent her right over the mare's back, and onto the ground again. Finally she had been up, for two minutes, until Bennett whistled to the horse. Insignificant penny's weight on her back or not, the mare was going to have her lump of sugar. The animal had headed for the gate—and Lyndell had headed for the ground. The mare had gotten her sugar, Lyndell had gotten the wind knocked out of her, and then a thrashing from Joshua Riddley, tears from her mother, and a moral from Bennett: "'At'll teach you to bite off more'n you can chew." It didn't. What it taught Miss Markham was not to get caught, and not to fall off.

She mightn't have the seals, but what Lyndell did have, besides her determination, was money and prestige. She had not met the situation in many years where her family name and a full purse could not work wonders. As much as she might deplore the hypocrisy and insincerity of aristocratic trappings, they were handy when dealing with prigs like Hammerly, to whom social standing and wealth meant everything. She also reassured herself with the fact that while a dead Miss Riddley might cause a local stir, a murdered Miss Markham would create a furor that Hammerly could not hope to avoid.

She no longer had to worry over Cheyne's well-being, and she felt confident of her own. As for Jasper, he would be safe until she could get to him at dawn. Lyndell acknowledged that concern for Jasper himself had not been a large factor in her early actions. But as much as she might wish to have him drawn and quartered, she would do her utmost to see no one else harmed him! The fear of scandal no longer mattered either. If the Marquis of Cheyne could not accept poor Miss Riddley with her weasel-principled brother and no dowry, then Miss Markham would just retire from society altogether. She'd live at King's Mark and raise pugs, and Aunt Hardesty and the others would recover as soon as a new scandal brewed. Of course, Lyndell did not really like the pop-eyed dogs, but for now she would concentrate her worry on waking up on time. As soon as Felicia's breathing softened, Lyndell pulled open the curtains, so the morning sun could come in. The bed looked too warm and soft, so she piled blankets around her on the chair, then drowsed a bit. She woke the first of many times with a trembling start, hearing a pug's asthmatic wheeze. Gads, who would have thought Felicia snored? At least there was no chance of oversleeping!

"Fine game, Hammerly. You almost had me, that last hand. Think I'll turn in now. What about you?"

"Oh, not so early. I'm used to Town hours, don't you know. Didn't realise it was so dashed boring in the country. What *do* the locals do? I think I'll stay by the fire here; at least the brandy is good."

Hammerly's plan suited Cheyne, who had time to go to his own room, fetch his pistol, put Farrow on the alert, and position the chair in Miss Riddley's room to face the door. He settled down to his uncomfortable vigil as Hammerly called out to the barkeep for another bottle. Cheyne, of course, could not hear the dandy offer Bennett a glass or insist on it, as a token of his appreciation for excellent service. And Cheyne, upstairs in Lyndell's bedroom, certainly could not see the white powder that trickled into Bennett's drink along with the wine.

Chapter Twenty-four

$\mathcal{T}$he note had said one hour past dawn. Was dawn sunrise or first light? Lyndell did not know. As soon as it was bright enough to see, she splashed some cold water on her face and put on her dress. She had not brought any of her own gowns to Felicia's room, so the brown bombazine would have to do, but she combed her hair till sparks flew and pinched her cheeks to offset the fabric's muddy tones, then covered it with her own emerald green cloak before creeping down the stairs. Bennett was asleep at the hall desk, his head on the ledger. He'd always tried so hard to protect her, poor dear, Lyndell was glad she didn't have to lie to him. The inn was still, except for his breathing, and every creaking step she took toward the front door—away from the light-sleeping Sarah—sounded like a thunderclap to Lyndell's ears. The door moaned like an actress in a Cheltenham tragedy, but Bennett didn't move, nor was there a challenge from the kitchen.

Lyndell was out, watching her breath make smoke in the air and hurrying back toward the stables, when Ajax barked. "Hush, you miserable beast," she shushed him, running up to him and pushing the dog back through the stable door. His bark was about to change to a welcoming yelp when she shoved her leather glove into his mouth. She led him to the loose box which had become his bed, hoping to calm him back to sleep, or at least keep him occupied. Ajax ran into the stall to begin shredding the glove, and Lyndell followed. There was Sam'l, sitting up on a straw pallet, rubbing his eyes. His blankets were all about, showing where he'd spent the night, instead of the nice room they'd fixed for him in the grooms' quarters overhead.

126

Lyndell smiled and told the boy to go back to sleep, she was just out for a walk. Then she bent to pet Ajax once more, telling him to stay there in his nest of old blankets and what looked a great deal like that old grey squirrel-lined shawl. So that's what Felicia had done with the ugly thing, given it for the dog's bed, wretched girl, rather than chance having to wear it again. What if someone came to claim it? But no, it had not been found upstairs in one of the inn's rooms, nor even in the common room; Lyndell remembered Mrs. Bennett finding it in the Quinns' closet, the only garment there, the only thing left in a closet that was later ransacked! The shawl was already a hotel for fleas when Hammerly searched the clothespress, when he examined the hollow tree. No wonder he thought Lyndell had the seals!

The lumpy seams ripped easily, the fur parting on its own as Lyndell tugged. Four, five, no, six seals fell into the straw, and a stick of dark red wax. Lyndell gathered them up into the pocket of her cloak, then reconsidered and pressed one into Sam'l's hand. "If I am not back in an hour," she told the boy, "give this to Lord Cheyne and tell him I've gone to the coach house at King's Mark. Bennett will know where to find him. Do you understand?" The boy nodded quickly. He understood fine, but would he tell anyone? Here she was, entrusting her life to a boy who'd said less than ten words this week! Lyndell didn't even know if he could figure an hour's time. Well, Hammerly still wouldn't kill her, not with one seal missing, and not if she offered to pay her and Jasper's way out, if she could return for a bank draft. She touched Sam'l's cheek one last time before leaving to pick her way between the hedges on the path leading to the manor. Lyndell turned and waved at Sam'l, still in the stable doorway. She took the final step into the hedge gap—and there was Captain Jamison, just on the other side. Lyndell's heart practised the quadrille in her throat for a moment.

"What . . . what are you doing here?" She noticed he was smoking a thin black cheroot.

"One of my men was at the pub last night." He jerked his head toward the inn; two stringy blond strands came unoiled. "He heard something about the murder and missing evidence, so I came to investigate. What about you, hm? What's Jasper Riddley's beautiful sister—if you are his sister—doing out so early? Meeting a man, sweetings? It wouldn't be Jasper, would it?"

His smirking presence made sense; she hadn't been downstairs last evening to hear the talk, but the captain was at least in full uniform for the first time, sword and all, and no soup stains on his front. Yet where were his troops, and why was he lurking (the only word that suited the ogling, drooly toad) in the shrubs before sunrise? Besides, even if she could bring herself to trust him, the note had been specific: "Come alone." She answered his insinuations with a cool, "What if I am? What business is it of yours?"

"Hoity-toity is it? You weren't so high in the instep when you were done up like an old spinster. Why don't we see if you can be a little friendlier to an old soldier, hm, sweetings?"

He took her arm and started to lead her away, still on the King's Mark side of the hedges, but toward the road. She was going to be late if this buffoon continued. She pulled away from him, toward the home wood path.

"I believe you mentioned government business, sir. I suggest you get on with it and let honest citizens go on their own way. Good day."

She did not get far before his hand was clamped on her arm. "You just don't know what you're getting into, sweetings. I tried . . ." He twisted her arm behind her back and propelled her closer to the road where two horses were standing, held by a hugely fat, dark man—Quinn! She started to kick and scream, which earned her a filthy rag stuffed in her mouth, making her almost retch, and a sharp upward jerk on her arm, nearly causing her to faint from the sudden pain.

"Anyone see you?" Quinn was asking.

"No one but the boy."

Quinn snickered. " 'E's nobut a dummy. I seen to that. Let's go. T'boss be waiting." Lyndell was hoisted up sideways into the saddle in front of Jamison, firmly pinned there by his arms reaching around her for the reins. A slap

128

on the face and a warning, "That's just a taste, if you don't sit pretty," kept her from struggling.

Lord, what had she gotten into now? Jamison was obviously in the plot, and how foolish of her not to have seen it in his watery, shifty eyes! Someone had to warn Hammerly or Quinn when the couriers were coming, and someone had to cover up any murmurs among the soldiers about delays or altered wrappings. And someone, someone in a position of authority, had to be turning a blind eye to the smuggling operations. Jamison. Lyndell wondered if Cheyne knew or suspected. Then she wondered if he would come. In time.

They were passing the open lodge gates of King's Mark, unchallenged. The gatehouse looked abandoned, but surely the grounds staff would be up and about . . . or old Tyler or the kitchen maids. Anybody!

Jamison and Quinn turned off the carriage drive long before reaching the house; Lyndell could clearly glimpse the tall red-brick chimneys. They picked their way through the ornamental shrubs, finding the short cut to the stables, almost as if they owned the place, she thought bitterly. They gave the empty stables a wide berth, going back in the trees to circle around to approach the carriage house from the wooded side. Not a soul was in sight, as opposed to all those times when she had had to acknowledge ten curtsies and seven head bobs just getting from the house to the stable. Never again would she let the place be so deserted, even if she had to adopt some indigent relations. They rode right into the carriage house where two horses stood harnessed to the dusty old family coach, not used in years. A few other vehicles, one without wheels, huddled in the gloom. Lyndell did not see Hammerly before she was dumped off Jamison's horse and into Quinn's hairy clutch, to be dragged to the equipment room. Quinn fairly reeked with the scent of garlic and sweat, and he grunted as he shoved her across the room toward Jasper, who had blood dripping down his forehead. Diccon sat, tied up, in another shadowy corner.

"Swine," she spat out, along with the foul rag, knowing she was insulting every pig in England. She was bending over, mopping Jasper's head with her handkerchief when Quinn growled, "T'boss says to check'n make sure she's got them seals." He grabbed at her while Jamison pawed at her body, for "places of concealment," he told her, and sniggered.

Jasper jumped up, behind Quinn, and brought both fists down on the fat man's head, shouting, "Get your filthy hands off her!" Quinn released Lyndell, shook his head, setting his black-whiskered jowls to flapping, and clouted Jasper above his ear. Riddley went down, almost out.

"Here," Lyndell said, flinging her cape at Jamison, "they're in the pocket, you dastard," then stooped to cradle Jasper's head in her lap. "Thank you," she murmured. "That was foolish, but sweet. I didn't know you had it in you."

Jasper managed a weak grin. "Neither did I."

Jamison tossed back her cloak, without the seals, slamming and bolting the door behind him and his apelike cohort. Lyndell was starting on Diccon's ropes when she first heard Hammerly's voice, without its Tulip's drawl.

"What took you fools so long?" he was shouting. "We've got to get them and the carriage out of here now!"

"Ah, y'know t'capting with a pretty face."

"A pretty face? Miss Riddley? What cork-brained notion do you have now, Jamison?"

"Cork-brained, is it? I'm thinking I've got a better use for Miss Riddley than sending her off a cliff in a coach with your precious evidence."

Hammerly snorted. Lyndell could hear his footsteps coming, the bolt being slid back. She stood up and faced the door defiantly.

He was wearing lime-green pantaloons and a purple waistcoat strewn with red roses. He held his glass-headed walking stick in one hand, and a pistol in the other. And he was cackling. After an instant's shocked silence, the wrinkled, purplish lips had opened in a squawky chortle, and it went on and on, almost insanely. Lyndell shrank back against the wall where Jasper was propped.

"Ah, how kind the fates can be," Hammerly finally got out. "Your servant, Miss Markham. Here we were, taking

130

the last, desperate measures, and salvation was sitting around the corner."

" 'Ere now, Gov, let's just get on w'it like we figgered. Make it look like they was headin' for the coast with the goods 'n some kegs, 'n end this bloody enquiry for good."

"Plans have changed, you fool. This lady represents one of the largest fortunes in the kingdom. The very building we're standing in is hers! And we don't have to harm a hair on her pretty little head, either. We just marry her and it's all ours. She can't testify against her husband, and I'd see that she wouldn't. Oh, it's too, too perfect."

Lyndell was too relieved he wasn't talking about over-turned coaches and cliffs to concern herself with his ravings, but Jamison was paying closer attention. He was getting redder in the face, and breathing in raspy gulps. "What makes you the one to get the girl and the fortune, hm? You were all set to kill them, if not for me. And what about Riddley? And him?" pointing at Diccon. "I say we send the two of them over, like we planned, and *I* get the woman. We can live like kings in Italy, if what you say about her money is true. Then neither of you has to worry about a thing."

Hammerly cackled again. "Stubble it, Jamison. You'd only waste the opportunities. With the Markham connexion I can reach the highest circles; no doors would be shut to me. While you—Pah, you'd never amount to anything but a half-pay officer gambling away your wife's dowry. You're nothing but low-born scum, Jamison, so don't get ideas above your station."

"At least I don't wear corsets and high heels like some stinking Nancy, you damned Macaroni." He lunged at Hammerly, ready to throttle him. "Why, you—"

The shot was deafening in the small room.

Chapter Twenty-five

"I will never, ever, marry you." Lyndell spoke quietly, determinedly, in the silence that followed Jamison's body slumping to the ground and Hammerly's pistol, now empty, clanking on the floor. Instead of fainting, as she wanted to do, or even casting up her accounts like Jasper in his corner, or being shocked witless, Lyndell found perfect clarity, and a last smidgen of courage. The man was a complete bedlamite, and she had to stall, to bargain, to delay whatever obscene plan he devised.

"Tongue-valiant to the end, eh? I think you'll change your mind, though. What if that was the only way of keeping Jasper alive, eh? Not that I relish having a rowdy innkeeper for a brother-in-law, mind you, but he does seem to hold some place in your affections. Too bad I didn't recall the connexion earlier, although I can understand your not bruiting it about. Relatives in trade, my dear, are not at all the thing."

"I'd rather have my relations earning an honest living than leeching off society," she countered, only to be met with, "An honest living? Jasper? How naïve you are. But you will marry me to keep him safe, for now."

"I'd rather die first."

"That, too, can be arranged, my dear. After the ceremony, of course. No, you'll be the perfect bride—rich and beautiful—and the most compliant of wives, one way or another. Too bad about Jamison, I could have had him tame you. That was his type of diversion, you know. Ah, well, there's always Quinn." Lyndell couldn't help the shudder that rippled through her. "Quite. And you needn't think your family will protest either, for I'll make sure they know there'd be an epic-proportioned scandal, without their cooperation. One way or another, Miss Markham, you'll be well and truly compromised."

"Sorry, old chap," came a deep voice from the doorway, "but I've already had the pleasure. Innocently, of course."

The marquis stepped into the room, a pistol held nonchalantly in his hand as he surveyed the carnage. "Miss ... Markham? Are you injured?" he asked, his dark eyes strained with anxiety. When Lyndell shook her head, he muttered, "How fortunate for you, Hammerly." He nudged Jamison's body with his boot, wrinkled his aristocratic nose at Jasper, still retching in the shadows, and returned his attention to Hammerly, while keeping a loose aim with the pistol, for Quinn's sake. "I have three men outside, all armed, plus a boy and a particularly nasty dog. How easy shall you make this?" He could have been offering for a dance, for all the emotion he showed.

Hammerly also stayed remarkably cool, merely nodding his acknowledgement of the odds. Perhaps it wasn't so remarkable, Lyndell decided, considering he'd just killed a man without an instant's hesitation. "Swords?" he asked, as if debating between a waltz and a quadrille. What a peculiar ritual! The marquis gave a half-bow and stepped over Jamison, pulling the captain's sword from its scabbard and slicing the air a few times to feel its weight.

"You mustn't!" Lyndell cried, but the marquis only nodded and told her, "It's the only way." He handed her the pistol, having to wrap her limp fingers around it, and squeezing them in his. He gestured toward Quinn. Lyndell moved the pistol in Quinn's vague direction as, horrified, she watched the marquis drag Jamison's body toward a wall. She knew Quinn was edging to the door, but her eyes would not leave the trail of blood smearing along the floor. When she did look up, Quinn was at the entrance. Maybe she could have pulled the trigger if he was moving toward the marquis, but away? Her hand fell to her side.

There was a clatter of hooves and a shout, barking—then a shot. Willy's voice called out, "Got him, Wesley. You couldn't have done better." Cheyne's lips tightened into

133

something between a smile and a grimace as he bowed once more to Hammerly.

Sir Frauncis twisted the eyeglass on his walking stick and pulled a wickedly thin blade from the cane, then attacked. No bow, no salute, just a mad lunge. Lyndell gasped, and this time the pistol came right up to center on the dandy's waistcoat, but the marquis parried easily. The lighter blade had the advantage of speed and manoeuverability, and in the hands of a master might have threatened the heavy sabre, but it was the marquis who had the agility, the stamina and the skill. There was some metal screeing against metal, but no real contact before Hammerly was clutching his side as blood poured over his fingers, the blade slithering to the floor.

And then Farrow and Bennett and Willy were all there, untying Diccon, holding a pad to Hammerly's wound. "You could have killed me easily," he gasped. "Why not?"

"That's why," said the marquis, his eyes on Lyndell, "though you'll never understand." He was taking the gun from Lyndell before she dropped it. "Give it to me, my girl. That's how Willy lost a toe."

"I say, Wes, you swore not to tell! What do you wish done here now? Can't just leave bodies strewn about, you know."

Cheyne had his arms about Lyndell's shoulders and was leading her to the door, but he paused. "No, I suppose not. Bennett, if you could fetch the magistrate and that discreet doctor of yours, I'd be grateful. I'm afraid you'll have to stay here till then; Farrow, see what you can do to keep Hammerly awake till I get a confession signed by him. And you"—to Diccon—"I don't know your name, but get Riddley cleaned up, will you?"

"As for you, sir," he addressed Hammerly, "I'm tempted to let you free once I have the guarantee of your confession, and your promise to stay abroad. Jamison and Quinn were guilty enough to satisfy Whitehall." Hammerly grimaced, but acquiesced. "I would like to avoid that scandal you mentioned." Another nod. "Yes, I thought so, especially when you'll remember how very, very easy it would have been for me to kill you . . . or would be in the future, if ever a mention of Miss Markham's name passes your lips. You do understand, don't you?"

"Yes, yes, a pox on both of you. Just leave me." He waved one lace-edged wrist at them, then he gave the ugly cackle again. "But you'll get yours too. With the magistrate and the doctor and the servants and the stable hands—you'll have to get married. B'God, cotched at last, a cold bride and a reluctant groom! You'll find what hell is, soon enough."

"Perhaps" was the only answer as Cheyne gently ushered Lyndell out. She hesitated this time, whispering to him until he turned back. "One last question, Hammerly. What did happen to Quinn's wife?"

"They were going to France . . . smuggler's boat. Revenuers started firing . . . men all ducked down but she jumped overboard. Couldn't swim. Too, too stupid, don't you know?"

Lyndell was too numb to reprimand Felicia for flying into Willy's arms while a strange man in an old-fashioned wig harumphed in the background, and she was too exhausted to wonder at the girl's dainty sprigged muslin and the pink ribbons in her curls. It was unseemly, of course, but Lyndell was simply beyond caring. Mrs. Bennett gathered her up, exclaiming at the state of her dress. It was covered in blood and dust and horse hair, with the hems sodden from the snowy walk home. Lyndell was trembling with cold and fatigue—and relief—when the marquis handed her a glass of something hot and, in his usual politely commanding fashion, requested Mrs. Bennett to see to a hot bath and a warm bed for her.

"Come, poppet. You'll feel better in no time. And I'm going to burn that awful dress," Sarah fussed. Lyndell would have protested, but the marquis raised the hand he was still holding and kissed it tenderly. "Go now, I have some details to take care of. I'll see you at luncheon."

Lyndell had a few details of her own to take care of once she was warm and clean and rested. The first was putting on her prettiest dress, a green shot-silk with ecru lace at the low neckline, the high waist and the scalloped hem. It was

135

a trifle too fancy for ordinary daywear, but not for this extraordinary day.

Her next business was with Jasper, and it was simple: how much and how far. Riddley still had a greenish tinge and was not really up to complicated negotiations, so he settled for less than Lyndell was prepared to offer—a tidy advance on a monthly allowance and passage to America—if he left that week.

"Damn generous of you, Dilly. You won't regret it."

"I already do. Leave today and I'll double the cheque."

The victory celebration seemed to be in full swing in the tap room, with bottles and huge platters set on the long tables. Sam'l, declared to be the real hero for his timely warning to Cheyne, was ensconced atop the bar, grinning, while Diccon was recounting his tale, an abbreviated version, as edited by Cheyne. The audience consisted of locals like the doctor and old Jake, the usual lunchtime customers, plus Lord Crowley and some recently arrived, well-dressed strangers, including the bewigged man seated between Felicia and Willy. Sarah and Bennett and the kitchen girls were busy serving, trying not to trip over Ajax who was adding his noise to the clamour of toasts and cheers and rattled dishes. The only one missing, besides Jasper, was the only one she wanted to see, so Lyndell turned to leave. It was Willy who shouted that his cousin was waiting for her in the front parlour, if he hadn't paced a hole through the floor yet.

"You are so beautiful, Lynn."

"Lyndell," she said, smiling, still standing by the door, noticing how handsome he looked in his dove-grey breeches, the diamond stickpin in his cravat.

"Ah, the ladylike Miss Lynn, and the hellion Dell, the most perfect combination a man could hope for."

And suddenly she was in his arms, pressing as close as she could so their hearts could touch.

"Gad, I am never going to let you go again!" he murmured between kisses, telling her of his horror at the peril she had been in. Then Lyndell expressed her own remorse,

136

at lying to him about her name. "At first it was because of Jasper. Not that I was ashamed he worked for a living, but that he was so spineless. And then ... then I wanted to trust you, but ..."

"But what, precious?"

"But you'd never said you loved me!"

"Loved you? I have loved you from the day I met you! Every independent, persnickety ounce, every little curl on your beautiful head. I even loved you when I thought you were a spy. I was ready to run off to Australia with you!"

"But, Wesley, you've only known me a short time! We don't really know each other. What if it's only midwinter's madness?"

"Do you doubt your love for me, darling?" he asked seriously, her face cradled in his two hands. The answer was in her eyes, so full of love and wonder that he grinned and said, "If you're so worried, we can have a long engagement: two weeks. That's all I'll wait, I swear."

"But how can I marry a man I've never even danced with?"

"Another big problem, my love." And he started humming "te-dum-dum-de-dum," and swirling her around the room. They ended up on the sofa, laughing, then embracing again, so enrapt that they didn't hear the banging on the door. They did manage to look up when the bewigged man stomped into the room and glared at the marquis.

"Disgraceful, I tell you, sir, absolutely disgraceful. A respectable chaperone indeed! Your uncle would be horrified at this whole episode. I can only hope, for his sake, that you're finally going to do the right thing."

As soon as the door closed behind him, the marquis kissed Lyndell again, that seeming like the right thing to both of them. In a few moments Lyndell remembered to ask, "Who was that man anyway?"

"Felicia's father, Lord Fullerton. Uncle George's good friend and Willy's prospective in-law. Tell me quickly, do you have any such dragons in your family?"

"Why, are you trying to back out already?"

"I'll show you how far I'm backing." And he pulled her down on top of him, their whole bodies in fiery contact.

"Dragons, griffins, sphinxes. If you've got them, I'll love them. Except maybe not Jasper . . ." he teased.

"What about King's Mark? Will you love that also?"

"Of course. Our second son will need a home too, won't he? But, sweetheart, if you are worried about my usurping your place here, don't be. I've been off to the wars, remember, so you'll have to teach me about managing. You'll have to help take over my estates, for our firstborn, and third and fourth . . ."

"Hmm. Wesley?"

"I am beginning to mistrust that tone of voice. What bee have you in your bonnet now, pet?"

There was, indeed, the tiniest seed of a doubt, not in her heart, but in her mind, planted by rumour and nurtured by Hammerly's vile tongue and Lord Fullerton's good intentions. She thought that if she didn't get rid of it now, it would grow and spread, like a weed choking out her newfound joy. "Wesley, I . . . that is, you aren't just marrying me because I have been compromised, are you? I don't care about the scandal at all, and it was mostly my fault in any case, so you don't really *have* to marry me."

"Yes, I do, darling," he told her, smiling tenderly, "if I ever want to see the sun shine again, or know how velvet feels, or be this happy the rest of my life."

"Sorry, Lord Wilton, the inn's shut down, temporary like. You might say it's closed for renovations."

An Early Engagement

To good friends and good neighbors, and especially Mrs. Stork, to whose house I would run away when I was running away from home.

Chapter One

Some marriages are made in heaven. Some are made in solicitors' offices between the pages of Debrett's *Peerages* and on county land maps. Some are even conceived in the minds and hearts of well-meaning fathers.

"A fine day's work, eh?" beamed the Earl of Stokely, who had the hearty good health of a country squire, vast acreage to field his sporting interests, and the continuance of his line assured if his heirs managed not to starve to death or end in debtors' prison.

"Indeed, indeed," congratulated his friend, the Duke of Aylesbury, a somewhat older, more reserved gentleman wearing a black armband. My Lord Aylesbury possessed an ancient title, a position of respect at court, and immense wealth. Unfortunately, he had but one child, even more unfortunately, a daughter. With a sigh of relief, he had just promised the hand of this daughter, Lady Emilyann Arcott, to his old friend and neighbor's eldest son and heir, Everett Stockton, Viscount Stokely. "At least I'll know the chit's future is secure. What was I to do about settling a motherless chick?"

The earl tried to look mournful in respect for the other's recent loss, but the proposed change in his own family's fortunes could not dim his enthusiasm for long. "No need to talk like that, Aylesbury, you're not in your dotage yet, you know. It's early days, but you'll wed again." The earl knew *he* would. He was already on his second wife.

The duke shook his head. "Not after my Cora."

"What, not even for the succession? You'd let that wastrel brother of yours come into the title? The man's a gambler, a cardsharp—a regular dirty dish. He is hardly received in company."

"Aye, Morgan is all that and worse, and that is why I need to see my girl provided for. I promised her mother that I would, for Lord knows Morgan won't have her best interests to heart. Now I can rest comfortably. . . . But enough of such gloom. This is a day for celebration. A toast, I say. To your son!"

"To your daughter!"

"May they have a long, happy life together."

"Health, wealth, and a parcel of grandbabies."

So the pleased papas repaired to the duke's study to affix their seals to a letter of intent for their men of business, to enter the engagement in the Aylesbury family Bible, and to have a few more toasts with the duke's excellent brandy. They left the youngsters, duly chaperoned, of course, to get better acquainted.

Viscount Stokely staggered a bit under the combined weight of his father's hardy slap on the back and his cheerful admonition to "go do the pretty with the little lady, my boy." Everett tugged uncomfortably at his newly starched collar, then he pulled the fingers of one hand through his dark hair, disturbing the slicked-down curls. Zeus, what did he know about courting? The bride-to-be was no help, growing fretful at his ineptness. It was obviously up to him to soothe the social waters. He cleared his throat manfully and stepped closer to Lady Emilyann, her duenna smiling encouragingly.

Viscount Stokely hesitated a moment, looking down at his fiancée all done up in fussy white lace. His clear gray eyes opened wider and he declared, "Gads, she looks like something that fell out of the nest too soon!"

The infant Lady Emilyann, hairless, red-faced, and indeed as scrawny as an unfledged nestling, did not appear precisely enamored at the betrothal either. She scrunched up her face and started wailing, angrily waving her arms in the air.

"Here now, don't do that," Master Stokely told her, "you'll hurt yourself." Without stopping to think, since rational thought would have told him this was no job for a six-year-old lad in nankeen shortpants, he reached over the side of her eyelet-decked bassinet and held her hand away from her face. The tiny fingers curled naturally around his. Perhaps it was the sound of his voice, or the bright red soldier Everett held in his other hand that caught her eye, but Lady Em stopped crying, looked up, and smiled a wet, gurgly, gummy baby-smile at her intended.

"I think she likes me," he said with wonder.

"A' course she does," Nanny told him. "She will love you and look up to you and you'll be a brave lad and look after her forever. She be yours to cherish, you know. Didn't your papas just say so?"

They had. He would. He did. "Hallo, Sparrow," he whispered.

Emilyann blew some bubbles and contentedly shut her eyes. Still clutching his finger, she went to sleep, exhausted by her hard day's work. After all, how many ladies manage to be christened and betrothed on the very same afternoon?

"Don't you dare cry, Sparrow. It's only a little scratch, and viscountesses don't blubber."

"No viscountess has her hair all in rats' nests and her skirts trailing in mud either," taunted Thornton, second son of the Earl of Stokely. "I don't see why she had to come along anyway, Ev," he whined, "she's just a baby."

"She's not a baby anymore, are you, Em? And if we're going to play at St. George and the dragon, we need a lady to save. Besides, she's more fun than you are anyway."

Lady Emilyann, five years old, stuck her tongue out at Thornton, who promptly announced, "I'm going to tell!" So her cavalier, a handsome eleven now, rolled his younger brother in the grass. And the mud. Master Stokely was birched, of course, and Lady Em was sent to bed without her supper, because Thornton always did squeal, but no matter. After Thornton had run home, they'd had another glorious day without him, out in the adjoining estates, begging gingerbread and cider from the cottagers, finding tadpoles and newborn sheep, fighting off countless Saracen invaders.

No one worried about them overmuch, except perhaps the young viscount's tutor, who would certainly lose his position if the earl ever found how little time his eldest son actually spent in the classroom. Lady Em's parent spent his time in London, immersing his grief in affairs of state, leaving his daughter alone except for a horde of doting servants, including Nanny, two nursemaids, the entire stable crew and indoor staff, and a rather totty-headed young female relation of his late wife's to serve as governess/companion to the little girl. Cousin Marietta was suitably grateful to Lord Aylesbury for such a comfortable position in his luxurious household; life would certainly have been very unpleasant for a gently bred female with neither pittance nor prospect. Marietta would have been a great deal more grateful, however, if instead of a child to watch her noble cousin had seen fit to give her a dowry and a London season. Why, the only company the man ever invited to Arcott Hall were dull old political cronies. No chance for her to meet eligible gentlemen! Here she was, stuck in the country, getting older by the minute, with nary a beau in sight. So she spent her days and, regretfully, her nights, sighing over the heroes in her Minerva Press romances, while Smoky, Viscount Stokely, looked after her charge.

"Smoky" was not Lady Em's first word, but it was close. The young lord was Master Stokely to the staff at Arcott Hall (when he was not that imp of Satan), but the syllables were too difficult for Baby's tongue, so he quickly became Smoky. The name stuck, partly due to Emilyann's insistence, partly to his clear gray eyes, but mostly to his knack for escaping his own governors and the harum-scarum household at Stockton Manor, with a new stepmother, new baby brother, Geoffrey, and the righteous Thornton to bedevil him. At Sparrow's home he was treated with respect, even devotion, plus all the treats a growing boy could cajole from a willing kitchen staff, and all the coy smiles he could win from Cousin Marietta. She couldn't help it; a girl had to stay in practice, didn't she? And he was such a charming scamp. As Nanny said, the boy was too smoky by half.

He thrived on all the attention, and so did Sparrow. If his

name wasn't her first word, he was there for her first steps. He taught her to write, and received her first letter. He read to her for rainy-day hours, and if the books had more to do with King Arthur's knights and their bloody battles than they did with good little girls who studied their Bibles, well, Cousin Marietta had no complaints. She was lost in *Lady Longacre's Liaison* or *The Web of Westfall* herself, books the children later disdained as too flowery, with not enough action. Marietta did insist on *some* ladylike accomplishments, though, especially close to holidays when her employer might be expected to visit and show an interest in her charge's progress. So Smoky received Miss Arcott's first pressed-flower picture, her first muddy watercolor, and her first wobbly curtsy. Emilyann herself drew the line, however, at stitchery.

"I'm not going to do this silly girls' stuff and you can't make me!" So she had to sit in a corner for an hour.

"I won't do it! I won't! Smoky's out riding and I want to go!" She kicked over the sewing basket, sending silks every which way, and got none of her favorite strawberry tarts for a week.

"I hate this . . . this bloody sampler!" She had her mouth washed out with soap, and Master Smoky got his hair combed with a footstool by Nanny for teaching her chick such language.

In the end Emilyann learned a few other female skills beyond needlework. A trembling lip, big blue eyes swimming in tears, and Smoky bribed his stepmother's abigail to finish the wretched piece, and the two went riding. After all, a lady of the ton needed to know how to sit a horse, too.

At first Emilyann rode in front of Stokely on his pony, a groom on either side. Then she was given a mount of her own, and the two were off, her silver-blond baby-fine hair coming undone and streaming out behind her, her pale complexion turning sun-kissed, and her laughter delighting everyone on two estates and in the tiny village of Arstock, which separated them. If some of the higher sticklers considered her behavior hoydenish, well, a female who was al-

147

ready spoken for had a great deal more latitude, no matter how young.

"Lady Em," Nanny would chide, "you cannot go galumphing down the stairs with your skirts all apelter and throw yourself at Master Stokely! What would your mother think, to see her lamb such a forward miss?"

"It is perfectly proper," Sparrow would announce in her best *grande dame* manner, "we are afancied."

Smoky called her a silly widgeon. "It's affianced, you goose. Fancy is something you'd better not ever be. Besides, one day I might forget to catch you when you come flying down that staircase, and then where would you be?"

"Then I'd be showing even more of my petticoats, I suppose. As if you ever would!"

"Minx." He grinned at her, then told her not to stick her tongue out. "I don't want any ill-mannered brat for my viscountess," he declared, effectively curbing that bit of waywardness.

If it weren't for the viscount, even Nanny admitted, little Emilyann would have grown up spoiled, headstrong, and hey-go-mad, without limits. Without love and affection and attention, either, except what she received from the servants.

Their attachment stayed constant even when Smoky was sent away to school. It was the young nobleman this time who needed the reassurance of his devoted friend, away from home and all he knew, with more restrictions on his freedoms than he thought possible outside Newgate Prison, and only few opportunities to employ his knack for disappearing from unpleasant tasks. So he wrote long letters home to Sparrow, and she read them over to the barn cats and the toy soldiers he'd outgrown and left in her safekeeping. In return, Emilyann filled her sometimes grubby pages with bubbling news of Queenie's foal and the vicar's hiccups—right in the midst of the sermon—and Cousin Marietta's latest book from the lending library, and love.

At the long vacations, Smoky's first stop was at Arcott Hall, before going home. Lady Em would come flying down the stairs, her sun-bleached hair coming unbound, and launch herself into his arms, laughing. He never did let her fall.

"I won't have it! Do you hear me, Stokely? I won't have it!"

"B'Gad, I hear you, Aylesbury. My whole household hears you. The whole county hears you. Blast if they don't hear you back in Parliament, where you dashed well belong, rather than haranguing a gentleman in his own home."

"Gentleman? A gentleman, is it? You insult the name, sir, with all your wenching and carryings on. Shameful, I say."

"Why, because you're a dull old stick with no fire in you? Confound it, you are turning into a Puritan. My Louise has been dead these two years. I'm not shaming her memory any."

"No more than you did when she was alive, nor your first wife either, chasing every light-skirt in Northampshire. But now you've gone too far. Aye, far enough that I hear of it in London! You are a laughingstock, man. The 'Eager Earl,' they call you."

"So get ye back to London, you old fool. It is naught to you."

"It is when you bring your profligacy home to me, you poltroon. My household, my family."

The Earl of Stokely was silenced, finally. He turned away, red-faced, and covered his embarrassment in pouring another glass of port, which was another mistake. A man needed a clear head to deal with the Duke of Aylesbury, especially when he was on his high ropes, and the earl hadn't had a clear head in ages. Stokely had always possessed robust appetites, and the passage of neither years nor wives had caused them to diminish. What did dwindle were his resources, so jaunts to London for the pricier pleasures were a thing of the past. Even the countryside was not such a fertile field for plowing, not for a bleary-eyed, bloated old philanderer with pockets to let. Attics to let, more likely.

"I must have been foxed."

"That's not an excuse, man, that's a condition!" Now, the Duke of Aylesbury may have led a celibate life after the

149

death of his beloved Cora. Then again, he may have not, but at least he was discreet. He was certainly no prude, not living in London among the decadent aristocracy, but he most assuredly did not bring those pleasures home to sully the eyes and ears of an innocent, inquisitive child. "In front of my daughter, by Jupiter!"

"Chit had no business being in the library. Why she couldn't play with dolls like other girls, I don't know. My little Nadine don't go tearing around on horses, playing at soldiers with the boys, or reading books, you can be sure of that."

Whatever else the earl may have said concerning the education of girl children was drowned out in the duke's roar. What they weren't supposed to learn, he bellowed, was how their governesses got tupped by ramshackle Romeos!

Cousin Marietta had found something better to do with her evenings than read tawdry romances.

"You'll not bring scandal to my doorstep," the duke insisted. "I expect a special license before the week is out. You may honeymoon at my hunting box."

"But listen, I can't afford another wife, especially one with dreams of London ballrooms in her cockloft. It ain't as if—" The sound of a fist being smashed down on the desk gave him pause. He may have been a randy old fool, but he wasn't gudgeon enough to face Aylesbury at twelve paces over any female. Marietta was a tidy armful, anyway, a bit scrawny and featherheaded with die-away airs, but a man could do worse.

. . . And some marriages are made in heat.

Scandal kept from his door, the duke meant to keep it that way. He was rid of Marietta; he'd be rid of the whole Stockton clan.

"That boy of yours bids fair to follow in your footsteps, and I don't want him near my girl."

"Come now, the lad's only sixteen. Wild oats, you know."

"I know it all! Do you think I don't keep track of everything that concerns my family? I know he's been sent down from school so many times they hardly recognize him there. His instructors say he's near brilliant—where he got

150

that heaven knows—but he lacks discipline. He'll end up another care-for-nothing loose screw, and I won't have it."

The earl grew even more red-faced, if possible. "The whelp's just army-mad. Always has been. I won't let him sign up, the heir and all, so he's just kicking at the traces. He'll likely buy his own colors when he's eighteen with the money his mother left him. I misdoubt I can stop him."

"What, did you think my girl would follow the drum?"

"Dash it, man, the chit's only what? Ten or eleven? He'll be ready to settle by her coming out."

"And if he's not? If he's so deeply in debt he's just waiting for her dowry? It won't do, man."

Damn, but the earl saw all that wealth slipping away. "Then maybe my second son, Thornton, would suit you for the chit? Lord knows he's sober and steady enough for a bishop." Lord knew where those traits came from, either, but the earl held out his last, faint glimmer of gold. Fool's gold, of course, as he saw by the duke's answer.

"I swear your first wife must have played you false, Frederick. That boy can't even keep up with Emilyann on horseback, for all his four years' advantage. He's nothing but—"

The earl may have agreed that Thornton was a priggish toad-eater, but enough was enough. His third son, Geoffrey, was a jolly, likable lad, but he was younger than Miss Arcott, with no chance of coming into the title or lands. The duke would never go for that, so Stokely had nothing to lose. Hell, he was getting a flighty new wife, a parcel of debts, and his heir's future to settle all over again. At least he deserved the satisfaction of spoiling the duke's holier-than-thou attitude with a few home truths of his own.

"There's to be no scandals in your family, eh? What about your own brother? The man's a regular here-and-thereian. You worry about keeping your darling's fortune safe from my boys, but Morgan Arcott would go through that money in a year, and throw your girl in the streets without thinking twice of it. And if"—he was in full spate now—"if you are thinking it will be so easy to settle your daughter to some high-born gentleman, think again. If ever there was a hell-born babe with more instinct for trouble,

151

I've never seen it. The chit is a regular tomboy and a hoyden to boot. I've never seen her with her hair combed or her face clean or her pockets free of frogs. She's on terms with every groom and dairymaid for miles, and has about as much ladylike decorum as my prize pig. Less, maybe." He didn't say that he'd miss chasing her out of his orchards and stable yards if she ever changed. He didn't say that everyone adored Lady Em for her cheerful deviltry and there wasn't an ounce of guile in the moppet. He just concluded: "If she don't blot her copybook, it'll be a miracle. And even if you get those haughty London hostesses to accept her, she ain't going to make anyone a comfortable wife, I'll wager."

"Don't bet on it, you cannot afford to lose."

It took a while for Lady Emilyann to figure how to smuggle letters into and out of Miss Meadow's Select Academy for Young Ladies in Bath. At last she received a reply to her most recent tear-stained missive. *Dear Sparrow,* he wrote. *Don't worry. I'll marry you anyway.*

Chapter Two

Under the British legal system, a person who stole a loaf of bread could be hanged or sentenced to a long imprisonment. He, or she, could be exiled to Botany Bay or one of the other penal colonies. Many such involuntary tourists died on the voyage or from hunger, disease, or the elements. Others survived and made the best of a harsh living. Some even fought hard to succeed in their new life—dreaming of the day they could go home.

For the crime of being a child—worse, a girl child—Emilyann Arcott was shipped off to Bath, to a school

152

devoted to the task of making young girls into model citizens, young ladies ready to make their bows to society. If it took mincing steps and modulated speech, Emilyann would do it. Dancing, French lessons, even the harp, she would learn it all, then go home, or so she thought in her childish naïveté. But Rome wasn't built in a day, and a hoyden wasn't made into a debutante overnight, and life wasn't fair. No matter that Emilyann outpaced her instructors, or charmed even the redoubtable headmistress with her eagerness to learn, she could not go home, except for an occasional long vacation. Gads, it was a life sentence!

And how she hated it! Some of the lessons were interesting, and she made friends among the less silly of her fellow students. She did not even mind the uniforms the others despised, never caring about her clothes so long as they were comfortable; she barely resented the rules about keeping them neat, for there was no chance to muss anything. She missed the country, the freedom, the rough-and-tumble of boys' play, the bustling activity of a productive estate. She missed Nanny and Cook and all her friends on the farms. She missed her dog.

She did not miss Smoky, who had himself been at school for ages and would soon join the army. Boys could have adventures! Of course she remembered his last promise, but without much hope for the future. Not even he could change the mind of the Duke of Aylesbury. No one ever had, in Emilyann's memory, and not for lack of trying. Her own tears and pleas and threats to starve herself hadn't prevented her continued incarceration at school. Instead, she was sent to a dragon of an aunt for one whole vacation, where she did nothing but read improving works and sew shirts for the parish needy. (Those who had one arm shorter than the other, who didn't take part in strenuous activities like breathing, which would have opened her pitiful seams, or those who did not require buttonholes, which were entirely beyond her. Miss Arcott might understand the functions of an orery, but the workings of needle and thread were true mysteries.)

She did not miss her father either. She hardly knew

him, except as some distant divinity to be worshipped, feared, and obeyed. Occasionally he would grant some benediction, like petitioning Miss Meadow to provide riding lessons for the girls, and sending Emilyann's own pony down to Bath. Mostly, however, he was an implacable force, in God-like charge of her life. Previously, Emilyann had childishly and cheerfully accepted his edicts concerning her future. Of course she would marry the man of his choice. That was as natural to her as her name. She was Lady Emilyann Arcott, betrothed to Everett Stockton. Here was her right hand, here was Smoky. What could be easier?

Things were different now. Among all the other gossipy, giggly young misses, some approaching their debutante seasons and freedom from Miss Meadow and lessons in deportment, Emilyann quickly learned that daughters, especially daughters of wealthy, powerful men, were only pawns in their fathers' chess games. The girls might read as many lurid romances as they could smuggle into school, dreaming of the dashing heroes who rescued the distraught damsels, but they knew they would wed the suitor their fathers chose, be he old and gouty, pock-marked, or averse to bathing.

Lady Em kept Smoky's letter, folded so many times the creases almost split, and dreamed her own dreams.

"Well, my dear, we will be sorry to lose you here at Miss Meadow's Academy."

That was a lie. The pudgy little headmistress would be sorry to lose only the duke's patronage and the money she had extorted from him for his daughter's schooling. Emilyann waited to see if Miss Meadow would be struck by lightning for such a monumental untruth. No such luck, so she courteously replied "Thank you." She would *not* tell the bigger whopper by replying that she would miss the school.

"I am sure you will make us all proud of you when you enter society." Now, that was coming too strong, Emilyann considered. Likely old Meadowlark was shaking in her boots lest any prospective parents learn what institution had had the molding of this particular pupil.

"Sixteen is a bit early, but the dear duke feels you would benefit from some local society in Northamphshire before your official presentation, and sooner or later we would have to see you off anyway. It is the nature of young things to leave the nest, try their wings, take their proper place. . . ." Miss Meadow was rushing through her standard farewell speech, most likely to get to the celebratory bottle of champagne that much sooner. Emilyann found no fault there; she had been eagerly anticipating this day herself for six years now.

". . . Remember that you will always be in our hearts."

Hah! That midget martinet might look like a cherubic chipmunk, with pouchy cheeks and button eyes, but her heart held all the affection of a flea! Emilyann murmured, "How kind."

"We will miss you."

Miss Arcott choked and needed a restorative sip of tea. That was the biggest rapper yet. Miss Meadow would be vastly relieved to see the last of Lady Emilyann Arcott.

She looked like the model student, hands folded demurely in her lap, blue eyes cast respectfully downward, light blond braids twisted into a pristine bun at the back of her neck—not a single hair would dare to be out of place. She wore a simple but elegantly fashionable white muslin gown that had been ordered from the most expensive dressmaker in Bath, with a percentage, naturally, accruing back to Miss Meadow's account. Her cheeks were appropriately pale, untouched either by artifice or vulgar sun-darkening. Smiling politely, repeating her "Thank-yous" in a softly sweet voice, Lady Emilyann was an angel, a lady, a debutante!

A wraith, a shrouded corpse, a blasted virgin being readied for sacrifice, she muttered to herself as she took another sip of tea. (A lot better quality than the brew served the pupils.) Lord, it had been a long time—for both of them. Emilyann had learned in her very first year that cooperating with the gaolers would not shorten her sentence. No knight on a charger was going to ride to her rescue ei-

155

ther. Smoky had charged off to join the army while his father and Marietta were on honeymoon. His letters were few and then, when he joined the Peninsular campaign and his knack for playing least in sight sent him behind enemy lines, even more sporadic. Lately, all she heard about him was when she managed to see his brothers at some neighbor's house during vacations. No, if anything was going to be done about her wretched condition, she would have to do it herself. It was not in her nature to be mopey and miserable, not when she could do something to enliven her days and make the gaol bearable. As the daughter of a duke, with a more than generous allowance and a natural friendliness that charmed the kitchen staff, the grooms at the hired livery, and anyone else she had no business being in contact with, there was a great deal Miss Arcott could do to subvert authority . . . and make Miss Meadow's life hell.

How many creatures had crept, crawled, and slithered their way into the schoolrooms? How many bushels, barrels, and bales of merchandise had found their way to the academy's kitchens with Miss Meadow's signature on the order forms? The clocks set back, the signs repainted naughtily, the Madeira watered at a social for local patronesses—the list went on and on because there was nothing Miss Meadow could do about it. There was only so much retribution she could exact before the duke withdrew his daughter and blackened the school's reputation. Miss Meadow would never admit defeat—nor refund a tuition. Not even the time the entire school had to be quarantined during the bishop's visit when a whole grade came down with measles—that had been painted on!

None of the other girls would ever squeal on the chit; she was a hero to them. Even the older girls who had already absorbed Miss Meadow's strictures on propriety and decorum, she thought, were not above giggling at Emilyann's fits and starts. The most senior students, those wise young debs who were about to make their curtsies to the polite world, realized it would be better to stay friends with one of the wealthiest heiresses in England. Furthermore, they liked her, with her gamin grin and big blue eyes and boundless energy.

156

Lady Em even had the instructors wrapped around her dainty little thumb, being polite, cheerful, eager to learn. Emilyann was quick to see the teachers were as much prisoners at the school as she was, with their miserly salaries, drab existences, reams of rules and regulations. Perhaps they were in worse straits, for she could leave eventually. Sparrow was never one to add to another's burden; she was a lady.

She was a witch, recalled Miss Meadow, shuddering at memories of pink dye in the laundry, scarlet ribbons appearing in the hair of every single student, in church, no less, and the magistrates even calling on her—twice! Magistrates, dear Lord. The sooner the hellion was gone, the better.

"Yes, well, we must not keep your father's coach waiting. I expect he will join you in Northampshire as soon as Parliament is adjourned. Then there will be local assemblies and house parties, and next year, London," she said reverently. London. It was the goal of a girl's schooling, the pot of gold at the end of the rainbow, where a miss could become a Toast, a Belle, a bride. She could also become a social outcast if her behavior was found wanting. Miss Arcott's behavior was wanting a bridle! In one last, desperate effort to inculcate six years of pleas for propriety, and incidentally save the reputation of her school, Miss Meadow placed a chaste kiss in the air near Miss Arcott's chin and said, "We'll be thinking of you."

"I'm sure you will," Lady Em said, dropping a perfect curtsy, and, behind her skirts, a lovely little green garden snake.

"Freedom, Nanny," Emilyann shouted, skipping into the old nursery. "Two whole weeks of freedom!"

Nanny put down her mending and adjusted her wire-rimmed spectacles to read the letters being gaily waved under her nose while Lady Em went on happily: "Father writes that Parliament is embroiled in another debate on the Corn Laws and so will not adjourn for at least another two weeks. And even better, Aunt Ingrid cannot come to Northampshire to chaperone me because that nodcock Bobo fell off his horse and broke an arm. Too bad it wasn't his head; that might have knocked some sense into him."

"Now, missy, you shouldn't be agloating over another's misfortune, and that bein't any way to talk of your cousin."

"Nanny, you know very well that if the wiser creature sat on top, Bobo would be wearing the saddle. Besides, he isn't really my cousin. He's only Uncle Morgan's stepson from Aunt Ingrid's first marriage. Thank goodness I have no blood in common with that bobbing-block."

She changed the subject at Nanny's frown. "Father sent Jake Coachman to look after us because Jake's arthritis is too painful for him to drive right now. He's been telling me the most wonderful stories about the highwayman they are calling Gentleman Jim. Jake hasn't seen him in person, of course, more's the pity."

Nanny harrumphed. "Fine watchdog your papa sent, filling your pretty head with such notions. Next thing you know, we'll be having you out on the highway with a mask and a pistol."

"Not to worry," Lady Em said, lifting her chin. "I'll have you know I am a lady now."

"Sure, and your lovely gown is allover dog hairs and grass stains already, and your hair is no-how, like a gale came through here. And I had it braided so pretty not two hours ago."

"Oh, Nanny, you know my wretched hair is too fly-away to stay tied for long, unless I sit perfectly still."

"And a fine day that would be, if I live to see it."

"Don't scold, Nanny. I mean to be good, truly I do."

"Aye, I'll bet you do, after your papa's letter. One hint of mischief, he says, and it's right back to that school for you. No parties or picnics, and no going up to London in the spring neither."

Emilyann twirled around, oblivious to the falling hairpins and ribbons. "Won't it be grand? The opera and plays and Vauxhall Gardens and Venetian breakfasts. Father says I'll even get to meet the prince!"

"And a whole passel of eager young bucks, too. I'll wager every eligible gentleman in London will be begging His

158

Grace for your hand within a sennight. Some what aren't so eligible, too."

Emilyann blushed, an easy occurrence for one of her fair coloring, and one which happened much too often for her peace of mind. "Do you really think so, Nanny? Do you really think I'll be popular? What if I have to sit out every dance on the sidelines with Aunt Ingrid, or, worse, if only Bobo asks me to dance?"

"You'll be a wallflower when pigs fly, child. And not just because of your papa's wealth. He would no more let a fortune-hunter come near you than he'd let Old Toby's plowhorse near his broodmares. But for the other beaux . . ." The old nursemaid shook her head, wondering if the duke knew what he was in for. "You'll do, if'n you just remember that pretty is as pretty does, and you have to please the mamas as well as the sons."

"Father said I might have a year to . . . to survey the field. I know that sounds vulgar, but that's how all the girls at school refer to it, and the season is nothing more than a marriage mart anyway. He promised he'd consider my wishes."

Nanny waved the letter. "And he promised right here that he'd marry you off willy-nilly to the first suitable *parti* if there was one whisper of scandal while you are here. No riding astride, no going into the village alone, no dicing with the stablehands, he says."

"Yes, and I am to stay away from Stockton Manor, although it seems harsh that I cannot pay my condolences to Nadine. That was a terrible tragedy, losing both the earl and Cousin Marietta in a carriage accident. They said he was foxed."

"A lady doesn't gossip, missy. And you know your father ordered that woman's name not be mentioned around here. At least you won't be getting up to deviltry with those boys. Master Thornton has taken orders and has his first vicarage, a fine living not far from London, and that rapscallion Geoffrey is still away at school."

"And what of Smoky? Is there any news of him?"

"He's Lord Stokely now, of course, but isn't making any

159

hurry to sell out. We heard he was mentioned in the despatches." Nanny pursed her lips.

"Why do you look so disapproving? There's more, isn't there?"

"There have been stories, stories not fit for your ears, lamb. Wellington's young officers make a habit out of cutting a dash, you know, and that lad always could charm the birds out of the trees."

Emilyann hooted in delight. "A rake? You mean Smoky is a rake? How exciting for him! Oh, I wish I could go visit with Nadine. She would know."

"Ladies don't gossip, missy. And Miss Nadine is too young for such goings-on. Although what I hear about her and that ninnyhammer aunt of hers who is supposed to be taking charge at the Manor . . ."

"I thought ladies didn't gossip, you old faker," Emilyann teased. "No matter, I'll hear all the *on dits* from Cook or Mrs. Finster in the village. Father said I was to have some new dresses made up, to give some of our trade to the local merchants, although I already have so many gowns I don't know when I'll get to wear them. But I'll wait till he returns home to ask him about a duty call to the manor."

She never got to wear the new gowns or make that call, for the duke never came home. It was raining. The right leader slipped and came up lame, so one of the grooms led it back to a farmhouse they had seen. The undercoachman could not handle the off-stride team, and the coach foundered in the mud, miles from nowhere, in the rain and wind and cold. The duke took a chill, which settled in his chest, which became pneumonia, which killed him in three days.

Chapter Three

*B*lack was the color of Lady Em's dresses. Black were her prospects. But not as black as her uncle Morgan's heart.

Like a sapling growing crooked in the shade of a larger tree, Morgan Arcott grew bitter in the shadow of his brother's money, power, and title. But for a trick of birth, Morgan would have been the chosen one, their father's heir and favorite, not the unfortunate younger son given an allowance and a good-bye.

Brother George got to marry the woman of his choice. Hell, beautiful Cora would have been Morgan's choice, too, if she would have looked at a green lad already in the hands of the cent-percenters. No, Morgan had to wed money, and a bride was found for him among the wealthy merchant barons. A Cit, no less, and a shy, frail, nervous female Laura was, with neither looks nor wit to sugar coat the pill. Morgan's father thought the responsibility of a young bride would mature his son. Instead, Morgan got her with child, got his hands on her dowry, and got himself back to London and the gaming tables as soon as possible. She lost the baby; he lost her fortune, but they both kept trying.

Worn out with three or four futile attempts to bear him a child—Morgan could not quite recall the exact number— Laura faded away mere weeks before her twenty-fifth birthday, which he most assuredly would never have remembered either, the date not being scribed on the back of the pasteboards, although certain other marks were.

By now their father had stuck his spoon in the wall and brother George was Duke of Aylesbury, no more generous nor less censorious than the old man, just younger. He was a rising star in political circles, his investments returning fourfold, his wife increasing. Morgan's interests also broadened as he added shilling for the gaming dens to cardsharping.

Morgan needed another wife. Oh, not for the comfort of a woman's warmth; he got all that from a different class of female entirely. No, he needed another investment in his career, another bankroll, but this time there were even higher stakes. George's Cora suddenly died of childbed fever leaving the one infant, Emilyann, a girl. Morgan found himself second in line to the title, with his grief-stricken brother vowing to remain a widower.

That was doubtful, even to Morgan. After all, George was still a young man with more sense and family pride than to leave the Arcott fortunes to an ivory-tuner. Nevertheless, the gambler in Morgan saw a chance, albeit a long shot, of getting his hands on the Arcott wealth, taking his rightful place in society, and topping that flat George at something, even if merely in begetting an heir.

Money and an heir. Those were the only two reasons Morgan could ever see for marrying, and he was desperate for both. Finding a bride, however, was not quite as simple this time. There was no wealthy duke spreading patronage, nor were Morgan's own prospects such that a wealthy Cit would trade his daughter on the chance of a title. Those middle-class merchants and mill owners were as canny as the money lenders when it came to Morgan's place in the succession.

As for finding a wealthy heiress among his own kind, he had a better chance of finding the lost mines of the Incas. He was not even invited to ton affairs, and chaperones in the park made their debutantes sidestep him like a pile of horse droppings.

Then he found Ingrid, a handsome widow with a handsome jointure and a small son: a proven breeder! Better yet, he discovered her while on a repairing lease to Cheltenham, where word of his unsavory reputation had not reached. He put on sober clothes and attended her at Sunday church; she

162

put off her widow's weeds and gaily accompanied Morgan to the theater. Even the lad was cautioned to stop drooling, stop fiddling with his unmentionables, and to leave the contents of the gentleman's pockets alone. With such fine behavior on all sides, a match was soon made.

Now, if *this* marriage were made in heaven the angels had a most quirky sense of humor, for the wedding was one of the few times Ingrid saw her husband that month, much less sober. It was the last time she smiled at him, as soon as she realized that not only would she have to pay for the wedding breakfast herself, but none of Morgan's noble friends were coming, because he had none. Beauregard spilled down his shirt whatever he did not manage to cram in his greedy little mouth, and promptly cast up his accounts on his new papa's boots. He also "found" a shilling that had somehow slipped from the vicar's topcoat pocket. Beauregard indeed, Morgan told himself too late, a jumped-up name if there ever was one. As soon as the happy new family removed to Arcott Hall, the only honeymoon spot available to Morgan on his finances, Emilyann and the Stockton boys renamed the sausage-shaped, light-fingered, slow-topped little toad Bobo. Only his mother could love him and, as it turned out, he was the only thing she could love besides Mother Church. Ingrid was a rampant reformer, an evangelical missionary out to save the world from the evils of gambling, drinking, and wenching—the only particulars Morgan was good at! So she would pray for his soul, that he repudiate the devil before it was too late and he burned in hell forever.

According to Morgan, hell would have been an improvement to life with Ingrid. As for begetting the heir, she did her wifely duty at first, praying the while. Morgan prayed, too, that he could muster up enough enthusiasm to get the deed done. When no child was forthcoming, Ingrid took it as a sign from on high, a punishment for her sin of ambition, hoping to better herself and her son's position in life. In her weakest moments she dreamed of becoming a society hostess. Heaven forfend! So she redonned her Puritan gowns and scraped her hair back in a bun and refused to attend plays. And she started getting headaches, especially

163

when Morgan came back to their lodgings in London from wherever he spent most of his time, remembering why he married in the first place. Gads, he kept asking himself, how could any woman who spouted of hell-fires and soul-scorchings be as cold as her northern forbears? Worse, she was clutch-fisted.

In all honesty, Ingrid had mentioned that the bulk of her wealth was held for Bobo, with her to administer, but at first—before the wedding—Morgan thought he could charm whatever he needed from her; if that woman had been in Eden, Adam would still be eating gruel in the altogether. So it was back to work, back to gulling greenhead boys into losing their allowances, back to weighted dice and shaved decks. Morgan played; Ingrid prayed.

Until, that is, one cold, rainy day when the right leader of the Duke of Aylesbury's coach slipped in the mud and came up lame.

"What do you mean, he left most of the money in trust for the chit?"

"What do you mean, he named Uncle Morgan as one of my trustees?"

Both together: "Damn and blast!"

Mr. Baxley, the late duke's man of business, wiped his forehead. Where to start? He turned first to the ashen child lost in a tentlike black gown. He had known her all her life; he moved the ink bottles farther out of her reach.

"My dear," he said gently. "You must know that your father loved you very much and he wanted the best for you. But you are not even seventeen; you cannot set up your own household. Arcott Hall is your home, your uncle is now its owner, therefore it is reasonable for him to be one of your trustees. I, ahem, was honored by the duke to be the other. According to the terms of your father's will, you will have a generous allowance, and of course the whole of your inheritance will be turned over to you when—"

"Just like that damn fool brother of mine," Morgan muttered, "handing a fortune over to a female! Soft-hearted, he was. More like soft-headed."

Emilyann jumped up, indignant to the slur to her father,

and nearly tripped on the unfamiliar wide skirts of her mourning gown. "At least he had enough sense not to leave it all to you to gamble away, you ... you basket-scrambler!"

"And you wonder why you need a trustee? Unmannered brat, you need a keeper! I've a mind to—"

Mr. Baxley interrupted hastily. "As I was saying, Lady Emilyann, you will receive control of the principle when you come to your majority, which is the age of twenty-five for females, somewhat older than for males." He paused while Em's unladylike snort told what she thought of that piece of jurisprudence, conceived by a man, no doubt.

"Yes, well, as I was saying, when you come of age, or when you marry, whereupon the management of said capital will devolve to your husband."

"I don't understand. Why wouldn't I get my own money then?"

Uncle Morgan grinned. "Ignorant chit. A woman's property always becomes her husband's."

"Aunt Ingrid's didn't," she answered sweetly, changing his grin to a scowl. "But no matter, I shall simply remain unwed until I am twenty-five and then I can be my own woman."

Morgan had gotten up to pour himself a glass of his brother's excellent brandy. "That should be easy," he said between sips. "No sane man would have you. Tongue like a viper, temper of a shrew, about as much sense of decorum as a mayfly, and looks ..." He just shrugged.

Emilyann and even Mr. Baxley, who was fond of her, had to agree with the last affront. Good grief, her father wasn't dead a fortnight, of course she wasn't in looks, what with the original shock and the funeral to get through. She had lost weight, giving her face a close, pinched look, with no color to speak of; she'd also lost her ready good humor and sunny disposition, having Uncle Morgan and his family thrust upon her in her grief. And her dress, well, it had to be black, of course, but it did not have to be the heaviest, scratchiest stuff ever made, with high neck, long sleeves, wide waist, and acres of skirt. The matching poke bonnet did not have to cover her ears, her forehead, and every

165

strand of her hair, but it did. Suffice it to say, Aunt Ingrid had the dressing of her now.

Mr. Baxley tut-tutted in sympathy. "It's early days to be worrying overmuch of marriage. You'll be in mourning for a year, naturally, and then you will have to be presented, et cetera."

Emilyann's mind wandered, wondering what kind of come-out she could look forward to, with Aunt Ingrid as chaperone. No dancing, no theater parties, no pretty dresses. No, she may as well wait for her twenty-fifth birthday. The only bright spot she could see, her thoughts coming back to the present, was that Uncle Morgan was not looking all that elegant himself. Surely that coat was second-rate and the pouches under his eyes were more noticeable, especially when he'd turned that greenish tint on hearing the terms of his brother's will. At least he was no happier about it than she was. Good.

Lord, how she despised the man. For years he had been bearing tales to her father about her misbehavior: sneaking off in the bushes with the Stockton boys, when they were only digging worms for fishing; boxing Bobo's ears, when she had been teaching the clunch to leave her possessions alone. She had been scolded sharply while he, Uncle Morgan, was permitted to dally with Dirty Sal down at the tavern, chouse the stablehands out of their salaries with stacked decks, and make off with a few dozen bottles from the duke's cellars on every visit. She would never tattle, of course, but Bobo would, or threaten to. Uncle Morgan always knew where Bobo got his information—the flabby little worm was too dunderheaded to figure such things, although he developed a fine sense of the principle of blackmailing. Morgan paid for his stepson's silence, loathing his niece more with every farthing. Since the funeral he had been gloating over her, peacocking around, demanding even she call him by his new title. He'd been hard put to show the least sorrow for his brother's passing, not when he was so busy eyeing each piece of furniture, and every painting and silver platter with a view to its value. He was bound for more disappointment. At least it appeared, from what Mr. Baxley was explaining, that while her father may have left Emilyann in an uncomfortable coil, he left Uncle Morgan worse.

"But you see, my lord—"

"That's Your Grace, damnit," Morgan snarled. He wasn't going to get much out of this, or out of the smirking scarecrow, but he'd get respect, by Jupiter!

"Yes, Your Grace," Mr. Baxley said. "His Grace, that is, the duke, ah, your late brother, was able to petition the court for such a dispensation. He did move in influential circles, you know." Inferring, of course, that Morgan did not. "With no male heir extant, no distant cousins or missing branches of the family, it is acceptable, although highly unusual, naturally, for the entailment to pass through the distaff side."

"Yes, yes, so the brat's son would be my heir instead of the property and the title reverting to the crown. But what of the rest of his money, man?"

"Ahem. Lady Emilyann's bequest was by far the largest, with some small pensions for employees, et cetera. The income from the estates follows along with the entailment, which consists of land, titles, the London house, heirloom jewels, et cetera."

Morgan banged his fist down on the desk. "Will you stop with the et ceteras and get on with it already! How much money will I have?"

Emilyann poured Mr. Baxley a cup of tea. He needed it. "Thank you, my dear. As I was trying to explain, Your Grace, the rest of the late duke's fortune was his own, to do with as he chose. He chose to leave it in trust for the next heir, either your son, if there should be one, or Lady Emilyann's firstborn. The money would be, again, held in trust until the birth of the child, then given to his parents to administer."

Morgan's ears perked up. "Ah, and I suppose I am one of the interim trustees there, too."

"No, Your Grace. There is a considerable sum involved, you know, and the duke considered it safest left with his financial advisers."

"Oh, well," Morgan said, almost reconciled. "I never

167

thought the old stick would leave me more than he had to. So tell me, how much am I worth?"

Emilyann showed great forbearance, merely plopping a lump of sugar into her tea with more noise than necessary.

"That's a difficult question, Your Grace. The holdings are extensive, certainly, but they also require a great deal of reinvestment to maintain."

"But if I sell the lot? How much then?"

"Oh, you cannot do that, my lord, it's all entailed. Otherwise His Grace could have left you out entirely."

Morgan could not dispose of the properties outright, but that did not stop him from trying to bleed the estate in any way he could: dismissing most of the household staff, not fixing the roof, selling off the racing stud. As he told his angry niece, he was not about to maintain the place for *her* comfort. He was long gone back to London and the gaming halls, taking Ingrid with him for a last-ditch effort to turn her up sweet enough to try for a child. She was not much more than forty. Stranger things had happened. Her conceiving would have been lucky; her cooperating would have been a miracle. A great many new temptations were open to Ingrid as a duchess. She prayed for the fortitude to resist. They took Bobo, thank goodness, after loyal Jake searched his luggage and restored the snuff boxes and pearl-handled silverware.

Morgan returned to the country occasionally after that to see how else he could beggar the properties to settle his losses. When Emilyann complained, he threatened to throw her out completely, except they both knew he wouldn't. He would only lose the heavy fees he extorted for "administering" her estate. So her allowance, which once looked so generous, had to go for Nanny's pension after Morgan turned her off, for making repairs to the tenants' cottages, and for buying wood for the fireplaces so the unused rooms of Arcott House would not succumb to dry rot from the damp ceilings.

Emilyann barely had enough funds for new dresses, which hardly mattered, since she was in mourning and never went anywhere or saw anyone. She could have

168

changed to gray or lavender for half-mourning, as the depressing year wore on, but her one effort at economizing by trying to sew up a new gown herself merely created more rags for rubbing down her mare—whose feed she also had to pay for out of her own funds. If nothing else, the long, lonely months made Em rethink her ideas about marriage. If living under her uncle's thumb was this dreary, she'd go to London as soon as the year was up and find a sweet boy she could manage who could overlook her lost-waif appearance and dowdy clothes in favor of her dowry. She would wed him before the cat could lick its ear. She'd grow to be like Cousin Marietta, finding her dreams of romance between the covers of a book, which was a sad enough fate for a seventeen-year-old girl to contemplate.

There were, of course, worse fates.

"Marry Bobo? You must be more addlepated than he is, Uncle." Emilyann laughed as she took a comfortable seat in her father's study. Morgan was already at ease behind the desk—her father's desk—and he was already half disguised, she guessed from the bottle and glasses and the half-baked idea he'd just proposed for her future. She laughed again. "I wouldn't marry Bobo if he was the last man on earth."

Morgan's eyes glittered as he poured another refill. "He is, as far as you are concerned. That way all the money gets tied up in one neat little package. Your money, the heir's trust, the estate, all in the family, heh-heh."

"Yes, and all in your greedy hands, I suppose. I do congratulate you though; it's a brilliant scheme, from your viewpoint. Unfortunately, Uncle, that horse won't run, I'm afraid, because there is just no way in hell you can make me marry that nodcock. My year of mourning is nearly over and I have decided to go to London to find myself a husband."

"And how do you propose to do that?" Her uncle snickered. "*I* ain't about to provide for your come-out, and you cannot do it on your own. Besides, in case you've forgotten, my dearest niece, I am your trustee. You cannot marry without my permission. Oh, you could run off to Gretna

169

with some romantic young fool just to spite me, but you better pick a well-heeled one, for you won't see a groat of your money until you are twenty-five. No, there will be no presentation, no pretty new frocks and geegaws, no half-pay officers or second sons. Just Bobo."

This was no longer laughable. Emilyann could feel herself beginning to perspire in the wretched wrong-season black gown. She got up to pace around the room, trying not to notice the new stains on the fine Aubusson carpet. By all that was holy, the man was serious!

"Come now, Uncle, Bobo could not want to marry me. He thinks I'm a bluestocking. Most likely because I know how to read. We wouldn't possibly suit." Now, that was one of the biggest understatements of Emilyann's life, but she was trying to maintain a little politeness, trying very hard not to lose her temper and start another shouting match with her uncle, who only ended up taking his anger out on the servants or the horses. "You remember, just this Christmas I had to box his ears to keep him from bothering the upstairs maid. He does not even like me."

"Nevertheless, he'll marry you. Soon." Morgan wore a self-satisfied smile. He picked up a piece of paper from the desktop and raised his glass in salute to the legal-looking document. "Special license. Damned expensive, but worth every penny."

Emilyann stopped her pacing. "You can keep me from London, Uncle, and keep me from marrying any other man, and even keep me like an indigent prisoner in my own home, but you cannot make me wed that slimy toad."

Morgan tossed down the remainder of his glass and stood up, coming around the desk to confront his recalcitrant niece face-to-face, bloodshot eyes to flashing blue ones. "You will, girl," he said dangerously, no longer smiling. "Because a lot can happen in what? Eight years till your majority? A lot can happen in a week, my proud lady. I can leave you here alone with Bobo, for one. He ain't no relation of yours, so your reputation would be in tatters. No man would ever look at you again, at least not in any honourable way."

"I don't give a fig for my reputation, and Aunt Ingrid

would never countenance such a thing anyway," she said disdainfully.

"Ingrid is in Cheltenham playing the grand duchess to her old neighbors. Then, too, perhaps she'd approve, to make the boy a lord. Enough of the ready, a handsome gift to Prinny, the heir's father's got to be a viscount at least."

"The *heir*? You think I'd ever let—that Bobo and I—" she sputtered.

"As I said, a lot could happen in a week. Maybe I would let dear Beauregard try to convince you. A lad his size can be quite persuasive. Not very polished in his address, I'm afraid, but Bobo was never one to concern himself over taking what others did not want to give."

He could not have meant what she thought he meant. Not even this dastard could be so low to threaten his own brother's child! Too angry to be frightened, too incensed to mind her tongue, she screamed at him: "You miserable, craven leech! That's all you've ever been, a dirty bloodsucker. No wonder my father left his will the way he did, so that you couldn't destroy everything he loved. It's only too bad he had to name you my trustee, but I suppose he was too high-minded to suspect even you of such abominable behavior. Trustee, hah! I wouldn't trust you to oversee a pile of manure, and you won't destroy me!" she raged unwisely. "I'll go live with Nanny. So there." And she shook her fist at him.

Red-faced with fury, Morgan shook his own fist inches from her nose. "And good riddance to bad rubbish. I'll declare you a runaway and pocket your bloody allowance. Then how will you and your precious Nanny live, huh, raising pigs?"

"Better that than living with them!" she shouted.

That's when he hit her.

171

Chapter Four

*N*o one had ever struck her before. Of course she had gotten her own back and snatched up the special license before fleeing to her room—expensive be damned! He could go through forty inheritances purchasing the blasted things before she would go along with his plans. She would burn it later, when she had enough patience to build a fire. Now she just had to get out of there, put space between herself and that worm. She did not even have a riding habit that fit her, thanks to him. No matter. Emilyann thrust her feet into her riding boots, tore open the confining collar of the black gown, rolled up the sleeves, and headed for the stables.

"Hey, Lady Em," Jake called from the side of the barn, where he sat polishing tack in the sun so his knotted joints moved better. "Where you goin' lookin' like thunderclouds? And no hat on neither."

"I'm getting out of here, that's all," she threw back over her shoulder as she led her mare out. "No hat, no saddle, and I don't need you to accompany me either." She mounted herself from a railing, hiking her skirts to straddle the horse and showing a deal of leg above the boot. "Don't worry," he heard on the wind, "I'll be back. Unfortunately."

Jake shook his head, knowing he'd never catch up, not when missy was on her mare Coco, not in that mood. Not that he could blame her, knowing the master was back. Jake spat tobacco juice at a passing beetle. Some master, hah! How this place was going to ruin, and young miss wasting away like some faded rose, all on account of that loose screw. "I should of been drivin' the coach that day," Jake told himself, not for the first time. He shook his head and spat again. "Damn, I should of. There be none of this nip-

172

farthin', nor branglin', and missy'd be all set up like the little princess her father intended. No jumped-up caper-merchant actin' like king o' the hill, neither." But he hadn't been driving and things had been going to hell in a hand-cart ever since, and hanged if he could think of a way out.

Emilyann rode and rode—and hanged if *she* could think of a way out. She did not notice the sweat, the twigs caught in her hair from low branches, the growing shadows, not even the early crocuses lining the hedgerows. She saw nothing except the passing miles until the mare's heaving flanks finally brought her back to reality. So she got off and walked, no destination in mind, no haven in sight, nothing but the need to put still more miles between her and her horrible relations.

Marry Bobo? Old Toby's plowhorses would dance at Almacks first, wearing white gloves and pearls. Her dear stepcousin had grown from a repulsive boy to an even less attractive man, only slightly better dressed. Now he stuffed his extra tonnage into the latest fads, like the yellow panta-loons he wore to dinner the previous evening, his legs like two giant sausages dipped in egg yolk. With an aqua jacket and puce waistcoat—all this in a house of mourning—the cocklehead resembled nothing so much as a silk balloon half inflated for launching.

"I only wish he would fly off somewhere," Emilyann told the horse as they tramped on. "But he's so stupid he couldn't find the sky if he had wings."

As nasty and light-fingered as ever, Bobo had added leer-ing to his list of charms. "Just what the world needs, an-other bacon-brained lecher." Coco pricked her ears but made no comment. "How could any woman think of mar-rying him?" Emilyann couldn't stand being in the same room with the slug. The thought of him touching her with his bloated fingers, kissing her with his damp mouth—"Ugh!" she exclaimed. The horse snorted in alarm so Emilyann stopped her marching to reassure the beast with a nose rub. "It will never happen. My father's heirs will not be slimy little mushrooms who paw at housemaids and have gravy spots on their shirtfronts. Never."

So she would not marry Bobo; that was the easy part.

But how? "Think, Emilyann," she told herself, hiking on, dragging her skirts in the dust. Mr. Baxley might listen, but he was in London, a long, expensive way away. Too, he was growing old, and might agree she would be better off wed. He would certainly never countenance her showing up on his doorstep like an infant in a basket—if she could afford the stagecoach ride. It best be a letter. There had to be somewhere she could go meantime, somewhere she could be safe. Nanny's little cottage was inviting, but Uncle Morgan was sure to just fetch Emilyann back, despite his threats to let her rot there in poverty. No, he would ride down like a marauding Hun to reclaim his missing meal ticket, then he would make the old woman's life hell. Emilyann could not chance his petty vengeance affecting anyone else. She realized that she'd been unconsciously headed for Stockton Manor this whole time, and heaven knew there was not much ill he could do there, not in the deplorable condition the last earl had left it. The only Stocktons in residence, however, were skitter-witted Nadine, at fifteen the biggest flirt in the county, and her equally flighty aunt, no protection at all. Those two were barely holding household and needed another penniless mouth to feed as much as they needed another leak in the roof. There was no other house in the neighborhood where Emilyann could just drop in and announce: "I do not like the husband my evil guardian has selected for me, may I stay here for eight years?" They would lock her in chains, right before sending a message back to Arcott.

"But I *can't* go back, I just can't," Emilyann wailed, dropping to the ground and beating her fists on her knees. The mare nudged her before ambling off to find a patch of new grass. "Fine help you are," the girl complained, getting up to fetch the reins before Coco remembered she was missing her supper. "You would most likely go home without me."

Home. No money, no friends, no loving family. Home, where Bobo would torment her and her uncle would batter her with words, meanness, and greed. She could stand up to his harassment—she was her father's daughter, after all—but how long could she endure this new physical abuse?

She could make one of the maids sleep in her room, and keep one of the dogs by her side and a pistol in her pocket, but she knew from that gleam in Morgan's eye that he would never give up. She would never be safe again. How long, dear Lord, could she live like that? How long before she took Bobo to wed ... or took a life, Morgan's or her own?

She buried her face in the horse's mane and wept.

"Hell's bells, Emmy, don't tell me you and the mare have parted company. I wouldn't have believed it."

She'd never even heard the horse and rider approaching, but she looked up quickly, wiped a dirty hand across her face, and smiled at her old chum Geoffrey, the youngest of the Stockton boys, now grown to a gangly sixteen-year-old, dark like all the Stocktons.

"Don't believe it, you clunch, Coco would never be so rude. But whatever are you doing home, Geoff? Not that I'm not delighted to see you, of course."

He waved one hand in the air with studied nonchalance as he dismounted, saying, "Oh, the usual." His wide grin ruined the effect.

"Sent down *again*? Oh, you great looby!" It may have been true, but it was spoken with a deal of warmth as the two shared a quick hug of affection.

"I say, though, Em, if you haven't taken a toss, why is it you look like you've been dragged through the hedge backward?"

"Now, that's a pretty thing to tell a lady," she said, stalling, bringing a blush to her friend's cheeks.

"You know I ain't in the petticoat line, Em. 'Sides, if you were hanging out for compliments, you'd be reclining on a sofa dressed to the nines, like m'sister Nadine."

Emilyann shook out her skirts in a cloud of dust, avoiding his eyes. "Uncle Morgan's home."

"Uh, right." Nothing more needed to be said, so they walked on, leading their horses. After a bit Geoff murmured, mostly to himself, "Damned lucky I didn't take the shortcut and miss you at the Hall."

"Dashed lucky," she corrected him automatically. "Aunt

175

Ingrid is visiting in Cheltenham, so you wouldn't have had to make your bows there, and I doubt dear Uncle was receiving. Only he and Bobo came for the visit," she added bitterly.

Geoffrey wrinkled his brow in an effort to figure out what wasn't being said, then he gave it up. "We've got company over at the manor, too. M'brother Thornton and his wife, Cynthia, stopped by on their way from London."

"Oh?" She couldn't drum up much interest. Reverend Thornton and his wife were as dull as ditchwater, with minds as stilted as the social conventions they worshipped. "Is he still hoping for a preferment?"

Geoffrey laughed. "Not after this week, I'd guess, to hear him rant about all of us ramshackle Stocktons ruining his chances of advancement. What a dust-up there was."

"About your being sent down again? What has that to do with—"

"That ain't the half of it. They were already up in the boughs when they got here, and well, there's no wrapping it in clean linens, the manor ain't in prime gig. Something about mice and cobwebs and the ceiling falling on Cynthia while she's in her bath. Aunt Adelaide got her all calmed down enough for sherry before dinner, in the 'good' parlour. Only Nadine decided it was a good time to show Thornton she's old enough for a season in London."

"Oh, no!"

"Oh, yes. Red dress, damped petticoats, painted cheeks, and tossing off Madeira like it was mother's milk."

"What did Thornton do?"

"You know that look he gets when he's going to start a sermon? Eyes raised to heaven, hands clasped in front of him, a big breath so he won't have to pause for hours? Well, he takes his big breath and sneezes—the dust, don't you know—and spills his glass all over Cynthia, who's hopping up and down and screaming so loud that *more* plaster comes down."

Emilyann was laughing so hard she could barely get out the words, but she just had to know: "What about Aunt Adelaide? Did she 'go off' as usual?"

Geoffrey grinned back. "Of course. Right over on the couch. I didn't hang around to hear anymore."

"Coward!"

"Genius, you mean. Besides, I thought you might want Everett's present."

"Smoky sent a present? Why didn't you say so, you gudgeon! How is he, and where, and is he coming home?"

"Slow down. He's fine, I think, from what I could get out of Thornton, who, incidentally, insists we call Ev Stokely now, as befits his title."

"Oh, pooh, as if Smoky would ever stand on his dignity!"

Smiling, Geoff handed her a rumpled package from his saddlebags. "Well, he is a captain now, in addition to being an earl. Here, this one's for you. He sent one for Nadine and Aunt Adelaide, too, and a bang-up knife with designs etched up and down the blade for me. . . . Thornton said it's called a *mantilla*," he explained as Emilyann unwrapped a gossamer length of sheer white lace and an ivory comb. "The Spanish ladies wear them in their hair."

Emilyann tenderly covered the lace again in its paper before it got soiled. "It's beautiful. Is Smoky still in Spain, then?"

"No, and that's what set Thornton off in the first place. Old Ev is in London, or he was, at any rate. He's supposed to leave tomorrow. He had two or three days' leave only, presenting papers to the War Office from Lord Wellington, so he could not come north."

"Just enough time to cut a swathe through London, I'll wager!"

"And have Thornton running to the bishop. Then Thorny thought he could give big brother a lecture on what was due the family name, and how he ought to sell out and see to the properties. I don't know what he thinks Ev can do, when we all know his pockets are as much to let as ever, what with paying off the governor's mortgages so we don't lose the estate altogether, and my allowance and—I say, Emmy, are you all right?"

Big tears were splashing onto the wrapped package. "I . . . I don't have a handkerchief."

"And that's why you're turning into a watering pot?" he asked, offering his none-too-fresh cloth. Years of living with his sister and aunt had cured him from turning into a blancmange at the sight of feminine weeping. "I never thought you'd be one to go all missish, damned if I did."

"Danged," she sniffed, before explaining about her father's wretched will and Uncle Morgan's greed and the threats, and Bobo.

"Why, that bleeding—sorry, that bleating bast—hell, Emmy, you know what I mean." He straightened his shoulders. "There's nothing for it; I'll go call him out."

"Don't be a cabbagehead, Geoff, he wouldn't meet a puppy like you, and anyway, you're not a good shot. Too bad I can't challenge him—I already thought of that—and it's just so unfair, being a woman and all. I can't take care of my own money, I can't decide where I'll live or whom I'll marry, I can't even defend my own honor!"

"Now who's being harebrained? You need a husband for all that. Tell you what, Em," he said after a long moment's considering, "I'll marry you myself. It won't be so bad," he conceded, "you're a dashed fine rider, for a girl."

Emilyann giggled. "Is that how you'll pick your bride, by how well she rides?" She reached for his hand and squeezed it. "But thank you for the compliment, and thank you for the offer, my good friend. You can rest easy. I won't take you up on it, for we'd never suit, you know. I'm a restless, managing sort and I like you too much to make your life a misery. It wouldn't fadge anyway. Uncle would just have the marriage annulled because we're both underage. If not, he could withhold his permission, so he would never have to release my inheritance to us. There's no way we could live, unless you've come into a fortune recently."

He grinned cheerfully. "Not a sou. I'm even below hatches till next quarter-day. There's no appealing to Thornton either. He's as tight as a clam when it comes to parting with the blunt. I already tried." He shook his head, rearranging the dark curls. "It's the deuce of a coil all right."

Emilyann kicked a pebble out of her way. "I bet Smoky would know what to do."

Geoff nodded. "Downy cove, m'brother. Even Wellington said so, asked him to join his own staff. Too bad Ev's not staying around long enough to set your uncle straight."

"He's leaving tomorrow?"

"That's what Thorny said."

"But he's in London tonight?"

That sudden note of hope warned him. "Don't even think it, girl. London's over six hours away. It took Thornton the better part of two days to get here, and putting up at an inn overnight."

"But he had the carriage, and Cynthia. If we took the horses, and rode cross-country . . ." She was thinking aloud.

Geoff gulped. So was he. "We?"

She didn't hear him, or pretended not. It was a good idea, maybe brilliant. It was also her only idea. She had enough of the household money left to change horses, and they could carry food and . . .

"Listen, Emmy, we don't really know that Ev didn't leave early. We don't even know if he can do anything about this mess."

"You said he was a knowing one."

"But he's got no time, and he sure doesn't have any of the ready to spare. If he did, he would have sent it down to Aunt Adelaide like always. And besides, a girl can't ride into London in the middle of the night! Even I know it just ain't done."

So it was that Lady Emilyann Arcott crept up the back stairs of her home and changed into some mismatched, foul-smelling, overlarge clothes pilfered from the grooms' room over the barn while Jake and the stable crew were at dinner. She used a likewise borrowed shears to lop off her hair any-which-way, consigning the hatcheted locks to the bottom of her wardrobe, with good riddance to the plaguey mop. While she was at it, she cut a piece of the drapery pull cord to hold up her falling breeches. She stuffed money in her sock, a pistol in her boot, and some bread and cheeses and apples into one of the deep pockets of her filched friezecoat. Into the other pocket she tenderly placed Smoky's gift, still wrapped for safekeeping. The coat

179

looked, and smelled, like something used to transport a poacher's booty but, she told herself, beggars—or borrowers—cannot be choosy. She rolled the sleeves up twice, crammed a moth-eaten cap over her shorn hair so the peaks and clumps didn't show, just a pale, ragged fringe around her face, and she was ready. She patted an odoriferous inside pocket of her coat one last time, to be certain of her "insurance." There, among leaves, hairs, and worse rested a kerchief wrapped around three papers: a parchment document with official-looking seals, a creased and tattered letter, and that miserable, misintended special license.

Captain Everett Stockton, Lord Stokely, mightn't have much money, and less time, but he did have something Lady Arcott needed desperately. Emilyann grinned. Wouldn't Smoky be surprised!

Chapter Five

"Cap'n Stockton ain't to home now." And never would be to the likes of these callers if Private Micah Rigg had anything to say to the matter. Rigg was his lordship's batman, valet, butler, and sometimes watchdog. It was a position the older Rigg much preferred to being cannon fodder at the front, so he was bound to see his employer stayed alive and well, and happy with the service he got. Which he'd never be, if Rigg admitted these two scruffy boys to his temporary quarters at the St. John's Hotel, an establishment favored by the itinerant military.

"But it's three in the morning," squeaked the smaller, dirtier lad out in the hallway. "Where could he be?"

The other boy kicked him. "Stubble it, Em. We said I'd do the talking, remember?" He tugged at his jacket and turned back to the mustachioed soldier. "I appreciate the inconvenience, my good man, but I am Geoffrey Stockton, Lord Stokely's brother, and I really must see him tonight. Could you tell me where he is?"

Brother, was it? Rigg raised his candle higher. This one did have the look of the cap'n about him, the same dark hair at least. The cap'n had given strict instructions that that other bloke, the starched-up religious fellow, wasn't to be admitted again, ever. He hadn't said anything about refusing any other brothers. "You wouldn't be the one as keeps getting sent down from school, would you?"

Geoff bowed. "The same."

Kinship to the officer showed more and more in the checky lad. He was likely in some bumblebroth or other, expecting his lordship to go bail, which he would if Rigg was any judge. Whatever the trouble, it could only get worse out on the streets of London in the middle of the night. "The cap'n's out with some officer friends," Rigg told Geoffrey, ignoring the grubby companion entirely. "It's anybody's guess where they are, but I expect he'll be in soon 'cause it's early reveille tomorrow if we're to be on time for the ship sailing. You can come wait in here, I s'pose, but *he*"—with a whisker-twitching grimace in Em's direction—"has to stay out in the hall."

"Why, you—" Em began, and Geoffrey kicked her again.

"I'll vouch for my friend," he said quickly, stepping around the short batman and dragging Em behind him by the sleeve of her coat.

There was a smallish room, with a bed, a dresser, and two chairs drawn around a table cluttered with books, papers, and bottles. When Rigg shut the other open door to the dressing room, where his own cot was set up, Geoffrey flopped down into one chair, exhausted. Rigg pointedly took the other. Em glanced yearningly toward the bed, but the batman's glare discouraged her quickly, and Geoff's grin did not help matters. She sniffed her disdain and found a place on the floor. At least the carpet was thick. She was so tired she let the wall prop her up until she caught herself starting to slip sideways, half asleep. She fumbled her way out of the bulky overcoat and curled up in it like a kitten,

181

using part as a blanket, part as a pillow. A short nap was all she needed, waiting for Smoky.

"Bella, bella señorita, mi corazon necessite," sang a remarkably loud, off-key baritone. Footsteps staggered to the entry and a hand fumbled for the latch before Rigg could get the door open and his master inside.

"What's that, shush? Me shush? Oh, company, you say? Good, good. I told the lads the night was still young. Here, who is it, Rigg? Don't look like any of the army fellows." He wrinkled his nose. "Don't smell like one either."

"It's your brother, sir," Rigg informed him, grabbing for his master's hat, sword, and gloves before they ended on the floor. "Your younger brother, Cap'n, Geoffrey. I'll just go fetch some coffee, shall I, sir?"

"Capital idea, Rigg, my brother's here."

"Yessir."

When the batman left and a grinning Geoffrey was being pounded on the back, Emilyann stayed quiet in her corner, horrified. She hardly knew this man! She had not seen Smoky in, what? three or four years, and then briefly, but how changed he was, how much older he seemed than his twenty-four years. She did not recall him being so large either, surely not so broad-shouldered under his scarlet uniform jacket. His hair showed some silver at the long sideburns, his face was pale and gaunt, with a new red scar following along his jawbone, and worse, Captain Stockton was more than a little disguised. She huddled back into her coat.

"Devilishly glad to see you, bantling," he was telling Geoff while tugging at his neckcloth. "If I had more time, I would have sent for you from school, but you wouldn't have been there anyway, right? Ain't it lovely how things work out? By the way," he asked, shrugging out of his jacket, "what was it this time? Wine, women, or song?"

Now, Geoff had declared himself the spokesman while on the road lest anyone recognize Emilyann for a girl; he desperately wanted *not* to be the talker now. His frantic glances in Em's direction brought no salvation.

"Your abysmal grades, eh? You'll come about. Give me a hand with these boots, will you?"

"It . . . it was the pig," Geoff blurted out, giving a pull on one well-polished boot, then the other as his brother leaned back in one of the chairs. "It was a runt, you see, and the farmer was taking it to market anyway, and the little thing couldn't keep up—oh, Lord."

Stokely had unbuttoned his shirt and was starting on his breeches when a squawk from the corner made him turn around. "That had better not be the pig, my boy," he said awfully, eyeing the pile of rags.

"It's Emph, um, hm."

"Gads, you'd never make a soldier. Speak up, Geoff, it's a what?"

"It's Emilyann."

"Holy Mo—" Pants were hastily fastened, shirt tucked in. "You imbecile, how could you bring her to London like this, to bachelor quarters? Don't you have anything in your brainbox at all? The pig would have been better!"

"That's not fair, Ev. When was the last time you tried to talk her out of anything?"

Indignant, Emilyann started to get up, but a thundering voice ordered her to "stay. I'll deal with you next, miss." Stokely ran his fingers across the scar on his cheek. Lord, what if his friends *had* come back with him? All he could see of her in the shadows were two huge eyes in a face that was ghost-white where it was not mud-streaked, topped with clumps of colorless hair. Arms and legs poked out from the rags like sticks, and an aura of what?—kennel, kitchen, swamp—hung over the whole corner like a bad dream. At least no one would recognize her for a lady. Hah!

"You still look like an unfledged nestling," he told her, finally beginning to see the humor of anyone mistaking this guttersnipe for a gently born female. He headed back toward the chair, apologizing that she improved with the distance, and where the hell was Rigg with that coffee anyway? "For I think I am going to need all my wits about me when I hear what you two cawkers are up to."

He was smiling. He was the Smoky she had always

183

known, but oh, dear, where to begin? It wasn't as if he was going to be happy with the idea, she could see that now. She sent a silent appeal to Geoff for help, and he nobly rose to the occasion.

"We, that is, Em, needs to get married."

The amiable gentleman was instantly replaced with a snarling beast, his hands at his brother's throat, lifting him clear off the ground. "Why, you—"

"Not me, Ev!" Geoff croaked, and was dropped.

The earl turned to Emilyann in disgust. "What was he, some good-looking stablehand, or some smooth-talking basket-scrambler? Or maybe he's already married. Is that it?" He sneered. "And what do you think I can do about it? I'm not exactly in prime fiddle to force a duel on some dirty dish so he'll marry you."

Now Emilyann found her voice. No one, not even Smoky, was going to talk to her like that. "Why you . . . you miserable mawworm, how dare you think the worst of me like that. As if I would . . . And here I came to you for help. Some help, a jug-bitten old soldier"—she emphasized the *old*—"back from a night of hellraking, giving orders and suspecting everyone else of behavior as bad as yours!"

She stood there, arms on her hips, blue eyes flashing, and he laughed, partly in relief that she hadn't been led down the garden path, and partly in memory of a tiny scrap of a girl giving Thornton what-for over some slight. He held his arms open. "Hallo, Sparrow," he said, and she walked into them, rags, aroma, and all.

"Hi, Smoky."

Rigg almost dropped the tray, coming back to the room to find his master holding the raggedy urchin. "That will be all, Private."

Rigg shut his mouth enough to say "yessir." He set the tray down with a thump and about-faced to march to his own room, shaking his head and vowing to burn that shirt the captain had on.

There, she was safe now, protected in Smoky's arms. She could tell her story, ending with "I really had no choice. I just couldn't stay there, not after he hit me."

He held her away from him and gently cupped her chin,

turning her face to the light. His eyes narrowed to steel-gray slits when he saw the bruise there, under the grime. "What did you do then?"

"I . . . I kicked him."

"Where I taught you?"

She just nodded, looking down.

"Good girl."

Geoffrey cheered. "I hope you put paid to *his* getting the heir, Emmy," he said, which earned him such a scowl from his brother that he decided a nap might be in order. Yawning mightily, he sprawled across Stokely's bed, his back to the other two.

"Such subtlety," complimented the captain, indicating that Emilyann take Geoff's vacated seat. She poured him out coffee first, and then, deciding a slightly fuddled Smoky might be easier to deal with after all, poured some brandy into his cup, too, while he was busy finding his slippers.

Smoky finally settled, the cup on his knee. "All right, my girl, let's hear what feat of derring-do you expect from me. I'm sure you've some feather-headed scheme in mind." He took a sip of coffee, only raising one eyebrow at the taste.

Then she said, "I want you to marry me," and he spilled the hot liquid down his shirt.

"Damn, Sparrow, you shouldn't say such things to a fellow."

"But I am serious, Smoky. I need you to marry me. You are old enough, and have a title and property and you're even a hero! There is no way Uncle Morgan could withhold his permission, not when my own father once approved."

His lordship stopped dabbing with his napkin at the brown stain to look at her again: a bedraggled, undernourished elf in ragpicker's hand-me-downs pouring coffee like a duchess.

He shouldn't have laughed. He knew it the moment her spine stiffened and a very determined nose, slightly tilted, lifted in the air. Maybe it was the alcohol clouding his mind, but damn if he didn't laugh again.

Lord Stokely may have been in his altitudes, but Lady Emilyann Arcott was very much on her dignity.

"Laugh now, my lord," she announced in a frigid tone,

185

unfolding one of her documents, the special license. "But marry me you shall. I don't think you'd find it funny in the least when I take you to court for breach of promise." She unfolded a second paper. "Our fathers agreed to the marriage in a legal contract."

"And rescinded it later."

"But not on paper." She unfolded her last page. "You wrote me a promise, swearing to marry me anyway."

"I was sixteen! You were a lonely little girl at school."

"It's evidence."

He was still smiling, still drinking coffee, another cup with additions. "It won't hold up in court, minx, and you know it."

"But it might hold up in the newspapers. If you don't agree to marry me, I'll see that all of London laughs at you. And if you don't care, think of poor, worthy Thornton, or Nadine, what a scandal in the family could do to her chances of making a good match."

One side of his mouth quirked up in a lazy smile. "Blackmail, Sparrow?"

She jumped up and stamped her foot. "I'll do it, Smoky, so help me I will."

The other side of his mouth joined in the humor, and she sat down again. They both knew she never would. Emilyann shrugged and smiled back at him. It was a good try, and she wasn't finished yet. Smoky sat quietly in a state of happy relaxation, enjoying the play of emotions across her face and cheerfully awaiting the next round of machinations. He did not have to wait long.

"You know, Smoky, Stockton is going to rack and ruin without you. Old Mr. Taylor, your estate manager, is going deaf, and even if he could hear, there's nothing he can do without money. He can't buy equipment or stock or seed or food for the workers' families when times are hard. I'll come into a great deal of money when I marry, and possibly more if there is an heir to my father's dukedom. Even without, think of all that could be done with a fortune."

"From blackmail to bribery, eh?" he teased. "You must have spent time with my sister. She's always writing that I

186

should marry an heiress so she can be presented at court with all the pageantry her mercenary little heart desires."

"Of course I know about Nadine's wish to go to London for her come-out. The whole county knows about it. And that's another thing, Smoky. Not just the money, but your sister is getting a sorry reputation, and your younger brother is going to need some occupation, surely not as a scholar, and your properties need someone to oversee them while you are gone. I could help."

"She's right, Ev," Geoff put in, giving up the pretense of not listening. "The place needs a lot of improvements, and I've got some capital ideas about modernizing. Been reading the farm journals, you know."

The captain opened his eyes wider. "No, I didn't know. From what I heard, you never read anything at all."

"That's just school. But the agricultural experiments . . ."

"See, Smoky, you don't even know what's happening at home."

"Don't start spouting about my selling out, either of you. I heard all I need to hear on the topic from Thornton. And I know little brother is returning to school so he learns more than to be a farmer."

"Too late," Geoff brightly declared. "They won't let me back in. So if you marry Emmy, the two of us can take care of the estate and you won't have to sell out at all."

"Thank you," Stokely said dryly. "The way the two of you handled this mingle-mangle, there will be nothing left to come home to. And what's this about Nadine? I thought Aunt Adelaide had the chit in hand."

So they told him about Nadine's flirts: the gardener's boy, the parson's rector, Squire Dickerson, and how whenever Nadine was likely to create a scene Aunt Adelaide would "go off."

"Gads, Dickerson's fifty if he's a day! You mean she just leaves the chit to make micefeet of her reputation?"

Emilyann was giggling. Smoky was rubbing that scar on his jaw. "She don't go off visiting," Geoff had to explain, "she 'goes off' in a near constant swoon. Always manages to land on a sofa or chair, too."

When they were finished laughing, Emilyann addressed

him again: "You see, Smoky, you need to get your house in order, and I can do it."

"But those are all the wrong reasons for marrying, poppet. It's not like buying a pair of shoes or hiring a housekeeper."

"But you are my only hope, Smoky. I have no other choices."

"You always have choices," he told her, reaching to pat her hand. Then he suggested that since it was almost dawn anyway, Geoff go fetch them some hot rolls from the bakery a few blocks away.

"What, and leave you two alone?"

"It's a little late for propriety's sake, bantling," Stokely told him, tossing a pouch of coins.

"Who cares for propriety? I'm just worried you'll murder each other."

"Well, little one," Stokely asked after the door was shut behind Geoff, "have you used all your ammunition?"

Blue eyes twinkled up at him. "I haven't tried tears yet."

"Heaven help me from the heavy artillery! Truly, though, Sparrow, I can fix things without such drastic measures. I can stay a day or two." He held up one graceful hand. "Old Hooky won't be best pleased, but the Corsican won't run over the allied forces without me there, at least not for the time it would take to see your Mr. Baxley and put the fear of God into your uncle and that jackanapes Bobo. I have friends about, men who have served with me, who would be eager to look after you. I'm sure I could locate other officers' wives who would be willing to act as chaperone, you know, be hostess for a season or two. As for the other, my family isn't your responsibility. The war won't last forever, then I'll come take charge. I'm not entirely below the hatches, you know, despite my father and old Taylor. So you see, you don't have to worry about anything; you don't have to fear anything."

"I wouldn't be afraid, Smoky, but I still wouldn't be free either. I couldn't travel or pick my own friends or purchase a horse for myself or even make sure my money is invested properly. Don't laugh. I've had nothing to do this past year but study such details. You've always made your own choices; why shouldn't I? I don't mean to set myself up as some independent eccentric, I just want to make some of the decisions in my life, just till you come home."

"I see what it is, you want the convenience of a spouse's name without having to put up with his daily presence. How fortunate your chosen husband is a soldier with a war going on."

"Don't tease, Smoky. I am serious."

"I know you are, pet, that's what worries me." He studied his fingernails. "What if you, ah, fall in love with another man while I am gone? You are young, you've never been out in the world. Maybe your head is filled with romantic dreams that could come true one day. It's entirely possible. What would you do then, leg-shackled to an old war-horse?"

"More likely you'll fall in love with an opera-dancer or something. Don't look daggers at me. I know all about those things. And I have thought it all out. We could get an annulment when you return if we find we do not suit. After all, the marriage will not have been consummated, will it?"

Smoky choked. "It most certainly will not!" The idea of bedding this tattered waif was thoroughly unappealing, nearly indecent.

"Well, that's all right, then, as long as Uncle Morgan thinks it's a real marriage. He'll know I spent the night here, and with your reputation . . ."

"My reputation is for a deal more discrimination, miss, and no, we shall not discuss opera-dancers and the like. Annulments indeed. What a topic for a delicate maiden. Who knows, you might get lucky and end up a widow."

"Smoky! Don't even joke about that!" She jumped up and took his hand between her grubby ones and knelt at his feet. "You have to come home."

"Of course, the heir," he said lightly, smoothing the irregular tousles of her hair. "Nice to know that someone will be praying for at least parts of me to come back intact."

"Now who's talking improperly?" she wanted to know, looking down to hide her blush.

He tilted her face up and, taking a serviette from the coffee tray, began wiping at the smudges there. "Is this what

189

you really want, Sparrow?" A brilliant smile was his answer, blue eyes shining.

"Good going, Emmy," Geoff enthused on his return. Pounding his brother on the back, he chuckled. "I knew all along you would do it."

"So did I," muttered the Earl of Stokely. He shrugged. "Well, let's do it, then. You and I, Geoff, are about to go ruffle a lot of feathers. Nothing like shaking a flock of stuffy old men out of their beds. Great Zeus, solicitors and sermonizers, and the sun's not even up. . . . And Rigg," he called louder, "you can stop listening at the door and get out here on the double. You've got a harder job yet."

The red-faced private stood at bandy-legged attention, eyes forward, chest out, even when the captain introduced him to the future Lady Stokely. His round chest swelled even more when his officer said, "Don't worry, my dear, I've trusted Rigg with my life countless times. You can trust him." But tears came to his eyes and the twin mustachios drooped when the captain gave his final orders: "Make her presentable, Rigg. I'll not wed a hobbledehoy ragamuffin in britches."

A short time later, on what was the start of a gorgeous sunny morning, Lady Emilyann Arcott was finally wed to Captain Everett Stockton, Lord Stokely. The groom was attended by his brother, his solicitor, and his batman. He wore his second best uniform, and his eyes were only a trifle bloodshot. The bride was given away by Mr. Baxley, her man of business; her matron of honor was the vicar's plump wife, who wept through the thankfully brief ceremony. The bride's cheeks were red from scrubbing, and she clutched a nosegay of violets hastily purchased from an early morning street vendor. She wore an exquisite white lace mantilla held by an ivory comb—and the bridegroom's lace-trimmed nightshirt. Her bare feet hardly showed.

Chapter Six

*M*arry in haste; repent at leisure. But in the middle of a war? Captain Lord Stokely spent the first hours of his marriage giving orders, deploying his ragtag troops, and signing papers. He affixed his name to the marriage license, a settlement deed, a new will, a quitclaim to his wife's property, and a power of authority, all in Emilyann's favor. He also sent off notices of the wedding, details omitted, naturally, to the newspapers, his brother Thornton, and, with great satisfaction, Emilyann's uncle, Lord Aylesbury. Next he saw his child-bride off on her way home, in a carriage, in a dress, with his brother, a maid, and a draft on his bank.

Her readymade dress was at least two sizes too big, the best poor Rigg could do—hell, cannons and bayonets were less scarifying to the bewhiskered batman than frippery doodads and snooty dressmakers. The front was looking better to him all the time. Emilyann's bonnet was an atrocious concoction of feathers, flowers, and fruit, but she wore Smoky's gold signet ring on her wedding finger and a brilliant smile on her pixie face as she listened carefully to his firm instructions about her future conduct.

"Well, that wasn't so bad," Stokely congratulated himself and Rigg, whose hands were still shaking. "We even brushed through in plenty of time to meet the ship at Portsmouth."

He hardly gave another thought to the matter, beyond a few chuckles, until rejoining the army and reporting back to his commander. Word of the nuptials had already reached him, and not for nothing was Wellington called the Iron General.

191

"I don't like it, boy, do you hear me? I don't like my junior officers involved in any havey-cavey affairs. You knew that when you signed on, didn't you?"

"Yes, sir."

"It looks bad for the army, bad for the country, bad for me, do you understand, Captain? My men don't rape and plunder; my officers do not ruin gently bred females and get wed in hole-in-corner fashion!"

"Sir, it was nothing like that. In truth, it was quickly decided, but there was a long-term understanding."

"And the gel ain't breeding?"

"Certainly not, sir." Stokely stood even straighter. Gads, did the old man think he was a child molester?

"Harrumph. She better not be or I'll have your resignation on my desk before you can say Jack Rabbit. I don't like my officers married even, don't like 'em distracted, don't like 'em overly cautious. She ain't goin' to be hangin' on your coattails, weepin' and beggin' you to come home, is she?"

"No, sir. My Em is pluck to the backbone. She has plenty of bottom."

"I don't like creatin' widows either, by George, and I hate like hell makin' orphans. You're a damned fine tactician, boy, one of the finest, but I won't keep any man at the front whose mind ain't on the job to hand. There's too many other lives at stake, you know."

"Yes, sir. That is no, sir. Thank you, sir. My, ah, wife is well provided for and shall not cause me any concern which might interfere with my duties."

"I ain't seen the woman yet who didn't . . . but you remember what I said. Carry on, Captain."

Stokely saw no cause for concern. He did not feel any different, being leg-shackled, nor was he crushed by any mounting responsibilities. Sparrow and Geoff would play at handling things, and he would take care of everything else when the fighting was done. A soldier learned fatalism early, never making too many plans for when the war was over anyway; too many of his friends wouldn't be going back home at all. No, things had worked out for the best, and the captain saw no difficulties. He had given Sparrow

192

explicit instructions: do not overspend what the estates could hope to pay back in the near future, for he would not live off her wealth; do not go near her uncle; stay away from public appearances until he was there to help her take her rightful place in society. If she followed his directives, there would be no problems beyond minor childish scrapes, and he could proceed wholeheartedly with the job of defeating Bonaparte. Why should he worry? He was an officer in the army. Everyone obeyed his orders.

It took Emilyann longer to get around some of Smoky's mandates than others, and some lapses were not entirely her fault, like seeing her uncle. She had to retrieve her parents' portraits and her clothes, didn't she? And Jake, and her mare, and a little bit of her pride. She waited to be sure Uncle Morgan had Smoky's letter and the London papers with her wedding announcement before visiting with Geoff and Nadine and two grooms. Smoky needn't have worried: Uncle Morgan had been passed-out drunk for three days. She gathered her belongings, offered positions to any of the staff who wished to join her, and left her hastily engraved new card, one corner carefully turned down to indicate that Lady Emilyann, Countess of Stokely, had called in person. Let him swallow that!

Then there was the issue of her not going out into society. As soon as word reached Northamshire, however, local society came to her. At first all the old biddies came, paying respects to the new bride, they said. Checking to see if she was increasing, more likely. She couldn't let the gossip-mongers ruin her good name, or Smoky's, she wrote him, by hiding and acting as if she had something to be ashamed about. She didn't, and wouldn't, so she had to be seen at the local assemblies. Furthermore, he wouldn't want her to be rude to the neighborhood gentry by refusing their company, so she had to accept dinner engagements and invitations to private parties, and then she had to repay the calls and hospitality, didn't she? It was good practice for his sister, too.

And do you know what? she wrote to Smoky. *Everyone seems to like me. I suppose that's what comes of being a*

193

rich, titled married lady. Even Squire Kimball has forgiven us for the orchard incident, and Vicar has not mentioned the ant colonies in at least a month. So you needn't be concerned that I am not fit for polite company.

Finally, there was the money. She was not about to live like a pauper anymore, not when she was a wealthy young woman. Her old home was turning into a crumbling mausoleum through lack of funds and attention; her new one would not follow suit. No more cheeseparing, no more dilapidated furnishings or cold and damp accommodations. But new carpets made the draperies look faded, and new, bright hangings showed how threadbare the upholstery had become. Simply taking charge of the household showed how the china was chipped, mice had gotten into the pantries, the linens were darned past redemption, and the servants needed new livery, especially if they were to be inundated with callers eager to find fault with the new mistress of Stockton Manor.

Coming out of mourning, Emilyann also needed an entire new wardrobe, since her schoolgirlish frocks were hardly suited to a countess, or her still slim but more mature figure. She could not spend days shopping and being fitted without taking her new sister-in-law, who knew more about fashions than Em ever would, or would care to, or dear silly Aunt Adelaide, who was so pleased to hand over the managing of the place. Of course those ladies needed new outfits, too.

Then there was the estate, and Geoff's pigs. She read his journals with more enthusiasm than she read Nadine's *La Belle Assemblée* and came to agree that hogs and turnips were indeed the crops of the future. Geoff came to learn not to let her make pets of the piglets, or he'd never get any to market. As for the tenant farmers, Emilyann believed with all her heart that those old friends who shared their lemonade and fresh bread with a hobbledehoy little tomboy deserved better conditions now that hers were so improved.

She also decided to reestablish her father's racing stud at Stockton, as an investment. Breeding mares, proven stallions, and likely young colts all took money, men to care for them, and decent stabling conditions. Of course she had

194

Jake to advise her, and he knew all there was to know about horses, as she wrote to Stokely, so there was sure to be a profit in a few years.

Smoky wrote a letter back, forbidding her to do any such thing as pour a fortune into four-footed gluttons, no matter how fast. Unfortunately, she replied, the mails were so slow, two mares were already in foal. Did he have any preferences for names?

Wife, he wrote, *I have received letters from my bank, my man of business, and my brother Thornton. What in hell are you doing?*

What she was doing was having the time of her life. She had a family and friends and looked better than she had in years. She kept busy using her head and time and money, all for good purposes, doing what she was born and bred to do, and coincidentally proving to Smoky that she could manage. Repent the hasty marriage? Not on your life.

"Repent, ye sinners! Repent your evil ways before your souls burn in eternity. Repent, I say!"

Hell and damnation, indeed. What in bloody hell was Morgan Arcott doing sitting on a deuced hard pew at one of the Reverend Brother Blessed's spiritual meetings? Trying to turn his wife up sweet again, that was what. Might as well try to teach a cow to sing. He repented, all right. He repented that damned marriage, letting the chit slip through his fingers that way. His sources of credit had dried as fast as the ink on the wedding lines, forcing him back to Ingrid, who was fool enough to give his niece her blessings—and a damned pricy tea service.

"Renounce the temptations of the flesh; that way lies perdition." Hah! The last time Ingrid was tempted by the flesh she had another serving of roast beef. With her hair scraped back from her sharp features, and her perpetual mourning clothes shaped like sacks, not even Old Nick would be lured by her.

"Reject the devil-worship of greed, money, and ambition. Repent! Repent!" Now, that was more like it, Morgan decided. Maybe Ingrid would begin to see the evil of her ways and feel the urge to share some of her wealth. Give to the needy, sister, and one of the neediest was sitting beside her. Clutch-fisted old bat could line Brother Blessed's pockets and let her own husband punt on tick. Damn! And double damn his brother. Now, there was a soul he'd like to see writhe in Satan's grasp. Repent, hell, Morgan wanted revenge!

He wanted the money, he wanted the heir, and he could not see his way to either of them now. At least his miserable niece wasn't breeding—his spies in Arstock kept him well informed—so there was no immediate danger from her. Those threats from Stokely held his hand from any thoughts of danger *to* her, especially since Emilyann's money would only go into the Stockton coffers now anyway. Besides, with any luck, and the Lord knew Morgan was due for some luck, that rackety hero of hers would get himself killed in the wars. No, his only hope was Ingrid, or getting rid of her.

"The true jewels of life are piety and purity; do not seek the false gems of earthly trappings."

Now, how did the fellow know Ingrid's diamonds were paste? Morgan had been selling off the Arcott jewels one by one, after having copies of the entailed heirlooms made for the vaults. Never mind hell, he'd go straight to Newgate for that if old Baxley got wind of it.

"Elevate your mind to the Almighty! Divorce yourself from the bondage of the body!"

Well, there was always divorce. It took time and a lot of money and made a scandal, none of which mattered if he had any grounds for getting rid of the sanctimonious albatross legally. Barrenness was legitimate, but there was the evidence, albeit weak, of Bobo. Adultery? Not even Golden Ball had enough blunt to hire some poor blighter to seduce her, for a crim. con. case.

"The devil reads your mind. You cannot hide your evil thoughts. Get them from you. Banish them. Cleanse yourself in a spiritual rebirth!"

A new wife, that was it. Morgan knew he was virile enough for a fruitful young bride if only he were free. Unfortunately, he was a coward. Just enough of Ingrid's preachings had roosted in the tiniest corner of his shriveled heart, just enough to cause a niggling, nagging fear of that eternal hell she was so sure of. The fear wasn't enough to keep him from shaving the cards, of course. A fellow had to get by, you know. But it did stop him short of killing his wife.

"And the Lord helps those who help themselves."

So bad oysters and loose saddlegirths didn't count.

"Let us bow our heads and pray for salvation that we may leave this mortal coil for a better life."

Morgan's *amen* was the loudest in the room.

Lady Ingrid Aylesbury returned to Arcott Hall in Northampshire for her health. She felt her life's work was in the city, where evil abounded, and Brother Blessed was there to give spiritual guidance, but even the staunchest warrior in the battle against sin had to rest from his wounds occasionally. She never did find out how those wild mushrooms got into her stuffed capon, or why the fireplace in her bedroom should be stuffed with rags. Perhaps it was all part of a divine plan to bring spiritual fulfillment to the ignorant masses in the countryside.

She burned every pack of cards in the house, those devil's hymnals, and threw Emilyann's collection of novels out in the trash bin, where the maids retrieved them and had the housekeeper read aloud about the Masked Marquis and Dimquith the Demon. The girls trembled in their cots at night and went stumbling to Ingrid's prayer meetings in the morning.

It was Ingrid's mission to spread righteousness, and her right as the highest-ranking lady in the vicinity to oversee the morals of the neighborhood. The path to salvation may have started at home, but it led straight to her niece's door.

There were to be no more social at-homes on Sunday, no gambling, no waltz lessons. Emilyann's bodices were to start no lower than the collarbone and her hair, in that deplorable crop, must be covered by a cap. She must stop riding about the countryside giving orders; that was man's work.

"And I'll wager I shouldn't dampen my skirts, either," Emilyann said, just to see her aunt's lips move in silent

197

prayer. Not that Lady Stokely's elegant new muslins and silks needed any artifice, nor would she be goosish enough to want clammy fabric draped to her legs, but Aunt Ingrid was so easy to send into the boughs. Ingrid had never approved of her niece, Emilyann knew, thinking her a wayward chit, not good enough for her precious Beauregard. But cropped hair indeed! One of the most expensive coiffeurs in London had come here to style Em's shorn locks into a halo of white-gold curls. Monsieur had gone into raptures; even Geoff had acknowledged it was better than that flyaway mop she used to wear. No matter, she nodded politely at her aunt, agreeing to anything that might shorten her aunt's visit. Then she could return to practicing the dances, for after the card party she was giving next week.

Ingrid's lips trembled, but she knew her duty, especially now that Bobo was safe. There was no one else to see the motherless child through the rocky shoals of marriage. "You poor neglected orphan," she told Emilyann, who looked around her elegant new morning room, searching for a destitute tot. Nanny was over in the corner with her mending, scowling. At least she hadn't fled like Nadine and Aunt Adelaide, at Ingrid's all-to-frequent visits of enlightenment.

"I always told Morgan you were not to blame for growing like a wild weed instead of a tender blossom. Never knowing a mother's care, it was too easy to fall into headstrong ways. Now that you are married, you need the guidance of an older woman. There are certain—"

"Too kind, dear Aunt Ingrid," Emilyann hurriedly interrupted before her aunt could start a lecture on wifely duties, as if her marriage to Uncle Morgan were an example of heavenly bliss. "But you really need not worry. My lord writes that he is quite pleased with me and all my domestic accomplishments."

That was not quite true. What Smoky wrote in his last letter was that he was happy Mr. Offitt was not threatening to sue him anymore over her last investment, and thank you for the socks, or were they mittens?

Aunt Ingrid was relieved, both that Stokely was not disgusted with the girl yet, and that she would not have to explain certain delicate matters. "Fine, fine. And you must consider yourself fortunate as a young bride, with your husband a soldier abroad, not having to put up with all that."

" 'All that'?"

"You know, what we were talking about."

Mittens?

"Of course you'll be denied the joys of motherhood."

Oh, *that*.

"Yes, the ultimate fulfillment for a woman, if she lives through it, of course. There was your mother, and Morgan's first wife, and Stokely's stepmama and . . ."

Emilyann suddenly decided to put "all that" off as long as possible.

"Nevertheless, I pray for the captain's safe return nightly."

"Thank you, Aunt. So do I."

Dear Smoky, she wrote, you are in our thoughts and our prayers. The fire at the granary was not extensive. Please don't feel you have to hurry home on my account.

Chapter Seven

"*I* don't see why we cannot go to London like everyone else," Nadine whined. She was sitting in the morning room, nibbling macaroons and practicing flirtatious looks over the top of her new chicken-skin fan.

Emilyann looked up from the journal she was reading, considering new designs—for plowshares, not gowns. "What was that?"

Nadine screwed up her face. "You heard very well, you just think you can ignore me. For the hundredth time, why can't we go to London for the Peace Celebrations?"

"For the hundredth time, we cannot go because Smoky specifically told us not to."

"Oh, pooh, you know he specifically told you not to invest in that shipping venture, either."

"That was simply because he did not have all the information to hand. When I explained how I made the captain's personal acquaintance and found the other investors to be very astute businessmen, Smoky agreed."

"After you had already made a handsome profit, you mean. And what about the fox hunt? You know Stokely told you that you could not forbid the hunt to pass through Stockton lands without offending the local gentry."

"He also told me not to hand-rear those fox kits, a full month after I had them weaned—and released into the home woods. What was I supposed to do? Let Squire ride down two half-tamed innocents waiting for a handout? Squire would have looked foolish. Besides, Smoky was not familiar with the hogs, and how upset they would have been with the horses riding past."

"Like when he told you to fix the drains first and then the thatch on the old cottages by the mill?"

"It was simply a matter of timing. You know very well his letter came after the thatchers were already at work." She waved her hand dismissively. "Smoky understood."

"Gammon. You just don't want to go to London because you're too content to wallow here with Geoff's pigs. Either that or you're afraid you won't take."

"Nadine Stockton, what a nasty, spiteful thing to say. Has anyone told you lately what a spoiled child you've become?"

"Yes, Thornton does all the time and your Nanny nags, too, and you are beginning to sound just like them! Even Aunt Ingrid is beginning to approve of you. Bobo says—"

"Bobo?"

"Well, yes. You know he is rusticating with his mama. I danced with him at the Finley-Bourns's ball. Oh, I think you were discussing that tiresome fence with Mr. Offitt at the time. And you were out with that man Jake at the horse auction when he came to call yesterday. He stayed to tea," Nadine said around another macaroon.

"Did you count the silverware?" Emilyann moved the dish. No wonder Bobo appealed to the girl: they would both soon be fat as flawns.

Nadine pouted. "Well, *I* think he's very nice. He's looking top of the trees, too. You don't have to smile. Just because you are skinny does not mean it is fashionable," she preened, wriggling her rounded dumpling of a body. "And Bobo knows everyone in London. You should hear him tell about the fireworks displays and how the streets were all lined with people when the tsar arrived and how there are more fetes every night than anyone can attend." Her fan waved furiously in her enthusiasm. "And I am stuck here in the country, where nothing ever happens. Emmy, I am nearly seventeen! I'll be on the shelf soon if I don't get to London and find a husband! Why, you were already married when you were my age. Of course, your aunt Ingrid says—"

"Aunt Ingrid has been entertaining some very odd notions lately," Emilyann put in hurriedly. "She hasn't been feeling at all the thing since Uncle Morgan's last visit; she's even complaining that her tooth powder tastes peculiar."

"But Bobo says even she is considering returning to London before the end of the victory celebrations."

Emilyann turned the page of her journal, tired of the discussion. "Yes, well, perhaps we shall get there, too, if Smoky comes home in time."

"He's been gone over a year this time," Nadine wailed, throwing down the fan. "All the other officers are returning. I don't see why Stokely can't."

Emilyann stood and picked up the fan. She smoothed the feather tips between her fingers and tried once more to stay patient with her sister-in-law. "He explained it very carefully, that it was an honor to be asked to help establish the peacekeeping forces in Belgium. Lord Wellington himself asked Smoky to stay on until a new command staff can be assembled. There were so many losses at Toulouse, you know, that experienced officers are in short supply. The Congress of Vienna will be convening shortly, anyway, and then it is just a matter of time before the peace is finalized and all the troops can come home. Since Smoky will be selling out, it only seemed fair to let the other officers have leave first, before they rejoin the army or go off to the American conflict."

"You know what I think?" Nadine asked with a sneer. "I think you're glad. I think you are going along just as you please, managing everything and everybody, and you don't even care if the war lasts forever. I bet you'd be happy if Stokely never came home!"

"Hateful little shrew!" Emilyann shouted back, shaking the fan under Nadine's nose. "Don't you ever, ever say such a thing! I have been waiting forever for Smoky to come home. And he will; he promised me. Just because he's the finest, bravest, most honorable officer there ever was, and won't go back on his responsibilities so some foolish little girl can attend her silly parties ..."

The fan didn't last long.

Nadine apologized sweetly. How could she have been such a wretch to dear Emilyann, who had done so much for her and the family? She would be content to stay in the country, she swore, even if all the local boys did have hay in their hair, except Bobo, of course.

And Emilyann bought her a new fan, with turquoise ostrich feathers this time, to dazzle the rustics. And she threw her first large entertainment, to encourage Nadine's local swains, except Bobo, of course. And she did a lot of serious thinking.

She was almost nineteen now, and she had never had a London season either. She would like to see the spectacles, too, and all the other evils Aunt Ingrid was always attering on about, like the theater and Vauxhall Gardens. The lands were prospering, her investments were earning returns, her remodeling projects were nearly accomplished— and where the deuce was Smoky? If she felt a trifle guilty for enjoying herself too much in his absence, she also reasoned that she had worked very hard on his behalf. Now she wanted to show him the fruits of her labors, convince him that he hadn't married such a ninnyhammer and an antidote to boot.

Of course he had responsibilities, and of course the peace

treaties would be signed soon, but perhaps, just perhaps, he could have come home for two weeks in the past year or so if he wanted to. Which was the rub, naturally. It was perfectly reasonable that she was not overeager to become a wife in deed as well as name, and understandable that she might be nervous about his return. But if he was not returning because he didn't want to return, if he would rather stay in some bloody war rather than come home and be her husband, if he was ashamed of her—then she would show him a thing or two. The Countess of Stokely did not have to vegetate in the backwaters growing pigfeed and crocheting, as if she knew how, during the biggest celebrations of the century, not on any overbearing soldier's selfish whim.

Dear Smoky, I hope this finds you well. Thank you for the package of Brussels lace you sent. Did you really watch the women making it? Nadine is busy steeping hers in tea for the aged look she swears is all the crack now. Nanny is helping me use mine to retrim a boring gown. See how frugal I have learned to be?

Speaking of saving money, I have been thinking of refurbishing the London town house so that it might be rented out rather than sit empty for years, growing stale and shabby. I understand houses are being let at remarkably high prices now, with so many dignitaries and hangers-on in town. I would have to supervise the work myself, of course, which would involve moving the rest of the household to London for a brief time, which I cannot but think would be to everyone's benefit, despite your worries.

I know you felt we should do better in the country for the time being, but I think you might not have considered all the facts of the matter. To wit, your sister is growing into a beauty, and unfortunately knows it. She really needs a bigger pond in which to swim, the local swains offering no challenge. I fear she is fixing her interest with Bobo, of all people. I cannot decide if he loiters about the place for Nadine's sake or Cook's excellent pastries, which interest they have in common. Geoff, meanwhile, is in danger of turning into the complete farmer, as you feared. It is all we can do to get him to change for dinner. I myself would not

203

find a little town bronze amiss, between visits to the ware-houses and linen drapers. I have been most eager to view the new British Museum with Lord Elgin's treasures, and to hear that soprano everyone raves about, La Catalani. You see, nothing exceptional. Aunt Ingrid is thinking of return-ing to town now that she is recovered from the carriage ac-cident, so we shall have the most rigorous of overseers. Aunt believes the peace talks need her blessing.

How are the treaty negotiations going anyhow? We hear so little, here in the country. Oh, and Nanny is sending you some handkerchiefs. Nadine says that I should write that I embroidered the monograms myself, but you would not have believed a word of it, would you? Which is by way of saying you can trust me.

There, I am sure I have overcome all your objections. Do you have any preferences for colors for the London draw-ing room, and was there any of the old staff you wished to see rehired?

Of course if your orders are changed, we would natu-rally be delighted to await your homecoming in Arstock, so do keep us informed. I hope that day comes soon, Smoky. As ever, Sparrow.

The mails were more reliable now that hostilities were over, and a letter could reach Smoky in Brussels in less than two weeks, Emilyann estimated, especially since he was no longer moving around with a marching army. He had won promotion to major, too, and the higher the rank, she was sure, the quicker the mail was sorted and delivered. So there were perhaps ten days before he had her letter, an-other ten before his response. She foresaw no difficulty; they would be making their curtsies at Almacks long before that.

As she told Nadine, it was all a matter of timing.

Major Lord Stokely thought bald men looked silly, other-wise he'd tear his hair out. He was drowning in paperwork, choking on conflicting orders, and being nibbled to death by the ducks of diplomacy. And his little peahen of a wife was going to London! She had dirty-dish relatives, a nearscandalous marriage, no looks, and about as much sense of self-preservation as a kitten. She would hate all the petty strictures and she'd flaunt whichever didn't suit her. Gads, those dragons of the ton would eat a spirited girl like her alive, and spit her reputation out in shreds. With no proper sponsor but a psalm-singing fanatic, and no chaperone except Aunt Adelaide, who could be counted on for a season-long swoon, Sparrow wouldn't be received in the polite world. The impolite world, filled with hardened libertines and fortune-hunters, would welcome a fresh-hatched chick like her with open arms. His baby-faced brother could be counted on to outrun the constable, and that sad romp of a sister needed a lot heavier hand on the reins than Sparrow's if she wasn't to disgrace them all. To top it off, Stockton House in London was a moldering pile that would take a king's ransom to restore. He would have sold it long ago if he could have found a buyer stupid enough. Of all Sparrow's cork-brained schemes, this one took the prize. Those unprotected innocents had no more business in London than he did behind a desk in Brussels. He couldn't leave Belgium; they couldn't leave Northamshire, period. That was it.

Do not go to London, he wrote. How much more explicit could he make it? He sent Rigg to dispatch the letter at once, then he came back to his office, loosened his collar, and put his feet up on the battered desk. He shook his head, smiled, thought how he'd ought to have taken a switch to the chit when she was nine, and wrote the letter over. This copy he sent to Stockton House, Portman Square, London.

Chapter Eight

So he thought they were innocents, did he? From his letters, with all of his do's and don't's, Emilyann gathered that Smoky thought she was still a nine-year-old scamp with a soiled pinafore. One mustn't gallop in Hyde Park, one must always be accompanied by a maid at least, one must not speak to a gentleman unless formally introduced to him. Goodness, *one* might think she hadn't learned anything at all at Miss Meadow's Academy. She surely had not been instructed in how to keep accounts, or how to trace a broodmare's bloodlines, or when to invest in consols or futurities, so what did Smoky think they taught there, anything practical? No, she had a head full of paltry rules and trifling data, such as how to greet each level of the peerage, how low to curtsy to each dignitary, and which fork to use at dinner. She knew how to discourage an overheated beau, and how to hold polite conversations with half-deaf dowagers. If she did not always choose to use this education in inconsequentialities, that was a minor point only.

I did not just sprout from under a cabbage leaf, you know, she wrote back to her doubting husband, meanwhile thinking that if Smoky was so sure they would land in the briers without him to watch over them, he should dashed well be there.

Emilyann had intended to keep a quiet profile in London: visit the modiste shops and booksellers, see the historical sights, look up some of her school friends, and take in a few concerts and plays. She would have to see about a presentation at court and their vouchers for Almack's for Nadine's sake, but she truly meant to stay on the outskirts of the ton, more an observer than a participant.

That was before receiving the reams of orders and advice from Major Lord Stokely. Now she was determined to make a splash.

When Emilyann and her entourage arrived at the Pulteney Hotel for a week's stay while the city mansion was being restored to glamour, the hotel staff sniffed as if the aroma of Geoff's hogs had traveled with them. A bit of name-dropping, a lot of largesse, and the little countess became a favored guest, and she hadn't even needed Smoky's instructions. Soon the best couturiers and the premier employment agencies and caterers to the elite were sending emissaries, leaving gratuities for the porter for the references, *certainement*. Bankers and merchants and carriage makers filed through her suite, and then, after she began making morning calls and leaving cards, dowagers and debs.

Many of her former schoolmates were easy to locate; anyone not already married was in London for the season, hunting. They wholeheartedly welcomed Emilyann back to their friendships as someone who was wealthy, titled, funloving—and absolutely no threat to their capturing a *parti* of their own. She even had a charming brother-in-law, a bit young but sweet. Of course they would be pleased to extend invitations to their balls and Venetian breakfasts.

To her father's friends, the diplomats and politicians who used to attend house parties at Arcott Hall, Emilyann was a cherished recollection, Aylesbury's moppet. She was as dear to them now as any young woman they did not have to feed, clothe, or provide with a dowry. They made sure their wives and secretaries put her on the lists for state dinners and soirées.

Even Aunt Ingrid was moved to do her part. Back in town for the Peace Celebrations, surely a praiseworthy occasion, Ingrid was convinced her cachet was all-important to Emilyann's success, not that being accepted by the leaders of the ton was on a scale with being welcomed to heaven by a band of trumpeting angels. Ingrid disdained such worldly pursuits for herself, of course, but her harumscarum niece was just as likely to set the town on its ear if not guided properly. Lady Aylesbury shuddered to think of

207

even more scandal and shame touching her family. It was her duty to see that Emilyann had the proper introductions and supervision. If, in the meantime, Ingrid was pressured into purchasing new gowns and wearing the Arcott emeralds now and again, it was all toward a higher good. She had to attend that tiresome marriage-mart at Almack's and those insipid come-outs anyway, if she was to find Bobo a suitable mate. Her husband might not be welcomed at routs and receptions and ladies' teas, but no one refused a duchess, no matter how eccentric.

When the house was ready, Emilyann was ready. She had the start of her new wardrobe, all bright colors and vibrant fabrics, not the sprigs and calicos suitable for country life. She had an elegantly appointed, well-staffed mansion, and a hall table full of invitations. She had an experienced abigail, a full cellar, and a still-healthy bank account.

What she did not have was the continued support of her most loyal followers. Nadine, Aunt Adelaide, Nanny, and Geoffrey all wanted to go home within the first month. Emilyann had been too busy showing Smoky how wrong he was about herself to see how right he had been about the rest of the family.

Don't let Nadine have her head, he'd written. But Emilyann hated checkreins; how could she impose them on another? So she made Nadine an allowance, hired a maid to accompany her, and made sure she knew the rules as well. She could trust Nadine not to jeopardize her own chances, she had thought. Smoky would have every right to call her a dunderhead or worse—if she ever mentioned the matter to him.

"Mrs. Drummond-Burrell said I had country manners!" Nadine howled, red-faced and weeping.

"She told me she thought you were too young to make your come-out. I had to disagree, naturally, but I thought we discussed how they did not do the contra dances here with quite as much enthusiasm as you were wont to see at the local assemblies."

"Sally Jersey said I was fast." Sob.

"Yes, but you knew you should not go onto the balcony

with the Mittleborough boy, or that Prussian Hussar, or that . . ."

"And Princess Lieven told Aunt Adelaide my dress was farouche. Auntie says that means t-t-terrible."

"I *told* you all the other debutantes would be wearing white. Cherry stripes are not at all the thing for a girl in her first season. Smoky even wrote that specifically. I remember reading it to you."

Sniff. "But you never do what Stokely says. Why should I?"

"Because I am older and married," Emilyann told the girl. She did not add that she had a better head on her shoulders, too. "Moreover," she continued instead, "I do try to listen to Stokely's advice."

"That's a farradiddle if ever I heard one. What about the carriage?"

Emilyann suddenly discovered a spot on the hem of her peach sarcenet gown. "I, ah, suppose you are referring to my new phaeton. In my previous letter to your brother I mentioned admiring Lord Findley's new equipage, and Smoky wrote back that a high-perch phaeton was too dangerous and too daring, and I was on no account to consider purchasing one. I never did. The seats are much too high to get into gracefully, you know, without showing an undue amount of ankle."

"But?" Nadine asked, smiling now.

"Oh, very well, you wretched girl. But he never mentioned standard phaetons, which are quite two feet lower."

"Don't you think that's cutting hairs?"

Emilyann grinned, showing her dimples. "Don't you think it's the most dashing thing ever?"

"Everyone in Hyde Park certainly did. The way heads were swiveling, I thought the regent himself was out for an airing."

"Oh, but he was. Prinny complimented me on my driving. I must remember to tell Smoky that, for he taught me, you know. Of course I had time to practice on the country roads, and Jake to give me tips, but—whatever is the matter now?"

Nadine was dissolved in tears again. "I can never go back to the park. Ever. They all laughed at me, Emmy!"

Emilyann bit her lip to keep herself from giggling. Nadine was the worst shopper in London, wanting every tasteless frippery she saw in the store windows. She just had to have the parasol with gold tassels, the red slippers with turned-up toes, that outrageous headdress with five ostrich feathers in a rainbow of colors . . . and she still needed a new shawl. All the ladies were wearing those brightly woven Kashmir wraps which were, unfortunately, much too dear for Nadine's allowance. Emilyann told her, Nanny told her, even Smoky wrote and told her, *Buy quality*. But Nadine saw a way for her allowance to go further, and bought a shawl of the cheaper dyed India muslin.

So there she was in the park with Aunt Adelaide, in the family chaise, at the appropriate hour of five o'clock, when the ton came out to see and be seen. Soon she was surrounded by a flock of young Tulips, with a scattering of military types. She decided to get down and walk, so her beaux might admire her glorious new ensemble better, the colorful scarf, a lemon-yellow jaconet dress with mulberry ribbons, the ostrich plumes floating above.

"I'm afraid it might shower, dear," Aunt Adelaide fretted. "Perhaps you shouldn't . . ."

"Don't be such a worrier, Auntie," Nadine told her, gaily twirling her parasol.

It wasn't a very hard rain, and did not last long. Just long enough for the parasol to collapse, the ostrich plumes to sag onto Nadine's forehead, the red tips of her slippers to droop into the mud with a squelch, and those bright colors of the shawl to run down her dress, leaving rivulets of dye streaming down her arms.

"I can never show my face in public again! I'm ruined, Emmy, ruined. I want to go home! Aunt Adelaide says she wants to go, too, and Bobo offered to accompany us."

"Bobo? Whyever would that overfed fop leave town at the height of the season?"

"His jackets don't fit so nicely with his arm in the sling, so he thought he may as well rusticate. I tried to tell him

210

he looked heroic— Are you all right? Shall I fetch some water?"

Emilyann held up her hand. "No, no, just fine. What, er, happened to Bobo's arm?"

"Oh, such a silly thing. He tripped on some loose carpet threads outside his mother's door. It's a miracle he didn't fall right down the stairs. Just his shoulder was bruised though, poor thing."

Poor thing, Bobo? No, Nadine could certainly not go home with that oaf. In fact, the best thing all around would be to get her fired off and married soon, before she landed in the basket altogether. That would take a little luck and a lot more management than Nadine was used to, or Emilyann wished to impose. The solution? Blame it on Smoky.

"Your brother insists you stay and have a proper presentation. He writes right here," she said, waving the shopping list, "that I have to make sure you have an acceptable wardrobe and more seemly conduct. If I don't he'll ... he'll sell the phaeton and the racing stock and make me live with Aunt Ingrid."

Nadine looked wide-eyed. "Can he do that?"

Of course he couldn't, and assuredly wouldn't. Didn't the rattlepate know her brother at all? Emilyann was not about to disabuse her of the notion of Smoky as ogre, though, if it kept the minx out of dark corners and got her into white gowns.

"But white is so boring. I suppose next you'll order me to fold my hands in my lap and sit mumchance through endless piano recitals."

"It would be more suitable, indeed, than going to a military revue with none but your maid and three half-pay officers!"

"But no one likes those dull girls. Even Papa used to say those colorless females were no fun."

"My dear Nadine, are you being guided by your father's conception of how a female should act? The whole county knew his preferences ran to blowzy women with painted faces and easy manners. You cannot be trying to live up, or

211

down, to his values, girl. No one marries those women, not even your papa."

"I shan't take anyway, I know it."

"Not if you proceed the way you've been going," Emilyann agreed. "But there is no reason you can't be one of the season's Incomparables. You know your dark looks are quite the fashion this year, pity us poor blondes, and your figure is everything pleasing if you just refrain from so many desserts. Smoky has set aside a comfortable dowry for you, and your breeding is unexceptionable. We can turn the lady patronesses up sweet with one or two demure morning calls, and the rest of the ton will forget the park incident as soon as Lady Bainbridge takes a new cisisbeo or Prinny insults another German *graf*."

"You really think I can become a Toast?"

"Definitely. If you will be led by those who love you and truly have your best interests at heart, then there is no doubt."

Aunt Adelaide had plenty of doubts. *She's just not strong enough for the rigors of the season,* Smoky had written.

"My heart, you know, dear. No, I don't feel at all well in this foul air. I fear for my health, I truly do."

Emilyann feared she might have to accompany her sister-in-law to every debutante do and young peoples' outing herself if she could not talk Aunt Adelaide into staying. "I thought you enjoyed the opera, and I know you were delighted to encounter that old friend of yours."

"Yes, but all the hustle and bustle can cause palpitations, quinsies, dyspepsia. I could succumb to any number of them, you know, if I don't return to the country."

"What a hum, Auntie. I saw you having a comfortable coze with Mrs. Richfield and tapping your toes. You didn't feel the least bit weak until Nadine went behind the draperies with that Austrian."

Aunt Adelaide reached for her vinaigrette.

"See? You needn't worry anymore. I have decided to take Nadine in hand myself, and she agrees to try to moderate her behavior. That is, Smoky insists. Since I am a married woman, I'm considered enough of a chaperone for

her, so you needn't come with us to all the big squeezes
if you think they might be too wearing. It's just that we
need you for some of those times when I may have other
plans. You know, those quiet afternoon teas you find so
pleasant, or the afternoon dance parties the young people
like so much when their mamas sit and gossip. I wish you
could see your way to staying with us, but you mustn't
jeopardize your health, of course."

"Oh, dear, so kind of you to concern yourself. And
you've been so generous, I keep asking Nadine what would
we have done without you. And to disappoint dear Everett.
No, no. The family must come first. You did say she
wouldn't wear those awful feathers anymore, didn't you?"

"I burned them myself, ma'am."

"I do miss my garden though. . . ."

So Emilyann had three rosebushes planted in the grassy
patch behind the house, and a bench installed. It was a fair
trade if she got out of another harp musicale.

Nanny was even easier to deal with. It was her opinion
that Miss Emmy should be in the country, where Master
Stokely ordered, waiting for her man like a good wife. Instead, she was gallivanting around town in a flimsy rig,
wearing her hems too high and her necklines too low, making too much of a stir for a respectable matron. Her little
lamb was trotting too hard altogether, so there.

Emilyann couldn't get Nanny a baby to mother, not comfortably, anyway, so she did the next best thing: she bought
her a puppy.

Geoffrey, at least, was no problem. *It's too easy for green
boys to fall into the wrong company in London*, Smoky
wrote, but Geoff hadn't. He had quickly made friends with
one of her schoolmate's brothers, young Johnny Remington,
who was such a likable, levelheaded fellow, with a nice
smile and even features, that Emilyann was considering
him for Nadine. Geoff and Rem went everywhere together
when they were not escorting their female relatives, poking
fun at the dandy set, and only halfheartedly emulating the
Corinthians. They seemed to be enjoying London and their

freedom as men about town, so Emilyann was surprised when Geoff approached her one morning in her study, saying that he wished to go home.

She put down the pen and closed the account book she'd been working on, with some relief. "What, is mutiny contagious?" she joked, not really worried. "I suppose you're worried about your hogs, is that it? You know Meecham writes every week, and follows your instructions to the letter. But I suppose we can get along without you for a few days if you are determined to see for yourself."

"It ain't a visit I had in mind, Emmy. I don't think I like this kind of life here, you know, nothing much for a chap to do."

"No? What about that mill, and the race to Richmond, and the new steam engine exhibit you wanted to go watch?"

Geoff set his mouth stubbornly, all too reminiscent of Nadine's sulks. "I ain't on leading strings, Emmy, and I want to go home."

Emilyann was sure she could bring that ready smile back to his face, the one where he reminded her more of Smoky than of his sister, even though his face had Nadine's roundness, and his hair and eyes were brown like Nadine's, not Smoky's darker colors. "I know what it is," she teased. "You want to get out of another night in knee breeches. Very well, you need not escort us to Lady Cheyne's ball this evening. Or is it that you're afraid you won't be able to outrun little Miss Rivington and her predatory mama?"

Geoff grinned sheepishly; he never could stay mad for long, and Miss Rivington did seem to be nearby whenever he took his sister anywhere. Then he noticed the account books, and remembered his mission. "No, Emmy, this place is just too dashed expensive for my tastes. I'd rather be home seeing the farms prosper than stay here, being a drain on them."

"I see," said Emilyann, thinking she did. Smoky and Geoff had agreed to maintain the latter's allowance, adding in the unused school money, until Smoky was home and the estates were earning more. Then they would see about a fair share of the profits, or even a manager's salary. Meantime, she supposed, keeping up appearances in the city was more expensive than they had planned. Her other investments were paying off well. "Why don't I write to Smoky about increasing your allowance?" she offered.

"No, Emmy, you've done enough, and it ain't anything I want you mentioning to my brother, not even a right 'un like Ev."

"Oh, ho, wild oats, is it? You've sown barley and wheat and turnips, so why not? From what I heard, Smoky did his share." She refused to consider whether her husband had put such ways behind him or not. "If it's a loan you're needing—"

"Stokely would have my hide, discussing such things with you!"

"But the problem is money?" she asked, her blue eyes looking troubled now.

"Ah, not exactly . . ."

She tapped her fingers on the account books. "Then what is it, *exactly?*"

She was like a dog with a bone, this fragile-looking sister-in-law of his. A big dog with a meaty bone, and she was never going to let go. So he told her, between his embarrassed pauses and her impatient prying, about the previous evening's event. He and Rem had decided to seek more excitement than watching the soboroidoo at White's and Watier's and had left for a visit to Drury Lane. They couldn't really afford the high fliers at the greenroom, but the night was still young so they left, this time to the Daffy Club and the Cocoa Tree, using Smoky's name to gain entry. Stakes were awfully high there, and they weren't much into gambling, so they wandered the streets awhile, until Remington recalled hearing about a place where the dealers were all women. . . .

They threw down a few pounds here and there at the craps tables, or at *rouge et noir*, admiring the females, tossing back a few glasses of Blue Ruin—"It's free at those places, don't you know"—and feeling very well up in the world indeed. And then . . .

* * *

"You got into a game of cards with *whom*?"

"Your uncle Aylesbury?"

"You clunch! Everyone knows what he is. No one ever plays with him but greenheads, and they never, ever win."

"I know, but I couldn't very well ignore him."

"Why not? I do."

"It's different in a club like that, with his friends all around."

"That makebait doesn't have any friends. He's such a cur, it's a miracle Aunt Ingrid hasn't prayed her way into heaven yet, trying to make her morality compensate for his lack of principles. I am ashamed he is my relative, and mortified that he wears my father's title, yet you play cards with him, you complete—"

"You don't understand, Em."

She did, though, understand how two well-mannered, friendly boys wouldn't know how to extricate themselves from such a trap. There was venom in her voice. "How much?"

"All of it. I lost the rest of this quarter's allowance, and the governor's gold watch. Rem went through his bank account, too, to the tune of about five hundred pounds. Your uncle—" At her glare he amended that: "Lord Aylesbury said he'd take our vouchers, but we had sense not to go that route."

"Thank goodness for small favors. So then you left, and now you are ready to slink off to Arstock and wait for next quarter-day before you can buy a friend a drink or send a lady a bouquet of flowers?" The quill pen snapped in her fingers. "I won't have it!"

"Nothing you can do about it, Em. Debt of honor and all that."

"There is nothing honorable about an old Captain Sharp chousing allowances out of farmboys. No, we'll just have to get the money back. And your father's watch."

"But—"

"But nothing. It's my family; I'll handle it. You get yourself ready to escort us to Lady Cheyne's this evening. The refreshments there are free, too."

* * *

By Jupiter, this was something Smoky should be handling! Emilyann fumed as she waited in her carriage outside Arcott House for Aunt Ingrid to leave for her four o'clock Tuesday afternoon prayer meeting. She was so angry at her uncle for being a dastard, at Geoff for being a trusting fool, and at Smoky for being right and being gone, she hadn't a thought to spare for the might-have-beens, seeing the elegant old house again. When her aunt's coach left, Emilyann marched right through the doors of her family's one-time home and demanded to see her uncle.

She did not know the new butler and he did not know her, but he recognized quality, and a blazing temper at that. He murmured, "The library," and stood aside.

"I want it back. All of it. Geoff's, Remington's, the watch. Now."

Uncle Morgan was still trying to keep his eyeballs from jumping out of his head at the door's slamming open. "Lower your voice, girl. My poor head!"

"Jug-bitten again, Uncle? My, my." She pounded her fist on the desk in front of him. "You'll have more than a headache if I don't get the money back."

As soon as he could take his shaking hands away from his throbbing temples, he took a better look at his caller. "Damn if you ain't growin' more like your mother in looks every time I see you." He reached for a bottle and glass. "And more like your father in temperament."

"Thank you. The boys' money?"

"Now, why do you think I should return the lads' blunt, assuming I still have it, that is? I won it fair."

"That word's not in your vocabulary. That's why."

"A matter of opinion only, girl. Won't hold up in court or anything, you know. No, I don't think you've got a winning hand there."

She did have an ace in the hole, however, besides a pistol in her pocket. She pulled a chair closer to the desk and sat down without being asked. "You're a gambling man, Uncle. What do you say we cut cards for it?"

His reddened eyes opened wider. "And if you lose?"

"I'll double the sum."

Morgan's trembling hand reached into the top drawer of

the massive desk—her father's desk, where he had transacted affairs of state—for a pack of cards.

"We'll use my cards, Uncle." Her voice was firm, her determination unwavering, her deck well worn. She shuffled competently, set the pile in front of him. "One cut. High card."

Morgan nodded, staring at the cards. He licked his lips, reached, cut. The ten of clubs.

Emilyann ignored his smirk. Her hand hesitated delicately over the cards for a moment, then she made her cut, a king. She gathered the cards back into her reticule and stood, expectant. Morgan rubbed his face with his hands, but did reach back into the drawer for a leather pouch and tossed it across to her. She did not move.

"It's all there, the watch, too. What are you waiting for now?"

"I just wanted to give you a little advice, Uncle. If this ever happens again—Geoff, Remington, any of my friends—I'll go straight to the magistrates. No, not to accuse you of fleecing the lambs. I'll simply mention Aunt Ingrid's jewelry, you know, the family heirlooms that were entrusted to your care."

His whiskey-flushed face turned a sickly green. "You wouldn't do it, girl. Think of the scandal."

"Still a gambling man, Uncle? Don't bet on it." She turned to leave, then went back and pulled some pound notes from the pouch. "Here, now you can get the roof fixed. A tile fell as I was driving up. It only missed Aunt Ingrid by inches."

"There's some missing, Geoff. Consider it well spent if you learned anything."

"Lud, Emmy, I swear I did! But how in blazes did you manage to get it back?"

"It was simple. I used one of his own old decks of cards."

When they stopped laughing, and Geoff stopped congratulating his sister-in-law for being the best and bravest, he asked, "Ah, Em, you won't, that is, you don't need to mention this to Smoky, do you?"

Tell Smoky she had gone alone to her uncle's house with a pistol and a shaved deck of cards to win back his brother's money? Hah! She wasn't *that* brave.

Chapter Nine

See? she wrote. *You worried for nothing. We are all settled in and having a delightful time. We are very well received, judging from all the invitations on the mantel, and Nadine spends hours each day deciding which we shall accept. We have heeded your dictates*—she crossed that out and amended it to *advice*—*and have elected not to travel to Vienna. Although the company does get a little thinner as so many travel to the gaiety of the Congress there, after being kept from travel on the Continent for so long, we feel there is quite enough to keep us content in London for the nonce. We hear the peace talks are stalled, while the festivities there increase. Our social rounds in London are flourishing well enough. . . .*

Indeed, the Stocktons' popularity could not have been greater. Geoff could be counted on to dance with the shyest girls, those who intimidated him least, pleasing the hostesses no end. A toned-down Nadine was delighted with the steady stream of beaux and flower baskets through Portman Square, and the smiles and nods from the callers' mothers. If her laugh was too loud on occasion, at least she was not considered a milk-and-water miss.

But it was Emilyann, the Little Countess, who was taking London by storm, to everyone's surprise including her own. Rounded brunettes or stately golden beauties were the fashion, until one small, thin, silver-blonde became the rage. Ladies were cool, reserved, bored—until a laughing, blue-eyed pixie charmed a smile out of the starchiest matrons and the most careworn Parliamentarians. And men, single, married, young and old, bucks and beaux, flocked to her like Geoff's pigs followed the slops bucket. She never made fun of the callow youths nor turned a deaf ear to the prosy old gents who were her father's cronies nor let a hardened rake go beyond the line. If anyone accused her of being a deliberate flirt, she laughed back. "But everyone knows I am only an old married woman, how could I lead anyone on?"

She never singled out one of her admirers, except young Remington, who gave her puppylike devotion in return for his purse back from Uncle Morgan. She refused to hurt his feelings, and she still had hopes of him for Nadine. Mamas of young lads realized their babes were safe; jealous wives saw their husbands secure in numbers; marriageable girls took lessons and were happy for a friendship that kept them in the vicinity of every eligible *parti* in town.

Emilyann laughed and danced and teased, and never lost her own sense of style, wit, intelligence, and charm. She was in no danger of becoming spoiled by her popularity; she was in no danger of losing her heart, either. She was pleased with her success and complimented by so many men's regard, but she held them all up to Smoky, and none met his measure.

She could not lie to herself that she knew her husband well: she had not seen him in over a year, and then for hours only. Childish dreams, girlhood fantasies, and his friendly letters (when he was not lecturing) combined to form an image of him in her mind and in her heart. He was wise and brave and kind and comical. He was tall and thin and rugged, with broad shoulders, black curls, and gray eyes that smiled down at her as he tied her bonnet's bow along her cheek on their wedding day. He had kissed her forehead and told her she was safe now. No other man ever gave her that feeling of belonging. Now she needed more than that, but only from him.

Have you any chance of coming home soon? she concluded her latest letter, then added: *Oh, Aunt Ingrid is recovering nicely. The footman who tripped on Uncle's foot, spilling the orange flambé in her lap, has been dismissed.*

*And just in case you hear one or two small rumors about
a race to Richmond after the masquerade, don't worry. I
won.* She signed it, *Your loving and obedient wife.*

Obedient? One or two small rumors? Hah! There were
nothing but rumors floating around Brussels. Half of them
concerned Napoleon's possible plans to leave exile; the
other half concerned Stokely's own wife!

The major hated unproved information. He always had,
volunteering to go behind enemy lines when he first signed
up, to find the truth for his commanders lest they commit
troop movements to ungrounded talk of enemy strengths
and positions. Later, on the command staff, he gathered
these reports from other men and helped plan the army's
strategies—with facts, not hearsay.

Now he was stuck in Brussels, playing nursemaid to
petty officials of the Allied forces, while Boney considered
wreaking more havoc on Europe. Damn, if he only knew
the truth! Why couldn't those bloody fools in Vienna stop
waltzing long enough to find out?

Then there was the talk about his wife. His wife, by
God! Half the time he forgot he even had one, and the
other half he wished he didn't. Every returning officer told
him what a lucky dog he was. Pride kept him from asking
for details; there was no way he could admit he hardly
knew his bride. Every weeks-late newspaper had columns
full of the latest doings of Lady S———, with this man's
escort, in that man's box. Spindly little Sparrow? What the
devil was going on? Carriage races and masquerades, indeed. Why hadn't the little madcap been tossed out on her
ear? Stokely didn't understand any of it, and liked it less.

If she'd only stayed in the country . . . Hell, if she hadn't
climbed that tree after him, he wouldn't have broken his
arm getting her down. Now there was no hope for a quiet
annulment, not after the stir she was causing. It wasn't as
if no one had heard of her or the marriage. She would be
ruined by the same blasted gossip that currently raged
around her. They were truly married now, for good or for
evil.

The major was not even sure if he minded so much.

There were times when she infuriated him, like spending her money to outfit his sister for presentation at the queen's drawing room. There were times when she terrified him, like when she wrote about wanting to be part of a balloon ascension. And there were times when he felt an aching loss: it should have been him giving Sparrow her first sight of Vauxhall Gardens at night, with the fairy lights and fireworks. He should have shared her first taste of iced champagne ... and her first kiss. Then he remembered letting her trail after him on her first hunt, braids flying, her whole dirty face lit with a gap-toothed grin. Sparrow was just a child, an adorable imp. That was why all of London embraced her, wasn't it, and forgave her all those fits and starts? But he was a man, not a monk, and would want more from a wife than a towhead tagalong. Lord, he was confused!

The British Army left in Belgium was well encamped and organized, provisions were flowing nicely, and the troops were in good spirits. Smoky knew to a man how many soldiers were billeted where and how much ammunition was on hand, so he decided the politicians and pettifoggers could be trusted, briefly, to watch out for the Corsican's return; he had to see about his wife.

The very correct butler raised his nose up, his chest out, and sonorously intoned: "My apologies, sir. The ladies are out for the evening. I shall be pleased to convey a message, or your card if you choose to leave one."

"Put on your spectacles, you old charlatan, and get off your high horse. It is I, Stokely, and I own the damn pile, so you may as well let me in."

"Master Everett, is that you? We weren't expecting—that is, welcome home, milord. Welcome home indeed." He took the major's hat and snapped his fingers for footmen to assist Rigg, now in sergeant's uniform, in with the baggage. "It has been a long time."

Stokely looked around the entry hall, the gleaming furniture, the vases of flowers, the attentive servants in perfect livery. "It certainly has. Where did you ever come from? I thought you retired to your sister's farm after my father stuck his spoon in the wall. However did Sparrow find you?"

The butler's lip twitched. "Through the advertisement, m'lord, in all the papers. 'Butler wanted,' it said. 'Mr. only.' I knew it had to be me wanted, and Lady Emilyann as inserted it. She was the only one who ever called me mister. Said it did not suit my dignity to be summoned as Butler."

"But it's your name."

"And my calling, milord. The family has always been in service." He couldn't suppress the smile. "It does confuse the callers, milord."

By this time they had reached the master bedroom, redone, Stokely saw, in elegant navy velvet hangings with gold accents. He could not resist asking, in his most non-chalant voice: "I, ah, suppose there are a lot of callers?"

"Yes, indeed, milord. We are very popular."

"And Sparrow, Lady Emilyann, she goes on all right?" Gads, he was quizzing his own butler!

"Oh, quite. I was able to advise her ladyship about a few matters that—"

"She took *your* advice?"

The butler poured out a glass of cognac and served it on a silver tray. He did not bother answering, instead commenting, "How upset Lady Stokely and the family will be to have missed you. Shall I send a boy after them? They are attending Lady Winstoke's fete, I believe. They would have stayed in, I'm sure, had they known."

"No, no, it's my fault for not writing. It was a sudden decision to come, and I arrived before a letter would. All I need is a hot bath and my dress uniform pressed, then I might drop in at the Winstokes' and surprise them."

"Very good, milord, I'll see to it at once." He turned at the door. "And may I say how gratified I was that you requested my lady to seek me out for the position."

"Did I . . . ah, thank you, Butler."

The ball was well under way when he arrived. It was one of those massive affairs where the hostess invites more people than can possibly fit into her house, for her party to be a success. The receiving line was long disbanded, so the major just stood at the top of the stairs leading down to the ballroom, looking for a familiar face. He could not see across the floor on account of the crowds milling around and the smoke rising from the multitude of candles. The musicians seemed to be on intermission, but the noise was like a barnyard, and the scents of perfume, flowers, and dancing bodies all combined to create a mind-numbing fog. He wondered how the hell *anyone* was expected to find his own wife in this mob.

Then he spotted Nadine in a cluster of giggling debs in white gowns. So Emmy really had convinced the chit to at least dress the part of pure maiden, although he recognized his sister's style in the rows of ruffles and frills. She was blooming, he could see, surrounded by a gaggle of rangy youths and a few scarlet jackets like his own. The minx was likely picking her partners by their bank balances, he thought, but she looked charming, without that discontented expression he was used to seeing on her face.

The major was attracting no small attention himself, standing in the entry in his regimentals, dress sword and all. His brother Geoff soon hailed him from across the hall, and tried to dash between the wedged bodies, nearly upending a fop balancing two cups of punch.

"Ev, it's really you! I couldn't believe m'eyes! I said to Rem here—oh, this is Johnny Remington, Ev. Rem, m'brother Stokely, you know, the hero, Emmy's husband. I said that looks—"

The major was trying to shake an embarrassed-looking youth's hand while still being pounded on the back by his exuberant brother. Geoff was broader than he remembered, and a great deal neater. Likely Butler was tying his neck-cloths for him.

"—best of all things great, I said. The fellows have been dying to meet you, read all about you in the war news, you know. There's McCall and Wister in the card room, unless you want some refreshment first. They set a fine table, lobster patties, you know, and—"

"Hold, cawker. I just got here! I've got to pay my respects to my hostess, and I really think I should like to say

224

hello to my wife." He was looking around, so happily missed Remington's fierce blush.

"You mean you haven't seen Emmy yet? What a shock, ah, surprise you'll be for her. I can't figure how you missed her though. She's right over there."

Geoff gestured to the near corner, where a group of people—no, personages—was given a respectful distance. Stokely instantly recognized Lord Castlereagh, temporarily back from the peace talks, in conversation with a tall man in the uniform of, yes, the Russian forces, dripping gold braid and decorations. Princess Lieven and the Russian ambassador were there, and Sally Jersey. Another man may have been the deputy prime minister, but he could not be sure from the angle. No matter, his eyes skipped on to the next group of partygoers. Geoff laughed. "No, there." He motioned back toward that first, select circle.

The Russian peacock turned—he had to be one of the princes, from the rows of medals—revealing a . . . a what? A dream? A sprite? A small, exquisite, merrily laughing woman, shimmering in a brilliant blue gown that was tied at one shoulder only, with a cloud of curls so light colored it could have been a halo but for the tiara set regally in their midst. Stokely swallowed, hard. Sparrow? It could not be.

The last time he had seen Emilyann she had been a scrawny, scrappy, filthy waif in boys' clothes, then a scrawny, scrubbed, wide-eyed child-bride clutching a bouquet of violets, wearing his nightshirt in that parody of a wedding. The last he'd seen of her, before handing her into the coach and sending her off to Stockton, she'd been a scrawny, shapeless imp in a too-big gown of some nondescript color, lost in her clothes like a little girl playing grown-up. Her faded hair was lopped off in odd angles and lengths so he quickly tied a limp bonnet over it, bringing a twinkle to those blue eyes, the only color in her pale face.

Well, she certainly wasn't scrawny anymore, nor the least bit colorless, and she definitely was not just playing at being grown-up.

"Better shut your mouth, brother, before something flies into it."

225

Stokely did not hear him. He went down the stairs in a daze, crossed the room as if the crowd weren't there, barely nodded to the notables in her circle, bowing slightly in case the Russian was indeed a royal, out of habit only, and as the band struck up for the next interval, said, "I believe this is my dance, Lady Stokely."

Emilyann turned, saw a truly handsome officer—and turned again. "Smoky!" she cried, her smile becoming even more radiant, and started to rush into his arms. Then she remembered herself, the company she kept, and how she wanted to show Smoky how sophisticated she was. So she amended her delighted call to "Stokely," sank into her most graceful curtsy to excuse herself from the gathering, and offered him her hand. He raised it to his lips, still trying to regroup his rattled perceptions, and led her onto the dance floor. His feet thankfully performed the waltz steps, for his mind was not sending directions, too busy absorbing this glorious woman in his arms. The pert nose and dimples were the same but the eyes were a more startling blue; he wondered how anyone could have considered her colorless with that creamy glow to her skin, especially that soft fullness above the gown's low-draped neckline.

His mouth was dry; his throat felt like a hedgehog had taken residence there. All he could think to say, confirming his place with the army and not the diplomatic corps, was "My God, Sparrow, you don't look like a plucked chicken anymore at all!"

Emilyann laughed, that same bubbly gurgle he remembered. She thought she would burst with pride; she thought the orchestra had stopped playing, her heart was beating so loudly. So she stopped dancing, coming to a stumbling halt still in his arms. And he stopped, too. And they just looked at each other for a moment until Smoky laughed, held his arms open, and lifted her right off the ground as she came to his embrace. He twirled her around, miraculously missing the other dancers. "My proper countess," he said, smiling, while she hugged what she could of him. Blushing, she stepped back and they continued the dance. Sally Jersey was seen to dab a tear from her eye, and Princess Lieven nodded knowingly. This certainly removed the last traces of doubt about the marriage. If ever there was a love match, it was this one. Every eye was on them, and Lady Winstoke's ball was a guaranteed smash.

Whose ball? It could have been a Red Indian rain dance around a gamy campfire for all the Stokelys noticed. They waltzed, they smiled, they stared into each other's eyes. Like moon-calves, Smoky decided, finally coming partway back to earth.

"I can't seem to get over the changes in you since I saw you last, and the house, and all—"

"You look different, too. Not as thin."

"Not as castaway and hung over, you mean."

"Somehow you do not seem as tall as I remember. Perhaps I grew."

She certainly had. "You even grew eyelashes."

That laugh. "No, I found a French maid with secrets no lady talks about."

He only half pretended to give her careful scrutiny, turning her around in the dance. "Nothing else looks like artifice to me."

"Well, you'll have plenty of time to discover for yourself."

Gads, he was flirting with Sparrow! "Not long enough, I'm afraid. I have only ten days, with travel. Things are becoming less settled instead of more, and I have to return."

"Oh."

He hated seeing her look down like that, and would do anything to have the dimples restored. "I suppose every man in the room has already told you how perfectly your gown matches the color of your eyes," he teased.

"Do you like it? You'd better, it's named for you. Stokely blue, they call it. Isn't that silly?"

"Especially when my eyes are gray." There, she was smiling again. "And you dance divinely."

"Now, why do you sound so surprised? I think you're just waiting for me to pull a frog out of my pocket or do something else outrageous. I'll have you know that hugging you in public was the most improper thing I have done since I have been in London."

"I should hope so! But you'll have to forgive me, Spar-

227

row, for thinking you are still ten years old. You've had years to grow up, and I seem to be seeing the results all at once."

"And?"

"Are you fishing for compliments now, minx? Very well, I am only sorry I am not home for good."

She was sorry, too, and sorry the waltz was coming to an end. "You dance very well yourself," she said as they walked to the sidelines. "Where did you find opportunity to practice during all the war years?"

He passed it off. "Oh, here and there. Do you think we might collect Nadine and Geoff and leave this crowd? Or we could send the carriage back for them. I can hardly hear myself speak and—"

"Oh, dear, I'm sorry, but I'm promised for the next set."

"Come now, Sparrow, the returning husband does have some precedence." His eyes narrowed. "You can just tell your beau that I have prior claim."

"Not this one," she said, giggling delightfully, and more so when she saw his frown. Meanwhile she was leading him, fully aware that many eyes were focused in their direction, toward a section of gilt chairs near the orchestra. She nodded toward a particularly corpulent gentleman who struggled up from his seat, smiling. Then she looked back at Smoky and winked, before sinking into a deep curtsy and murmuring, "Your Highness, I believe you bespoke this dance?"

Smoky made his bow to the prince regent, and whispered in her ear as he stood aside: "Where did you learn to flirt like that?"

"Oh, here and there," she tossed back over her shoulder with another gamine grin.

Chapter Ten

*H*ow could a deuced ball go on so long, and how could a man who organized the movements of whole battalions, their cannons, cookstoves, and camp-followers, have so much difficulty gathering three youngsters in one place?

They were supposed to meet in the marble hallway after saying their good-byes and collecting their wraps. But Nadine wanted just one more dance with an exquisite in a puce waistcoat, and Geoff was promised to Lady Huntington's niece, a squint-eyed miss who would never find another partner for the quadrille. Then he had to make his particular friends known to Stokely, who was himself drawn into innumerable greetings, belated congratulations on his marriage, and discussions of the Vienna talks and chances of a lasting peace. He found himself committed to calling at Carlton House, Whitehall, and, almost, a certain boudoir of a politically astute widow. Emilyann's cough put a stop to that.

Everyone laughed when he introduced her as Emilyann Arcott and he had to be reminded that she was Lady Stokely. Her glittering eyes told him he'd damn well better not forget again, especially in the presence of dashing widows in dampened gowns who wanted to hang on his arm. He quickly extricated himself from Lady Bramby's efforts to renew acquaintance, seeing Emmy's slippered foot tapping the ground. He was not about to test if her famous temper had undergone the same drastic change as her looks, not in public anyway. He grinned at this new possessiveness of Sparrow's, until more of her admirers kept claiming her company for dances, just when he thought they were

229

ready to call for the carriage. Sauce for the goose, her look told him. He stopped grinning.

"You do not mind, I am sure?"

In a pig's eye he didn't, but he nodded and bowed to the Russian. He did not want to start an international incident.

"My dance, Major." He saluted smartly. He did not wish to return to the army as a private either.

"I, ah, that is, Lady Em promised, I, uh . . ."

A man would have to have a harder heart than Stokely's to refuse that Remington boy, gazing at Sparrow with such moonstruck adoration. So that's what all the blushes were about. He agreed resignedly, and was awarded such a sweet smile from his wife that he vowed to get her home right after this dance, even if Mad King George himself appeared in his nightshirt and asked her for a waltz. He grabbed Nadine lest she skip off again, and joined their set.

When the dance was finished he grimly placed one hand on his wife's elbow and the other on his dress sword. This time no one interfered with their progress toward the door.

Aunt Adelaide woke at all the commotion, and the servants darted about, hoping for a glimpse of the master. Soon they were snug in the new Egyptian salon, where cool black and white upholstery complimented the old black marble mantel. Only two chairs had crocodile heads for armrests, he was relieved to note, and the rest were comfortable, normal furniture. Stokely lounged at ease near the fire, his feet up on a footstool, with a glass of fine cognac in his hand, put down, he was assured by his wife, before the French conflict.

"I claimed these bottles from Arcott Hall when I went to fetch Mama's jewelry, as part of my personal effects that were untouched by the entailment, before Uncle could swill them all down. For you must know I would not support the French by buying smuggled wines, not while you were fighting against them."

"Emmy's so loyal," Nadine told him, "she wouldn't even let us buy French laces, there being no way to know if they came in under the blockade. That's why we were so delighted with the trims you sent from Brussels. You should

230

see the divine ensemble I've contrived. It's white, of course, but I wore it to—"

Nadine babbled on, mostly to Aunt Adelaide, who kept her hartshorn nearby, for the excitement of his homecoming, while Geoff tried to get his attention on the Northampshire property and the hogs. Emilyann sat quietly, letting the others talk, seeing that the teacups were filled, the biscuits passed.

Stokely leaned back. How cozy this was. Here he thought he had to return to ride herd on a pack of unruly children, but now he began to think there were a lot more benefits to this being a family man than he had considered. It might take some getting used to, having a wife and all, but as he looked at her again, it seemed much less of another burdensome responsibility and a lot more like a dashed fine idea.

"Yes," he told Geoff, "I was hoping we could all get up there for a time during my leave. Invite Thornton, look over the new plantings, and decide on the next improvements." And get to know my wife, away from this blasted fish bowl, he thought.

"Capital! When do you think we can go? I'll write to Meecham to inform the household staff, and see if we can't get up a hunt for the weekend or—"

"Not so fast, bantling. I have an appointment with the regent and his advisers tomorrow, though what they think I can tell them about the current situation is beyond me. I promised to call on the Home Secretary this week, and of course I must check with the War Office to see if they have any news, or commissions for me. Perhaps early next week . . ."

Nadine was looking mutinous, but it was Emilyann who said, "Oh dear, I am afraid we cannot leave town then. That's when our ball is planned, and the cards are already sent."

"What ball is that, Sparrow?" Stokely asked quietly. "I thought we agreed that there should be no come-out ball for Nadine until I was home?" And until he could afford to provide for his own sister without Emilyann's money.

"Of course we agreed, Smoky." She couldn't help add in all honesty, "That is, you issued a decree and I acknowledged it. That's why this is not a formal presentation. We had a small dinner following the queen's court, with just a few select friends, and a little dancing after, for you must know Nadine could not go out in company without some bow to the ton. But that wasn't a ball. Why, there were less than two hundred people there."

He blinked. "Strange, it sounds just like a ball to me."

"Not compared to this one," she said, laughing. "But Nadine's name is not even on the invitations, so don't get in a fidge. It was just time for us to repay all the hospitality we've been shown. It wouldn't be polite otherwise."

"I did not doubt for a minute there was a good reason for it."

She flashed her dimples and told him that sarcasm was not becoming. Plus he would enjoy it immensely, and how proud she would be to have him stand in the receiving line with her. Nadine chimed in about her new dress and the spectacular decorations, and Aunt Adelaide noted how much more fitting it was, having the master of the house host his own ball. "Not that Geoffrey is not an adequate substitute, of course," she added. "We do depend on him for everything, you know."

Stokely's eyes narrowed. Just how much substituting had his young brother been doing? The boy had turned into a good-looking young man, and he and Emilyann had always been close. Now this year, rebuilding the farms, coming to London, entering society, they were thrown even closer together. . . . Maybe Aunt Adelaide was trying to warn him about something. Every other man seemed to have laid his heart at Sparrow's feet, why not Geoff?

Then, "Hell and damnation, Emmy," Geoff said. "Why do we have to have another blasted party just now that Ev is home?"

"You mind your tongue, Geoffrey Stockton," she scolded. "I will not have such language in my drawing room. And we have to have this ball, you gudgeon, especially now, so Smoky can see that *some* of us can behave like ladies and gentlemen."

"You've been hanging around your aunt Ingrid again."

So they were still squabbling like brother and sister. That was all right, then.

"... have a good idea, though, Geoff. Why don't you and Smoky go up to Stockton as soon as he is free? You can make better time without us and all the baggage we would need, and you'd only be in the way here anyhow. There is all the cleaning to see to, and the caterers will be in and out, and the florists and the extra staff. As long as you promise you'll show him the stud farm, and get back in plenty of time for the ball, that is."

Geoff thought it a great notion, "Capital," of course, and urged Stokely to consider it. Even Nadine and Aunt Adelaide were in favor, likely so he could not veto any of the expenditures. It would mean being away from Emilyann for most of his leave time, though, and didn't she seem a bit overeager to get rid of him? In fact, now that he noticed, she seemed nervous, anxious over his decision, then relieved when he said that he might go, pending the outcome of his meetings. Jupiter, he had to get a hold on himself. First his own brother, now these nameless suspicions. Incredibly, he was jealous. It was totally without foundation, he knew, except that any man would find her irresistible, particularly sitting curled in the chair with her slippers off and her stockinged toes peeking out. There was only one way to slay the green-eyed monster, he decided, and that was to make her his once and for all. He'd end this nonsense, and this new yearning, this very night. He yawned mightily and loudly.

Be careful of what you wish, Nanny had always said. You might get it. A confused Emilyann understood the old saying better now. She had wanted Smoky home and proud of her. Here he was, cutting up her peace, criticizing her actions, and already making plans to institute changes. The family and the servants alike instantly deferred to him, and even her own maid was casting coy glances at Emilyann as she neatened up the room. Em dismissed her, to stand in front of the fireplace, pretending to fuss with the logs, but really just staring at the flames.

She had wanted him to see her as a mature, sophisticated

233

woman, and that part of the wish had come true also, judging from *that* look, which she was quick enough to recognize after her months on the town. When a man's eyes rolled and his breath came quicker, he was more liable to make an improper offer than call for a restorative. Smoky's offer could not be improper, of course, since they were married, after all, but admiration based on what Aunt Ingrid would call lust was not what she wanted from him. It couldn't be any foundation for a solid relationship, especially when she felt no inclination whatsoever to pursue her marital duties, especially as her aunt described them, and certainly not with a virtual stranger. In some ways he was her beloved Smoky; in others she hardly knew this tall officer with the commanding presence. No matter what, he was an experienced man of the world. She could never please him anyway. Not like a Lady Bramby, she thought, angrily poking a recalcitrant log back into the grate. Well, he was tired tonight and he was traveling with Geoff soon, and— No, she wouldn't be in a hurry to make any more wishes. She jabbed the logs again.

"Ahem. Is it safe for me to enter? I knocked, but you did not answer."

There he was, standing at the connecting door of their rooms, looking even more devastatingly handsome in a paisley dressing gown, open at the neck to show dark curls on a broad chest. She wouldn't look. "Smoky? What are you doing here?"

"I live here, remember?" He smiled in amusement.

"I don't think so."

"Would you care to put the weapon down and explain that?"

She blushed, and he caught his breath seeing where the blush started at the neckline of her nightgown, a flimsy pale blue affair that already had his blood racing. When she moved to put the metal poker back in its stand, the fire silhouetted her outline through the sheer fabric. He took another deep breath. His eyes shifted toward the bed, done up in gold and navy, complimenting his room's color scheme, except for—"What's that on the bed?"

Emilyann laughed, relieved to have a distraction from his

overwhelming proximity, even at the other side of the room. She moved farther away, toward the bed, almost furtively. "Oh, that's Pug. I wrote you about the puppy I bought to keep Nanny company, remember? She didn't care for him somehow. There's no accounting for taste, I guess. And he's such a cute little fellow, I let him stay in here. I couldn't bring any of the hounds to town of course, but he's the perfect companion for the city." She petted the little dog, who snorted in pleasure and tried to wag what tail he had. Instead, his whole rear end wriggled. "Of course Pug is not a very good name," she went on, knowing she was babbling and unable to stop, "but Nanny called him that, and Geoff only wants to call him Piglet. The hogs are the only thing on his mind sometimes and—"

Why was she so nervous, he wondered, coming to get a closer look at the pup, and her bare shoulders. "What do you mean, I don't live here?" He sat down on the other side of her bed.

Her bed! She shivered. "Well, you are not staying and you said we needn't, that is, not until you were home for good." She got very busy, checking the buckle on Pug's collar.

So that was it. He let it pass for now. "And we also said that you would love, honor, and obey me. I believe those were the exact words?"

"You're not still angry about the ball, are you?"

"Not precisely angry, more perturbed. I didn't want you spending so much money, you know."

Thankful for the change of topic, she looked him in the eye and said, "But it's my money, Smoky, and I am having a wonderful time with it. There's lots more left and I have some new ideas about investments. You did say I might manage my own finances for now, remember? You signed all the papers."

"And you agreed to keep the investment in Stockton to a minimum, so I could hope to repay it eventually."

"Pooh. The farms are already repaying the outlay for equipment. We shall recoup the other expenses soon enough. It would be very wrong of you to insist on controlling how I use my money, just because you have the legal right, when you are not here to help make the decisions."

"I'm not an ogre, Sparrow. I wouldn't insist on any of my rights, you know."

They both knew he wasn't talking about the money. "Thank you. I just, that is, I, ah . . ." She rubbed Pug's velvety ears.

"You're afraid, Emilyann Arcott, and you may as well admit it."

She stamped her foot. "I am not! It's just that I don't know you very well and—"

She was frightened—of him! None but an untouched maid would be as jittery as an unbroke colt. He felt like whistling! Never had he been so happy over another's fear, and how could he ever have doubted her? She was as true as an arrow, as solid as a rock, and his. He rolled over on his back, grinning, cushioning his head on his crossed arms. "I never thought I would live to see the day. Used to be you would follow me anywhere, into caves with bats and spiders and snakes, up to the attics to search for ghosts."

"Smoky, I am not that little girl anymore!"

"I wouldn't be here if you were! No, now you're a worldly sophisticate, quaking in your boots"—he glanced over—"no, in your satin slippers, to think of your husband's attentions."

"Don't you laugh at me, Smoky. This isn't like exploring spooky old places. I just think we need more time, to get to know each other."

"I'm not laughing at you, poppet. I'm laughing at myself for being an egotistical fool. Here I was congratulating myself that my little wife had turned out to be a beautiful, desirable woman who would fall into my arms at my first appearance." He reached out and took her hand, tugging her to sit down on the bed next to him. "Life is never so easy, and I am sorry for frightening you, or taking you for granted."

He was also sorry for losing something he never treasured enough. He was, however, a British soldier, and the British hadn't surrendered yet. Major Lord Stokely would just have to woo his own wife.

"You are beautiful, you know," he told her, stroking her hand lightly.

"Fudge. I just have style. People are inclined to think me something special because they like to approve of wealthy countesses."

And still unspoiled. So much for winning through flattery. "It's growing colder. I don't suppose you'd care to continue this discussion under the covers?"

"Smoky, you said!" She snatched her hand back and jumped up, breasts heaving.

His sigh was not entirely feigned. "Well then, what about a good-night kiss?" Who knew where that could lead?

She shook her head, smiling. Damn if the chit wasn't up to snuff after all. "No? What if I said Mr. Butler advised it? I understand you listen to him."

She grinned, stuck her little nose in the air, and solemnly parodied: "I regret, my lady, that it would not be in our best interests."

"It's been a very long day." He got up, reluctantly conceding for now. It was going to be a long night, too. "We shall continue this discussion tomorrow, Sparrow, you may be sure of that." And he went through the door, turning once to fix the image of his lovely bride sharing that enormous bed with a silly, wrinkle-faced puppy—when she could have had him. She was right, there was just no accounting for tastes.

Lady Emilyann, Countess Stokely, had wished her disturbing, amusing, aggravating husband would go to his own chambers. Now she clutched the little black-faced dog tightly, undecided if she felt like laughing or crying. She did a little of both. Another wish had been granted.

Chapter Eleven

In another bedroom, in another part of town, after news of Stokely's return had filtered down through the greater and lesser haunts of social London, another husband entered his wife's bedchamber.

"Morgan, is that you?"

It was three o'clock in the morning. Who the bloody hell did she think it was?

He raised his shielded candle. The shadows parted to reveal statues of martyred saints bleeding stone tears. Maybe Ingrid was expecting St. Peter. She lay rigid on the bed like the lid of a sarcophagus, flannel gown buttoned to her chin. Sure as hell wasn't waiting for young Lochinvar.

"It's terribly late. Did you want to . . . ?"

Not by half, he didn't, not in view of the reproachful saints. "No, no. Sorry I disturbed you. Go back to sleep." He looked around again. No, not even a pound note left out to tempt a burglar. His wife's evening devotions were well-established: mirror, safe, prie-dieu. Heaven alone knew the combinations.

"What's that you've got, Morgan?"

"This? Oh, it's just a pillow. I, ah, thought you've been looking peaked lately. Fellows at the club recommend elevation, uh, that's it. Raise your head so blood don't pool on your brain. I can see you've plenty of others there, if you need, so I'll just toddle on."

"How thoughtful. Are you sure you wouldn't . . . ?"

If he couldn't hold a blasted pillow over her head while she was awake and staring at him from those gimlet eyes, he damned sure couldn't do *that* either. He left.

Chapter Twelve

Stokely was minded to pursue the discussion with his wife. Actually, he meant to discuss the pursuit of his wife, with seduction in mind. Lady Stokely was equally as resolved to avoid the assault on her senses and defenses.

The heavy artillery was on Stokely's side. He was the master tactician, the wily campaigner, and, if not a practiced seducer, at least a veteran of the boudoir battles. Women might not find him irresistible, but they did a fine job of pretending. Emilyann, on the other hand, was practically a Johnny-raw at this type of heart-to-heart combat, and predisposed to hero-worship her adversary anyway. She did have her indignation for armor, however: if he wanted to be her husband so badly, he could sell out and stay home. Otherwise, well, she was managing very nicely without him, thank you.

Smoky was rolled up, horse, gun, and saddle. Outclassed, outmaneuvered, and out in the cold.

"A bachelor party, Geoff? That will last all night? I'm sure Smoky would love to go with you."

"That's just capital, Ev. I told Old Chadwick you'd stand buff. He wanted all the fellow benedicts he could find."

Stokely started to demur, but his wife generously thought he should have the fun of a night on the town after so many months away. "I intend to make an early evening of it anyway, after all the excitement yesterday." She yawned delicately.

"I thought I would stay in tonight, actually," the major ventured. "I'm a bit done in myself."

"Oh, in that case I'll have to invite Aunt Ingrid over. You know she is looking forward to seeing you again."

This was after a day cooling his heels outside government offices, and fruitless speculations inside them about the chances of war breaking out again. Then there was dinner with his brother Thornton and his wife. At least Thorny was still the same top-lofty, sanctimonious prig. No surprises there. But an evening with Ingrid before he could get his wife alone? He surrendered, and raised his coffee cup in a toast to superior forces. There might be time for a cozy chat before breakfast anyway, if he could ditch little brother. The image of Emilyann at daybreak, warm and rosy with sleep, would cheer him through the night.

Unfortunately he and Geoff were set upon by Mohunks outside the club where the party was being held. There were only four of the footpads, so Stokely could not work off all of his frustrations, just enough to impress his brother past belief, and leave Stokely himself in no condition to grace his wife's bedchamber.

The next day he had to call on his banker, his tailor, and a crippled officer cashiered home. He also had to converse with the magistrates concerning his strewing the city streets with injured bodies. He was not amused, on returning home, to find that his wife was riding in the park with some French émigré aristocrat, prior to dinner and a musical evening at the home of one of Nadine's fellow debutantes. They couldn't miss the occasion, Emilyann regretted, because his sister was scheduled to perform.

"It is already listed on the program. Nadine showed me, and she was so proud. She's been practicing her piece for weeks, you know, and I cannot disappoint her. I'm sure you have much more interesting things to do, for I don't expect you to accompany us to these dreary affairs, nor will I hang on your sleeve. Married couples don't need to live in each other's pockets, you know."

He also knew that those musicales never lasted long, there being a limit to what even the most doting mama's ears could take. So he visited a few of his clubs, then went over some papers in the library until he heard Mr. Butler welcome the ladies home. He clocked an hour after hearing Emilyann's cheerful good-nights before he, too, went upstairs. He donned his robe and gathered the bottle of wine

240

and two glasses he had set out earlier, and tapped on her door.

"Come in," she called ever so sweetly.

His heart doing a fandango in his chest, he pushed through the door. Emilyann was sitting up in bed in that same sheer blue gown, her lovely shoulders bare—and brown glop slathered all over her face!

"It's for my complexion. I told you my maid knew a lot of secrets."

She was gone by the time he came down for breakfast the following morning, on a myriad of errands, her note said, getting ready for their party. They were promised to the Seftons' ball that evening and it wouldn't do to offend such an influential hostess, but Emilyann would be pleased with his escort if he cared to go.

At least Stokely got to dance with his wife. Twice. Then he got to watch every puppy in London drool over her hand, and every rake and Redcoat, every silver-tongued park-saunterer, try to turn her up sweet. And she laughed up at them, and twinkled her blue eyes and floated in their arms like a rose in the breeze—until Stokely went on the offensive.

"Ah, Lady Bramby, how nice to see you."

See her? You could see *all* of her, Emmy raged, her gown was so transparent. And her cheeks were rouged, and her toenails were painted, and "I'm very tired, Smoky, would you mind terribly if we went home?"

He did not mind at all, delighted with his strategy—until his lady wife pretended to fall asleep in the carriage. His hand, under cover of the lap robe, inched up her thigh, but the minx whimpered drowsily and curled up in her corner of the seat, all snuggled in her cape. Outflanked again!

One more day before he left for Stockton, and Emilyann agreed to a drive in the park.

"What, no excuses, appointments, prior engagements?"

Lady Bramby wouldn't be busy either, not for the most handsome man in London. In addition to being out of evasive maneuvers, Emilyann felt she deserved Smoky's company, with all the subterfuge she'd been through. After all, it was daytime and she would be safe. Excepting, of course,

241

the runaway carriage that thundered down on them after they got out to stroll along the track. They heard the shouts and cries, the neighs of frightened horses, and then there was no time to think. Smoky shoved her off the walkway and turned. Emilyann scrambled up to see him standing in the path of four frantic horses and a heavy carriage careening behind it. She screamed just as Stokely leapt for the back of the nearest leader and reached down for the fallen traces.

Aunt Adelaide was so upset by the tales of the day's events that Emilyann decided she better sit up with her that night, in Aunt Adelaide's room, of course. Of course.

Stokely left for Northamphshire with his brother in the morning, but he was not going to be good company.

The trip to Stockton was uneventful, if you discounted the wheel coming off the carriage. Geoff was thrown clear as the coach tipped, luckily onto a grassy verge. Stokely, who was driving, managed to grab the seat rail with his left hand and hang on to the reins with his right, pulling back with all his force to halt the plunging horses.

White-faced, he came back to find his batman Rigg stumbling out of the carriage. "Knocked me head over horsefeathers, sir, but nothing's broke. I'll survive."

Geoff was dusting off his buckskins when Stokely reached him. "I'm beginning to think civilian life is not as dull as it's cracked up to be," Smoky told him, using his handkerchief to dab at a trickle of blood on his brother's forehead. "Footpads, runaway horses, flying coachwheels. The front was never this dangerous."

"And you ain't even been to Almack's yet. At least you don't need to worry about getting into the Four-in-Hand Club when you get back. I never saw driving like that! Wait'll I tell old Rem."

"I, ah, don't think we'll mention this around town, Geoff. Wouldn't want to upset the ladies, you know."

"Lord, after the dust-up yesterday, I can't blame you. Still . . ."

The two brothers rode bareback to the nearest inn on the coach horses, leaving Rigg with the carriage while they fetched help. Later, when the carriage was righted, the wheel restored, fresh horses put back in the traces, Rigg took the major aside.

"Found this when I was walking around a bit, sir," he said, holding out a beefy hand with a bent piece of metal on the palm. "Linchpin from the wheel, Major."

Bent was to be expected, fresh file marks on the ends were not. Stokely rubbed the old scar on his chin. "Remind me to hire some new grooms when we get home," he told the other man quietly, outside Geoff's hearing. "I'm sure you can find a few of the lads from the old battalion in need of a position."

"Yessir, men that can keep their eyes open."

"And their mouths shut."

"Beggin' your pardon, Major, but it wouldn't be a devil's divorce, would it?" The grizzled little soldier had never gotten over the ragged stableboy who married his master. The chit had come on a piece, true, but a body never could trust a woman, much less one in britches.

The furrow on Stokely's brow smoothed, and he laughed a rich, hearty laugh. "You mean Sparrow? She was with me yesterday in the park, for one thing, and she doesn't hate me enough, for another. She mightn't be content on a short lead, but I pray it is nothing as personal as this. Then again, if I did happen to incur my lady's displeasure, her style leans more toward putting a bullet between my eyes. No, Sparrow would never resort to something underhanded like this." He laughed again.

The bewhiskered batman just grunted. Women, bah!

Nothing much happened in London while the Earl of Stokely was away, except his wife realized how much she missed him, and how foolish she had been to deny herself his company. She went about her duties getting ready for the ball, but kept seeing his gray eyes laughing, his mouth quirked up in a smile at her. Her knees still threatened to give out when she recalled him jumping in front of those galloping horses—and the quick kiss he had given her after.

She consulted with the chef, she stood for another endless fitting for her dress, and she counted the days till his return. Oh, yes, and the wheel came off her phaeton.

Luckily Nadine had gone with Aunt Adelaide to match some ribbons while Emilyann conferred with Gunther's again, reconfirming her order of ices. Luckily a vegetable cart was delaying traffic, so she was driving at less than her usual up-to-the-bits pace. One moment she was perched daintily on her seat, the next she was sprawled on the pavement, but with the reins still in hand. Her man Jake, riding behind as groom, shouted a commanding "Whoa," and the lovely grays pulled up instantly before Emilyann could be dragged beneath the coach. Her horses were high-bred, fast, and showy, but steady as bricks, well-mannered, and schooled to the inch. She wouldn't raise them any other way; Jake wouldn't let her drive any he hadn't trained. None of those high-strung, unreliable prads for Lady Em, who hugged each of her matched grays and told them what dears they were. Her knees were scraped, her gown was ripped at one sleeve, and her bonnet was missing altogether. Perhaps she would visit Gunther's tomorrow.

"Oh, and Jake, there is no reason to mention this back at home. Aunt Adelaide would have conniptions, you know, and Smoky would . . ."

Jake already knew the master's opinion of the phaeton, thank you. He didn't allow as he needed his ears warmed again. Not that any of it was his fault, mind. Jake misdoubted even the earl could have sweet-talked Lady Em into a ladylike chaise, and he *had* convinced her that a red and gold racing curricle was too flashy. As for this accident . . .

Jake left a street urchin to hold the horses while he and Emilyann went to see the damage. The wheel was in perfect condition. The shaft was fine. The linchpin was missing altogether.

"I think we'll hire a few more grooms, Jake. You know, for the party and all the coaches there will be in the street."

Jake allowed as how that sounded like a fine idea to him. He knew a few likely chaps from the Black Dog Inn. So what if they did not know a horse's hock from his hindquarters, they were handy with their fives.

Then Lady Stokely whirled around. "But where is Pug? My goodness, I forgot all about—" She flew to the tiny, still figure at the curb. "Jake, do something!"

Two days after Stokely's return from the country there were more grooms than horses in the stable behind the house. They had to draw straws to see who would wear the livery until more could be delivered. Jake scratched his head and kept mum. After a go-around between the military types and the locals, he sent some of the latter out as groundskeepers with instructions not to set foot on the grounds, not knowing Aunt Adelaide's roses from rutabagas. What they kept was watch on every entrance to the house. The tack gleamed, the stalls were swept thrice a day, and no one came or went without Jake knowing about it. And Pug had round-the-clock nursing.

Chapter Thirteen

"*I* thought that with the ball tomorrow, and you so recently back from the country, we might stay in and have a quiet night tonight."

Stokely would have given his right arm and his favorite horse to hear those words from his adorable wife, looking fetching in a low-cut, high-waisted gown of emerald lutestring. She was trying to sound so blasé, propositioning her husband in front of his family at afternoon tea, with her lower lip caught between her teeth in an effort to hold back her blushes.

"I'm sorry, my dear," and he prayed no one knew how sorry, "but Geoff and I have other plans this evening."

"You what?" The teapot was set down with a resounding thud. Emilyann had been composing that speech for days, rehearsing to find a middle ground between friendship and fast talk. She did not want to sound overeager; Smoky was already too full of his own consequence and she was not ready to back down completely, just make a few concessions. There could not be much danger in kissing one's own husband, she had concluded, deciding to become available for that long-delayed discussion. And he had other plans?

"Sorry, but you've been so busy, and I thought you would want us out from underfoot. . . ."

She had almost laid her heart at his feet and now he was about to walk over it, likely on the way to some light-skirt's door. The tea in Emilyann's cup could have turned to ice from the chill in her voice: "I shan't wait up."

"I did not expect it, my dear," he said, leaving in a hurry.

"Whew," Geoff said once they were out on the street, "I knew you were a brave man, but that was close. I don't mind telling you, Emmy on her uppers ain't a comfortable thing. Best of good fellows generally, for a female, of course, but when she gets her wind up . . . Did you see Nadine cram that last almond cake in her mouth and race Aunt Adelaide for the stairs? Emmy didn't seem to like our shabbing off like that."

"You just have to know how to handle her."

Geoff grinned. "Like bolting? 'Sides, I don't see you handling her at all. Ain't my business, of course. . . ."

"No, it's not."

His irrepressible brother just grinned wider. "Well, can you at least tell me what this is all about, and where we are going? If I'm to be in Emmy's black books, I deserve to know why."

Stokely threw his arm around Geoff's shoulder and told him, "We are going sight-seeing, my lad. Big brother is going to show you a side of London you've never visited, I pray. And if you ever go back without me, being on Sparrow's bad side would look like heaven compared to what I'll do to you."

They started in the clubs, and proceeded through the gaming hells, to the dives, to the alehouses of the slums, to the stews. Always Stokely asked a few questions, put a few coins on a counter, and sat at a table for a few minutes, nursing a glass or a mug or a bottle. Sometimes a man would come whisper a name or two, for another coin. Other times a woman would come, asking a different question, in hopes of earning Stokely's favor. He sent the women away with a smile and a coin, more often than not. It was information he was after, nothing else. Someone had hired those thugs who attacked him and Geoff on the street, someone had rigged his carriage to crash, and that same someone had likely whipped a team of frenzied horses in his direction in the park. He wanted to know who that someone was, and soon, before he had to return to the Continent, leaving his family open to more attacks.

" 'Pon rep," Geoff commented as he took a breath of fresh air outside one foul ken, "we're lucky to get out with our skins."

Stokely smiled. "We were in no danger. I used to spend a lot of time here and there when I was supposed to be at school and later, after I signed up but before I was sent to the Peninsula, and then on leaves. I got to know a lot of people in the army, too. That barkeep with one eye, Corcoran, was with us at Valdoz, and the beggar outside that last tavern."

"You're at home to a shade here," Geoff said a little enviously. "It's a wonder you ever left. I mean, you didn't have to go in the army, being the heir and all."

"What, should I have stayed and been like our father, becoming another old reprobate living beyond his means, draining the estate for his own pleasure? If I stayed here, I would have, too. Gaming, women, drink. It would have been too easy for me to fall into that trap. Then where would you and Nadine be, or the lands? I didn't have Emmy to go bail for me like you did. No, she didn't tell me, Butler did. Not all the details; I suppose he couldn't hear everything through the keyholes."

"Pompous old busybody," Geoff muttered, but Stokely was not listening.

"I don't know," he reflected, "maybe I did have Sparrow then, I just didn't realize it."

He did not have the name he wanted either. He had some

leads for his night's efforts, and people on the lookout for him, but no proof and not enough to make up for what he was missing: an evening with Sparrow in neither a teasing nor bashful mood, but possibly willing to talk. He would not hope for more, now, just the warm, willing woman he knew she could be. And tomorrow was that blasted ball.

The ball was the culmination of Lady Stokely's season, proof of her stature as a lady of quality. It was a grand affair, with half the ton present, admiring her, her home, her ability to organize a function this size. She was one of those popular hostesses whose invitations people craved, and best of all, Smoky would be there to see it.

Pride, that was what it was, and let Aunt Ingrid say a prayer for her if it was such a sin. Emilyann knew her house was in order, flower-decked and spotless, refreshments lavish, servants well trained. Her guests could have no complaints.

She herself was in looks, in a new gown of blue satin with a silver net overskirt. Every male guest had told her, if she hadn't read it in Smoky's eyes before they stood to make the receiving line. And how splendid he looked standing next to her, for once out of uniform in a coat of dark blue superfine stretched perfectly across wide shoulders, and black satin knee breeches enclosing muscular thighs. His weathered tan and the bit of gray at his temples made him seem even more distinguished than the pale, pomaded fops who passed for gentlemen of the ton. Geoff on her other side was saying just what he ought to each of the young debs who tried to catch his eye as they passed through the line. Emmy only had to grip his hand twice before he disordered the starched cravat over which Mr. Butler had labored so lovingly. Nadine was charming tonight, too. She would never be a tongue-tied miss, and she was sparkling in her tiered gown of white lace, which still fit, remarkably, after all the nervous eating she had done this week in anticipation of the event. Lady Stokely's heart nearly burst with the glory of it all, her wonderful family, her delighted friends, her magnificent hero-husband. Let Aunt Ingrid say *two* prayers.

248

Smoky led her out for the first dance. "My countess," he said with pride matching her own, kissing her wrist. "I hereby demand all your waltzes and the supper dance, no matter who else asks. I don't care if it's the prince or the tsar or Bonaparte in person. Actually, I'd like to have a few words with that chap myself, so if you find him hanging about your skirts . . . No, not even him. The waltzes belong to me."

His eyes told her more, that *she* belonged to him. Blushing at her own thoughts, and his knowing smile in return, she nodded. Her enjoyment of the night was complete now, and she could just as happily have retired from society altogether, returned to the country to raise pigs and pugs (and maybe little gray-eyed tykes). Of course there was Nadine to settle, and Smoky still hadn't resigned his commission, but she had hopes of talking him 'round. But tonight, ah, tonight Lady Emilyann would twirl in her husband's arms. In the waltz, of course.

The only note to mar her contentment of that first dance came when Stokely asked: "What the devil is Aylesbury doing here?"

"Aunt Ingrid has been very kind to us. Did you notice she is out of black for once, in honor of our ball?"

"Yes, instead of wearing black buttoned to the neck, she is wearing gray buttoned to the neck. At least she is not preaching to the company."

Emmy teased: "No, that's the entertainment for during supper."

"All well and good, my girl, but what about Morgan? You know I told you to have nothing to do with him."

"Yes, but he is my uncle, after all. I couldn't very well not invite him without setting people to talk, or upsetting Aunt Ingrid."

"He's a rum touch and she knows it as well as you do. I don't want him near you, especially now."

"Why now?" she wanted to know.

Perhaps it was concern which made Smoky revert to Major Stokely. The officer in him was not used to being questioned, or having his orders disobeyed. "Because I say so, that's why."

Hmm, Emilyann reconsidered. Maybe just pigs and pugs.

Their second dance was not quite as enjoyable. Emilyann had received congratulations from the Almack's hostesses, adulation from her usual coterie, a pinch from the regent, who stopped in for a moment, marking her party a true success, and censure from her husband.

"What do you mean letting that chaw-bacon cousin of yours hang around my sister?" he asked, taking her in his arms for what should have been a delightful experience.

"What do you mean 'letting'? That's why we came to London in the first place."

"Then why did I find her in the refreshment room helping Bobo stuff lobster patties into his pockets?"

"At least it's better than the silverware. And I gave Mr. Butler strict orders that Bobo is not to go into the cloak room, so you needn't worry about him going through the guests' coat pockets for loose change."

"Egad, I only have to worry about him stealing away my sister. Whatever were you thinking about? Next you're going to tell me you had to invite him, too."

"No, Nadine did," she shot back, eyes flashing, giving up the pretense of a smile for the attentive watchers on the sidelines. "Why do you not take her to task, my lord?"

"Because you said you could watch out for her, my lady."

"I am. That's what this whole ball is about, finding her eligible men to choose from."

"Well, he ain't one of them, madam, your cousin or no."

Emilyann vowed to strangle the wretched girl right after this dance. Meantime, she had a bone to pick herself. "May I ask what you were doing in the refreshment room, Stokely? I haven't seen you in the ballroom since the quadrille you had with Nadine. Perhaps you think that's suitable behavior for a host, but I do not. I am sure Sally Jersey expects you to pay her court, and little Miss Whitlaw hasn't had a dance yet except for Geoff. I don't like wallflowers at my party."

"Oh, but it is *your* party, madam. I could not have sprung for a third of the champagne you have flowing like water. Besides, I have more important things to consider than the Jersey's ego or Miss Whitlaw's stammer. General Fanshawe is here, and he has reports that Napoleon's army is regrouping, and the Corsican will be breaking out of exile any day."

"I don't see why you don't just sell out and be done with it. All this stupid talk."

"Yes, I know. At your ball." The music ended, he bowed, clicked his heels, and walked away.

Lady Stokely was not proud of that exchange.

By the supper dance Stokely was quietly distracted. More reports had come in with guests from the War Office.

Emilyann was not-so-quietly furious. "I just had a conversation with Squire Kimball," she hissed as they took their place on the floor.

"What's that? Oh, yes, very nice of you to invite him and the missus up from the country. I had a chat with him myself, earlier."

Emilyann stepped on his toe, not entirely an accident. At least that got his attention. "I know," she went on. "And you told him you had no wish to purchase that lower acreage, where the orchards used to be."

"That's right, I don't."

"But I do," she ground out, putting her foot in quite the wrong place again.

Stokely came to a stop, looked down at her through narrowed eyes, and said, "If you make a scene here, Emilyann Arcott, so help me I'll put you over my knee."

"I think you have forgotten again, my lord. That is Emilyann *Stockton*, not some little child. And it is not myself who is causing the difficulty." She gestured to the other couples who were nearly tripping in their efforts to avoid bumping into them.

He took her hand again, she winced, and they resumed the waltz. "We shall speak of this later."

They certainly did not speak during supper. The wines were excellent, the food superb, the conversation nil, until dessert. Stokely turned to her and said, "Since you are al-

251

ready in such a taking, I may as well tell you that I fired that man Gannon you hired as gameskeeper at Stockton."

"You fired Gannon?"

"At least we know you hear me when I say things. I was beginning to wonder, my dear. I did tell you the man was a lazy good-for-nothing drunk. And you hired him anyway."

"I thought he would be good for the job." She actually thought he would be too incompetent to harm her precious foxes.

"There are no pheasants, no grouse, and almost no chickens left at the tenants' farms."

"I'll bet there are fewer rodents, too."

"And more hungry cats going after the birds." He offered her a dish of syllabub. "It looks delicious. . . . I hired Hebert."

"What? That man is a . . . a trapper!" She couldn't think of anything worse.

Stokely took a spoonful of his dessert. "And I told Squire to organize a series of hunts. In the home woods."

The syllabub did not look as good in his lap.

Chapter Fourteen

*W*hen Stokely returned downstairs from changing his clothes, he happened to notice the Duke of Aylesbury, his unloved uncle-in-law, look over his shoulder in either direction, then enter the library. The library's door was closed, which should have informed guests that the room was not open to the public. Stokely reached for the sword that should have been at his hip. "Damn," he muttered, and moved quietly down the hall.

By the time the earl softly pushed the door aside, Morgan was standing near the mantel, examining the decanters lined up on a small side table there. He jumped when Stokely cleared his throat, and put his hands in his pockets.

"Ah, it's you, nevvy. Just came to, uh, blow a cloud."

Stokely noticed one of the cut-glass stoppers was out of its bottle. "And have a glass in private? What, is Aunt Ingrid keeping a watch in the refreshment parlor?"

"No, no. Not at all. Just wanted a little quiet. Balls ain't in my line, you know."

"I'm surprised you came, then. No matter, now that you are here, perhaps you'd care to take a glass with me."

"Honored I'm sure, but no thank you. Got to get back to the wife."

Stokely's eyes narrowed. "But I insist," he said, pouring two glasses from the opened bottle. "After all, I do not believe you have ever drunk to my marriage."

Oh, but Morgan had, bottles and bottles. Not exactly *to* the marriage, but certainly on its account. He had no wish to do so tonight, however. "Sorry, lad, my, ah, stomach has been bothering me."

"Brandy is just the thing to settle it, then." Morgan found himself in a leather chair, a glass in his hand, and his very large, very serious nephew-in-law sitting across from him. He shrugged. "To you and Emilyann." The men clinked their glasses together and raised them to their lips. Stokely's glass was empty. The level of Morgan's drink had hardly changed.

"Come now," said the earl, refilling his own glass and noting Aylesbury's eyes glitter. "You can do better than that. Another toast. To the family." He emptied his glass again, after touching it to the duke's, but Morgan's hand seemed to shake, and the liquor spilled out.

"How clumsy of me."

"Yes, wasn't it?" Stokely's voice was smooth, satisfied. "I begin to think you do not like my taste in wine. That could be construed as an insult to my hospitality, you know. I am almost tempted to take offense and call you out."

"Not at all, not at all. Merely an accident." Morgan made to rise, but a hand shot out and gripped his arm in an iron-hard clasp. Morgan looked down to see wine dripping from

253

Stokely's sleeve, where the earl had been pouring it. Morgan slumped back in his chair.

"Exactly." Stokely carefully wiped his hand with his handkerchief. "I find it strange how many of these 'accidents' there have been lately, don't you? Especially when I wrote to you once concerning my wife's welfare. Forgive my immodesty, but I consider my own continued existence also necessary to her well-being." He paused to contemplate the ruined cuff of his new shirt. "Peculiar thing about your family, you and Emilyann anyway. Neither one of you seems to take my orders seriously. You would not last long in the army." He looked up and there was cold death in those gray eyes, a promise of implacable vengeance in the low, steady voice. "You will not last long in London."

Dead men have nothing to lose, so Morgan shot back, "Go ahead and make your threats, you sanctimonious cockscomb. You're a fine one to talk, marrying a chit out of the schoolroom to line your pockets with what should have been mine. We paupers cannot afford scruples, eh, but your notions are a little nicer than mine? I think not, nevvy." He waved a liver-spotted hand at the room, the house. "I see the way you live, how your sister's fixed on buying a title with her dowry. That was Emilyann's dowry, what should have been mine!"

"It was never meant to be yours, you old fool, and it will never *be* yours. I'll see you rot in hell first. You're forgetting who forced Sparrow into the marriage, Aylesbury. It wasn't me. I never coveted her fortune. *I never sought what was not mine.* The money she spent on the house will be repaid, yes, and Nadine's dowry and the price of every blasted pig at Stockton if it takes me the next twenty years, and you shall never see a groat of it. You stupid bastard, haven't you even figured out that if you kill me, the money goes to my brother Thornton?"

"But not the heir's fortune. Dead men don't make good fathers."

Now, that struck the earl funny. He wished he could have shared that joke with Sparrow: Uncle Morgan wanted to keep him out of her bed as much as she did. He smiled, thinking that in the mood she was in tonight she'd be more dangerous than Morgan's wildest imaginings. She would be even harder to placate if he ruined her ball—and the new carpet—by spilling Morgan's blood all over them.

"I'll tell you what," he said. "I am going to give you another chance, and a good piece of advice. The chance is this, and my last warning: one more accident, one more clumsy attempt to harm me or Emilyann, and you die. I wouldn't even bother calling you out. You better hope we live to ripe old ages and die of natural causes. Have I made that clear?"

Morgan had almost stopped quaking. Damn, he needed a drink. None of *those* drinks, of course. He swallowed the fear-taste and nodded.

"And here's the advice: get yourself the damn heir. I don't care a rap for the money; it would be the boy's anyway, and I fancy my son taking over my title, not yours. So do it, man. The babe doesn't have to be from the right side of the blanket, you know. Get yourself a by-blow somewhere, and enough proof that you're the father to stand up in court. I'll not contest your petition to have the child declared legitimate as long as you don't try to foist Bobo on us."

Morgan wore a speculative look. "Never liked the bobbing-block m'self."

"Well, there you go. A little bedroom action, a little legal action, and one-two-three, you'll have a new little Arcott to corrupt and a whole new fortune to gamble away."

The idea had possibilities, maybe even promise. Morgan could do it, all right. There was that new dealer at Mrs. Corbett's. Nice, but not too nice, of course. Good head for cards she had, too. It might even be refreshing to have a son with some intelligence for a change. Yes, he was liking the notion better and better.

Lost in the happiest thoughts he'd entertained in years, Morgan did not realize he was being led, not back to the ballroom, but through the corridor to the front door. Stokely had his arm around the older man's shoulder, for all the world like a loving nephew escorting a relative to his coach. He nodded affably to any of the guests they passed and paused only to whisper a few words to Mr. Butler in the entry while Morgan dreamed on. The innkeep's daughter out in Richmond? What about one of the tenant farmers' daughters at the Hall? Healthy, wide-hipped, yeoman stock might be just the ticket.

"I'll do it," he declared, chortling. He pumped Stokely's hand up and down, ignoring the two strapping footmen who now flanked him and would until he was off the premises.

Stokely smiled and stepped out of the light before more of the company noticed his soiled sleeve. "Good," he said just before he went back inside, just before he made his final thrust, like a knife in Morgan's back. "Good. Now all you have to do is convince Aunt Ingrid to house your bastard."

"Cor," said one of the footmen as he slammed the door of the hackney carriage. "I ain't never seen no duke cry."

Stokely hurried back to the library, where he threw open the window, stepped out to the balcony, and proceeded to empty all five bottles of very old, very fine wines, unintentionally murdering one of Aunt Adelaide's rosebushes. Then he went upstairs to change his clothes again, just as the strains of the next dance began.

It was a waltz, and Emilyann's partner was missing. She was being stood up for a dance at her own ball, by her own husband! She almost dragooned young Remington into partnering her, then noted little Miss Whitlaw sitting forlorn on one of the gilt chairs at the edge of the dance floor. She sent a very disappointed young man in that direction and went to join a laughing group around Lady Jersey.

"What, not dancing, my dear?" that lady asked. "I thought you two lovebirds would be waltzing again for sure. Such a romantic dance." She tittered. Everyone in the place knew the Stokelys were more like fighting cocks than lovebirds tonight. What a diversion!

Emilyann seethed but smiled. "I had to see about a small matter in the kitchen. The duties of a hostess come first, of course."

"Of course, my dear, and I must congratulate you on performing them so well."

Emilyann nodded politely. If she told this old cat what

256

she was thinking, they'd never see the inside of Almack's again. She bit the inside of her lip as Lady Jersey went on, living up to her nickname of Silence. "And it's a pleasure to see Stokely taking on his new responsibilities as host also. So kind of him to go after Lady Bramby when her flounce tore. At least I think he did. We saw him headed toward the library just after she left, didn't we, Ferdie? Thoughtful boy. You know, I had my doubts about him as husband material, such a shocking rake he used to be, don't you recall, Ferdie? Why, I remember . . ."

Emilyann remembered another errand in the kitchen. "We can't seem to put out enough of those spun-sugar confections. Count Andreovich loves them so, I'll just go find some more."

What a surprise, there were no candied violets in the library. There were no erring husbands, either, but there were two empty glasses, and the doors to the balcony were open, letting in the cool night air. Emilyann stepped out to look, but the balcony extended too far in either direction for her to see past the library's meager light. Of course, they would have found a dark corner somewhere. She pulled the doors shut with a snap, rattling the glass, and turned the key in the latch. If they were out there, let them freeze. Lady Bramby had been wearing little enough anyway.

Emilyann was not a heavy drinker, but she needed Dutch courage tonight if she was to get through the rest of this awful party. She found a clean glass and—and all of the bottles were empty. Heavens, what kind of orgy was Stokely throwing? She kicked his stupid old desk. He'd been castaway on their wedding night, too, and Geoff looked green this morning after a night out with him. If Stokely was that kind of man, she told herself, he was not worth her tears. So why was she crying?

Because her foot hurt, she answered herself, and because what should have been one of the happiest nights of her life just couldn't get any worse.

She was wrong. It could.

After the last of the guests made their departures and Emilyann had thanked the staff and ordered the clean-up

257

left for tomorrow, she limped up to bed. Marvelous, she thought, her maid hadn't even waited up for her, and those tiny buttons down the back of her gown would be devilish to undo. It was not as if the girl were overworked either, or underpaid, Emilyann considered angrily, about to wrench the offending buttons apart. She hated the ugly dress anyway; she would never wear it again.

Then the last person she expected—or wanted—to see was in her doorway, asking, "May I help?" Stokely had been bidding farewell to the men from the Foreign Office the last she saw, ages ago. Now he was in her bedroom, wearing his dressing gown and a tentative smile. He could just take that quirky grin and—

"Thank you, no, I'll ring for my maid. She should have been waiting here."

"She was. I dismissed her."

Emilyann took a deep breath. "*You* dismissed *my* maid?"

Smoky nodded, meanwhile moving out of throwing range just in case. At least life would never be dull. "I wanted to talk."

She put her hands on her hips and pursed her lips. "Well, that's all of a piece, isn't it? You order my servants about, you ride roughshod over my plans, overrule my decisions, and make me a laughingstock at my own ball. Well, you, you, authoritative ass, you can just go back to Lady Bramby, see if I care."

"What, was Sydelle here tonight? I'm sorry I missed her. Pleasant lady, always even-tempered."

"And I'm not, I suppose?"

He grinned.

"She wouldn't be either, married to an insufferable, arrogant brute, to say nothing of any *lady* dressing like that. Her gown was so sheer you could tell she had no underpinnings on beneath."

"Then I am doubly sorry to have missed her."

Now, Smoky might tease, and he might rage, but he would never lie to her; Emilyann would have sworn on that. "You did not see her tonight?"

He took a seat on the chaise longue. "I said so, didn't I?"

She sniffed. "That doesn't change things. How dare you

258

cancel the negotiations I had going with Squire Kimball? I've been after him for ages now, and you queer the deal within minutes. We needed that land for the new breed of hogs Geoff and I have been studying."

"I cannot afford it."

"I can!"

"But that is your money, not mine. I don't care if you dress every horse in London in a green bonnet, or buy every break-down hackney nag for your racing farm. That is yours. The land is mine, and I will not have my wife bankroll it. Which sentiment I believe I expressed frequently and forcefully."

"Of all the overblown, prideful—"

"You're the one standing there in a dress that won't unbutton rather than let me help."

She ignored that. "And what about Gannon? You had no right to fire him without a by-your-leave."

Stokely brushed at a piece of lint on his sleeve. "No? I thought I had a great many rights, even if I choose not to exercise them all the time. I gave you your head in a large field, Sparrow, I did not give you the ordering of my life. You did not buy me, you know. I *do* live here, or there at Stockton, and I have every right to make sure my properties are well tended."

"And they are!"

"In nearly all instances. Perhaps I never expressed my gratitude to you for how well you've managed. Stockton has never been in better condition, and all the tenants sing your praises."

"At least someone does," she muttered. It was becoming harder to maintain her anger. That was the way it always was with him, blast.

He looked around. "Where's the dog?"

Oh, dear, in all the bustling about, she had not even had time to check on poor Pug!

"He's in the stables with Jake."

"Good, that's where he belongs."

"And you don't even like my dog!"

He laughed. "Anything else in your budget, Sparrow? I'm sure I have wronged you woefully, so you may as well

259

have at it now while you have the opportunity. I'll be leaving soon."

He shouldn't have reminded her. The ball! "You left me there without a partner at my own dance!"

"I was occupied, my dear."

"Occupied? Your brainbox must be occupied by a family of squirrels! Everyone knew we were to have the waltz. All the old tabbies were snickering behind their fans."

She was mussed from her struggle with the dress, and she had kicked her shoes off as soon as she entered the room, and she was in a kitten-fit again, so Emilyann looked more like the hoyden he was used to than the cool countess he had been seeing. Stokely thought he might like this fiery woman better. "Does it matter so much to you what a bunch of old quizzes think?" he wanted to know.

"I wanted to make you proud. Oh." She had not meant to say that at all.

He smiled and moved over to make room next to him on the chaise. He patted the cushion and she sat, just close enough for him to take her hand and carry it to his lips.

"And I am, my dear. I am proud of you with or without anyone else's approval, with every curl in place at tea or on your hands and knees dicing with the stablehands." His hand moved to her shoulder, gently stroking.

"You saw!"

"And I wished I could join the game. I have always been proud of you, you must know that."

"Even when I sound like a fishwife? And you cannot approve of my dumping the syllabub in your lap. I regretted it instantly, you know."

"You always do, Sparrow. And yes, even then, when you looked so righteous, like a Greek goddess casting thunderbolts at offending mortals." By now his hand had moved to caress her neck, her back, and damn those pesky buttons, he thought. Why did they make the bloody things so small?

"I am sorry, Smoky, truly. I know I can do better. It's just that . . ."

"I know, I am overbearing and officious, and I should have consulted you first. I am sorry, too, my dear."

260

"Oh, but I am headstrong and willful. Nanny has told me so a million times."

"Only Nanny?" he teased, pressing her head against his chest and kissing the top of her pale curls, incidentally having two hands free to work on the back of the gown. "Why, if I told you not to jump off the balcony, you'd do it just to spite me."

She laughed, a little breathless. "And you would expect me to obey you even if the house was on fire."

"What a fine couple."

Her hands had moved, tentatively at first, along the silky lapels of his robe, then to the dark hair on his chest. Was that warmth from him, or her?

"You know, Sparrow, I think we *could* be a fine couple, if we tried."

"Hmm," she agreed dreamily. "We'll have lots of time to work at it."

His hands stopped their explorations. "Ah, not much time for now, I'm afraid."

She pulled back, out of his embrace, where he could see how flushed she was, how utterly kissable. "Oh?"

Oh, hell, he thought. "All those rumors flying around, you know. That's what we were so busy discussing the entire night. The peace won't even make a hundred days, it seems. I'll have to be returning. Soon." Her brows were raised. "Sooner than I had hoped."

She stood slowly, uncurling like a stretching cat. "Just how soon?"

More like some wild jungle cat with prey in sight, he decided. "Ah, tonight."

"Tonight, and you weren't going to tell me, and you were just going to—"

"Do you want me to fetch some pudding for you to throw? How about that vase of flowers? You notice I did not put on my uniform yet, just in case I had to change again. I wish you would think of poor Rigg, though."

"How can you tease, Smoky?"

"Why, you were wishing me to the devil not five minutes ago. The devil or Lady Bramby, I forget which."

"It was Lady Bramby and I would have torn your heart out with my fingers!"

He held her face in his hands. "Then you do care?"

"Silly, I wouldn't be jealous otherwise."

"And you know I wouldn't be angry if I didn't worry about you so much, don't you?"

She nodded, and tears started to fill her eyes. Smoky kissed each lid in turn. "I don't suppose . . . ?"

"Would you still leave?"

"God, Sparrow, what a question."

She stepped back. "Come home soon."

She was exquisite, like some fairy creature in an enchanted forest, and he wanted her more than he'd wanted anything else, ever. He wanted to wipe away that sad look and make her laugh and blush and get furious and silly. Gads, she was his own wife! He'd hurry home all right.

"Godspeed, Smoky."

Chapter Fifteen

*M*eanwhile, in that other bedroom:

"Morgan? What do you want? We already did that this week."

"No, no, just wanted to talk," he said, pulling a chair closer to the bed, where Ingrid lay with one long, heavy braid like a sword at her side.

She pushed the nightcap out of her eyes and fixed him with a piercing stare. "You're drunk."

"No, I swear. Wanted to tell you, Ingrid. I'm a changed man."

He still smelled of yesterday's mutton and still had hair growing out of his ears. She raised herself up on her elbows and said, "Yes?"

"I got to thinking at that ball, seeing my niece and her husband so well set, seeing young Bobo doing the pretty with the young girls, how fortunate we were. As a family, you know. And I got to thinking, maybe we should do more for other people, other, ah, families. You know, charity." He had trouble saying the word; it was not much used in his vocabulary. He looked at his wife for signs of approbation and went on although she looked at him blankly.

"Well, you are always nattering—uh, going on about doing your duty, bringing true belief to us lesser mortals. Savin' souls, Ingrid, couldn't be a finer ambition. Now, I say to myself, Morgan, you need a goal like that, doing something for others. Charity, that's it, good deeds to atone for the wrongs you've done." He checked to see if she was swallowing this. She was nodding, so he continued.

"And I asked myself, where can I do the most good? Lot of causes around London, you know. Climbing boys, crippled veterans without pensions. They're always debating such in the Lords, you know, always asking for money for 'em."

She wondered how he knew what was debated in Parliament at all, since he never went and hardly read a newspaper beyond the racing journals to her knowledge. She decided it was money he wanted, thinking he could get another check out of her by appealing to her generous nature. "I already contribute, Morgan," she told him to dampen that dream. "I send two pounds every month to Brother Blessed's Orphanage and Boardinghouse for the Needy."

Great gods, she sent good blunt to a bunch of dirty rugrats? "Very bountiful, m'dear. I'm sure the little tots remember you in their prayers. But it was more practical help I was thinking of, not just the cash. Too easy to write a chit and forget about the need." He was certain he'd heard her say that.

"I am sure Brother Blessed would appreciate if you went down and helped care for the orphans, though I cannot see what—"

"No, no. There are so many people devoting their energies to the foundlings. I was thinking of other charities, you

263

know, workhouses, dole hospitals ... homes for unwed mothers."

"You want to send money to encourage women who are no better than they should be?"

"Not the money, recall. Practical help, that's what those unfortunates need. Food, medical care, shelter. I, ah, thought we could offer room to a few of the girls. Heaven knows we have enough space in this old barn."

Ingrid sat up straight at this. "You want me, a God-fearing, churchgoing woman, to take one of those, those soiled doves into my home?" she shrieked. "Do you know how those women got that way?"

Morgan thought he remembered.

"It's a sin, do you hear me, and I won't let any light-skirts cross my door. Even the housemaids know I won't tolerate such goings-on, walking out with footmen and such. I know where that leads, and I won't have it."

"Uh, and if the girl wasn't such a stranger, do you think you could reconsider?" Her frigid silence told him the chances of that, so he tried another tact: "Wouldn't you like to hear the patter of little feet again? Those nurseries up-stairs have stood empty for a long time and ..."

When he finally got around to it, confiding Stokely's grand scheme, the money, the title, and all, Ingrid had only one comment to make. Very succinctly, very sincerely, and with every chance of success, she uttered: "Go to hell."

Chapter Sixteen

Smoky left, not knowing of her love. Emilyann could not tell him she loved him, not when he hadn't said it, not when she could hardly say it to herself. She whispered it into Pug's soft fur when she went to visit, as if telling the little dog a great secret. Dogs were good for that, they never gossiped and they never laughed, even when the secret was such a piece of silliness. Of course she loved Smoky. She always had. Her hero-worship had evolved all it could—he was a hero, after all—but without the blinders of infatuation. She saw Smoky for what he was, kind and courageous, strong and warm-hearted—and pig-headed, overbearing, used to command, devilishly handsome—and gone.

Emilyann thought of the gentle, biddable husband she had thought to marry, and laughed. Pug wagged his tail. Smoky was none of those things, and she would not have changed him for the world, even if she could, except possibly to make him less overprotective. He left so many instructions—for her well-being, he said—that she may as well be a china doll wrapped in cotton and placed on a shelf until his return. As if she did not know to check her saddle girth, or was widgeon enough to ride out unaccompanied by Jake or one of the new grooms. She was not to attend masquerades or walk on the balcony during balls, although she did not think this was entirely for her safety, and hugged to herself the thought of his jealousy. She was not to spend time alone with Uncle Morgan, ever, and mostly she was not to travel to Belgium, where the ton was assembling.

First Smoky gave orders: she must not become one of those empty-headed pleasure-seekers chasing frivolity at the fringes of war. Then he reasoned with her: Brussels had not enough accommodations for the influx of tourists, with so many fleeing Paris; no one knew where Napoleon would make his final stand and Brussels could be too close; worrying over her would be a distraction from his duties. Finally he pleaded: *Please stay in England,* he wrote, *so I can come home to you.*

She had no desire to go abroad anyway, but what about *her* worries? Emilyann asked the dog. Smoky should be safe, she believed, unless the gudgeon volunteered to rejoin the army in France, which sounded just like what he would do. And she had all his other commands to consider. He

265

called them "wishes," of course, as in "I wish you would be more cautious with your investments," and "I wish you would discourage that paperskull Bobo from hanging around Nadine." The first was easy. With the uncertainty of the peace continuing, speculation was too uncertain. There were vast earnings to be made on munitions and grain shipments if war broke out again, but Emilyann thought it indecent to profit from the spilling of men's blood, especially if even one drop were Smoky's.

Bobo was more of a problem, or Nadine was. Emilyann sent Geoff home to see about the harvests and replanting for the winter feed, and to find a replacement for that new gamekeeper. Aunt Adelaide went along to keep house for him, she said, and to see her garden again, but they all knew it was a surfeit of Nadine, not a dearth of day lilies, sending her off. Emilyann would have followed herself, except that news reached London long before it filtered to the shires, and she could not bear it if the armies were engaged without her knowing Smoky's whereabouts. She tried to send Nadine with Geoff and her aunt, but the minx refused. She adored London and declared she was never going to rusticate with the pigs again. With the foreign diplomats scurrying off, though, all the young officers reenlisting, and every second son hurrying to sign up, the field of eligible gentlemen was shrinking. The nobility returned to their country homes, and London grew sadly flat after the revelry of the victory season. Even that nice Remington boy left town for a country house party at the home of little Miss Whitlaw, she of the squint, stammer, and spots—and three thousand a year, plus a very pleasant personality. There were just enough dinners and parties to keep Nadine on the go, showing off her new clothes, and just enough suitors to admire them.

Stokely had refused four offers for his sister's hand on the night of their ball, claiming she was too young. Two of the offers were above reproach, a baronet and a plain mister with good prospects. One proposition was not quite respectable, the penniless son of a French marquis, and one laughable, Bobo. Nadine was in alt at the quantity and

266

quality of her court—and preferred Bobo. Now, with the depleted ranks, it was even harder to keep her from him.

Emilyann did her best, inviting Thornton's shy curate to dinner, begging Lady Vinn and her nephew to share their box at the opera, driving with Nadine in the chaise instead of her phaeton so they could offer rides to gentlemen strollers of their acquaintance. Nadine still preferred Bobo.

"What do you see in that lumpfish?" Emilyann asked one day, frustrated in her not-so-subtle efforts to dislodge the nodcock from her tea table.

"We have so many things in common," Nadine replied, licking the crumbs of the last crumpet off her fingers.

Yes, like a love for garish colors and a fondness for strawberry tarts. "But he can hardly dance, never brings you flowers or makes pretty compliments."

"That doesn't matter. We have such a good time together."

"What do you find to talk about with him?" Emilyann had never been able to exchange more than five words with the cod's-head, words like "Put that down" and "Take your hands off me." She was appalled when Nadine giggled and answered, "Oh, we have better things to do than talk."

So Emilyann never left them alone, and was forced to attend those dreadful musical entertainments so dear to dowagers' hearts, where they could show off their daughters' accomplishments with little expense. The refreshments were just ample enough for the guests, if you discounted Bobo's pockets, so Emilyann usually came home hungry, in addition to irritable.

She did not dare let them go off riding together, so they were forced to amble along the paths instead of tearing across the greens. Neither one had much of a seat, and Bobo's poor mount was practically carrying double anyway, so Lady Stokely couldn't ask it for more exertion. As a result, Emilyann was not burning off enough of *her* energy, and was restless, agitated over her concern for Smoky, and aggravated at the whole situation.

It was no surprise, therefore, when she accepted Bobo's offer to try out the paces of a spirited new gelding.

* * *

After his last misstep, Morgan was forced to attend three prayer meetings to get back into Ingrid's good graces, if not the Lord's, and to get back on her list of household expenses. He had no choice. There were no more jewels to be put on tick; Arcott would yield nothing until after harvest time; and that nipfarthing Baxley would not answer his letters. Moreover, the kitchen cat had died after eating some of Ingrid's breakfast gruel that tasted "off."

"Get ye hence, Satan! Do not place temptation in front of me."

No chance of that. The crone on the hard pew in the row ahead had the widest-spreading—

"Renounce the greed, renounce the avarice, renounce the temptation to value the pence and shillings over prayer and salvation."

Easy for Brother Blessed. He hadn't tried paying the cents-per-centers off with an appeal to their immortal souls. "Pray on the Almighty's time," they said. "Pay up on ours."

"Sloth is a sin. The devil spins among the idle like a great poisonous spider, ready to capture souls and suck their life's blood from them till they hang like empty husks in the web of everlasting hell."

Hmm. But where could one find a poisonous spider? Morgan did not suppose you just went off to the woods and started digging. Too much work. No, there must be places where one could procure a black widow. He'd have to look into it.

"And like the serpent said to Eve . . ."

Or a snake. Morgan didn't like the creepy things himself, but if he could manage to get an asp into Ingrid's bed . . . This Brother Blessed wasn't half bad.

"And I say pluck the devil from you, like a thorn in the flesh! Repeat with me, brothers and sisters, Satan, get ye hence!"

"Here, Bobo, get ye hence."

"Huh?"

"Go on, already, take the horse over to Lady Stokely's. She's waiting for you for that picnic to Richmond."

"She don't like me."

"Of course not, you looby. No one likes you."

"Miss Nadine likes me."

Morgan couldn't understand that, but got a deal of satisfaction to think of that arrogant Earl of Stokely's own sister ending up with Bobo. The chit didn't have much of a dowry, but if she was willing to have the gapeseed, Morgan was happy to help, getting back at Stokely in the bargain. He feared the man, he feared hell, too, but he feared debtor's prison more than either of them. He had decided long ago that if he would be damned for the thought as well as the deed, he may as well get on with it, for he had thoughts aplenty. He may as well be hanged for a sheep as a lamb. Hell, he could be hanged for a wolf if he managed it, with Bobo's help.

"Here, if you want that Nadine chit, you have to get on Emilyann's good side, you know, so she will convince Stokely to approve your suit."

"Huh?"

Morgan tore at his hair; the bay gelding skittered around, eyes rolling, ears back. "Just take the horse to m'niece. Say you won it in a card game and you think it's too much horse for you. Maybe for her, too. She never could resist a challenge so she'll take it on the ride."

"But, Da, I don't want to ride all the way to Richmond. You know I get light-headed from bein' tossed around in the saddle too long."

"You got light headed from being born, dolt." He thought a moment, then added, "They are bound to have a picnic hamper along. Wouldn't set out without nuncheon. Cold chicken, likely, and Scotch eggs, cider, and cheese, maybe some of those tarts."

"That's all right, then. They've got a fine chef, though I don't see why we have to go all the way to Richmond when Nadine don't mind sittin' in the kitchen watchin' Cook roll out dough and stuff."

Morgan shoved the gelding's reins and a bag of sugar cubes into Bobo's pudgy hands. "Here, don't try to think. Just give it some sugar to keep it quiet till you get to the Stokelys'. The nag's already got a side-saddle on, so

Emilyann won't have time to think about it. And don't mention my name."

Bobo gingerly fed the restless gelding two cubes, then crammed five into his own mouth with horse-slobbered fingers before mounting his own steed, a sleepy, swaybacked chestnut. He rode off in stretched buckskins and lavender waistcoat, leading the fractious bay with its lady's saddle and, under the blanket, Brother Blessed's thorn in the flesh.

Why not? Emilyann asked herself. The bay was fidgety, in a sweat already. They both needed a good run, she decided. Jake was resting with a headache that morning, a loose window shutter having blown down and struck him last night on his way home from the Black Dog. And Smoky had not ordered her to stay off any rawboned brutes. He hadn't seen the need. She grinned, whispered sweetly in the bay's ear, and rubbed its forehead. "We'll do fine, sweetheart," she told the gelding, checking the girth and tightening it a notch. Her groom, one of the new men Jake had found, stepped back as the horse sidled and crowhopped. Emilyann laughed happily and mounted from the stable block.

She sat lightly in the sidesaddle and held the bay in close check until they were out of the city proper and had met up with the rest of their group, mostly Nadine's young friends and their beaux. The grooms followed a little behind with the hampers. And the chaperone, the proper married woman the matrons had entrusted with their precious chicks, decided to set a faster pace.

Emilyann touched the gelding with her heel and it was off like a flash, her laughter echoing back to the horrified group. When she tried to pull in, however, to wait for the others to catch up, the bay decided that although the discomfort could not be outrun, it might be dislodged. The horse reared. Emilyann shortened the reins. It bucked. She grabbed for its mane. Then the gelding did a hundred-and-eighty-degree turn, all feet in the air, and so was Lady Stokely.

The dismayed grooms had dumped the hampers to ride to her assistance, and the young people set their horses to

270

a gallop to reach her quickly, Bobo bouncing along. When they reached her, Emilyann already had the reins in hand and the saddle unbuckled, just waiting for a leg up.

"This fellow needs to learn some manners," she told an ashen-faced Nadine. "And I cannot do it in a side-saddle. Deathly contraption anyway." She left the blanket on, as a sop to convention.

"But, Em," Nadine wailed, "our vouchers to Almack's!"

Emilyann looked at her sister-in-law and grinned. "You hate the place anyway, remember? Stale toast and lemonade, that's all they serve. Don't worry, maybe I'll break my neck."

She got on and stayed on, her hands wrapped in the gelding's hair, her legs firmly clamped to its sides, wide skirts of her habit raised to show a stretch of stocking above the riding boots. They left the others far behind in a mad dash through hedges and spinneys and streamlets. The gelding never settled down, however, not even when its flanks were heaving and both horse and rider were drenched in sweat. The horse stayed frantic, and Emilyann finally gave it up rather than founder the animal. The beast was incorrigible; it just was never going to be a good ride. She climbed off at a farmstead and tied the reins to a rail, pulled off the blanket to rub the horse down while waiting for her party. What a fool she had been—again. Hell and damnation! "You poor darling," she crooned to the horse, tears streaming down her dirty cheeks.

The riding party was ruined, of course. The food was spilled, the girls were tittering about Emilyann's daring, and Bobo was still casting up his accounts behind a shed. Emilyann was no sight for an inn, so she thankfully accepted the farmer's wife's offer of cider and fresh-baked bread before herding her group back to town.

They left Bobo behind, his ears ringing, to lead the bay with a cob the farmer was willing to rent. Emilyann sat stone-faced on the swaybacked chestnut and Nadine whimpered. Emilyann could not tell if the girl was missing Bobo or the scattered hampers, and did not care. "And if I ever see you talking to him again, I'll box your ears, too."

* * *

271

"So what if she forbade you the house, you gossoon, there's parties and theater and the park. She can't keep the girl from you entirely."

Morgan and Bobo were in the library at Arcott House, sharing a bottle of Blue Ruin that Morgan had smuggled into the house under a sheaf of hymns. Ingrid was upstairs resting after a trying morning in which the suit of armor in the foyer had fallen on her, the valiant knight's spiked mace quite destroying her new black shawl.

"But Da, they had such nice teas at Stockton House. 'Sides, she says you're never to call there again either."

That was nothing new, except that his niece did not know Stokely's orders. Morgan had already had the door slammed in his face twice over there by that uppity butler and a bunch of footmen who looked more like boxers than servants. No matter, he had no more reason to call on Emilyann; she couldn't be increasing, not after that ride. Morgan lifted his glass in a toast to the gelding.

"And she says she's goin' to write to Stokely."

The whiskey tasted like sawdust and spit. Brother Blessed would be proud of the way Morgan prayed for the saints to preserve him from the devil.

Emilyann wrote to Smoky only about the ride. There was no reason to fret him with foolish suspicions, so she just said what a delightful outing it had been, the most fun she'd had in ages, and how she missed the country. And him.

Chapter Seventeen

Then came Waterloo. It was a smashing victory or a crushing defeat, no one knew which. Emilyann and Morgan

272

Arcott both avidly scanned the casualty lists, but there was no news of Smoky. Then word started to come back to England of the actual battle, and Major Lord Stokely's name was mentioned often. He'd left headquarters when there was no one else to send command decisions to Marshal Blucher and the Prussians. He'd borrowed a horse from the Twelfth Cavalry when his was lost, and he'd rallied a battalion of Scots' Greys until a junior officer was found to take charge. He had been seen at Quatre Bras, and again helping to fix a cannon position—and not since.

Emilyann haunted the War Office, battalion headquarters, and even Prinny's councillors' chambers, seeking word, but no one knew where Smoky was. One general patted her hand, like telling a child her puppy would come home when it got hungry. The others looked at her with sympathy, their averted eyes declaring her a widow before the official pronouncement. She wouldn't believe it.

She also would not take part in the delirium of the new, this-time-final victory celebrations, not in the face of such grievous losses, such grieving uncertainty. The ton rallied back to London from their estates, and the fugitives from the revelry in Brussels joined the new galas in town. Emilyann questioned them when she could: yes, Stokely had been at the Duchess of Richmond's ball on the eve of the battle, no, he had not danced, and no, they had not seen him since. Shocking disarray there, you know, casualties all over, none of the amenities. Nothing like home. Another cup of tea, dear?

So she stopped going out. Fireworks and illuminations held no attractions; there was no one she wanted to dance with at the balls; military reviews only reminded her of how handsome Smoky looked in his regimentals. She should have told him, dear Lord, she should have showed him how much she loved him. Perhaps she would be carrying his child by now, a piece of him to hold if— No, he was coming back.

Geoff wrote, cheerfully insisting Stokely would turn up. He always did. And Nadine went her own way, under the wing of one or another of her friends' mothers, declaring that since they had not heard any bad news, why borrow

273

trouble. If Bobo was at all of the same functions, Emilyann decided, so be it. Perhaps his real personality would emerge and Nadine would be as affronted as the rest of the world. Emilyann always found that Bobo grew on you, like mold.

Curiously, it was Aunt Ingrid who brought Emilyann comfort. Her prayers did not seem so absurd anymore, and her belief that they would be answered was reassuring. She would sit quietly while Emilyann brooded, reading her religious tracts or embroidering a new altar cloth. She accompanied her niece on the calls to government offices, and insisted Emilyann go for outings in the park for fresh air and come down for tea, lest she waste away with worrying.

The two women became so close, in fact, that one day Emilyann was tempted to ask Ingrid about her suspicions.

"Don't you think that a lot of, ah, peculiar accidents happen to you, Aunt?"

Ingrid was holding her head at an odd angle. The window in her room had flown open in the night somehow, and chilled her neck into an uncomfortable position. As she told the younger woman, it was a miracle she did not get influenza. "What's that, dear? What kind of things?"

"Oh, things like that locknut coming off the carriage chassis, or the canopy falling down off your bed while you were in it. Remember last year when the stair rail had been greased?"

Ingrid set another stitch. "The servants these days aren't to be trusted, you know. I told that footman precisely how to rehang the chandelier, but no, it fell the very next day, as soon as I slammed the front door."

"But other people don't have so many of these odd occurrences, Aunt Ingrid."

"The Lord is testing me, dear. Like Job. And my faith protects me."

"What about the fire at your prayer meeting? If belief was such good protection, how could a fire start there of all places?"

"But, dear, I told you there was no real fire. Someone must have mistaken wisps from the incense burners for smoke. Of course those of us in the front pews did not know it at the time, and there was a regrettable panic until

274

Brother Blessed recalled us to our faith. The Lord would guard His flock, he said, and so we prayed. As I mentioned, there was only the one casualty from the first rush to the doors. Your uncle should be up and about again in a few weeks, the doctor says."

Emmy grinned, the first time in days. "Perhaps I should go to the lending library and fetch him some books to occupy his mind. Improving works, of course."

Ingrid's face cracked, like a chunk of granite splitting—goodness, the woman actually knew how to smile—and she echoed: "Of course."

Finally the courier came. The major had been found, alive, but just barely. A farmer returning to his homestead after the battle and the looting had followed a trail of blood to his barn and the wounded British officer. He did what he could, until an army doctor could be sent out and the wound, a saber gash from Stokely's ribs to his thigh, could be dressed. The field surgeon decided to leave the officer there, unconscious and unidentified, lest the massive wound reopen. Supplies were sent, and medicos when they could be spared, until the day Stokely revived somewhat and through his delirium managed to say his name. Then his frantic batman, who had been searching the field hospitals and helping with the gruesome task of mass burials to make sure his master was not among those sorry piles, came to take over the nursing, and messages could be sent home.

The latest report was that the wound might not prove mortal if the fever did not kill Stokely first.

"I have to go to him," Emilyann declared, clutching the memo and pacing around the drawing room. Nadine quickly moved a footstool and a firescreen out of her way.

"Of course you do," replied Aunt Ingrid calmly, sitting with her embroidery as usual. "It is your duty as his wife to bring ease to his suffering, to succor him in his moment of need. Haven't I been tending to your Uncle Morgan? I have been reading to him from the Bible like a faithful helpmate, seeing to it myself that he had nothing to eat but gruel and barley water, lest heavy meals retard the healing process."

"Yes, but I swore to Smoky that I wouldn't go to Belgium. I gave my word."

"But, Emmy," Nadine said, "he meant you shouldn't follow the other British tourists to the parties and festivities there."

"That's right. I said I would not go for the fun, and this is not frivolous at all." She had also promised Smoky not to put herself in danger by journeying to a battlefield, but the battle was over, and she was in enough danger here in England in any case. She looked over at Aunt Ingrid, who was placidly sewing the altar cloth, sincerely believing her faith could be worn like a protective mantle. Em said nothing about her fears, just "I'll do it. I'll go."

"And I shall accompany you, of course," Aunt Ingrid said in a voice that allowed no argument. "You cannot travel alone, naturally, even with trusted servants. That thought, I am sure, would cause dear Stokely unease. No, I shall go with you, to lend you countenance and also to bring aid and comfort to the many wounded. I see it as my duty to tend to the soldiers' spiritual well-being."

"I think they might need blankets more, Aunt, but—"

"And I'm coming, too," Nadine put in.

"Not on your life," her sister-in-law told her. "Smoky would kill both of us."

"Not if he's that sick. And I cannot stay here alone, you know."

That was true. Em shuddered to think of all the trouble Nadine could get into on her own. If Aunt Ingrid went, too, Emilyann could not even deposit the plaguey chit with her, even if that was Bobo's own home. "No, it will have to be Stockton. I'll send you with the chaise and—"

"I won't go. Besides, Em, I really can be a help. You cannot sit with Stokely every hour of the day yourself. Or else I can help Aunt Ingrid with the other wounded. I'm not just a china doll, you know. I have seen lots of injuries and illnesses in the country. I can help, truly."

Em was undecided, but Aunt Ingrid thought it a good

idea. "Let the gel come along. It will be good for her. She needs some depth."

"You were not thinking of bringing Bobo, ah, Beauregard, along, were you, Aunt Ingrid?" she asked, looking at Nadine suspiciously.

"No, some of us are not meant for travail. He is not a good traveler, you know. Otherwise I am sure he would want to assist Stokely. Moreover, he must remain to care for his stepfather in my absence. Quite devoted he is to Morgan, you know. Such a good boy."

Emilyann swallowed her reply and turned to Nadine. "There will be no parties, and you cannot take your pretty clothes, and I want to leave as soon as Jake can have the carriage loaded and arrangements made."

"I know all that, silly. I *do* have other interests beside balls and clothes, you know. I'll go see Cook and make sure she packs plenty of supplies so we don't have to make frequent stops along the way, and some restorative pork's-foot jelly, and whatever else she thinks an invalid might need."

Em was already making lists. " 'Toinette can see to the packing, though we won't know for how long. We can have a trunk shipped later. I'll send one of the footmen to the apothecary. Tan-bark infusion, I think. He'll know. We had better bring extra linens, muslin for bandages . . ."

"I'll take care of the last, dear," Aunt Ingrid said, neatly folding her embroidery into the work basket. "The Ladies' Guild has been rolling bandages throughout the war. I brought some home for Morgan to do while he lies abed. The devil makes work for idle hands, you know." She tied her bonnet strings and continued, "I shall fetch those and my necessaries, leave instructions for my staff, and make my farewells to my family. I shall be back within the hour, unless I cannot find that stack of hymnals I meant to bring to the Gates of Hope alms-house."

Emilyann stopped listening, hurrying through her own lists and notes, sending maids and footmen every which way, trying not to think of Smoky lying in a pool of blood on some barn floor. Mr. Butler could take care of writing to Geoff, and someone would have to get to the bank to cash a check for traveling money, and make a draft for whatever bank they would need later. Mr. Baxley would know. When were the packet boats scheduled, and could they guarantee a passage? If they had to wait another day ... Emilyann said a quick prayer.

"Perhaps Morgan recollects where I left the hymnals."

The hymnals were safe in the butler's pantry. None of the pawnbrokers would take them. And Morgan was safe in his bed, gnashing his teeth. He was bruised, bandaged, and bad-tempered, even more than usual. Here was his golden opportunity, Emilyann and Ingrid together, in the same coach, on the same packet from Dover. An accident, a hold-up, a hole in the bottom of the bloody boat, and his problems would be over. If he could go along, how easy it would be to jostle Ingrid at the rail of the packet, bump into Emilyann during the crossing. And he could be the one to shout "Man overboard!" just a few minutes later.

Instead, oh, the injustice of it all, he lay in bed, both legs in splints, with only that attics-to-let Bobo for company. The tub of blubber could sink a boat by sitting in it, his fond steppapa groused, so instead of making futile plans, Morgan took a leaf from Ingrid's book, and prayed.

He always knew that religion business was a hoax. Damn boat wasn't struck by lightning at all.

Chapter Eighteen

Brussels was in chaos. Dazed men in tattered uniforms lined the curbs outside in the drizzling rain because there were no beds for them. Men with slings, crutches, bandages were everywhere, and no one seemed to be in charge. The hotels were all filled, mostly with tourists who had thought Brussels would be safe from the conflagration and who had been stranded minutes from a war zone by lack of transportation. They were leaving as fast as possible, but their rooms were taken by wounded officers who could pay to leave the horrid field hospitals.

It was already growing late in the day when the travelers found an establishment at least serving tea. Aunt Ingrid and Nadine needed a break, Emilyann decided, while she considered where to start to find rooms, or Smoky. Aunt Ingrid had already struck up conversation with a respectably dressed, middle-aged woman at a nearby table who directed Emilyann to the British Consulate. Mrs. Hammersmith, as she introduced herself, was an adjutant's wife, the officer presently lying abed upstairs.

"Hammersmith will do, hardhead, don't you know. It's the other lads who need help. We've been doing what we can, the wives who follow the drum, and some of the English tourists who stayed have been regular troopers. Some haven't, of course, afraid of gettin' their hands dirty." They could all hear the question in her voice, and Emilyann was quick to assure their new acquaintance that her little party was here to help.

"Never heard of your major, dearie, sorry to say, but I'll make inquiries for you. Someone's bound to know where they billeted an earl. You come tell me where you're staying, and I'll start asking questions."

The harried junior legate at the embassy knew of only one empty property, a mansion on the edge of town belonging to a Bruxelloise Count d'Charteret who had sided with Napoleon. He was going to stay at his country property for now, for his health.

Emilyann and Jake found the manager, a weasely, garlic-breathed churl who growled that the place wasn't for let. Money still ruled, though, even in hell. Especially in hell.

By the time Emilyann had settled negotiations, Aunt Ingrid was already surveying the possibilities of the enormous barracks of a house. The luxuriousness of the furnishings was absurd, considering Emilyann's mission, and the fact that most of the servants required to keep up a place of this size had long since fled. Mrs. Hammersmith, who had come along to point the way, was confident they'd be back as soon as word went out that their wages would be paid. She and Aunt Ingrid set the grooms and footmen to dragging palettes and cots around, turning the downstairs rooms away from the family apartments into recovery wards. Nadine, naturally, went to oversee the unloading of their provisions and the organization of the kitchen to feed any number of hungry men.

It would do. Mounts being in even shorter supply in Brussels than rooms, Emilyann and Jake tacked up two horses from the carriage team with the count's saddles.

"For the exorbitant rental I am paying the man," she told the disapproving manager, "the saddles should be covered in gold leaf. Now, get out of my way and stop interfering, unless you wish me to write to the count myself." She looked at the scurvy little lout and narrowed her eyes. "I wonder if he knows precisely how much gold I just handed over."

There would be no more trouble from that quarter and at last, at long last, Lady Stokely could start trying to find her husband. The embassy had been no help, but directed her to army headquarters. Headquarters sent her to the Quartermaster's Office, which passed her on to Command Operations, then Battalion Chief and Captain of the Watch. Night Watch, it turned out, because so much time was wasted, every petty officer searching through lists and scraps of paper and duty rosters. They all knew of Major Lord Stokely, everyone praised his bravery, and they all had heard he was still at that farmhouse, somewhere. Thank God she was spared searching the field hospitals at least, but Lady Stokely's temper was not appeased. Her family would have known to step back when Emilyann's eyes flashed like that and her hands clenched into fists. The desk sergeant just shuffled some more papers.

"Is this the way you treat your heroes in this army?" she started, pounding that same desk until the papers flew around. "You *lose* them? Do you think Lord Wellington is going to be happy to know you have misplaced my husband? When I tell Uncle Arthur—"

Uncle Arthur? The sergeant began to see his career flash before his eyes.

"You and the rest of the imbecilic bureaucrats sit on your padded seats filing documents while your wounded men lie in God-knows-what backwater, and God better know, because you sure don't! Well, I—"

It did not take long. The poor sergeant promised to have an address and directions delivered to Hotel Charteret by ten the next morning. Eight at the inn?

"Yes, sir, ah, ma'am. Here at dawn."

The tired sergeant told them they'd never get the heavy carriage down the rutted country lanes to the farmhouse, so they rode again, carrying what supplies they could tie on the backs of the horses and in saddlebags. They would make better time this way, too. The farm must have a dray to get produce to market, or Jake could ride back to rent a pony cart if they found Stokely could be moved.

The farm was not too far off, as the crow flies. But horses and humans needed paths and road signs and landmarks to find their way. They took wrong turns and had to slow the pace as the dirt roads turned to mire in the persistent rain. They had to skirt the nightmare scenes of the past battle or, horror-stricken, guide their reluctant mounts through.

It was midmorning when they reached a neat white-washed homestead. No dogs barked, though, and no one came out to answer their calls. Emilyann did not wait for Jake to hand her down, or even to tie her horse. The old man clucked but secured both mounts and followed her slowly, pulling his damp collar closer around him.

"B'Gad, it's Lady Stokely! I never thought you would— that is, I am right glad to see you, ma'am." Micah Rigg came to the door to see about the commotion. Stokely's batman looked even more grizzled and unkempt than the last time Emilyann had seen him. His gray mustachios drooped, he hadn't shaved in days, nor changed his clothes nor slept, it appeared.

"The major . . . ?"

"I'm that sorry for losing him, ma'am."

281

"My God, he's not dead!"

"No, he's resting peaceful now," he told her, pulling a chair out from the kitchen table when her knees looked to give out. "I mean losing him in the battle. The smoke and rain and all. Then all those field surgeries and temporary billets. I thought I would go pure crazy. Now, like I said, he's resting, but it won't last. Medicine wears off, he starts burning up again, and starts throwing hisself around. The sawbones says we can't give him more, or it'll kill him for sure." Rigg sat down himself, that is, he collapsed into another of the wooden chairs, with a "Pardon, ma'm. It's that run off my feet I am."

Emilyann nodded, and poured out some of the hot tea they had brought in a towel-wrapped jug. Jake was bringing in wood to rekindle the meager fire in the cookstove. "Wet," he muttered.

"Aye." Rigg sipped his tea and shut his eyes. "I was going to get to it as soon as the major dropped to sleep. We was managing better till yesterday, when the farmer loped off. Said he went to fetch his wife back from her papa's up north, safer, you know. But the French ate his pigs and the British ate his cows, and the horses trampled everything else, so I don't know if'n he'll come back." He wiped a hand over his whiskers. "Doctor's not due back till the end of the week, if he gets here. I didn't see how I was to make another night, ma'am."

Emilyann patted his hand awkwardly. "I'm sure you did everything possible, Sergeant. We're here now. Everything will be fine."

Rigg looked at her hand, so white and dainty, and shrugged. "I got to admit I never thought to say I was happy to see you, ma'am. But the major's been a-calling for you, and if you could just keep him easy in his mind when he gets those restless fevers, I figure time can do the rest."

"He will recover, won't he?"

It was Jake who answered, "Here now, missy. We come this far, ain't we?" Then he told the tired batman to get some rest, he and the little countess would watch over the major. "For I reckon I've had enough experience doctorin' man and beast in my time to see the master through. And

282

don't worry none about missy," he said, happily ignorant of the circumstances of the first meeting between his mistress and the soldier. "She's got more pluck than pretty manners, most times."

This was no peaceful sleep, no matter what Rigg tried to tell her in reassurance, before the exhausted batman himself passed out on a cot in the kitchen, the only room beside the bedroom where the major lay. Smoky's cheeks were clammy, his color yellowish, his skin drawn tight over the planes of his face in a grimace of pain. He looked like Death.

Emilyann brushed the dark hair off his forehead and his eyes opened. It took a bleary moment for them to focus on her, and still seemed to take most of his concentration. "Sparrow?" His voice was no more than a whispered croak.

"Hallo, Smoky. I'm here."

He waved a hand that trembled like that of an old man, and she caught it and raised it to her face, and told him again, "I'm here now."

"I thought . . . I told . . . not to come?"

"Yes, but then you called for me."

"I remember . . . 's all right, then. Good girl." And he went back to sleep.

Emilyann bathed his face while Jake brought in the supplies, and she made broth while the coachman changed Stokely's bandages. "It's a nasty cut, make no mistake," he reported, "but I've seen worse. He'll do."

The next time the major awoke, Emilyann got some nourishing soup down him, and on him, and he tried to smile for her as she wiped his chin. She busied herself with the bowl and towel so he would not see her struggle to hold back the tears. His sunken eyes never left her, though, and he seemed more lucid.

"Hush," she told him when he wanted to talk. "Save your strength for tomorrow."

"No. You weren't supposed to come. You promised."

"I promised not to come for the fun and parties. Let me tell you, Everett Stockton, this is not fun."

"Know that. I'm sorry, Sparrow."

"You great goose. I like it better when you shout at me."

"You never listened anyway. . . . You shouldn't be here. Too dangerous."

"No, Smoky, the war is over, and I have Jake and Rigg to protect me." That seemed to please him, so she went on. "And Aunt Ingrid is back in town, too, organizing prayer meetings and saving souls, I am sure, so you needn't worry over the proprieties." She was not about to tell him his sister was here also; she was trying to ease his mind, not send him into a rage. But mentioning Aunt Ingrid reminded her that her scratchy relative would be anxious for news, or Emilyann's return, before nightfall.

Smoky's three nursemaids discussed the problem in the kitchen when he nodded off again. Emilyann flatly refused to leave, especially since one of the men would have to accompany her. Jake felt that since he was well rested, he should stay on with his mistress, while Rigg, who had had a few hours' sleep, knew the roads better and would know where to hire a gig to carry supplies back from town. Rigg could report to the ladies at Charteret, get a decent sleep there and, in the morning, check with headquarters and gather whatever stores he thought they might need, including a new uniform. Rigg did not want to leave his major, but knew when he was outgunned. And His Lordship was improved by the lass's visit, no doubt about that, and her man Jake seemed handy enough for a horse doctor. So he left with one of the horses and a list from Lady Stokely. "And remember the lemons. Smoky always liked lemonade, so we brought them all the way from England just in case there were none to be had here."

Stokely began to sweat not ten minutes after Rigg left, and an hour before his next medication. Great dropules formed on his forehead and soaked the bedclothes. Emilyann and Jake both worked to keep him covered when he wanted to throw the blankets off and dry when his sheets became drenched. This was no place for maidenly modesty, Emilyann found out quickly, bathing her husband to bring the fever down. Jake had to hold the major to keep him from thrashing around, but Emilyann's voice seemed to soothe him the most, though he was beyond responding. He would call "Sparrow," and she would tell him yes, she was there, and he would lie quietly for minutes, until the shaking started again.

At last it was time for his next dose and Emilyann and Jake were both drained when Stokely finally sank into a deep stupor.

"Whisht, lass, it's gonna be a long night," Jake told her, wiping his own forehead before sitting down to the meal of cold meat, bread, and cheese they had carried with them. Rigg had set out a jug of ale and the remains of a rabbit pie. "Best you get some sleep now, an' you're able. I'll wake you when things get bad, then you can sit up with 'im whilst I rest a bit."

Jake made sense, and Emilyann realized she had hardly slept since that courier came with the message. It was strange, with Smoky lying there so deathly still, how she felt relieved, as if just seeing him were reassurance enough. She might never have seen him again. Yes, she would sleep for a few hours, but she dragged Rigg's cot into the bedroom and curled up in a blanket that smelled comfortingly of horse.

She did not move when Smoky woke the first time and asked for her.

"She's right over there, Master Stokely," Jake told him, holding the candle up so the major could see the blond-haired bundle in the corner.

Smoky's lips almost curved in a grin, and he slept that way awhile. The next time he roused, he was troubled. "You . . . ?"

"It's Jake, my lord," the old man told him, keeping his voice soft in order not to disturb Lady Em. "You remember, the old duke's head coachman. You used to pester me to let you drive the four-in-hand."

"I remember. Jake, you'll look after her, won't you, if . . ."

"I allus does, Master Stokely, when she lets me. You're the only one as had any reins on the filly when she gets the bit 'tween her teeth though, so you better be back in the saddle soon."

"Headstrong girl, my Sparrow. Shouldn't be here. You'll take care ... ?"

He did not know Jake when he woke next, wet and trembling. Jake was trying to sponge him down, determined that Emilyann should get as much rest as possible. The major started throwing himself around, however, and Jake put his arms on him, lest he fall off the bed altogether.

"No!" Smoky shouted. "No, you filthy grave-robbing bastards, I'll not let you have my watch!" Even in his delirium the officer was strong enough to throw Jake's arms off and swing out and clout the old stableman on the chin. "I'm not dead yet, you damn vulture."

Emilyann jumped up, wide-eyed, and screamed for Jake to leave the room. Couldn't he see he was upsetting Smoky? She ran to kneel on the bed next to him and clasped his face in her hands. "Smoky, wake up, dearest. No one will hurt you, Smoky. You're safe now."

"Sparrow?"

"Yes, it's Sparrow. I'm here. You're safe." She kept repeating it, stroking his face, until the tension left his muscles and he relaxed against her. She got him to take some more broth, and put a fresh case on the pillow, then sat down next to him again when he struggled to talk.

"I want to tell you. All that time ... trying to get somewhere safe ... warm, out of the rain ... trying to hold my guts together with my hands ... I was laughing, Sparrow. Know why? 'Cause all those years, all those battles and skirmishes, I came out with hardly a scratch."

She touched the scar on his jaw, more noticeable now that he was so gaunt. "That's not just a scratch. A few inches more ..."

"You don't understand. No one cared. Then I finally had something to go home to, don't you see?"

"Yes, Smoky, I see. I cared. But why were you laughing?"

"So I wouldn't cry, Sparrow. So I wouldn't cry."

Smoky rested a few minutes, his head cradled in her lap and one hand holding hers. Then his face grew troubled and he asked her to go send Rigg in to him.

"Rigg has gone back to town for supplies and things. He'll be back in the morning."

"Then get your man Jake, will you, Sparrow?"

"He's fast asleep, Smoky. What is it?"

Smoky raised his other hand from under the sheets. It was covered in blood. "I think you better wake him."

"Me? I can't do that, Jake. You know I can't." Her voice was pleading, unsteady.

The old man held up his hands, the knuckles bent and swollen with arthritis. "Well, these fingers can't hold a needle steady enough, and my eyes ain't what they used to be neither, lass, so it's either you start stitchin' or we sit around hopin' he don't bleed to death afore that batman of his gets back."

"I vote for Sparrow," her husband put in, waving Jake's flask.

"And I'm quite sure you've had enough of that, my lord, what with the laudanum and that other stuff that smells like spoiled eggs," she answered, snatching the flask away. "Smoky, I just cannot do it. It's not that I'm going missish on you, you know I wouldn't. But remember all the samplers we paid your mother's maid to finish for me?"

"You still owe me twenty-five guineas. Maybe it was forty-five."

"And they tried and tried at Miss Meadow's, but I never got the hang of it, Smoky. The plaguey thread is always tangling and the knots come undone and—"

And Jake was already boiling water and laying out a gruesome array of scissors, knives, and powders from a pouch in his saddlebag.

"You old windbag," Emilyann accused him. "You said you could do whatever was needed. I wouldn't have brought you else."

"That's why I said it. Now, here, watch close. Tarnation, girl, open your eyes or you'll be sewin' him to the bed."

Emilyann felt bile rise in her throat as Jake pulled the bandages back and she saw the great gaping wound for the first time.

287

"It looks worse'n it is," he assured her. "At least you don't have to sew up any intestines or anything."

She excused herself for a moment to be thoroughly sick outside. When she came back, Smoky gave her a drunken, lopsided grin before sinking into unconsciousness, and she took up the needle.

"Smoky mightn't like looking like an altar cloth with little crosses up and down him," she murmured, "but, by heaven, where is Aunt Ingrid now that I need her?"

Chapter Nineteen

"And your aunt says she's praying for the major. And I says all to the good; he needs all the help he can get."

Rigg was back, all spruced up, his mustachios neatly trimmed, driving a donkey cart. "Beggin' your pardon, ma'am, but it's a hell of a thing for a cavalry man to be reduced to," he told Emilyann, but it was the only rig for hire in the town that wouldn't get bogged down in the muck. Rigg brought food and supplies, a few chickens, a change of clothes for Emilyann, who still wore her crumpled riding habit, and news from town.

"It's settling down now; provisions are coming back in finally, and more of the men are being shipped home, those that can travel. Oh, and little sister sends her greetings. She is busy entertaining the troops, though they be officers mostly."

Emilyann glanced nervously toward the bedroom, and Smoky. "She's not doing anything too outrageous, is she?"

"What, with the preacher-lady there? No, she sings church songs to them, and reads from the Holy Book. Of course, as soon as Lady Aylesbury heads out on an errand

288

or somewhat, they switch to little ditties and waltzes and some novels the gel brought from home."

"Nadine is not left unchaperoned, is she? That doesn't sound like my aunt."

"Now, how could the gal be unchaperoned with you billeting half a battalion at that palace? Every English lady in this country sits in your parlor of an afternoon, 'specially those what has daughters, doing their share for the lads' morale."

"That's all right, then."

"Sure, and I used some of the money you gave me to have that rat-faced concierge unearth a few bottles for the men from that count's cellars, and a couple of packs of cards. They're all fine." He looked at her more closely through shaggy brows, noting the dark circles under her eyes. "But how are things here?"

The major was awake when Emilyann took Rigg in to see, and he was wanting to know about their conversation. "I didn't hear you mention my little sister, did I?" he accused her.

"Little sinners, Smoky, Aunt Ingrid is reforming the little sinners. That's what you heard." When he raised one eyebrow she hurried on, "I think I'll ride back to town this afternoon to see for myself. Aunt Ingrid sent the wrong dress, anyway, and I—"

"Wear something blue, Sparrow. And tell Nadine to toe the line. I'm not grassed yet."

Later, when Rigg went to change the bandages, he squawked, "By all that's holy, Major, what the hell happened to you? You got more lacings than an opera dancer's corset."

"There was a little difficulty last evening. That nightmare, I suppose." He looked down, admiring Emilyann's handiwork. "Lovely, ain't it? We're aiming for tapestries next."

"Cor, I hope you were unconscious at the time."

"Most of it. I did wake up when she finished."

"You mean the chit did this? I mean, Lady Stokely?"

"Aye, and knocked off a swig after, like a regular trooper."

"I thought all women knew how to sew. Thought they was born with it, like a dog wagging his tail."

The major laughed, and Rigg could have forgiven her anything for the sound, even making his major look like a Christmas goose that had been trussed by a jug-bit chef. "Well, it don't seem to have done you any harm, at least. Seems you look a mite better, in fact. Having the lady here must have done the trick."

Either that or Jake's whiskey.

Smoky was healing. There was no doubt of that, nor that it would take a long convalescence before he was fully recovered. He was awake longer now that the laudanum dosage could be cut back, although the pain was still intense and he could not be moved. The fever never came back so violently, but he remained too debilitated to hold a spoon and too weak to care. He fell asleep during Aunt Ingrid's visits, albeit Emilyann thought he was shamming. Nadine's one visit certainly exhausted him, with all her chatter of the young officers whose recovery she was overseeing.

"Gads, the chit's got no taste," he told Em after she hustled the younger girl out, seeing how weary Smoky had become. "She thinks Lieutenant Andrews is cute. He's got freckles and no chin, and his ears stick out. Last time was Chippy Harrington, and he has spots." So he encouraged Sparrow to spend time with the ladies back in town, to keep an eye on his sister, and because he hated to see the shadows under her eyes and the paleness of her face from sitting by his bedside for hours on end. He sent her, although he dreaded the thought of her laughing with the military youngsters who must be predisposed to adore her anyway, living on her bounty as they were. As if anyone would *not* adore Sparrow, knowing her lively charm, her enchanting dimpled grin, those blue eyes of summer and sunshine. He sighed.

And Emilyann went back to town occasionally so Smoky could not see her anguish at his pain, her frustration at not being able to do more for him. There was less to do anyway, once the farmer Merced came back with his wife, after Emilyann sent word that she would help rebuild the little farm, in gratitude for Merced's kindness to Lord Stokely. Now the pair stayed with neighbors but came every day to take charge of the cooking and cleaning and keeping the fire going, in addition to seeing to new plantings and stock, so the major's nursemaids were tripping over each other in the small house.

In town Emilyann made sure Nadine did not go beyond the pale, but she had not taken a misstep, not with the men considering her an angel, and Aunt Ingrid only just reconsidering her opinion of Nadine as an imp of Satan.

Ingrid herself was seeing that Nadine's silliness did more to lift the officers' spirits than her own preachings, although not in the long run, of course. But for now she was toning down her fanaticism and finding friends among the English gentrywomen who accepted her as a kindhearted lady, not a dicked-in-the-nob eccentric who had to be tolerated because she was a duchess.

No matter the time Emilyann spent with her family, she hurried back to Smoky each evening, just to touch him in his sleep and watch his chest rise and fall, and make sure her love kept him safe. She sat for hours, memorizing his already well-known features, that firm jaw and not-quite-straight nose. She had to be there, she told her protesting aunt, because when he groaned with pain and drug-induced bad dreams, her voice still calmed him better than any other's.

For his part, Stokely fought sleep rather than dream of Sparrow laughing and singing with those park soldiers back in town, maybe getting up impromptu dances for the men so *they* did not fall into the doldrums. He tried so desperately not to dream of his wife in another man's arms that he ended up falling through grotesque webs to that other terrible nightmare of cold and blood and rain that would not stop. He was wet and—

"What the hell do you think you are doing?"

"Why, I am bathing you, of course, silly."

He grabbed for her hand that held the sponge before it could go any lower, and pulled the sheets up. "You shouldn't be doing that."

"But I've been taking turns with Rigg and Jake for weeks now, Smoky. They need their rest, too."

He still held her hand. The damn water was dripping on his chest. "But you're a lady."

She mopped at him with a towel and laughed, telling him, "No, I'm not, I'm your wife, remember?"

"I remember you are not quite," he said, which brought color to her cheeks.

To cover her embarrassment, Emilyann teased, "It's nothing I haven't seen before," and his hand clenched her wrist again.

"Who is it? I'll kill him."

"Are you feverish again? Shall I fetch the laudanum?"

"Couldn't you have waited, Sparrow?" he asked bitterly. "Or did some rake catch your eye?"

"A rake? Do you think that I . . . ? Why, you . . ." And she mashed the sponge down on his nose till he sputtered, then she wiped him off tenderly. "You really are a clunch. I meant that I had seen *you* these past weeks, with bandages and without. Besides, you forget that I am a country girl."

"I don't recall a lot of naked men running around the countryside in England either."

"Silly, I mean the animals. The milk-and-water misses in the towns may pretend not knowing where lambs come from, but every farm-bred girl knows when the cows are brought to the bull to be serviced or the stallion stands to stud."

Smoky lifted the sheet again. "Bulls? Stallions? My dear, are you in for disappointment!"

She fled the room, blushing furiously, while he laughed and laughed, despite the basin of water overturned on his head. Smoky was definitely healing.

Stokely was sick of being sick. He was tired of lemonade, bored with the same four bare walls, and irked at not being able to hold his wife. He was heartily disgusted with his dreams, especially the one where he could hear someone pounding nails in his coffin, so he decided to take no more laudanum, and then had to face *that* nightmare, after

292

which he was even more blue-deviled, with more energy-draining pain. And the same bad dreams.

Emilyann tried harder to cheer him, bringing books and a chess set and all the news from town.

"Nadine is in alt. There are starting to be small dinner parties among the English and the returning local gentry. Nothing ornate, mind, out of respect for the wounded, but with England in the throes of victory celebrations, some festivity was called for."

"Never fear, Nadine could find a party in the Antipodes, dancing with the penguins."

"She even found a local modiste with the latest fashion plates from Paris, so we are having new things made up rather than sending home for our fancier gowns. I told her she might have a small evening entertainment herself next week, to repay our hostesses, since I am hoping the doctor permits us to move you soon, and then you wouldn't want any such commotion around."

He wouldn't want any of those other officers around either, but he didn't picture Sparrow tossing them out in the streets.

"Nadine and the count's fancy chef have been concocting menus for days. He is a true *artiste*, and I have half a mind to bribe him to return to England with us. What do you think?" she asked brightly.

Smoky thought she only had half a mind at all, to be asking someone who had not tasted the chef's cooking, being limited to gruel, gruel, and more gruel. He muttered something impolite, which she ignored, as she had the rest of his ill humor.

"You shan't mind our socializing without you, shall you?"

He minded a great deal, and also her insensitive, patronizing attitude, so he grumbled, "It must be costing you a fortune."

"I won't argue with you about it, Smoky, if you are looking to start an argument."

"Why, because I'm sick?"

"No, because you're too pigheaded. Geoff writes that the

harvest was excellent, and he is getting high prices for the market stock, so you are well out of dun territory."

"Aye, and into petticoat financing."

"It's always the money, isn't it?" she asked sadly, and he reached for her hand, saying, "It's *your* money."

"Not according to Papa's will and English law. Those papers we signed give me a handsome settlement all my own, so I do not mind either. I might have if it was someone else, but—" She caught herself before she confessed too much. "Anyway, if you want to be so stubborn, you can pay yourself back after a few years of hard work and good management."

"That's fustian. What do I know of managing an estate, much less hogs? All I know about pigs is bacon and gloves, Sparrow. I'm a soldier, dash it, not a farmer. There's no place for me in England."

She brushed a dark curl from his brow, tried to smooth out the frown lines there with a hesitant kiss on his forehead. He looked up into those incredible blue eyes, so serious now and troubled. "Forgive me, my dear, I suppose I am just feeling sorry for myself," he said, reaching to touch her soft cheek. "It's just that you did not have the luxury of choosing where you and your fortune landed. You should have had a chance to look over the eligibles, fall in love, make a choice. You could have had your pick. You should not be tied to an invalid."

Emilyann tried to make light of it. "But, Smoky, I am the one who forced you into the marriage, remember? You should have been free to return home as the conquering hero and find a beautiful heiress to restore your fortunes."

"But that's what I did." He turned away, knowing that was how all of London looked at the marriage.

"You . . . you really married me for the money?"

"I may as well have."

Devastated at the crumbling of her dreams, Lady Stokely rushed back to town. She looked so stricken, Nadine assumed Stokely had taken a turn for the worse and started weeping.

"Stop that yammering, you peagoose. He's fine and he is

294

your brother, so you can go keep him company for a change. Tell him I am tired and need a rest. Tell him I have to see about travel arrangements home now that he is improving. Tell him anything you blessed well please, because he will believe only what he wants to anyway."

So Nadine went, and Stokely shouted at her; Aunt Ingrid went, and Stokely claimed a headache. He threw his breakfast pap at Rigg one day, and when the batman sent in Merced's wife with lunch, the major scandalized the farmwoman by refusing to wear his nightshirt. The farmer himself Stokely cursed—for being a farmer. After a few days only old Jake the coachman would volunteer to sit in the room with him sometimes, and Jake hardly said a word, just sat mending a bit of harness or polishing a piece of brass, and chewing his tobacco.

Just to make conversation, the thoroughly bored and sullen convalescent finally asked Jake about a noise he heard at night sometimes. "I thought it was a dream, my coffin being nailed shut. But I hear it repeatedly, even when I waken. Who the hell is hammering when a sick man is supposed to be resting?"

Jake kept polishing. "I 'spect you mean a little tappin' sound."

"It's not so little in the middle of the night, dammit."

Jake spit into a bucket he kept handy. "I 'spect you mean Pug, then."

"What, that ugly little mutt of Sparrow's? Why in the world did she bring him to Belgium with her?"

"Couldn't leave him, he was that poorly."

"Blast it, man, will you finish the story! Heaven knows I've got nothing better to do than listen, lying here in this miserable bed. What happened to the dog and what's he doing, learning drumrolls for the infantry?"

Jake looked at the major, and saw the same resty youth he'd always been. He put down the leather and the rag, spit again while Stokely fumed, and told how the pup had fallen off the carriage one day and gotten his leg mangled by the coach wheel.

"Gotta be put out of his misery, I says. Pup looks up with big brown pop-eyes and missy looks up with those

295

pretty blue ones of hers all misty and says 'Can't you fix it, Jake? Please, can't we try to help him?' " He shrugged. "What's a body to do? So me and the boys did what we could, stitchin' and sewin' and feedin' the little mite brandy. Recovered, too, he did. 'Course he's only got three legs now. So the boys renamed him Peg. I made him a brace from harness leather, and whittled him a new leg when you was sleepin'." Jake spat again. "Little fool was fallin' over when he tried to show the other males his territory, if you know what I mean."

Smoky did, and got the point. "This mightn't be a moral lesson, like the prodigal son or something, would it?"

Jake went back to polishing. Smoky went back to brooding. That little bleater was standing on his own legs, no matter how many. And Jake was likely here because Emmy had begged him to "fix" her peevish husband. And if that tapping went on at night, she must still come to see him.

"Old man, can you whittle me a cane? One with a donkey on the handle maybe."

Stokely called for newspapers, stationery, and his clothes. He was going to see about a position with the Foreign Office, or perhaps the War Office in London, to avoid any more travel. He was going to make investments to repay his wife as soon as possible, and he was damn well going to stand on his own two feet to woo her back.

Chapter Twenty

They traveled home by slow stages for Stokely's sake, and the journey was still agonizing for him, even when he rode in the second coach with Rigg instead of the carriage containing his prattlebox sister, his wife, whose dimmed spirits were a reproach to him, and Lady Aylesbury, whose tombstone, he felt, should read: *She Meant Well.*

They were all happy to halt the trip in London rather than continuing on to Stockton, which would have taken three or four more days at their current rate. Geoff came down and enlivened the household, and Aunt Adelaide fussed. Thornton did his best to depress the high spirits of the younger members of the family as unsuitable for Stokely's recuperation, but Geoff and Nadine reestablished their contacts in the ton and began the rounds of routs and assemblies, morning rides and afternoon promenades.

The regent's own physician ordered Stokely to bed for at least a week, and he was glad to go, albeit the room he was given was on the ground floor for his convenience, and not attached to his wife's suite for his comfort. The faithful Rigg was in attendance and the household staff stood ready to cater to his every whim. His siblings were good for a few minutes of gossip or talk of pigs, depending on which was coming or going, and his wife breezed in and out of his room with brittle courtesy. She did not want to tire him, she said.

Emilyann did not want him to see her hurt. He had his pride about the money, she had her pride in wanting to be loved for herself. She knew Smoky was fond of her in an offhand, brotherly way at least, and he had shown definite interest in sharing her bed, but she wanted much more. So she started racketing about town to show him—what? That she did not need him, that others found her desirable, that a woman grown did not die of shattered dreams. She felt like a china shepherdess broken by a naughty child and glued together clumsily. She was afraid that if she moved too fast, pieces would crumble; too slowly and everyone would see the cracks.

As she told Smoky, she had to keep an eye on Nadine, and, furthermore, it was not good ton for a wife to be in her husband's pocket.

The Earl of Stokely, for he was already writing letters resigning his commission and was no longer to be called major, scowled and bided his time. As soon as he was able, and before the surgeons thought he should, he was calling

297

on cabinet members, government officials, bankers and brokers, and his tailor. The uniforms were packed away and his other clothes would have to be altered to fit his gaunt frame. He walked with his cane when possible, both to rebuild the wasted muscles and because riding a horse was still forbidden to him and getting up and down into carriages was too painful. He looked with envy at Emilyann's phaeton, like a child with his face against the glass of a confectioner's shop, and practiced going up and down stairs when she was not around to say him nay.

He also walked to his clubs to hear the latest news, and found that he was it. Thanks to Nadine and Geoff, all of London had heard of his heroic wounds and Emilyann's valiant nursing, and the gossips were wondering why the Little Countess was not sitting dutifully by her injured husband's side. No one forgot, it seemed, the fireworks of their last public appearance together, and the tattlemongers were holding their collective breaths.

Emilyann also got wind of the *on dits*, and found she did not like her marriage being held under public scrutiny. She also resented the speculative looks she received from dissipated libertines. If Stokely wasn't interested, they seemed to imply, his lady was fair game. She could handle the encroaching toads, but would rather show a handsome husband than a cold shoulder.

"Do you think we might hold some form of entertainment?" she asked Smoky one night as they met for sherry before dinner. "Nothing too strenuous, of course. No receiving line," she told him solicitously. "Perhaps a musical gathering."

"Not if Nadine is going to torture the pianoforte," he answered, "but I think that would be ideal. I cannot get around yet to the balls and such, and there are men I would like to speak with who are too busy during the days. I have been wanting to talk to you about that, Sparrow." He filled her glass while she waited.

"What would you think if I took my seat in the Lords? Someone has to speak for the returning veterans, and their pensions, and then there is the reform movement. Petersham thinks there may be a position as an undersecretary next year if I prove myself this term."

Emilyann was pleased to see him looking excited about something again. He was beginning to fill out and looked elegant in his black satin jacket and dove-gray pantaloons, and all the better for the enthusiasm of his plans. "I think that would be wonderful, Smoky. You'll have to see about the child labor laws and those awful workhouses, and the climbing boys and—"

"Hold, my dear," he said, laughing. "I have not told them yes yet." He studied his glass, swirled the liquor around to see the glimmers in the fire's light. "You do know it will mean being in London most of the year, and you have been talking of returning to the country any time these past weeks."

Emilyann dreaded his next words. Here would come the part, she thought, when he politely ordered her to ruralize, so he might resume his rakehell ways in town. Behind nearly every profligate in London was a wife in the country, raising babies and roses. She was not about to become one of them.

"I do enjoy the country, but I have always aspired to become a political hostess," she lied. She never once thought of it until now, but let him wriggle out of that!

He did not squirm a bit, raising his glass to her and saying, "I knew I could count on you."

"Then you want me to stay?"

"Of course. I want you by me. I would not take the position if it displeased you."

Dinner was announced just then, and Emilyann, seated at the opposite end of the polished table from her husband, savored his words more than the turbot in oyster sauce or glazed squab. He really did care!

A few nights later Smoky asked if he might accompany her and Nadine to Almack's.

"Whyever would you want to go there?" Geoff asked. "It's deuced dull, and you have to dance with all the fubsy-faced females."

"Not I," claimed his brother, waving the silver-topped

299

cane. "I have but to limp in, in my knee breeches, of course, then I can adjourn to the card rooms."

"But they play only for chicken stakes, Ev. You could go to White's or Boodle's, or Crocker's even."

"Yes, but my beautiful wife will not be at those clubs, so I shall go to Almack's and practice my fiercest jealous-husband looks."

Trying to keep her voice as light as his playful tone, Emilyann inquired, "And shall you be jealous?"

He turned serious. "I pray I have no cause to be."

Lady Stokely's maid was putting the finishing touches to her mistress's toilette that evening when Smoky rapped on the door. Antoinette curtsied, giggled, and left. Emilyann was in a gown of soft blue crepe with a gauze overskirt that had sequined butterflies embroidered on it. Another butterfly rested in Emilyann's cloud of tousled curls. Stokely had to catch his breath a moment.

"What are you doing here? You should never have attempted the stairs!"

It was definitely not the stairs that had him breathing so hard. "I brought you something," he managed to say, handing her a long box. "I realized I'd never seen you in the family diamonds. You had the combination to the safe, didn't you?"

"Yes, but I never felt I should—oh, Smoky, they are exquisite!"

"I'd rather see you in the sapphires, your eyes, of course, but your maid thought these would be more suitable for this gown."

"That's why the wretch was acting like a schoolgirl with a secret all night." She lifted out a bracelet and he came to help her do up the clasp, kissing her wrist while he held her hand. Emilyann gasped at the delicious sensation, and blushed when he chuckled, turning away in confusion.

With her back to him he placed the necklace around her throat, and kissed the nape of her neck. She trembled.

"Let me see, Countess."

She turned, and now he was shaken to see how perfectly

the center stone nestled in the curvature of her breasts, above the gown's low neckline.

With his eyes fixed on that diamond, Emilyann worried that he intended to kiss her there, too. She nervously turned back to the mirror, admiring the effect. "And they are even real," she surprised him by saying.

"Of course they are, widgeon. Did you think the family heirlooms were Austrian glass?"

"The Aylesbury ones are. Uncle Morgan has been turning the gems into paste, for the money."

"That old court-card will stop at nothing. How you got such a loose screw in your family is beyond me."

"How you got Thornton in yours is just as strange."

"Touché. But what are you going to do about the jewels?"

"Oh, I have taken care of that. I have an arrangement with Uncle's, ah, jeweler."

Smoky adjusted his cuffs. "I assume you mean his pawnbroker, and I most assuredly do not want to hear how you came to do business with him. I have enough gray hairs as is."

She smiled and told him, "But you look so distinguished. Anyway, I have been buying the pieces back whenever I could, and the trip to Brussels gave me the opportunity to poke around Aunt Ingrid's jewel box and switch them for the copies."

"You'll make a politician's wife yet. But tell me, poppet, did you mind not having the Arcott heirlooms?"

"I minded seeing them go out of the family, but I never expected to have them, you know, and I do have my mama's things."

"And the Stockton heirlooms. Why did you never take them out of the safe?"

"They were yours and I, ah . . ."

"And I forgot to give them to you, slowtop that I am. Forgive me, Sparrow. They are not mine, however; they belong to the Countess of Stokely."

"But I didn't think I ought to wear them."

"I cannot imagine why. You are the loveliest Lady Stokely ever, and I could not be more proud to have you wear them."

There were no juicy tidbits for the tale-waggers at Almack's to chew that night. Lord Stokely was the lion of the evening, and his wife, the sparkle in her eyes matching the glitter of her jewels, hovered at his side. She urged him to sit down, to use his cane, to rest, nagging "like an old married couple." He teased and carried her hand to his lips again, just to see her cheeks grow rosy. She danced with some of her admirers, but mostly she made them known to her husband if they were unacquainted, and the glow between the lady and her lord discouraged the most self-confident seducer. She was also determined to bring Smoky to the attention of her father's cronies, those men with influence in political circles. Uncle This and Dear Lord That were brought to Smoky's chair. Stokely's evident chagrin at his wife's meddling did more for his career than his war record. Those hide-bound old men who used to dandle little Lady Em on their knees saw her dimples and her tender affection for this hero of hers; they saw Stokely's eyes follow her every movement when she was gone from his side, and their own hearts were glad. Their old friend, the late Duke of Aylesbury, would have been happy with this marriage, as proud as if he'd arranged it himself.

The current Duke of Aylesbury was at *point non plus*. During his wife's absence, when he could have been free of her pontificating and pestering, his own incapacitation kept him at home. He was thrown into his own company more than he liked, and found he could not even play cards with himself, left hand against right, because both hands could read the shaved decks. His only consolation was in dismissing half of the household staff—nobody ever went in all the rooms anyway; who cared if they were clean?—and using their wages to buy gin. There was nothing left in the cellars, he had checked them ages ago. Gin it was, cheap gin, and lots of it.

It came to pass on one cold, dark night when no one came to light a fire in his room, likely because he had fired anyone who could, Morgan Arcott gave his body to the bottle and sold his soul to the devil.

Funny, he thought, Satan looked like one of those crouching gargoyles he remembered from his grand tour. Notre Dame, maybe. Ugly memories were all he got out of the grand tour anyway, that and the French pox. The devil's eyes were fires—cheap help in hell, Morgan mused—and his voice was like coal rumbling down a chute.

"What do you want?" Morgan asked.

"It's not what *I* want," came the reply, as if from a distance, "it's what you want. I heard your prayers, and I came to help."

"I know about your help. You helped Adam right out of Eden, didn't you?"

The devil waved a taloned hand. "This ain't Eden, Morgan, and I can do better for you."

Now Morgan knew he did not have a snowball's chance in, well, hell, of going to heaven, so what did he have to lose? If Old Nick didn't already hold markers on his soul, the system was in trouble. "So what do I have to do?"

"Remember that old saying about the Lord helping those who help themselves?" The archfiend did not wait for a reply; he was off on a gripe of his own. "It's a lie. *I* started the myth. Get people thinking for themselves, I told Him, and they are bound to stray. 'That's a gamble I am willing to take,' He said."

Morgan gaped. "God gambles?"

The devil smiled, not a pretty sight, all yellow fangs and threads of saliva. "I cheat, of course. Is it a deal?"

When Ingrid came home, she was on a tear: the house, the servants, her beloved Beauregard led off the straight and narrow. Home? She would have been at home in the Inquisition. Hell, she would have been at home in a hair shirt, even if she was looking better, from what he could see through bloodshot eyes. Something about her dresses, maybe, or else she was wearing her hair in a softer style. Her heart had not grown any softer, that was for sure. Morgan found himself and a packed bag at one of his clubs before the cat could lick its ear, certainly before he could ask for a loan.

Chapter Twenty-one

"*I* think I shall ask Rigg to move my things upstairs today," Stokely announced at breakfast. Geoff was already off for a few days to a horse fair at Epsom and Nadine was gathering sustenance and the last of the Bath buns for a shopping expedition with some friends.

"How is it you can go up the steps today when we had to come home so early last evening?" she asked around a mouthful of muffin.

"Almack's can weary anyone, minx," he told her, but Emilyann, sipping her chocolate, wondered if it was wise. "You really were quite done up by the evening, it seemed."

Smoky detected a note of disappointment in her tone and grinned. "I intend to have an easier day, so I think I'll be able to manage by tonight." The look he gave his wife said he'd crawl if he had to.

"I don't see what all the pother is about," Nadine said on her way out. "Your room downstairs is closer to everything you need, after all."

Smoky choked on a bit of toast, and Emilyann excused herself hurriedly to see Cook about the menus. She kept busy all day, going over her accounts and making lists for the musical reception she planned. If her mind was not fully on her tasks, she told herself, it was merely due to the distraction of things being moved and commotions in the hallway. It had nothing to do with Smoky's knowing smile or the tender kiss he had placed on her lips before breakfast. Nothing whatsoever.

No one noticed that Nadine did not return from the shops until teatime. "Dratted girl," Emilyann fumed, "she knew I invited those Durhart twins just for her. I cannot even tell them apart, and they haven't ha'pence of conversation between them."

Luckily the Durhart brothers did not stay long, with the object of their call not present, for shortly Aunt Ingrid rushed into the room, offending Mr. Butler by slamming the door behind her. She was waving a note in the air and shouting, "Ruined, ruined. My baby is ruined."

Stokely and his lady exchanged glances. Someone had finally clapped Bobo in gaol for prigging their watch or something. No one except Aunt Ingrid would be surprised, or distressed.

"I just knew it would happen! That hoyden of yours has led poor Beauregard into sin. Oh, whatever shall I do?"

Emilyann led the distraught woman to the sofa and Aunt Adelaide handed her a cup of tea. "So soothing, my dear. I always find—"

"Damn and blast!" Smoky looked up from the note he had been reading. "She's really done it this time. Here, listen to this: 'Have taken Nadine to Gretna. Only way. Don't worry.' "

The next sound was a loud thud as Aunt Adelaide hit the floor.

"But why would they do that?" Emilyann wanted to know as she and Stokely struggled to get his aunt onto a sofa. "Nadine knew we would not stand in her way if her heart was really set on it. We might not have been thrilled at the match"—Stokely coughed—"but in a year or so . . ."

"And I even told Beauregard I thought the chit was coming along. He could have done a great deal better, of course."

"Aunt Ingrid," Emilyann cautioned, "Nadine is my sister-in-law."

"And my daughter-in-law!" Ingrid wailed. "She will never be accepted. Dear Lord, I will never be able to hold my head up again."

"Hold off on the dramatics, ma'am," Stokely told her, studying the letter. Lady Aylesbury sniffed and even Em thought he was acting with high-handed insensitivity, but he never was one for Cheltenham tragedies. "This does not sit right with me. They cannot have been gone long, so why would the clunch—pardon, ma'am—leave a note where we could find it? Why would they leave in the middle of the day at all, when they would be missed so soon?"

Emilyann glanced cautiously at her aunt and said in the politest terms she could think of, "Bobo never was one to, ah, worry over practical matters."

"You mean he hasn't got the brain power of a bedbug. And this is just like some fool romantical notion Nadine might enjoy."

"I told you the girl was no better than she should be," Aunt Ingrid countered. "Novels, hah!"

Rather than listen to the two of them trade insults, Emilyann went up to see if Nadine's things were missing, or if 'Toinette knew anything. This suggestion won her an approving nod from Stokely, who was rereading the note, and muttering that he didn't know the bacon-brained Bobo could write.

When Emilyann returned with the maid and Aunt Adelaide's restoratives—hartshorn, vinaigrette, feathers for burning, a flask of . . . rum?—Stokely was already calling for the carriage, a change of clothes, his pistols.

"Nothing much is missing that I can tell. Even her jewelry is left here, and there is a ten-pound note in her glove drawer."

"That's what I thought. Nadine would never elope without her wardrobe, not voluntarily anyway. I am going after them, my dear. Don't worry, I shall bring them back safe and sound. They cannot have much of a lead."

"I am going with you," two voices chorused.

"No, I'll make better time without you."

"But you'll need help, Smoky. You cannot take a lot of servants along or this will be all over London," Emilyann said, and added, "You'll need me to lend countenance to this affair."

So they set out in one carriage, Jake driving, Rigg up beside him with a rifle. Their first inquiries netted the information that yes, a young couple fitting the description had passed by, on the North Road, all right. They were not trying to hide their tracks, it seemed. Ingrid was not-so-quietly

306

praying on the seat next to Emilyann while Stokely laid his pistols on the other and reloaded them.

"This is all my fault," Emilyann lamented. "I should have watched her better."

Aunt Ingrid sniffed her disdain and murmured something about bad breeding which, thankfully, Smoky either did not hear or chose to ignore. He reached for his wife's hand and gave it a reassuring squeeze. "Never think so, Sparrow. She was never meant to be your responsibility, my love. You've looked out for her interests like she was a chick of your own, and I can never repay you for that either. Except possibly by wringing the chit's neck when we find her." He tugged on her hand until she moved to the seat beside him, where he could put his arm around her shoulder in comfort, and draw her close. "And you taught her more about being a real lady in this year or so than anyone else has managed in seventeen."

And right there, in the hurtling carriage with Ingrid sitting in her black gown like a vulture across from them, Smoky thoroughly kissed his wife.

At the next stop Stokely decided to ride ahead, over Emilyann's loud objections. He felt he could better concentrate on the problem at hand if his wife weren't in his arms. The prayers and Ingrid's carping about Nadine were trying his already strained nerves, but he told the ladies, half truthfully, that his leg needed to be exercised or it would tighten up. With night soon falling, they needed to cover ground more quickly.

The only horse available at the posting house was a likely-looking animal, but with a sadly ragged gait. Before the aching earl could resume the coach ride at the next change, the nag unfortunately ran out of wind. Stokely and his mount fell behind the carriage, which probably was the only thing to save them all when the three highwaymen rode out of the woods, firing.

Rigg nicked one of them, who rode off, and the pistol in Stokely's waistband dropped the second dead in his tracks before the bandit could pull open the carriage door. The third man was already around the other side of the coach, pointing a heavy pistol, before Smoky could get him in sight. Then a shot rang out, and the highwayman fell, clutching his shoulder.

"I told you missy was pluck to the backbone," Jake said to Rigg as the two tried to calm the frightened horses. Emilyann was calmly reloading the pearl-handled pistol drawn from her fur muff while the earl tied the injured attacker, who looked a great deal like one of the footpads who had assaulted him and Geoff on the streets of London.

"You are lucky," he told the man, binding the cove's shoulder with the thug's own greasy neckerchief. "My wife always did pull her first shots a bit to the left. Of course, she never misses with her second. Do you want to put it to the test, or shall you tell us where your employer is hiding?"

When they went to leave they found Ingrid on the side of the road, on her knees.

"Rigg will go around back," Stokely commanded when they reached the deserted hedgerow tavern, dark except for a faint candleglow in one window. "Jake holds the horses quiet and keeps an eye on our friend here while I try the front door. You"—he indicated Emilyann—"stay here with your aunt."

Limping badly, the earl made his stealthy way along the building's side, ducking under windows and keeping to the cover of shrubs. He bit off an oath when he bumped into his wife inside the door of what was obviously the common room of the old tavern.

"Welcome, nevvy, welcome." Morgan chuckled, shifting the aim of his pistol from Nadine, tied in a chair and gagged, to Emilyann. Cursing, Stokely dropped his own gun.

Ingrid rushed to Bobo, unconscious on the floor, with an ugly bruise on the side of his head. She immediately began weeping and calling on divine intervention to save her baby.

"Ah, motherhood." Morgan sneered. "But that was the gist of the whole matter, wasn't it?"

The man had obviously shot the cat. Empty bottles testified to the battle for Morgan's mind. Morgan had not put up much of a fight, Stokely decided. It was only a matter of keeping him pacified, he figured, until Rigg could find a way in from the back. Emilyann had other plans.

"You'll never get away with this, you know."

Stokely tried to shush her. He would like to shake the little fool for arguing with a madman who held a gun, but he kept his hands in the air so Morgan would not feel threatened. Emilyann was in full spate now, though, and he could see Morgan's face growing redder with fury.

"Do you think Mr. Baxley doesn't know about all the so-called accidents? Well, he does, you addlepated old tosspot. You won't live to see the next Duke of Aylesbury, you'll hang before my son is even born, you scurvy piece of offal, you makebait—"

Morgan leveled the gun vaguely at her heart. "So you want to be first, eh? I thought to have you all trussed up before lighting the place, but I can see I have to change my plans." He turned blurring eyes to Ingrid, keeping the gun mostly pointed at Emilyann. "You were right, m'dear, it's hard to find good servants. No one wants to work to get the job done. An honest pay for an honest day's work. Hah-hah. Those fools have ruined my plans countless times, aye, and taken my blunt ne'ertheless. Well, I'm done with them. Have a better ally now.

"Yes, niece," he continued, "you can see the fires of hell firsthand, as it were. I've seen them, you know. They're in little eyes on the great cathedrals, all over. Burning. Burning. Now you'll see them, pesky brat, then it will be your crippled hero's turn."

The gun kept wavering. He needed two hands now to hold it steady, and his eyes shut to pull the trigger.

Emilyann pulled the little pistol out of her muff just as Smoky dived to push her aside and knock the gun out of Morgan's hands. Both guns fell to the ground, but not before discharging both shots. One grazed Smoky's shoulder, the other his cheek.

"Of all the cork-brained, misbegotten moves," Smoky started while Emilyann began shouting, "You knew I had the pistol, you ninny. What did you think—"

Then they were in each other's arms, laughing, hugging, and even weeping a little in relief.

Rigg coughed, bringing their attention back to the dingy room. He was dragging the third highwayman behind him. "Sorry for the delay, Major. I had to take care of this fellow before I could see to the rear door. Everything satisfactory here now?"

They looked around. Uncle Morgan was flat out on the floor, and Aunt Ingrid was still bashing him over the head with a grimy long-handled cookpot from the fireplace. "I'll show you hell, you jackass!" *Whap!* "You want an heir so badly you can go—"

"Aunt Ingrid!"

Whap! "How's that for an eye for an eye, you spindleshank ale-spigot? The devil's on your side, eh? Well, here's one for him, too." *Whap!* She put the much-dented pot down only when Bobo groaned, and Emilyann and Stokely both said amen.

"What will happen to Uncle Morgan now?" a very tousled Lady Stokely asked later, safe in her much-bandaged husband's lap, at a comfortable inn some miles down the road.

Stokely's injured shoulder was not keeping him from holding her tightly. He smiled. "Ingrid mentioned a new interest of Brother Blessed's. He is sending missionaries to bring the word to some new native outpost. Esquimeaux I think they are called."

"And Uncle is going along? The Lord certainly does work in mysterious ways."

"His choices were that or Newgate. Bedlam maybe. He would have to relinquish the title and any future claims to the dukedom in any case. Otherwise you would never be safe."

"Nor you, as my husband." She shivered at the thought and Smoky pulled her closer. He brushed a kiss across her head and set her a little away from him so he could look into her eyes.

"As for that, my dear," he said, "we have to come to some kind of terms. I mean, now that the threat is gone, you do not need me anymore, except for target practice, of course. Therefore I, ah, will agree to the annulment if you wish, so you may have your freedom and your fortune back."

So he was going to be noble, was he? "I was going to say the same thing to you. Now that we need not be married, you must be wishing your carefree bachelorhood restored, so I would agree to the annulment. After all, I did trick you into the marriage. I knew you were disguised and I kept your cup filled with brandy so you would not be thinking clearly. And I threatened to sue you for breach of contract and libel you in the newspapers and ruin your family. I would not have done any of it, of course."

"Don't you think I knew that, peagoose? I've known you all your life."

Emilyann hoped he did not know how strangely her body was acting, growing warm and cold, tingly and numb. "Well, but I cannot hold you to a promise made while in your cups."

"I have a harder head than that, Sparrow. I knew what you were doing, and more important, I knew what I was doing."

"Then why did you marry me? You certainly did not love me."

"No, I have to admit I did not love that ragtag brat, not in the way you mean. I was not in the marriage mart, in any case, not with the war going on. On the other hand, I never thought of marrying anyone else. You were mine, always, to cherish and protect, and if giving you my name was what it took, there was no big sacrifice. Then when I realized you were all grown up, I stopped feeling brotherly altogether. You knew that."

"And you do not want an annulment?"

"Not on your life. Lord, when I think of your precious life, facing that lunatic's pistol . . ." He ran his fingers through his disordered hair. "Confound it, girl, don't you ever listen to orders?"

"Don't you ever stop giving them, my lord?" she asked sweetly.

"I cannot help worrying, Sparrow. I don't know what I would do if anything happened to you."

"And me you," she told him, gently touching the bandage and placing a shy kiss on his cheek.

311

"Besides, where else could I find another woman who could stand to look at my body?"

"Your body is beautiful!"

"Not so very beautiful, after you made your mark with chicken scratches up and down it."

"I am very proud of my handiwork, I'll have you know."

"So you did look after all," he teased, grinning before his gray eyes turned serious again. "Then you will be my wife?"

"Silly, I am your wife."

"But I never proposed to you, and you never answered. You are supposed to tell me what a great honor it is."

"And you are supposed to go down on one knee."

"You would only have to help me up, Sparrow. But, truly, we have been engaged by managing parents and wed to avoid another relative's machinations. We've never been consulted, really, and you have never had a choice. And I'll most likely always limp, and have more scars, and I can't promise to stop acting like a drill sergeant or resenting your fortune, but, Lady Stokely, I am humbly asking you to be my wife, in every way, forever, because I cannot live without you."

"And you truly love me?"

His lips met hers in answer, in a long, burning kiss that spoke of yearning and sharing at last. "More than life itself," he said finally.

"Then, Lord Stokely, if you don't mind that your countess will never be a meek, even-tempered, obedient little female who hardly bends the rules, and your son will have to be a duke, then I would be honored to be your wife, in every way, forever." This time she showed him, with her innocent, eager passion.

"And you love me." It was more a statement of his wonder than a question.

"I have loved you all of my life, Smoky. I am not about to stop now."

. . . And some marriages are made just where they should be, in the hearts and minds of joyous lovers.